UNTAMED FATE

MAGIC SIDE: WOLF BOUND, BOOK 2

VERONICA DOUGLAS

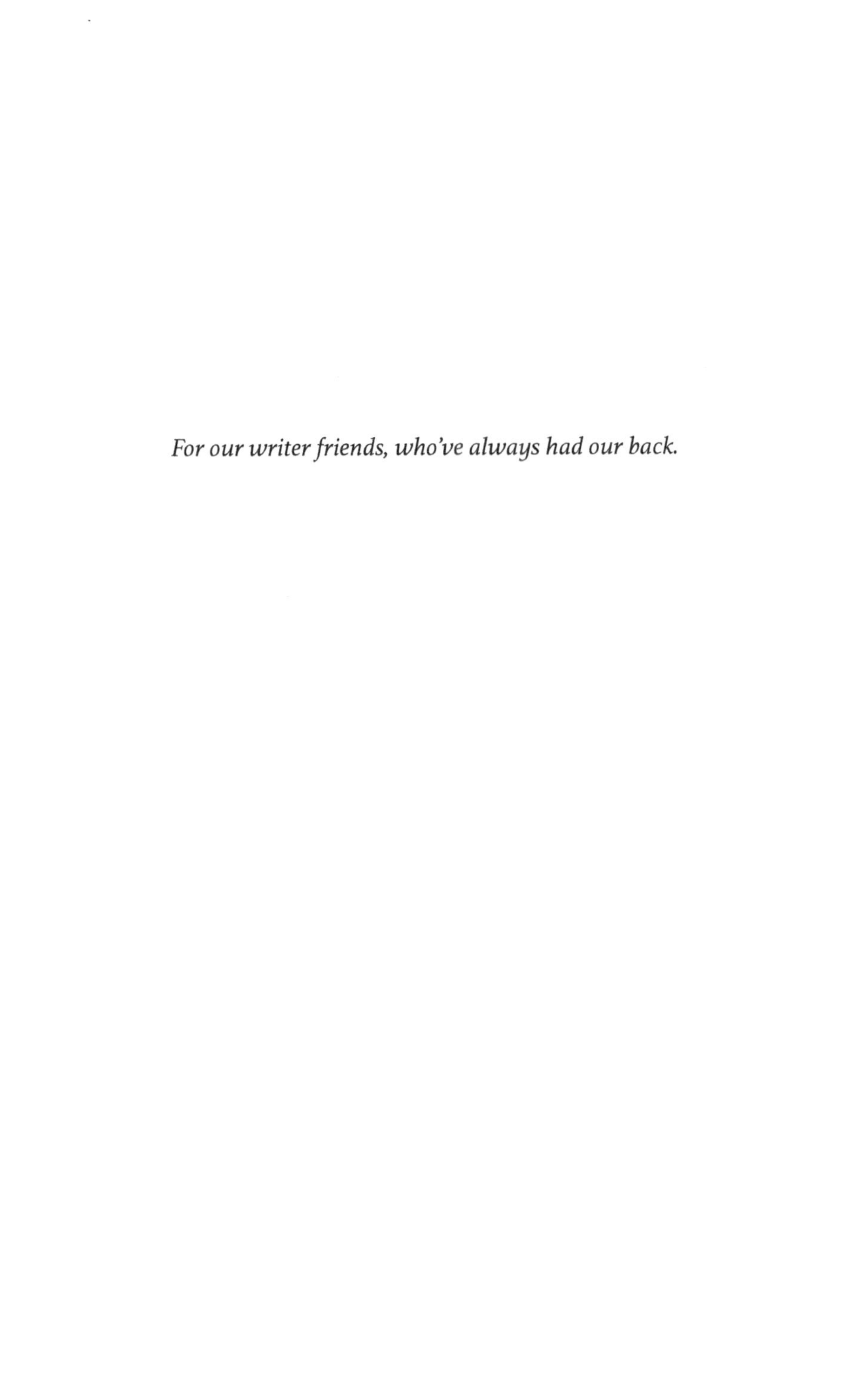

For our writer friends, who've always had our back.

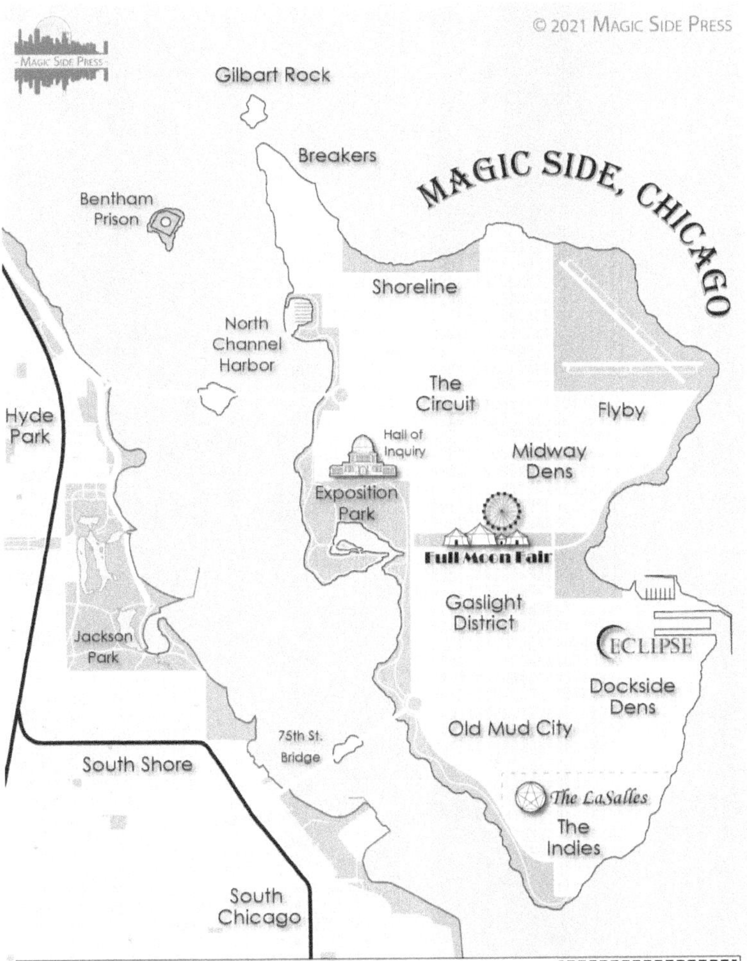
© 2021 Magic Side Press
Magic Side Press
Magic Side, Chicago
Gilbart Rock
Breakers
Bentham Prison
Shoreline
North Channel Harbor
The Circuit
Flyby
Hyde Park
Hall of Inquiry
Midway Dens
Exposition Park
Full Moon Fair
Gaslight District
Eclipse
Jackson Park
Dockside Dens
Old Mud City
75th St. Bridge
South Shore
The LaSalles
The Indies
South Chicago

WELCOME TO MAGIC SIDE, CHICAGO!

Having trouble getting around?
Ride Magic Side Surface Lines
Always efficient, always free!

Buy One Dog
Get One Free

Sammy's Italian Gelato & Chicago Dogs

(limit one per customer)

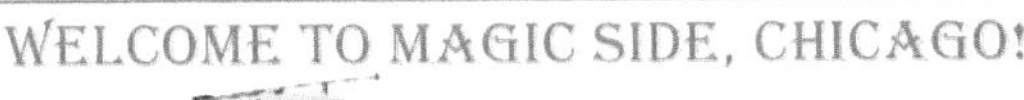

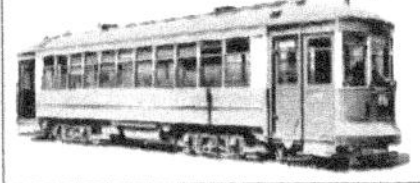

1

Hoots and hollers erupted through the crowd as one of my teammates careened out of the slanted roller derby rink and crashed into a water cooler. Cups and Gatorade sprayed everywhere.

What the hell was I thinking? I'm going to die out there.

Last week, I'd been nearly murdered by a horde of blood demons and a psychopath werewolf with a vendetta against my family. He was dead, but the twisted sorcerer who'd helped him was still on the loose. Having narrowly escaped with my life, I'd decided to immediately risk it again by stupidly agreeing to fill in for Zara's busted-up roller derby teammate.

There was a blast of sparks and another roar from the crowd, and the ref blew his whistle. "No claws, no magic, ladies!"

My skin chilled. Apparently, they played the game pretty rough here in Magic Side. Worse, our opponents were the Dockside Dens' team, Bitches with Bite. I was *so* over werewolves. They'd hunted me, harassed me, and were still following me around town as bodyguards. Now I had to skate against them.

I pressed my fingers to my temples. Had I really kissed their alpha, Jaxson Laurent? What had I been thinking? He was breathtakingly hot, but I hated the pack, I *hated* Jaxson, and by the looks in their eyes, they all hated me, too.

The only potential exception was my frenemy, Sam—Jaxson's closest confidant and the team's lead jammer. From the way she grinned every time she whizzed past me, I was pretty sure she was planning on eating me alive.

Pulse racing, I leaned over to my cousin Casey, who was sitting beside me on the bench. "This was a terrible idea."

"Are you kidding?" He grinned. "This was the best idea Zara ever had!" Since the match had started, he hadn't taken his eyes off Rayne, the she-devil he had the hots for, as she zipped around the track. She was our team's jammer and looked *amazing* on skates. I wasn't sure Casey had actually blinked yet

He was a damned fool. Nothing about this situation was good. I was fresh meat, and the werewolves knew it. There was no way they were going to pull any punches with a LaSalle girl in the rink.

At least these werewolves weren't actively trying to kill me. Yet.

I took a deep breath, trying to calm my erratic nerves, but it was fruitless.

There was a part of me that was always on edge these days, plagued by a low, simmering dread. The nameless, faceless blood sorcerer was still out there, lurking in the shadows and the corners of my nightmares.

I clenched my fist. Maybe he was coming for me, but I refused to live my life in fear. Not after the insanity I'd been through.

Instead, I was going to bravely die in a horrendous roller derby accident.

I squinted against the bright lights that swept over the rink. With the fog machines and the dark atmosphere, the place felt like a WWF wrestling arena. The bleachers that lined the walls of the large warehouse were packed, and the crowd pulsed with excitement as those without seats crammed themselves around the padded railing of the rink.

Sam whizzed past wearing black racing shorts, a matching tank with white claw marks on the front, and a silver helmet with a removable star cap. Rayne followed a few seconds behind, devilish tail swishing and determination pulling at the corners of her fiery red lips. Before she could pass, Sam planted her hands on her hips, signaling to the ref to call the jam.

A whistle pierced the clamor of the crowd, and both teams slowed and crowded into the pit.

Zara skidded to a halt before me, sweaty and cheeks flushed. "You're up, Savy."

She wore our team's signature outfit—black shorts, a pink jersey, and retro knee-high socks—with fishnet stockings to top it off. She gulped from a Red Bull and offered it to me.

"No, thanks, I've got enough adrenaline pumping through my veins. I don't need to give myself a heart attack." I leaned forward to check my laces, but mainly to hide my nerves.

Another whistle had my stomach churning, and Casey clapped me on the back. "Time to kick some ass, wolfsbane."

Clipping the straps of my white helmet, I glared at my idiot cousin. "Don't ever call me that."

"Feisty! Make me proud." He winked at me, and I spun, skating unsteadily after my teammates onto the rink.

Zara had given me a crash course on the rules, and I'd spent a whole day watching YouTube videos so that I wouldn't make a complete fool of myself...though my chances of abject humiliation were still decent with only a few practices under my belt.

"You should have told me who we'd be up against," I whispered to Zara as I eyed my opponents.

She raised a brow at me. "You getting cold feet already? I

figured you'd want to kick some werewolf ass after all they've done. Now get in position, and don't make me regret this."

Oh, she would *definitely* be regretting this.

I lined up beside my three teammates. We were the blockers, and our goal was to thwart Sam from getting past us while ensuring that Rayne got through and to the front. The werewolf team would be doing the opposite.

I narrowed my eyes at Sam, who was shooting the shit with Rayne as they positioned themselves behind us. As if sensing my attention, she met my gaze with a flash of amusement.

I *did* want to kick some werewolf ass, starting with Sam. I'd saved her from the clutches of the blood drainers, and we'd had a bit of a bond, but our last conversation had ended with her telling me to keep my dirty little LaSalle hands and lips off her alpha. Not that I wanted anything to do with him, but being told what to do pissed me off like nobody's business.

The whistle sounded over the din of the crowd, and the two jammers barreled toward us and into the line of blockers. One of the wolves shoved me aside, so I elbowed the bitch and pushed through the morass of sweaty bodies, my sight laser-focused on Sam. Two of her teammates had managed to open a space for her. Leaning low, I knocked one of them down and smashed my shoulder into the other, planting my body in the gap that opened in the line.

Sam plowed into me, pushing me back several feet. "I was wondering when you'd come out to play."

I growled through clenched teeth, locking one of my toe breaks. Though she didn't look it, Sam was a mass to be reckoned with and had rock-hard abs. Where the F were my teammates?

Zara was caught in a shoving match with one of the biggest werewolves, while another pink-jerseyed woman screamed as one of the wolves bit her. Was that even allowed?

Pain shot through my side as Sam's elbow rammed into my kidney. Before I had time to shout, she spun around me and broke through the line.

Shit.

I used my weight to slam into the muddle of bodies surrounding Rayne, and using my ass—since hands weren't allowed—I managed to make a gap for her to pass. She shot through and booked it after Sam, who was several seconds ahead.

Pushing and shoving the other team, we followed our jammer. The Bitches with Bite were several points up on us and would likely win, which made me want to play extra dirty.

Like a pack of entangled ferrets, we rounded a bend in the rink, and I shunted one of the shifters. She hurtled into the padded railing, and the crowd went wild.

One down. But not the one I had my sights on.

Excitement and adrenaline coursed through me as I lengthened my stride and formed a line with my teammates. Sam and Rayne were coming up behind us, and I really wanted to take Sam out.

Sam wove between two of her blockers, trying to skirt around us, but Zara and I pushed ahead using our outstretched arms and asses to cut her off.

Cheers rocked the warehouse as one of our blockers grabbed Rayne by the wrist and slingshotted her around the pack. Free from the chaotic cluster of jostling and cursing women, she flew forward, her long strides propelling her ahead.

Sam growled from behind and burst through Zara and me with a laugh, nearly taking my arm off and causing Zara to lose her footing and swerve into the pit.

My adrenaline surged, and only one thought filled my mind: *Get even.*

Biting back the pain, I sped after Sam, hunting for blood. I'd been on the bench the whole game, and with seconds left to play, this was my only chance to blow off a little steam.

Sam slowed slightly as she glanced over her shoulder, and I used my speed to cut the corner and propel myself into her. My hip crashed into hers, but she stayed upright. She elbowed me in the ribs and shoved me sideways with a wicked grin just as the ref blew the whistle.

I crashed into the railing beside the rink, and the impact drove the air from my lungs. My teeth ached, the beds of my fingernails itched, and I was ready to murder. That, or collapse and moan a bit.

Hands gripped my arms, and I blinked as faces from the crowd flooded my vision. Then Zara was beside me, cursing at the bystanders and pulling me back into the rink.

The taste of copper filled my mouth, and I touched my lower lip, wincing at the sting, my gums throbbing.

"What happened to your mouthguard?" Zara asked, looking at my busted lip with concern.

Dang it.

Zara shook her head but clapped my back. "You did good, Fury. You've got some bite."

My enthusiasm drained as I checked the sorry state of the scoreboard. "But we lost. Big time."

"Eh, we were never going to win. The Bitches with Bite have been undefeated for the past two years," Zara said, guiding me to the pit.

Sam and her teammates circled the rink, pumping their fists and hollering at the overexcited crowd. As they neared, she winked at me.

Irritation simmering, I skated into the pit, only to be enveloped in Casey's arms. "You kicked ass! Way to represent. Next time, aim for her face."

I shook my head, a part of me hoping there *would* be a next time because I'd actually had fun. Skating on eight wheels might be my jam after all.

My teammates were surprisingly upbeat after losing the match. Each of them congratulated me on my first game, and a few told me to come back next week. Our team skated around the rink as we congratulated the Bitches with Bite for their win.

"Ready to go? Drinks are on me," Casey said as I pulled off my skates and slipped on my tennies.

My lip was still bleeding, and I probably looked like a sweaty vampire. "Where can I clean up first?"

Zara pointed to a hall between a pair of bleachers, which were rapidly clearing out as people filed for the exits, heading to an afterparty or bar, no doubt.

"I'll meet you guys in the parking lot," I said, and headed toward the bathroom.

The cement floors were sticky with beer and spit and God-knows-what else. Three women exited the ladies' room. "Nice jam tonight, girl! Hope to see you on the rink next week."

"Thanks," I said, laughing, and stepped through the scuffed gray door. The bathroom was empty apart from the overflowing trashcans and paper towels strewn across the ground.

I examined my reflection in the cracked mirror. My lower lip was swollen and tinged pink with blood, and my cheeks were flushed and damp. Though I'd only been in the rink for one jam, the excitement and nerves of the night had made me sweatier than a pig.

I splashed some water on my face and swished the last remnants of blood from my mouth as I tried to wash away the cocktail of residual emotions from the game. I'd lost my cool and probably owed Sam an apology, even though I was the one with the fat lip. When Sam had whipped past with her cocky laugh, my brain had fried, and I'd had the irresistible urge to chase after and hunt her down.

I grabbed a handful of paper towels and dragged them over my face, feeling a modicum of relief. Suddenly my heartbeat skyrocketed, like I'd been hit with a dose of epinephrin. I gasped and stumbled back from the sink as I glimpsed my reflection.

Staring back at me were a pair of honey-gold eyes. *My* eyes.

No, no, no.

Pressing my eyelids shut, I inhaled slowly and counted to ten.

It's not real.

This had happened right after I'd killed Billy. I opened my eyes again, and they were a steely blue—their natural color. Was I losing my mind?

Maybe it was just PTSD or something. I'd been hunted and hounded by werewolves, and my mind was starting to play tricks on me.

"Get a hold of yourself, Savy," I muttered as I tossed the paper towels in the trash and pushed through the door.

I needed to figure out what the hell was going on with me. But my gut told me that the answer was tangled up with the sorcerer, and until I discovered who he was and hunted him down, I'd be shit out of luck.

My hands were shaking when I saw Zara and Sam down the hall. They both looked at me, and I balled my fists and put on a fake smile.

"You okay?" Zara asked.

"Yup. Right as rain. Just had to gurgle some water."

"Great. Casey's waiting outside. I'll meet you guys in a few. Nice game tonight." She turned to Sam. "Check ya later."

I didn't wait for Sam to speak but beelined for the exit at the end of the warehouse that led out into the back lot.

Sam appeared beside me. "What's up with you? You seem...off."

"Maybe it's because you just bodychecked me into the crowd.

Or *maybe* it's because your pack is a bunch of lying, murderous, psychos hellbent on destroying me and my family."

Sam chuckled. "You're being dramatic, and you know it. Billy was a wildcard."

"Right, and the others he recruited? Lemme guess, they were just flukes?"

"There's a lot of bad blood, but only a few acted on it. Jaxson has hunted down anyone in the pack he thought would be a risk." Her tone grew serious, and a shiver skated down my spine. What had he done to the traitors?

"Anyway," Sam continued, "sorry about your lip. I figured we both needed to blow off some steam tonight. Are we good?"

I gripped the doorknob of the exit and glared at her but only saw truth in her eyes. Sam was the one member of the pack who I'd grown to like, though she was prickly as hell and our last conversation still stung because it was the truth: *You and Jaxson can't ever be a thing. Just stay away.*

I sighed and stepped out into the orange-lit parking lot. "Yeah, I've got no beef with you, just—"

My breath left my chest in a rush, and my pulse quickened. Instead of the bodyguards Jaxson had trailing me, I saw *him*.

"Jaxson *freaking* Laurent," I hissed, my gaze locked on the devil beast himself. Six and a half feet of man-hunk under those blue jeans and dark V-neck. He was leaning against the hood of his truck with his arms crossed and a sinfully sexy scowl on his face, like he was annoyed that I'd kept him waiting. His eyes drank me in before flashing gold. My skin flushed, heat pooled low in my belly, and I silently cursed.

"Remember what I told you about smelling like a rare piece of steak? Lock your horny thoughts down, Savannah," Sam chided.

Balling my fists, I tried to channel my embarrassment and irritation and turn it into calm. I failed.

"Did you know he'd be here?" I seethed through clenched teeth, hoping my anger would mask the heat under my skin.

She smirked. "Of course. He told me to make sure I took some of the fight out of you."

Funny. I was just getting started.

2

Jaxson

Savannah Caine burst through the back door of the warehouse and out into the deep yellow-orange light and shadows of the parking lot.

She stopped short and fixed me with a venomous glare that sent my blood pulsing.

Striped thigh-high stockings sheathed her long legs, offering a delicious stretch of skin that disappeared into the trim of her black racing shorts. She wore a vivid pink top with *Hell on Wheels* emblazoned across the front. It was low cut, and beads of perspiration glistened on her chest.

I could smell it, and I wanted to push her up against the wall to taste it. I dug my claws into my folded arms to get control.

Fuck. This was why I'd stayed away.

Sam stepped out beside her and flashed me a reproachful look.

As if I needed reminding that she was off limits. Savannah was a LaSalle—a member of the twisted family that had gotten my sister Stephanie killed. And as if death and destruction somehow ran in their blood, Savannah had slain Billy, my sister's fated mate.

Yes, he'd been a monster, driven to madness and revenge after Stephanie's death. Billy had kidnapped, murdered, and conspired with a blood sorcerer. He had to be stopped, but it hadn't been her right to put him down.

That had been *my* duty. But Savannah didn't understand a thing about us. Or care to.

A creeping frost wound around my heart as Savannah strode toward me with her gym bag in hand and a fire burning in her eyes. Sam mouthed, *Watch out*.

The red-haired vixen homed in on me like a heat-seeking missile, stopping inches from my chest. "What the *hell* are you doing here, Laurent? I thought we had to stay away from each other."

Her eyes were murderous, unsheathed daggers.

I didn't bother moving a muscle in response, just leaned back against my truck with my arms crossed. "I have information. Are you going to listen, or are you going to try to stab me?"

She dropped her bag onto the pavement. "I don't have a knife, so you might as well start talking."

Her body vibrated with repressed fury, and her magical signature was on full display—the scent of tangerines and the feel of cool water flowing over my skin. It was like fucking nectar, driving me wild. I could smell her anger and resentment, and beneath it all, an undeniable undercurrent of desire.

I'd forgotten what it was like to be around her. A continuous assault on my senses. Contradictions piled upon contradictions. She was a beautiful nightmare.

My eyes dropped to her mouth. Her lips were full and soft, though the bottom one was cut and swollen. A stain of blood brightened the surface, and I could almost taste it. Blood that was special, that the sorcerer had wanted.

My muscles tensed with desire and protectiveness. "You're hurt. You ladies must play rough."

She sucked on her torn lip. "We can take it. Now quit checking me out and tell me why you're lurking in the parking lot."

I uncrossed my arms and tried to focus on the information burning in the back of my mind instead of the alluring line of her mouth and the fire she stoked in my chest. "We've identified the faceless man, the blood sorcerer who was hunting you, thanks to your sketches. You drew a tattoo of a triangle with the number 37 on his neck. It's an old prison tattoo. His name is Ulan Kahanov, and he's a murderer and deviant sorcerer."

Her breath caught as her pupils dilated. "Do you know where he is?"

"No. But his most recent residence was the maximum-security prison on Bentham Island, just offshore of Magic Side. He escaped a few months ago when the prison was breached. We would have identified him earlier, but the Order archmages were keeping the missing prisoner a secret to save face. The place is like Alcatraz—it's supposed to be impregnable."

"Then how did he break out?"

"It was attacked by a genie. Others escaped too, but Kahanov is—as far as the Order is willing to admit—the only one who wasn't caught. We've had one of the Order's best hunters tracking him for the last few days, but he's an elusive bastard."

"Wait a minute, how long have you known? Why am I only finding out now?"

"Because you didn't need to know the details." My irritation flared, but I kept my emotions locked down.

She scoffed. "If I matter so little, then why are you bothering to tell me?"

I was still uncertain how much to tell her. Certainly not the truth.

"Things have changed," I said. "You're in a lot of danger, Savannah. Kahanov is on the move, and I think he's going to make another play for you. I want you to come back to Dockside. I'll put you up in a safehouse until we bring him down."

She crossed her arms. "Oh, *hell*, no. Not on your life. I'm not going back into werewolf witness protection."

Anger simmered under my skin, and I fought the urge to throw Savannah over my shoulder and drag her back to the Dens. She had no fucking clue what kind of danger she was in. Not only because of the threat I'd received from Kahanov, but also because her blood was special. I'd ferreted out the traitors in our pack, but there were still rogue wolves running loose in Wisconsin who might come after her for it.

"I'm trying to protect you, and I can't do that when you're holed up in the Indies. Be reasonable," I growled, heat creeping over my neck. The LaSalles had refused us access to the south side of the island, so my surveillance teams had to stop at the border, which made it damn near impossible to keep a watch over her.

"I *am*. If the blood sorcerer is coming for me, then the safest place for me *is* the Indies, with the LaSalles. You know it. I know it. That's final."

I ground my teeth. It was all I could do to keep my claws in. But I knew that look in her eyes. She'd rather drive her car off a cliff than change direction.

"Fine. Then I'm doubling your guard for when you're outside the Indies." I turned and started to open the door of my truck. "I'll let you know when we bring him down."

She shoved my door closed and pinned it shut with her hand. "So what, you're just leaving me in the dark? Out of the investigation? That's bullshit."

My gaze dropped to her neck, her pulse thrumming like a hammer in my skull. What I wouldn't give to drag my teeth across her sweaty skin. Give her a reminder of exactly who she was dealing with.

"To keep you safe," I snarled, eying her hand on my door. "Do I need to remind you what happened the last time you were involved?"

Her eyes flashed—maybe a glint from the streetlamps—and she reared back. "What *happened*? I stopped a killer and prevented an attack on my family. Without me, God knows how many other people Billy and his freaks would have killed."

Her vitriol and resentment were almost overwhelming, and her words were acid splashed in my face. She'd killed my brother-in-law, and I wanted to hate her for that. And maybe I did. But she wasn't wrong. We wouldn't have stopped him without her help.

My voice cut through the air like a knife. "Get your hands off my truck."

She grabbed the lapel of my shirt instead and jerked. "I want in, Jaxson. Make it happen. I need to know why he's hunting me."

My wolf surged at her defiance, and I had to fight to keep him down. I glanced up, hoping this wasn't all on display, but apparently, we were the postgame show, and our conversation had drawn a bit of a crowd. Sam's pupils were dilated, and every werewolf in the parking lot had tensed.

A warning growl escaped my throat.

I was certain that Savannah Caine was the only person in Magic Side who would dare touch me like that. It was an affront to everything I stood for. And yet, everyone understood that somehow, rules didn't apply to her. She was like a rogue wolf, brave and fierce, but hard to trust and impossible to count on. I wouldn't put it past her to march into the Hall of Inquiry and start demanding things from the archmages.

"Hands off my shirt," I said, pitching my voice low but firm.

She released it and blushed. Unfortunately, by challenging my authority, she'd just made it that much harder for me to say yes. But maybe I'd bite.

I shoved my hands in my pockets and bent to her ear. "Lucky for you, Ms. Caine, our hunter has questions she wants to ask you. Meet us at the North Channel Harbor tomorrow at three p.m. If the Order will give you access, you can even join us on our way to Bentham Prison."

"What's at Bentham?"

"Murderers, butchers, and psychopaths, as well as a blood-thirsty devil that we need to talk to. I'm sure they would all welcome a visit from a beautiful redhead."

Savannah tensed, and I could sense her rising trepidation.

I nudged her with my alpha presence, letting her know she was dismissed. "Sleep well, Ms. Caine."

She spun and stalked back to her car, giving me a delightful view of her long legs and tight shorts. My breath stopped as my gaze landed on the back of her pink shirt. Below her nickname, *Fury*, was the number she had chosen—37.

She knew that the bastard Kahanov might be scrying, and she'd coopted his mark. Talk about sending a message. The woman certainly had stones, but she was toying with powers she didn't understand.

I slipped into the cab of my truck, heart pounding, as all the things I hadn't told her raced through my mind. At the heart of them had been the message Kahanov had somehow left on my desk—a small note, written in blood:

You have three days to hand over Savannah Caine. If you don't, I will make your pack pay. One way or another, when the bodies are piled high enough, you will submit.

My veins burned, and I struggled to restrain my claws as my fingers dug into the steering wheel.

The pack was everything. Everything I was, and everything I stood for. But I would never submit. I was going to hunt the bastard down, no matter what it took. Then I would wrap my jaws around his throat and savor the sweet taste of his blood.

3

***

Savannah

Three hours later, Casey and I stumbled through the front door after a heavy night of celebration in which I'd done my best to forget about Jaxson, the sorcerer, and the sword hanging over my head. I just wanted a night to be normal. Every muscle in my body ached, and I was dead beat. It was a relief to finally be home.

Home.

A funny thought. Two weeks ago, I hadn't known the LaSalles existed, and now I was living with them. I hadn't meant to linger, but my Aunt Laurel had insisted. Also, I was broke, jobless, and apparently still very much the target of a madman, so it made sense.

I dragged my tired ass up the stairs to my bedroom on the third floor, then locked the door behind me and flicked on the lights.

My room was obviously inhabited by a madwoman.

First off, the decorations were bizarre—though to be fair, that was on Aunt Laurel. The deep red Persian carpet didn't mesh with the palm trees on the heavy yellow curtains or the ship's wheel mounted on the wall. What was the theme? There had to be one.

On the other hand, the more clearly insane feature of the room was my collection of sketches, which littered every available surface—a couple of my friends and my godmother, several of the night fair and the fortune teller. And a lot of Jaxson. He was everywhere.

But the images that drew my attention were those lurking in the shadowy corner of the room, overflowing from the old writing desk onto the ancient radiator and dresser.

The faceless man.

Ulan Kahanov. I knew his name now.

I'd drawn him over and over, trying to recreate everything I could recall of my visions. I'd never seen the blood sorcerer in person, only while scrying. I remembered the fall of his clothing, the broad set of his shoulders, and the details of his surroundings. But his face was always a blur, a messy smudge on the paper. I'd kept on sketching, hoping that somehow my memory could get around the veil cast by his anti-scrying charm.

It had been a fruitless task.

I wasn't spending another night with the monster scattered around the room. With a flurry of motion, I scooped up the papers and shoved them haphazardly in the desk drawer. "I don't care what you're up to, I'm not letting you dictate my life."

My gaze landed on the dozens of pictures I'd drawn of Jaxson. They were some of my best work. While the illustrations of the sorcerer were scribbled with desperate, frenetic energy, every detail of Jaxson's face and body had been replicated with soft, meticulous strokes of the pencil. His strong jaw and handsome beard, his dark, wavy hair and radiant eyes. The powerful contours of his body.

What had I been *thinking*?

There was no way to forget the embarrassment and regret on his face after he'd kissed me in the woods. It still made my cheeks burn with shame and fury. I was, after all, just a dirty LaSalle. A sorceress with dark, tainted magic.

He thought I was so insignificant that he'd cut me out of his investigation. Treated me like a pawn. Kept me on a need-to-know basis. So why the hell was I drawing pictures of that jerk and leaving them around the room?

That was the million-dollar question.

"You don't get to dictate my life, either," I murmured, snatching the jumbled sketches off the dresser and bedside table and shoving them in the drawer with the creepy sorcerer, face down. I slammed the drawer shut with a satisfying thunk. "Enjoy each other's company, assholes."

Feeling slightly relieved at having completely and deftly rid myself of all my problems, I headed to the shower. I peeled off my sweat-soaked uniform and undies and dropped them on the mildly fragrant pile of clothes in the corner of the bathroom. I'd practiced three nights in a row and desperately needed to do laundry.

A quick shower drained the last of my residual adrenaline, and soon after, I slipped naked between the sheets and fell asleep on the rickety old bed.

The dreams came quickly, as they always did.

Carnival music echoed softly through the darkness, and a deep dread settled in my bones. I looked around, finding no source in the pitch-black void that surrounded me. But when I turned back, I was face to face with the fortune teller, who sat cloaked in shadow.

She reached out of the darkness and drew a card. The Wheel.

Her lips moved, but the sound of her voice lagged moments behind. "You cannot outrun your fate, Savannah. They're coming for you. Beware the wheel of fortune. It does not stop. Time is ticking. You need to learn who you truly are so that you can stop the ones who are coming."

She'd spoken those words to me before, in another dream, before I'd known who she was. From before I'd discovered my magic and my life had become a living nightmare.

The darkness of my dream began spiraling around me, sucking me down like a whirlpool. My pulse raced. I fought against the pull and staggered back, and suddenly, I was outside the fortune teller's tent at the Full Moon Fair.

The ebony night hung overhead, but the moon and stars were blotted out by the thousands of floating lights that lit the fairgrounds. I was alone, but muffled voices chattered and shouted around me like the echoes of ghosts.

I searched for any sign of the monsters who were after me—the rogue wolves, the demons, and the faceless man. Nothing moved, but I could feel that they were out there, hunting, drawing close.

Something tugged on my chest. An invisible thread. Instinct called to me. Find Jaxson.

I ran through the tents into the great empty expanse of the Midway. The floating Ferris wheel towered over the fair, the only landmark I knew. I ran toward it, searching, following the string pulling on my breast.

Something moved in the corner of my vision. I stopped and turned, recognizing him in an instant.

Jaxson.

Waves of desire and heat coursed through my body.

His claws were out, and his eyes shone radiant gold. A sheen of sweat covered his bare chest and powerful arms, and the signature of his magic overwhelmed my senses. The scent of moss and deep forests. The taste of smoke and fresh snow.

With a sudden movement, he vanished behind the corner of a tent.

My feet pounded over the matted grass as I raced to catch up. "Jaxson!"

I slipped between the tents and looked both ways. For just a second, I saw him down the line, and then he disappeared around another corner. With a shout, I pursued, pulled onward by that invisible thread.

I swung into the gap where he had turned and skidded to a halt.

Something wasn't right. The dream had changed. The shadows were all wrong. They pointed at impossible angles, as if they were drawn to the flickering lights overhead. The hair on my neck stood on end as my muscles tightened, and my palms grew damp.

A dark shape slid across the white canvas. The shadow of a man. Not Jaxson.

I spun.

A thin figure stood before me, radiating malevolence. His face was an inky smudge, a greasy blur that vibrated as he slowly turned his head.

The blood sorcerer. Ulan Kahanov, the faceless man.

We stared each other down alone between the long line of white exhibition tents. He tilted his head in an unnatural way, and my stomach turned. "Why, hello, Savannah. Imagine finding you here, all alone. Abandoned by Jaxson again?"

My heart strained, and a feral voice snarled in my head, Wake up!

The faceless man stepped forward. I tried to run, but my muscles were taut, and I couldn't move.

"I'm dreaming. You're not here," I hissed and dug my fingernails into my palm. Pain shot across my skin, but I didn't wake up.

"Yes, you're dreaming, but that doesn't mean much if I can still reach out and touch you." He brushed my face, and a sickening shudder worked its way through my nearly paralyzed body.

A gust of wind ripped between the lines of tents, and the canvas shook. On the horizon, the floating Ferris wheel collapsed and slammed into the ground, sending flames exploding into the sky.

Then it began to slowly tilt and roll toward me.

The sorcerer gripped my jaw with his hand, tearing my attention back to him. "You will come with me!"

Wake up! the voice in my mind howled.

I bolted upright with a jolt, heart pounding. I'd torn off the covers, and sweat drenched my bare skin. My aching palms were covered in blood. I swung my legs out of bed, staggered to the bathroom, and flicked on the lights. Running the tap, I watched as water and bright red blood spiraled together down the drain. My palms stung beneath the flow, and I bit my lip. I'd really dug my nails in. I didn't think they'd grown that long.

Once my hands were clean and the blood had slowed, I splashed water over my face and neck. It was cool and refreshing, like the icy trickle of my own magic. Breathing deeply in and out through my nose to calm my nerves, I grabbed the hand towel and dried my face.

When I looked up, the girl in the mirror had bright yellow eyes.

I blinked.

Pure blue. It had been an illusion, just like in the bathroom at the rink. Was it any wonder I was seeing things with werewolves hounding me day and night?

I rested my palms on the porcelain and fixed the naked girl in the mirror with a hard stare. "Get a grip, Savy. It was just a dream."

But I could still feel the sorcerer's clammy touch on my skin, and a shudder quaked through me.

You're in Aunt Laurel's house. You're safe.

With fear and frustration burning the back of my neck, I plopped down on the bed and ground my teeth. "I'm hiding from a psychopath in my aunt's house and relying on a jerk to solve my problems."

What a terrible plan.

I wasn't an idiot. In my heart, I knew I wasn't a match for

Kahanov. I needed the protection of both Jaxson and my powerful, but likely insane, aunt.

But I believed the fortune teller's words, even if they only existed in my dreams. I couldn't outrun my fate. Something was coming—I could feel it in my bones.

It was like a giant storm looming on the horizon. And I was woefully unprepared.

The dream was a warning. I needed to discover what Kahanov was up to, and I needed to master my magic so that I didn't need Jaxson or my aunt or anyone to protect me.

And figure out who I truly was, whatever the fortune teller had meant by that. Piece of cake, right?

Maybe tomorrow I would get some answers.

I reached out with my hand and focused my will on the shadows in the room. The icy sensations of my magic trickled over my skin, and slowly, the shadows began to dance and move.

My cousin could control fire, and I'd met all sorts of magical people with wonderful powers in my short time in Magic Side. For whatever reason, my magic was as cold as death, looked like smoke, and had the power to control darkness.

I sucked in a deep breath. "I really, *really* hope I'm not evil."

I pulled the shadows around me like a cloak, then let them swallow the room. If only I could make it all go away—the faceless man, the constant nightmares, and the relentless fear lurking in my head.

All that, and Jaxson Laurent.

4

Savannah

Five hours later, I staggered down the stairs in a desperate search for coffee.

Casey was sitting at the table eating a bowl of Fruit Brute, which featured a howling werewolf on the front. I was certain it had been out of production for years, yet he'd bought it from God-knows-where just to troll me every morning.

"Do you know anyone who makes sleep potions?" I groaned as I poured myself a piping hot mug of black gold from the pot.

I would have asked Uncle Pete, but he was out of town. Not that I wanted to drink one of his foul concoctions.

Casey nodded and mumbled through a mouth of cereal, "Yeah, they can knock you out for days."

"No, I mean, if you drink it, it's like you've actually slept, because I need to pound a couple of those."

"Another rough night?" my aunt asked as she whisked into the room.

Casey met my eyes.

I hadn't wanted to face the music quite so early, but I knew I couldn't outrun this. My mind still echoed with the fortune teller's warning, and I could almost feel the sorcerer's nails digging into my chin.

I sighed and poured myself a bowl of cereal as I filled my aunt in on what Jaxson had told me.

When I was done, she pursed her lips and put a kettle on the range. "I find it strange that Ulan Kahanov was the one hunting you."

"Why?"

My aunt tossed her long silver hair over her shoulder. "I knew of him. He was a creepy bastard, for certain. But from the little you've told me, this doesn't seem like his style. He was a loner known for experimenting on his victims with blood magic, but only one at a time. He worked with demons, but never anything coordinated like the attacks so far. Nothing so dramatic."

"Prison apparently changed him." I twirled my spoon reticently around the bowl. Fruit Brute was awful, but the sooner the box was empty and out of the house, the better.

Casey slurped a spoonful of bright pink milk from the bowl. "Maybe the rogue wolf that Jaxson put down was the one actually pulling the strings. That could be good news for you. He's dead."

I hadn't told my family that that rogue wolf was Billy, Jaxson's brother-in-law, or that *I'd* been the one to kill him. Instead, I'd helped the pack sweep everything under the rug. Now, I wasn't sure whether that had been the right choice.

My aunt nodded thoughtfully. "That could be. Our family didn't have any serious interactions with Kahanov that would warrant a target on your back. He was just another monster, brought down by the Order. However, half the packs in the Great Lakes hate us for manufacturing wolfsbane. Maybe they caught him after he escaped from prison and tried to use him to get vengeance."

I shrugged. Billy had planned on murdering our whole family, but I knew for certain who was pulling the strings—Kahanov, the faceless man...who might not be so faceless in my nightmares if I asked the Order for a photo.

I put my head in my hands and rubbed my temples. "I'm just exhausted from being hunted. I can't have a night out without being followed by a pack of werewolf bodyguards, and I can't stop worrying that some deranged blood sorcerer is going to send demons after me."

My aunt nodded. "I completely understand."

Then she left.

I shook my head and went back to my bowl of cereal. The LaSalles were a strange bunch.

Moments later, my aunt returned and slapped a thin leather album in front of me. Lifting an inquisitive brow, I carefully opened it. Inside were faded newspaper clippings and photos. The first headline read, *Local LaSalle Girl Slays Rampaging Ogre!* There was a picture of a girl, not more than fifteen, standing by the smoking corpse of a monster.

I flipped the page. *Malign Magic Mingles as Malicious Mage Meets His Match!* The faded color photo showed a red-haired girl on the steps of some public building. My aunt.

She leaned in and spoke softly. "That was Edwin North, a particularly heinous criminal and a pervert. He messed with the wrong girl."

My mind whirled. An album of monsters and villains she'd overcome. Or to think of it another way, people she had murdered.

What was *my* death toll now?

"Savannah, you have power—deep, untapped resources of magic. I can feel it vibrating around you. It's a gift, but it means you will be hunted and challenged all your life. Get used to it. You have to face down your fears and not let them get in the way of the magic around you." My aunt touched my hand and smiled when I looked up. "I don't keep this book because I'm proud, or because I need trophies. I keep it because sometimes *I'm* scared. For myself, for my husband, for my son, and now, for you, too. It reminds me that the gods gave me the talent to protect myself and the strength to overcome anything. You have that strength. I know it."

I swallowed and nodded as I turned the page.

A fierce, bearded face looked back at me with dark, half-mad eyes. The headline above the little black-and-white photograph read, *Victor Dragan Dead at Last. Laurents and LaSalles Overcome the Dark Cloud Hanging Over Magic Side.*

My aunt tensed. "Dragan was the worst. Absolutely deranged. And I disintegrated him at the end."

I scanned the article. "You worked with the Laurents—the werewolves. I thought you hated each other."

"Dragan was a demented aberration—half sorcerer, half werewolf, driven mad by a dark split in his soul. The pack came to us for help. We thought it could be a new beginning, but Alistair Laurent, Jaxson's father, betrayed us not long after we brought Dragan down. A treachery so deep that it still cuts my bones."

With a sharp motion, she turned me to face her, eyes blazing with unbridled fury. "Never trust a wolf. When it comes down to it, they will always choose pack over justice, pack over truth, pack over anyone else—and that includes you." Her shoulders dropped as she gave a heavy sigh. "That, more than anything, is why I don't like you working with Jaxson. He may be helping you now, but one day, he will have to make a choice, and you'll be on the losing end. I guarantee it."

My gut twisted. Some part of my soul knew it was true.

"You can only ever rely on yourself, Savannah. That's why you need to master your power."

I'd been practicing sorcery with Aunt Laurel every day, but I couldn't manage too much yet. So far, I'd found that I could release bursts of power, control shadows, and snuff candles. It seemed so small compared to the blood sorcerer, compared to what Casey and my aunt could do…but it was more than I'd ever imagined two weeks ago.

I looked down at my right hand and drew in a little of my power. It appeared as dark wisps of shadow that trickled over my skin and stung like ice water. "I'm not even really sure I understand what my magic is."

"You need to know who you are to understand what your magic is, and what your magic is to understand who you are. Right now, you're searching for both. That's why we're going to accelerate your training."

The last time my aunt had wanted to accelerate my training, she'd tried sucking my magic out with a doohickey that, if dialed up to full strength, could consume half of Magic Side.

I stirred my cereal nervously. "Please tell me that this doesn't involve the Sphere of Devouring again."

"No, don't worry. We're only going to be summoning a few demons."

My spoon froze halfway to my mouth, and bits of fruity cereal slowly dribbled off into the bowl. *Why did my long-lost family have to be insane?*

5

Savannah

Half an hour later, and after much protesting, I found myself in my aunt's "workshop," a massive candlelit room in the bottom of an old, elaborate red stone building. The floor was inscribed with dozens of interlinked magical circles, rings of arcane runes.

I slowly stepped across the black stonework, deliberately avoiding the magical sigils. I had no idea if anything would happen if I stepped on them, but I wasn't about to experiment.

"These look similar to the ring that contains the Sphere of Devouring," I said uneasily, then met my aunt's eyes with an accusatory stare. "As well as the circles of blood the sorcerer used to summon blood demons."

Aunt Laurel swept effortlessly across the floor to the center of the room, her silver hair trailing behind her. "Circles are powerful tools for containing and controlling magic. Some of these are for focus, others for protection, and some for summoning demons and other spirits."

My stomach churned, and it felt like something was trying to push its way out of my chest. Probably the massive boatload of doubts I had about this particular venture. We needed to talk about this before things got out of hand.

I steeled my nerve. She was my aunt, but also as intimidating as a dragon.

"Aunt Laurel, I don't want to be rude—you've been so kind and opened new worlds to me—but we need to have a frank discussion. I have some sort of twisted shadow magic, and you're about to summon demons. These both seem..."

She raised an eyebrow. "Diabolical? Evil? Sinister? Like witchcraft?"

I gave an apologetic shrug. "Pretty much."

She strode over and grabbed my shoulders. "Savannah, these are labels that people use to try to take your power. Don't ever let anyone take your power or make you doubt yourself. Magic is a tool. It can be used for good or bad."

"But summoning demons? That seems, like, always bad."

"Gun violence is a plague in Chicago. You're a good shot. Does that make you evil?"

I grimaced. "I hope not. I just worry..." I held up my hands and summoned my magic. Dark, smoky shadows twisted around my fingers.

"Would you rather make leaves grow and flowers bloom?"

I looked at the inky darkness drifting from my hand. "Maybe? Could I do that?"

She shook her head. "I know a young woman, like you, who had power over plants. She nearly brought a blight on the whole world. There are two sides to every coin."

I let the magic dissipate.

"Savannah, you're strong, and you have a good heart. Trust it." She clapped her hands. "Now, let's summon some demons. Casey, fetch the coal."

My head spun.

Having a conversation with my aunt was like listening to an

airline captain come over the intercom and say, "Sorry about the turbulence, folks. Everything is going to be okay," followed shortly by, "Good news, there are enough parachutes for everyone, and the flight attendants are standing by to help you put them on."

A scent of nutmeg filled the room as a stream of light poured from my aunt's hand into the runes of one of the circles. The sigils illuminated one by one until the whole circle was lit and crackling with magic. "This is a circle of protection," she explained. "As long as we're in here, we'll be protected from the demons."

Casey dumped a hefty bag of coal into a wide brass brazier set into one of the other circles.

"The coal is an offering, used to lure the demons and give them form in our world," my aunt continued. She flicked her eyes to me. "Kahanov would have used blood to summon the blood demons that attacked you. A lot of it."

Memories of the blood drainers with all their tubes and IV bags brought bile to my throat.

At my aunt's command, Casey lobbed a fireball into the pile of coal. Bright orange flames flickered in his eyes as he grinned at me. "You're going to love this."

Why didn't I believe him?

Laurel gently shoved me inside the glowing circle of protection, and Casey joined me. She strode to the burning heap of coal and poured her magic into it until the surrounding circle of runes glowed bright red.

With a swift gesture, she raised her hands, and all the shadows of the room swung toward her. She began chanting and weaving her hands, and the world twisted around her silhouette. Vertigo squirmed in my belly, and I grabbed Casey's arm as the room spun.

As my aunt's voice rose in tempo, the air crackled with

power, and the scent of brimstone burned my throat. The fire seemed to suck the shadows inward.

No doubt about it—this was definitely diabolic magic.

An ear-splitting screech echoed through the room, and a sinister form rose from the flames, clawing at the air.

My aunt scurried back to the circle of protection just as the lighting in the candlelit room returned to normal, leaving a flaming demon perched atop the pile of coal.

It was about two feet tall.

"That's it?" Casey asked.

"Baby steps, Casey," my aunt responded.

I was too busy trembling. My very own aunt had just summoned a creature from hell.

The thing screeched, glared at us, and then scampered on all fours across the room and ran up one of the walls.

Holy shit.

"What am I supposed to do?" I asked, my voice not quite as steady as I'd have liked.

"Extinguish it. Like you've practiced with candles and fire."

I bit my lip, uncertain what to think. "You want me to...kill it? After we just summoned it?"

She shrugged. "You can't really kill demons, at least not in the way we think of death, not without a lot of trouble. They just disappear and go back to whichever hell they came from. I'm sure it's unpleasant for them, but they're embodiments of chaos. This is like recess for them."

I raised my hand toward the creature on the wall, but hesitated. "Isn't Zara a demon?"

Casey snorted. "Half-demon. There's a big difference. As in real death. So don't kill her, no matter how mouthy she gets."

I licked my lips as the thing jumped down and scrabbled over the stone floor, then slammed against the steel exit door.

"Actually, you make a good point, Savannah," my aunt mused. "Why don't you negotiate with it?"

She shoved me out of the circle of protection. The instant I was out, the thing screeched and charged at me, flames billowing from its coal-like eyes.

Heart racing, I bolted for the opposite end of the room, desperately trying to summon my magic. Icy shadows swirled around me, along with the memories of being chased by blood demons. I tried to call the long, dark shadows that stretched across the room to smother the monster, but I couldn't concentrate.

Searing pain lanced through my skin as the devilish thing's burning claws raked into me. With a yelp of surprise and despair, I spun and sent a burst of uncontrolled dark magic at the monster. It flew backward with a sizzle.

Casey hooted. "Nice shot! Now extinguish it before it extinguishes you!"

The thing charged, but feeling more confident, I backpedaled, calling the shadows. Streaks of darkness coiled around my hand and slithered across the floor. I waved my fingers, and the shadows moved like a black fog, but before I could strike, the burning thing leapt to the wall, and then plunged down onto me.

Its claws dug into my shoulders, and its touch burned like pressing my hand to a hot grill. I screamed and lashed out with my magic, sending the demon careening across the floor.

I struck out with the shadows, pushing them toward the demon. The shadows slithered and darted like serpents, and the creature's flames flickered and began to fade. It screeched and struggled to get away, but I showed no mercy as I willed the darkness to extinguish it.

Suddenly, it vanished in a puff of smoke, leaving an unearthly chuckle hanging in the air. It was laughing? How was I supposed to interpret that? *You got me this time?* or *I'll be back?*

I shook my head in wonder as Casey started applauding. Chest heaving, I placed my hands on my knees.

"You got it, Cuz! Nice job," he shouted.

"Yes. Well done. Now try more," my aunt quipped, and then began chanting again. Seconds later, the room twisted, and demons began leaping from the flames.

I was still bushed. This was too much.

My heels pounded on the stone as I darted toward the circle. Casey shoved me back before I could get in.

"What the hell?" I shouted as I dodged away from the clutches of a diminutive yet deadly, charging fire demon.

Casey dramatically put the back of his wrist against his forehead and gave a plaintive and deeply sarcastic cry. "Oh, save me cousin. I can't protect myself with my weak fire magic. It's useless against fire demons."

The trio of fire demons darted toward me, and I retreated as quickly as I could, trying unsuccessfully to repel them. "Casey, you asshole!"

My aunt Laurel grinned. "You make a good point, son. As a specialist, you're woefully unprepared for a battle like this."

She clapped her hands, and he was ejected out of the circle of protection with a yelp.

"Oh, shit!" he cried as the demons converged on their juicy new target.

Chaos ensued. Blasts of magic filled the room as we tried to contend with the fiery devils. As soon as one was down, my aunt summoned another.

Finally, I screamed, "Enough already!" and pointed my hand at the burning pile of charcoal and ash. The shadows converged like serpents and extinguished the flames. Unfortunately, the little bastards didn't disappear.

Well, it was worth a shot.

Deprived of their burnt offering, one charged at me in a rage, and I stumbled back. My foot caught on a seam in the stone, and I slammed down onto the hard floor, sending a jolt of pain up my tailbone and through my spine.

I gasped as the burning beastie lunged, but before it landed on me, my aunt clapped her hands again, and the red glowing circle vanished. A surprised screech erupted from the flaming demon as it poofed out of existence, along with all the others.

Pulse hammering in my temples, I flopped back onto the mercifully cold stone as bits of ash rained down around me. I was more drained than I'd ever been in my life, but the glowing warmth of triumph trickled through my veins.

I'd lived. And I'd actually slain demons with my magic. Not bullets. *Magic.*

Casey dropped to the floor and rolled onto his back, chest heaving. "Holy shit, Mom. Are you nuts?"

As fit as he looked, he was really out of shape, and she gave him a kick. "Practice outside your specialty, you little pyromaniac."

Then she headed over to me and helped me up. "You did so well. Wasn't that fun?"

My mouth was dry, and I didn't have the strength to respond. My family was comprised of demon-summoning lunatics who were definitely into the dark arts.

Seemed about right.

My phone alarm began to buzz. I swiped it off and glanced up at my insane family. "Shit. I lost track of time. I've got a date with a devil."

6

———————

Jaxson

I parked my truck in the lot at Old Channel Harbor, got out, and slammed the door harder than I'd intended.

I had two days to hand over Savannah Caine, or the sorcerer was going to make my pack pay. How, I didn't know, but I believed his threat. I could watch over Savannah, but I couldn't watch over everyone in my pack.

That meant I had two days to bring him down.

I wound my way through the lot over to the two women waiting for me by the dock—Nevaeh and Amal, both agents of the Order. I didn't trust the organization, but I'd trust both women with my life.

No sign of Savannah. Maybe she wouldn't show.

"Good to see you, Jax," Amal said as she stepped forward and clasped my arm.

She'd spent her childhood torn between Chicago and Cairo, and we were old friends. She'd been like a sweet little sister then. Now, she was one of the deadliest assassins I knew.

I tilted my head to Neve, whose red hair gently floated in the still air—an enchanting quirk of being a powerful djinn, a genie of the winds. "Nice to see you, Detective Cross."

She smiled. "I've been out of town, but I heard you're the new alpha around here."

I'd helped her and Damian Malek, one of Magic Side's wealthiest and most dangerous underlords, overthrow a demented mage who'd managed to tear open a portal to the hells and had been amassing a demon army. This was after he'd unleashed a water genie on Bentham a month ago, allowing five prisoners to escape—including Kahanov.

Since I'd taken over as alpha from my father, we'd faced one crisis after another. I'd hoped Billy's death had been the tragic end of it, but now, I worried that was only a prelude. "Any new leads on the sorcerer?"

Amal shook her head. "I lost his trail in Italy. Sorry, Jax."

"Then this visit better pay off. We need a lead. Fast."

I'd told them about the note, as well as most of the details surrounding the abductions and blood demon attacks.

"Is Savannah supposed to be meeting us?" Neve asked. "You had me get clearance for her."

As if mentioning her name summoned the she-devil up from the pits of hell, Savannah's Gran Fury peeled into the parking lot with the radio blasting. The werewolves I'd assigned to her protection detail followed shortly behind in a black SUV.

She was late and loudly broadcasting that the world revolved around her. I clenched my fist. Just the sight of her made my blood pressure rise. She was insufferable and obstinate...and frustratingly arousing.

Savannah climbed out of the car and strode over to us. Her white T-shirt was tucked into high-cut jeans that accentuated her curves, and I had to dig my claws into my palms to keep my head straight.

Amal leaned close and whispered, "A new love interest?"

"Never. She's a LaSalle," I snapped, too quickly. Unfortunately, Amal could probably smell the desire that plagued my mind the minute Savannah showed up.

Her hips swayed as she crossed the parking lot, and I forced my smoldering arousal down, reminding myself that Savannah was the reason my pack was under threat.

I tensed as she drew near. "Nice of you to show. At last."

"Better late than never." She shot me a glare, then extended her hand to Amal. "Hi, I'm Savy. You two must work for the Order."

Amal shook Savannah's hand. "I'm Amal, and this is Neve. We're hunting Kahanov. It's good to meet the woman he's after. I've got a lot of questions for you."

"Likewise," Savannah said.

Neve shook her hand as well. "Your illustrations helped us identify him. You're quite the gifted artist."

Savannah's expression darkened. "That bastard turned my life into a nightmare. Even if I never saw his face, it's hard to forget the details of someone like that."

A jolt of anger and protectiveness tightened the muscles in my arm. "Let's go," I growled.

"What's at Bentham?" Savannah asked as we headed toward the two-prop boat waiting for us in the marina. "Jaxson mentioned a bloodthirsty devil."

Neve nodded, her mood suddenly dark. "Kahanov escaped from Bentham with the help of a devil known as the Ripper. He might know what Kahanov's plans were. It's all we've got to go on, so we're going to bash him around a bit until he coughs up something useful. He's a real bastard."

A cold wind whipped around us, and the boats at the dock started bobbing gently in the breeze. Neve had a temper, and when it rose, so did the storms.

We boarded the black Order patrol boat and sped across the

harbor toward Bentham Island. Over the roar of the engines, Amal and Neve relentlessly grilled Savannah about Kahanov, his magic, and what she'd seen while scrying on him. But silence fell when we approached the massive prison, and Nevaeh whistled low as we pulled into the recently outfitted dock. "What a change. The last time I was here, this place was crumbling into the lake."

"What happened?" Savannah asked.

"A water genie hit it with a tsunami and cursed its defenses." Neve pointed to a faint shimmering dome in the air above the prison. "That spell protects Bentham. When it came down, five prisoners managed to escape, despite a half dozen backup measures. Kahanov is the only one still on the loose."

The captain killed the engine and secured the boat against the concrete jetty. Neve stood and levitated onto the dock, while Amal leapt up. Savannah's eyes rounded, and her jaw dropped. "Holy hell, that's...awesome," she said, then stood and placed her foot on the gunwale. Amal and I both extended our hands to help her up, and Savannah paused.

Amal smirked. "I won't bite."

Ignoring me, Savannah took her hand, and Amal pulled her up to the jetty with a swift tug.

"Let me guess, you're a werewolf," Savannah said to Amal.

"That's right. The best kind, too."

"Wolfborn, like Jaxson?"

"Gods, no." Amal frowned. "I shapeshift into a wolf with magic, which means I can do it with my clothes on."

Savannah looked her up and down. "I've seen some of Jaxson's people do that. Does it work with guns, too?"

"Anything I'm carrying."

"Yeah. That seems better than the other option with all the twisting and bones snapping." Savannah gave me a wry smile. "If I had to be a werewolf, I think I know what I'd choose."

She'd probably choose death. Her reproach for our kind was blatantly obvious.

The guards at the gate had been expecting us, but it took ten minutes of running background checks before they let us pass wearing visitor badges. Finally, they stepped aside and waved us into the highest-security prison in the US.

Half a dozen men and women in tactical uniforms were waiting to escort us. I heard the chatter in their earpieces as they led us down a bare concrete corridor lit by fluorescent bulbs —*Level B is secure. Three-twenty-four has been subdued.* Even with the spells and design of the prison, the guards here had their work cut out for them. Bentham held some of the world's most dangerous Magica criminals.

We took an elevator ride down to Level E and were escorted past a dozen cells with iron doors. The guards stopped in front of a door with a glowing number 36 in a triangle.

Time to meet the Ripper.

Savannah's shoulders tensed as she glanced toward cell 37, which had once held Kahanov. She held herself strong, but I could feel her unease and smell her rising trepidation. A desire to go to her rose in me, but I fought it down. She'd all but forced me into bringing her here. She could handle herself.

Savannah looked back to cell 36, jaw set. "Kahanov and the Ripper were neighbors."

Neve nodded.

"Give this one a wide berth," the guard said as he unlocked the door with an iron key once he finished dispelling the magic charms.

"Oh, the Ripper knows better than to pull any tricks," Neve said as she stepped into the well-lit cell. The prisoner inside locked eyes with her and then scooted against the wall of open bars at the far end.

Beyond them was an empty circular space with an observation tower in the center that magically monitored all the cells that encircled it. The prison was a panopticon, more commonly known as the donut, for that reason.

"Stay back, you cursed woman!" the devil yelled.

I was glad to see him squirm. The *Magic Side Gazette* had nicknamed him the Ripper for the way he tore his victims' bodies apart. The last person he'd murdered happened to be in the Dens, and though it wasn't a pack member, it had happened in our territory.

I flexed my fists, and my knuckles cracked with the anticipation of breaking his nose.

"Quiet. We just want to talk," Neve said coolly.

"Not with you in here." His signature smelled like rotting corpses and tasted of tar, and his body quaked with fear.

Amal shot forward and had her claws at his throat before he could twitch a muscle. "Then you'll talk to me. We're looking for Kahanov. He got away with you and the others on the night of the twenty-third. Any idea where he might be?"

"You mean he's still out there?" He let out a piercing cackle and clutched his sunken chest. "The fates must have smiled upon him, then, because that's a surprise."

"Oh, really? And why's that?" Amal asked.

"Why would I give you information, filthy lycanthrope?" he snarled.

"Because if you don't, I'll ram my claws into your eyes and rip off your balls. Then I'll have my friend Neve here suck the breath from your lungs." Amal's cheery voice betrayed the wrath she could unleash.

The devil's eyes bulged, and he raised his hands in acquiescence. "There's no need for violence. I'll tell you what I know, but maybe you'll put a word in with the guards on my behalf. I haven't seen the sun in a month."

"Maybe." Amal stepped back and crouched in front of him. "Tell me about your escape."

The Ripper's catlike eyes flashed to me before settling on Amal. "Kahanov and I escaped together. But you already knew that."

"How did you coordinate the escape? Were you two friends? Where did you intend to go?" she pressed.

"So many questions." The Ripper smiled, but Amal's claws extended, and he froze. "We weren't friends, but he was my neighbor, and when you're in this place long enough, you take what you can get. The plan was his. I helped him slip past the guards, and once we got free, we were supposed to meet up with the Viper. She was going to get us out of Magic Side."

"The Viper?" Amal glanced back at me, but I hadn't heard the name before.

"Can't tell you anything about her. We never managed to meet up. Kahanov ditched me the second we reached the northern dock. So instead, I did what I do best." A bloodthirsty grin spread across his face, and I couldn't restrain myself any longer.

I stepped forward and punched him, careful not to break his jaw but ensuring I felt his nose crunch. He howled and clutched his bloody face.

As the Ripper's cries subsided to the whimpers of a wounded beast, Amal gave me a sharp look, then folded her arms and continued her interrogation. "Where was the Viper going to take you?" Irritation colored her voice, but she kept her cool.

"Don't. Know," he replied, his answer distorted by the hand he used to stanch the bleeding. "Like I said, Kahanov ditched me, and I wasn't privy to the details of his plan."

"Is that all you have for us?"

The Ripper nodded but I sensed his lie, and my patience was running thin. I unleashed my alpha presence and let my claws extend. Amal tensed, and the devil shrank further into the corner, averting his eyes. "S-stop. I've told you everything."

I took a step closer, and his skin turned ashen. "You were surprised that Kahanov was still on the run. Why was that?"

"B-because. He was half mad. I didn't think he'd last long on the outside." The devil's voice trembled with fear, so I pulled back my power.

"Half mad how?"

"It started a few weeks before we escaped. His mood changed, and he became obsessed with the LaSalles. Like, *deranged* obsessed. He'd been here too long, and he finally broke."

"Did he know the LaSalles personally?" Savannah asked, appearing by my side.

The Ripper dragged his eyes up her body and grinned, a terrible expression considering the condition of the rest of his face. "Don't know, beautiful. He never spoke of them before he went nuts."

"Then we're done here." The way the devil was looking at Savannah made me want to snap his neck, and it was all I could do to maintain control. I grabbed Savannah's arm and towed her out of the cell.

"What are you doing, Jaxson?" she snarled as she tore free of my grasp.

I narrowed my eyes and stepped into her space. "I said we're done. You shouldn't be talking to that bastard. He's a fucking monster that ripped women like you apart."

She flinched like my words had slapped her face, and she crossed her arms. "So now what? We still don't know where he is."

I cocked my head as Amal's voiced echoed into the hallway. She'd resumed her interrogation about how the escapees made their break.

I returned my attention to Savannah. "Amal and I are going to track down the Viper."

"You and Amal? So you're leaving me out of this again?"

I set my jaw and mirrored her crossed arms. "I have no idea who the Viper is, but if she's working with monsters like the Ripper and Kahanov, then she's probably a monster, too. The fact that he was able to coordinate with someone on the outside suggests Kahanov has connections in Magic Side. I'm not walking you into danger. So go home, sit tight. We'll deal with him."

"No." She shoved me, but I didn't budge, so she strode down the hall a few paces before turning back. "Why the hell are you so invested in protecting me? I'm a LaSalle, and you've made it clear you couldn't care less for me."

I slowly crossed the distance. "Because Kahanov is an asshole, and I'm not going to give him what he wants."

She raised her chin defiantly. "Then maybe you should just toss me in his empty cell. I'd be nice and safe, and you'd know where I was."

"Maybe I should."

She bared her teeth, and the silence stretched between us. There was something about the fire in her eyes and the scent of her rage that made me want to slam her up against the wall and take her mouth with mine. She gently bit her healing lower lip, and I imagined what she might taste like. *Pure fucking heaven with a bite of poison.*

My wolf strained in my chest, and it was all I could do to steady my breathing and repress my desire. Why was I letting this unbearable woman get under my skin?

Amal emerged from the cell, and the guard slammed the door.

Savannah glanced at Amal and Neve talking, and then whispered, "If I have to cower in a cell, then you're just handing

Kahanov all the power. Please, let me help you hunt him down. Maybe it's risky, but I need this, and I can help. You *know* I can."

Her body trembled with repressed rage and frustration. I looked deep into her eyes, measuring her will. They flickered with something I couldn't quite put my finger on at first—not hatred, nor desperation, nor fear.

I leaned closer and breathed in her scent, searching for answers. It always drove me wild, but even as desire overwhelmed my mind, a shock of recognition cut through the fog. I understood the emotion now—the call of the hunt. The compulsion to relentlessly chase. To tear down your prey. To take its life.

I knew that emotion well. It was strange from a sorcerer, but I could respect the need. It would also ensure that Savannah was under my watch.

Grinding my teeth, I relented. "Fine. Tomorr—"

A metallic thud echoed through the door of the cell beside us, and Savannah jumped at the noise.

The door to cell 35 was sealed with five arcane locks. Someone had posted a sign beside the window slit: *Do not talk to the prisoner.*

I stepped up to the door and slid the slit open. A shadow moved inside—a hulking figure, sitting in darkness. His signature resonated with power. Even through the magically sealed door, it vibrated the air around us. It felt like flames across my skin and smelled of fresh tobacco and amber.

"What do you want?" I growled.

His head turned slowly, and he spoke in a rough voice laced with danger. "If you're looking for Kahanov, you're not going to find him."

"And why's that?"

The inmate shifted, and his words echoed out of the shadow. "He was gone before he even escaped."

7

———

I spent the evening filling Casey in about our visit to the Ripper and complaining about thick-skulled werewolves. "I told you Jaxson was an ass," was my cousin's most frequent response.

At least Jaxson had agreed to let me help. For now. I was certain that at the slightest sign of peril, he'd try to stuff me in a box. What kind of monster would shove a woman into a jail cell just to protect her?

Screw werewolves.

By midnight I was out of complaints, and we were nearly out of whiskey, which was probably a bad sign for the morning.

I remorsefully dragged myself upstairs and into bed, but I tossed and turned. Nightmares flooded my mind.

I was alone in the twisting halls of Bentham. The lights flickered, and the sound of footsteps followed me around every bend.

The Ripper was coming.

I raced from level to level, but no matter how many stairways I descended, the glowing numbers of the cells stayed the same.

One door was always open. Number 37. Every time I checked, no one was inside.

I searched the empty cell. "Where are you, you fucker?" I screamed.

Kahanov's breath traced over the back of my neck. "In your room, right beside you."

Gasping, I sat up in bed, chest heaving. I pressed my eyes closed and tried to calm my breath, but when I opened them again, it was no better. I felt like I'd run a marathon, and sweat covered my skin.

Just a dream, I thought, slumping back down onto the soaked mattress. Another nightmare.

The echoes of the sorcerer's voice in my mind made my skin prickle, and an ominous sensation of being watched crept along my spine.

Had the sorcerer been scrying on me?

I was wearing my charm, so he shouldn't have been able to watch me. I went to touch my necklace, but my arm didn't move. It was leaden and useless, like I'd been sleeping on it.

I looked frantically around the room. Dim light from the waning gibbous moon filtered through the curtains, casting soft shadows across the furniture. Something wasn't right, but I couldn't put my finger on it. Then a slender shadow moved along the walls, and my stomach knotted as trepidation wound around my heart.

I told myself that it was just the shifting curtains or the branch of a tree outside...but then, with a soft, slow motion, the old rickety mattress sagged beside me. I tried to whip my head around to the right, but my body only moved as if pushing through molasses.

Deep dread squeezed my lungs and throat as I looked into the blurred, inky face of the intruder.

The faceless man.

He sat there beside me on my bed, head cocked curiously to the side.

I opened my mouth to scream, but he quickly placed a finger to my lips. "Come, now, we don't want to wake anyone up. It's the middle of the night."

My cry burned in my lungs, but no sound came out, no matter how hard I pushed.

The blur followed his face, just like when I'd scried. But his appearance was different—his body distorted the air around him, stretching the shapes of everything like fabric pulled tight over an object beneath. It was as if, somehow, he were pushing his way through a picture of my room.

A familiar voice snarled in the back of my mind. *Wake up!*

Shit. It was still a dream.

I forced words out of my leaden lips. "I. Am. Still. Dreaming...You. Aren't. Here."

He brushed my hair from my shoulder and whispered, "Yes, Savannah. You're dreaming. But your eyes are wide open because I want you to see what happens next. Don't worry. Soon, you'll be with me."

Rage fogged the corners of my vision, and I pushed a hiss from my frozen lips. "Soon, you'll be dead."

His hand paused. "Oh, Savannah, you have such a penchant for irony."

The faceless man rose, strode around the end of the bed, and examined the random sketches scattered over the furniture. "You do art things. How quaint."

With his back turned, I felt his hold over me slip... just a little.

Although I couldn't move my hands, I thrust spite-laden words from my mouth. "We'll find you and kill you. We know who you are."

He chuckled. "Oh, I doubt that. If you did, you wouldn't have quite so much sass. But it's no surprise you don't know the truth.

You don't even know who *you* are, Savannah. And you can't control your own body."

The faceless man waved his hand, and my right arm threw off the covers of its own volition. Terror wound around my thundering heart. He gestured upward with his hands, as if coaxing a small child, and my legs slipped over the scratchy sheets and out of bed.

Wake up! the voice in my soul cried.

But instead, I stood, adorned only in my skimpy nightclothes. At least the sorcerer wasn't looking.

"Are there any pictures of me?" he inquired, turning my way.

Fuck.

I nodded against my will.

He made little walking gestures with his fingers, and I staggered over to the desk with ungainly steps. My mind whirled. What was happening? Was I sleepwalking? Why could he control me?

"Show me what you've been working on," the shadowy man purred.

Every nerve in my body screamed in protest, but I opened the drawer and pulled out the crumpled papers.

This can't be happening.

I held out a fistful of the sketches I'd drawn of Jaxson. My heart leapt a little, glad that even out of my control, my body knew how to deliver a snappy *fuck you*.

The faceless man shook his head. "What rubbish. We know you can do better."

He waved his hand, and I ripped them and tossed them in the trash. Resentment and regret drowning my thoughts, I pulled out the drawings I did of him.

"Much better. Spread them out."

I did as he instructed.

"My, you are quite talented. But Savannah, you've got my

face all wrong. You've just made a smudge. I think it's time for you to see it for real."

I gritted my teeth. "If I wanted to see an asshole, I'd just bend over in front of a mirror."

He laughed. "So much fight. Such a strong soul. I doubt I'd have any chance of doing this if I didn't have your blood. But I do, so let's go."

Shit. Those bastards had taken it when I was trapped in the sanitorium.

Kahanov waved to the bedroom door.

My neck burned, and my teeth ached. My heart had lost its rhythm and was pounding erratically in my breast. Despite my fury, despite my fear, I obeyed. Straining with every step, I walked over and undid the latch on the door.

The pained voice in my head whimpered, *Wake up, Savy!*

But I couldn't. Sweat trickled down my spine as I opened the door and stared into the empty hall. I tried to shout, but my voice was locked again. But maybe Casey had heard my door. Maybe he would hear my footsteps or me talking to myself.

They were fool's hopes. The house was silent except for my labored breathing.

The sorcerer laid a hand on my shoulder. "This is where I leave you. Your ride is waiting. Better go catch it."

My mind screamed. Fighting my own body, I began padding barefoot across the creaky wooden floorboards to the stairs. I took each stairstep deliberately, sleepwalking my way down to the second-floor landing. Then the first. Pictures of long-dead LaSalles looked back at me from the walls and emotionlessly watched my descent. My ancestors, impotent to help. Content to watch me go.

Finally, I reached the entry hall. The sorcerer was nowhere to be seen, but I still obeyed his will.

I unlocked the five latches on the front door one at a time.

Then I swung it wide and stepped out onto the porch. Six more agonizing steps took me down to the sidewalk and another dozen took me to the curb.

Then my body stopped with an unsteady jolt.

"Remember to look both ways," the sorcerer's distant voice echoed in my mind—an intrusive, violating feeling—unlike the familiar snarl that echoed back in response.

But despite my rage, my head turned left. Then right. I was truly alone.

My foot lifted off the still warm pavement and stepped onto the dry, dusty asphalt of the street.

I stopped short when I reached the middle. Every part of my soul screamed in agony, but I couldn't move a muscle more. I just stood, petrified, beneath the deep yellow glow of the streetlights.

Then a shadow swept over me, and my already pounding heart accelerated to a breakneck pace.

With an ominous shudder, the street shook as something landed behind me.

I couldn't turn my head or even tilt my eyes, but I still could sense the overwhelming power of the thing. The signature of its magic smelled of deep, sickly pungent flowers and tasted of overripe fruit. It sounded like the deafening buzz of millions of cicadas and felt like sap creeping over my skin.

As I stood there, unable to move, an enormous, blurry shape methodically moved into the corner of my transfixed gaze. Something of unimaginable size and horror.

Step by shuddering step, it shifted into view, blocking the light from the streetlamps.

A shudder quaked through me.

Not real. It couldn't be.

But it was. The thing crouched on six spindly legs that were sheathed in fur and glistening mucus. Its head was almond shaped, ringed by hundreds of eyes. Two pairs of wings haltingly rose from its segmented back. They were decrepit, moth-like things, decorated with hypnotic, iridescent patterns.

Wake up! commanded the voice in my soul.

But I didn't, and I stood motionless as the thing's long, narrow head slowly split open vertically like a Venus flytrap, revealing rows of teeth and a fine purple tendril of a tongue that unwound and snaked toward me.

I would have wet myself, but I didn't even have control over that. I was a statue.

Its hot, wet, reeking breath rolled over me as its tongue slipped across my chest and neck, leaving a trail of mucus. But rather than bite me in half, the monster withdrew its head, arched its back, and curled its hindlegs underneath its body, then reached forward with a pair of glistening, clawed talons.

A howl tore through the back of my mind, the piercing wail of despair of a chained beast. But for a second, my eyes had enough freedom to turn away from the horror and look up into the night sky.

Behind the monster, a pillar of rising clouds boiled into the shape of a black wolf against the starlit sky.

What the fuck?

I will free you, if you free me. The words boomed in my mind.

It wasn't the voice of the sorcerer or of the monster. Or the voice in my soul that kept urging me to wake up. It was a voice that shook my thoughts and being to my very core.

There was no way for me to respond, only desperate, confused hope.

Suddenly, agony jolted through my body, and a knife-like pain shot through my fingers and teeth.

I screamed. With my own voice this time. Moving my own mouth. My body was my own again.

Heart near to ripping out of my chest, I spun as the nightmare's talons lashed out. They gouged into my arm and shoulders, but I didn't care. I could move. I was free. But how?

I charged toward the monster's sickening maw and dove beneath its reach. Pent-up adrenaline surged through my body, and I hurtled forward with a speed and strength that was far beyond me.

But the thing spun far faster than something its size should have been able to move. Its jaws snapped open, and it screeched with a dissonant cry that warped the air around me.

I dodged and dove across the pavement, screaming at the top of my lungs. Pain burst from my knees and elbows as gravel cut into my skin, but that didn't matter. I just had to live.

Its savage claws gripped my flesh, and I felt my body rise into the air. Then I slammed into the grass. Gasping for breath, I rolled to the side. The ground shook as talons sank deep beside me, barely missing my skull. Half crawling, I scrambled over the grass, desperately searching for any kind of cover, but I was trapped against the side of a moonlit house.

Use your magic.

How?

The nightmare loomed above me and spread its glistening jaws wide.

Summoning every ounce of strength in my body, I abruptly turned and charged back toward it. Its head snapped down, but I dashed beneath its centipede-like belly and darted for our neighbors' bushes. As I ran, I called the darkness to me. Ice water flowed over my skin, and shadows and streams of darkness wound around me, the only trick I knew.

As the thing spun, I crashed over the hedge and rolled across the grass. Then I clambered to my feet and ducked into shadows cast by the adjacent house. I called the shadows to me, every ounce of darkness the night had to give.

Panting but trying not to make a sound, I pressed my back against the wall. Darkness floated around me like a deep mist—though somehow, I could see through it.

The thing was searching. Its flytrap-like head snapped toward me, and I stifled a wail.

God save me now.

Its attention didn't waver. Could it see me?

Of course it could. It was a nightmare. Certainly, it could see me cowering in the shadows, magic or no. But it didn't move to strike or look way.

Hope sparked. Maybe it couldn't see me through the magical veil of darkness that I'd pulled around my body. But I was certain it knew I was here. It could probably smell my fear.

Then don't be afraid.

I steeled my soul. I was *fucking* Savannah Caine.

When I was a waitress, before I'd known any of this was real, I'd pancaked the first werewolf that had attacked me. I'd fought off blood demons, blood drainers, and more werewolves. I had a body count before I had an ounce of control over my magic. My pulse slowed.

The thing turned its head. Then a bunch of gills opened up.

What the fuck?

I assumed those were some stupid sensing organs for situations when it couldn't see the hapless victim it wanted to devour.

Suddenly, it screeched, and its head snapped away from me as a roaring ball of fire slammed into it.

Casey.

The monstrosity shrieked again, and the air reverberated with power and magic. It reared back to strike, but streams of flame poured toward it, billowing around its form.

Casey shouted above the roaring fire, "Savannah!"

The thing's wings unfolded, but as it began to rise, a black shape swept around its back and leapt into the air. Moonlight glistened off the set of savage claws that sank into the nightmare's flesh. A golden inferno of fire raging around him, Jaxson climbed hand over hand up the monster's spine, using his claws like pitons.

Where the fuck had he come from?

With a single swipe of his claws, he shredded the wings on the right side of the thing's body, and it fell.

He was at its throat in a second and shredded its neck and gills with his claws.

"Stand back, Laurent!" a shrill voice commanded. My aunt.

Jaxson leapt away from the gurgling beast as a green bolt of energy burst from the shadows of our porch.

The nightmare's corpse twitched, and emerald veins of light crackled across its body. The air around me shook, and with a thunderclap, the thing's form sucked down into nothingness.

Just like that, it was gone.

Stillness settled over the street, leaving Jaxson, Casey, and my aunt alone.

Then they began calling my name.

I pressed my back against the wall and shuddered with silent tears as their shouts echoed along the street. Jaxson's voice pulled on my chest, and I wanted to run to him, but I couldn't move—though this time, it wasn't because of the sorcerer's spells. The deep weight of the emotions churning in my heart had frozen my will to move.

Everything *felt* wrong.

I would never be able to unsee that abomination looming over me. The scent of rotten fruit still hung in the air, and I trembled at the memory of the monster's tongue tracing over my skin.

But that wasn't what was dragging me back into the shadows.

Kahanov had taken control of my body. I'd been a puppet. A toy, offered up to a monster.

I bared my teeth as an animalistic rage rose within me. My bloodthirsty thoughts echoed in a single chorus: *Never again.*

8

Jaxson

My body quaked with rage, and my wolf tore at my chest, demanding to be set free.

I scanned the street as the blood on my claws began to smoke and evaporate, leaving behind the sickly aroma of over-ripe fruit. The scent made me weary, dulling my thoughts.

What was that thing?

Casey's voice shook me from my dark thoughts. "What the hell are you doing in our territory, Laurent?"

I slowly turned my attention to the fool LaSalle, who had a ball of flame hovering in his hand. "Watching out for Savannah. Someone has to."

He started to speak, but I turned on him and silenced him with my presence. He was a mosquito.

Laurel LaSalle, on the other hand, had me worried. She hadn't said a thing, but her eyes hadn't left me for an instant. Her gaze was almost painful, as if it were slowly peeling the skin from my body.

"The moment we find Savannah, you get the hell out of here, understand?" Casey hissed.

"Gladly."

He started bellowing Savannah's name again, but I snarled at him. "Quiet, asshole. She's here and afraid. Shouting isn't going to calm her."

"How do you know?"

"Because I'm a wolf, and I can smell her."

But it was more than scent. Something was pulling me toward her, a sixth sense leading me on. Had that always been there?

I crossed a yard and paused, then slowly stepped over to the shadows in the lee of a house. They were too black. Too deep. "Savannah? Are you there?"

No response came, but I didn't need one. I could hear her thundering heartbeat and smell her fear.

"The thing is gone. You're safe." I stepped forward, but Savannah swept out of the darkness, away from me and from her cousin. The shadows clung to her, trailing her like a long black dress, moving softly in the glow of the streetlights.

It was beautiful.

"I will never be safe."

Her voice rang with anger, but I could tell it was covering for terror. I sensed she wanted to run toward me, but she just kept moving away.

Casey came over and reached for her. "Hey, it's going to be okay, Savy."

She spun away. "No, it is *not*."

He shrugged. "Look, the bug is dead, and we all lived. It's nothing a belt of whiskey can't fix."

"What do you know? Nothing," she spat, maneuvering around us like boxers in the ring. "Kahanov just invaded my dreams and made me sleepwalk out here. Then he tried to feed me to a horror from the abyss. I am *not* freaking okay, and I don't think I'm ever going to sleep again."

Shocked silence hung in the street.

He'd invaded her dreams?

That fucker. My body shook as I tried to repress my wolf, and my hands and face ached as I held back the shift.

"Holy shit," Casey murmured, eyes wide.

I wanted to go to Savannah, but I suspected the moment any of us took a step forward, she would back away—she was on edge, a tiger against a wall. Perhaps the others understood as well, because not one of us moved.

Finally, Savannah licked her lips. "Do any of you know what the hell that was? It was under his control and sent to capture me."

"It was a demon, though not one I've ever encountered. Come back in the house, and we'll figure this out." Laurel's voice seemed like a placid lake, but that was just a well-controlled veneer concealing a torrent of anger that made the hair on my neck stand on end. Her signature was oppressive—bees buzzing in my mind and a choking scent of spices. How Savannah could stand to be around them, I didn't know.

I pushed my alpha presence toward Savannah, trying to calm her unease. "Clearly, Kahanov is capable of far more than blood magic. I warned you that staying here would be danger-ous. You should come back to Dockside, and I'll put you in a safehouse with an armed detail."

Casey gave a bitter laugh. "No way in hell is she going back to Dockside with you. She's safer here, and you know it. Bullets and claws aren't going to do shit against that kind of thing."

I spun on him and snarled. "You annoyed it. I ripped its throat out."

"All the more reason she's not going with you," he retorted.

Savannah stepped forward, fists tightly balled. "Stop talking about me like I'm not here! Both of you!"

Casey flinched.

Laurel moved to the railing of her porch. "I can show you a way to protect yourself, Savannah, so that never happens again."

"How?"

"When we trained this morning, you took cover in a circle of protection. I can make one around your bed that will shield your mind—that includes your dreams as well as protection against mind reading and scrying. It'll take time, but I can show you how."

My wolf rose in protest, but I reined it in. As much as I wanted to take Savannah away from there, I couldn't guarantee that Kahanov wouldn't hijack her dreams again.

Savannah looked between us, then met my gaze. "Yes. That's what I want. Teach me to protect myself."

I took a step forward. "Savannah—"

"We've got this, wolf," Casey spat.

I twisted and narrowed my eyes at the asshole. "Obviously, you don't, LaSalle."

Savannah moved up the stairs beside her aunt. "Jaxson, I'm staying here."

Bitterness wound around me. Fine. If that's what she wanted, so be it.

I turned to go, but she spoke. "Casey, Aunt Laurel, give me a minute?"

With reluctance, they headed inside.

Savannah stared down at me from the rail, wrapped in her cloak of shadows. "I saw what you did. Thank you."

I set my jaw. I wasn't going to be patronized. "He'll send more, whether you're sleeping or not. We need to figure out what that is. Could you draw it? Like you've done before?"

"Yes."

"Good. Send me a picture, and I'll pass it on to Neve. I'll let you know what she finds."

Savannah nodded and turned toward the door. She paused

as she held it open, letting the yellow light spill out. "You can't protect me from this, Jaxson. You know that, right?"

Then she disappeared inside and shut the door.

By the next morning, shit had spiraled out of control. Three members of my pack were in the hospital. They'd gone to sleep, and no one could wake them.

I had no doubt that this was the result of another sort of dream attack and that Kahanov was to blame. His powers had grown. But how?

Dark thoughts percolating in my mind, I stormed through the halls of the hospital. With a nod of my head to the security guard, I entered the restricted wing where the sleepers had been taken. I had to see them for myself, to face the consequence of my choices.

My phone dinged, and I stole a glance as I pushed through a set of double doors. A text from Neve: *Got Savannah's drawing this morning, and I tracked down what the demon is. Come to the Archives. You're not going to be happy.*

Of that, I had no doubt. I checked the time—almost 11:30—and sent a quick response: *Meet you at noon. Let Savannah know.*

Regina was waiting for me outside a curtained hospital room, along with a doctor and Lily Duvoir, the curse diviner, who was dressed in a long flowing blue skirt with stacks of bangles around her arms. I was surprised she'd agreed to come. She rarely left her home in Dockside.

I tucked my phone away. "What's our status?"

The doctor looked at his chart. "We have three of your werewolves here. They're in comas. We haven't found a way to bring them around with magic or modern medicine."

I pushed aside the privacy curtain, revealing a young woman

with short black hair who was sleeping peacefully. My heart caught. "Shit, it's Cara."

Regina nodded.

Cara was a green recruit, but enthusiastic, and I'd believed in her enough to put her on the team that I'd sent to hunt the rogue wolves in Wisconsin last week. She was there when we stormed Billy's cabin. Now she was comatose.

Had Kahanov picked his victims at random, or had he seen her up there somehow and was seeking revenge?

I scrubbed a hand across my jaw and cursed. This was my responsibility.

Rage and frustration fought for control of my emotions, and my wolf stirred. I dug my fingers into my palms and forced it back. I had to keep my head clear.

"What are we dealing with here?" I growled, my voice teetering on the edge of lupine.

The curse diviner stepped up beside me. "I've examined them all. It's a sleeping curse."

I looked from her to the doctor. "Fine. How do I break it?"

Lily shook her curly dark hair. "I don't know. I think the girl is trapped in a dream, perhaps a nightmare. To break the curse, you might have to enter her dreams, but how that would be done, I haven't a clue."

"And the others are the same?"

Regina nodded. "Sleeping soundly, just like her. Sometimes they move a little or moan or cry out, but they can't wake up."

Not good.

I looked from one woman to the other. "Savannah Caine was attacked in her dreams last night. The sorcerer made her sleepwalk. Did that happen to any of the sleepers? Were they attacked in some other way?"

Regina crossed her arms and lifted her head toward Cara.

"According to her mother, she came in late and just went to bed like normal."

I took a deep breath, seeking an increasingly elusive calm.

Kahanov had appeared in Savannah's dream. Had he entered Cara's dreams and trapped her there? The consequences were staggering. If the bastard could attack my pack in dreams, then he could attack anywhere. We were under siege from an invisible assailant who was going to put my wolves to sleep one by one until I submitted.

Regina handed me photos of two other pack members. The other sleepers, trapped in nightmares.

This was the consequence of not handing over Savannah.

Every muscle in my body wanted me to shift and to hunt and to kill.

There will be a time for that, I told my wolf.

I needed more information. "Can I talk to Cara's mother? Is she here?"

The doctor led me to a woman sitting alone in a waiting room, who rose when we entered the room. "Alpha."

I inclined my head. "I'm sorry about Cara. She's a good wolf."

Her mother looked away and covered her mouth.

I pushed my alpha presence toward her. "It's going to be okay. I'll do everything I can to get her back."

She nodded slowly as my presence took away her fear and pain and amplified the true power I had over my pack—their trust.

I placed a hand on her shoulder. "Tell me what happened. Was she attacked? Any sign of a demon entering the house?"

She shook her head and wiped her eyes on the backs of her hands. "Cara came home from a night on the town and was quiet all evening. I thought she was just sleeping in late, but when I checked on her, she wouldn't wake up. I called 911 right away."

The scent of her emotions tore at me. Despair. Anguish. Hopelessness.

My pack was hurting, and that cut worse than any knife wound.

I tried to coax more information out of her, but the anguished woman had little to give. Eventually, Regina laid a hand on my arm, and I caught the meaning in her eyes.

I stepped back. "I'm sorry to ask so many questions. I'll let you get some rest. And I'll do everything I can to lift the curse from Cara."

"Thank you, Alpha."

I turned to leave, but the woman caught my arm. "It's silly, but I had a dream about this."

My heart froze. I'd only been asking about Cara. "What do you mean?"

"A man came to me in my dreams...he was tall and thin, and I never saw his face. He said my daughter was in trouble, and that..." She paused and averted her eyes, and I sensed deep shame.

"What did he say? Tell me. It's important."

She swallowed and wouldn't meet my gaze. "He said that you'd failed us, but that you'd know what to do to make it right."

Fury wound around my heart. That fucking bastard Kahanov.

She quickly grasped my hand, sensing my rage. "I know it was just a dream, and this isn't your fault, Alpha. But I'm praying that you do know what to do."

Hand over Savannah Caine.

I nodded. "I'll get to the bottom of this."

I left, and Regina tailed me down the hall. Once we were out of earshot, I pulled her to the side. "This is Kahanov, for certain. He's trying to force me to hand Savannah over."

"Will you?"

"No."

She frowned, and I could sense her dissent.

"You think it's the wrong decision? Kahanov is a terrorist. I won't negotiate."

She averted her eyes. "It's the right call. For now."

I followed her look back down the hall to the worried mother sitting alone in the waiting room.

What a fucking mess. Regina was my second in command. That meant she could question, doubt, and consider all options. But I couldn't. I was alpha, and I wouldn't bend before him.

"I'm going to the Archives to chase a lead. You need to get the word out. Find out if anyone else has been attacked. Get someone to interview the last people to see each of the victims awake, as well as anyone who was approached by a faceless man in their dreams."

"On it," she said with palpable relief. She was more comfortable when she had a clear plan to pursue.

I turned and headed down the hall. As I walked, I texted Damian Malek, one of Magic Side's underworld bosses. *I'm calling in a favor. I need to find the Viper, whoever the hell she is. ASAP.*

Savannah, Amal, Neve, Regina, Damian. One of them was going to find something that pointed to what Kahanov was up to.

And once I knew that, I would relentlessly hunt him down and make him beg for mercy. I would become *his* nightmare.

9

Jaxson

Fifteen minutes later, I double parked my truck in front of the Hall of Inquiry. I slammed my door and climbed the stairs of the massive limestone building. It was neoclassical in style with a wide columned entry and massive brass doors—a beautiful façade erected to convince everyone that everything was in order, that everything was under control. But I knew the truth. This city was run by monsters and mages and crime lords, and always one step away from the brink of destruction.

Savannah and Neve were waiting for me on the top steps, two redheads side by side. Neve's burgundy tones made Savannah's hair look like flowing flames, verging on orange.

It was almost impossible to take my eyes off the LaSalle woman. She wore pale blue jeans and a black moto jacket that hugged her curves in all the right places. I took in her form, my gaze lingering on her lips. Lips I had tasted before.

Something about her put me off balance. No one had ever had that effect on me.

Frustration drowned my desire the moment she spoke: "You're late this time."

I glared at her and turned to Neve. "Three werewolves went to sleep last night and never woke up. They've been hit with some sort of sleeping curse. Kahanov must be behind it, just like the attack on Savannah. Tell me you have some idea what's going on."

"Maybe." Neve led us through the front doors and deep into the Hall of Inquiry.

Now that she was out of the sun, I could see that Savannah's face was drawn, and worry dragged on her shoulders.

"Are you all right?" I asked gruffly as we crossed over a skybridge to the Archives building.

She set her jaw. "I haven't slept, I'm five coffees into the day, and my brain is running a million miles a minute—all I can think about is how I'm going to hunt down Kahanov and skin him alive."

My lips curled into a dark smile as a wild heat spread under my skin. This woman was resilient as all hell. My wolf approved, and so did I.

Her tired eyes widened as we pushed through the massive door of the library, which was decorated with moving carvings of scientists and scholars, myths and monsters. She opened her mouth to speak, but when she saw the library, her jaw dropped.

The Archives was much bigger on the inside than it appeared from the outside. A domed roof soared over a vast cylindrical chamber lined with books.

Savannah leaned over the balcony railing and looked down into the room below, a deep pit with imps flying in and out carrying books. "Belmont's library was the size of a Taco Bell and only open on Wednesdays and Thursdays and every other weekend."

Neve opened her mouth and then snapped it shut.

We followed her to a back room with a large leatherbound

book spread wide on the table. The pages were yellow, and the thing looked like it had been printed in the nineteenth century.

Neve gestured to Savannah's drawing of the monster that was on the nearby table. "I found a description of the demon that attacked you last night in *Carter's Bestiary of Strange and Infernal Abominations.*"

She flipped the pages to a bookmark and held the book open wide, revealing a delicate ink sketch of a gangly, six-legged creature with a flytrap head and four mothlike wings. Its jaws were open and dripping, and a long snakelike tongue lolled out. It matched Savannah's drawing almost exactly.

Savannah looked away. "That's it."

I nodded, recalling the acrid taste of its blood when I tore its throat out.

A subtle quake shook Savannah's body, and I could sense her revulsion and fear. A jolt of protectiveness pushed me toward her, but I stopped short and tightened my fists. She'd already chosen who she wanted protection from. Who she trusted. And it wasn't me.

Neve gave Savannah a warm smile. "With the sketch you sent me, the monster wasn't hard to track down."

"What did you learn about it?"

"It's a noctith demon. Fun fact: they breathe poison gas that puts people to sleep. They're classified as a third order demon, though technically, they're not really demons...more of a beast native to the Dreamlands."

"What are the Dreamlands?" Savannah asked, her voice laced with wonder.

"A realm of dreams, sort of like one of the fae realms but different. Most of the information is myth and anecdote. The best source is a book written by a witch, *The Grimoire of Nightmares.* But when I went to look for it in the Archive of Bound Tomes, it was gone. Stolen."

I started to open my mouth, but Savannah beat me to the punch. "The Archive of Bound Tomes?"

Neve nodded. "It's the section of our collections where they chain down particularly malicious and deviant books. Like a prison for knowledge."

A confused expression crossed Savannah's face. "Chain down deviant books? I don't think I..."

Neve smiled and closed the leatherbound tome. "Books of magic can be tricky things. If you cram enough spells and secrets and forbidden knowledge together in one place, sometimes the book will...well, sort of wake up and take on a personality of its own."

"But it was stolen?" Savannah shot me an anxious look. "Was it Kahanov?"

"The moment I discovered the book was missing, I called security and had them do a facial recognition search for Kahanov between now and the day he escaped. They got a hit on the cameras in the Archives."

She held out her phone and hit play on a recording. The video feed showed the Archives in complete disarray. Open books were scattered across every available surface, and people were rushing everywhere.

"When was this?" I asked, certain it had to be when the Archives was hit.

"The day he escaped. This place was flooded at the same time the marid attacked Bentham Prison. It was a distraction. Four hours later, Kahanov showed up."

A few seconds into the clip, a bright box appeared on the screen, isolating a figure who was moving warily through the shadows. For one second, he glanced up, and the video paused.

"That's him?" Savannah asked, a soft tremor in her voice. She'd never seen his face. Nor had I, but I clenched my fists and burned the image into my mind. *Got you, asshole.*

"Yes," Neve said quietly. "That's Kahanov. I can send you other pictures."

Savannah swallowed hard and nodded.

Neve slipped her phone into her pocket. "He went directly to the Bound Tomes and freed the grimoire. Then he vanished with a transport charm. He knew exactly where he was going...I wonder if the book called to him, somehow."

"That's creepy," Savannah said absently. "What powers does it give him? Other than summoning these noctith demons?"

Worry clouded the sky blue of Neve's eyes. "I don't know. I've gone through the archivist's notes on the thing. It's a guide to the monsters and realms of the Dreamlands. It promises, of course, unimaginable powers to those that learn its secrets and sleep with their head upon the book."

My pulse accelerated. "Could he use it to invade the dreams of others? To stop my wolves from waking?"

Neve nodded. "According to the notes, yes. It can grant the power to infiltrate and shape the dreams of others. Possibly more."

"So he hacked into my dreams?" Savannah asked.

"And into those of my wolves. How do we wake them?"

There was a long silence, and Neve frowned. "I'm sorry, Jaxson, I don't know—but that doesn't mean the information isn't out there. I'll keep digging in the Archives."

Savannah looked between us expectantly, like there had to be more that could be done. "I'm not sitting around while people read books. What can we do?"

Neve's expression darkened, and a slight breeze rose around us. "Find him, and don't sleep until you bring him down."

"Right." Savannah swallowed. "Simple as that."

The scent of her despair tore at me, and I knew she needed something to cling to. And for no conceivable reason, I wanted that to be me.

I stepped close, and she shivered as I let my alpha presence surround her. "We've learned quite a bit. Kahanov wants to toy with us through dreams and have his minions do the dirty work. He's never attacked you himself. What does that suggest?"

Savannah tilted her head and gazed up at me. "He's afraid of direct confrontation?"

"Exactly. He's weak or afraid we might best him in a fight. We need to hunt him down. Thanks to Amal, we know he's in Italy and on the move. That tells me that he needs something beyond the grimoire. We just need to get to it first."

"How?"

"We find the Viper and see what she knows." I nodded subtly to Neve. "I asked an old ally with deep connections to look into it. My guess is we'll know where the little snake is in less than twenty-four hours. Until then, Neve looks for a way to break the sleeping curse, and we rack our brains for every other possible clue we've overlooked."

I poured my alpha presence into Savannah and Neve, drowning their doubts with a torrent of strength and conviction.

If only I could drown my own.

10

Savannah

"You look like hell," Casey observed, as we drove through the Indies that evening.

"Thanks. Between the nightmares and demon attacks and hunting down the asshole trying to kill me, I haven't had a chance to do cucumber therapy on my eyes."

He turned right, into an old parking lot. "Hey, I get it. Seeing that thing last night messed me up. Your brain's got to be scrambled eggs by now. What you need is a stiff drink, and then two or three more."

"What I need is a bed, some sleeping pills, and a night of dreams without evil creeps breaking into them."

"Don't worry, you'll be fine," Casey said almost convincingly. "First, we do my plan, and then you do yours. And since your bed has a circle of protection, you'll be able to sleep off the hangover peacefully. The only dudes popping up in your dreams will be the ones you put there."

"I'm hoping for a total of none."

He glanced over at me with a cocky expression on his face. "None or just one?"

Fucker.

I ignored him and looked out the window. As gorgeous as Jaxson was, I did *not* want him in my dreams. I had enough on my plate as it was, and I didn't need to be fantasizing over the domineering alpha-hole whom I couldn't have even if I'd wanted him.

The fading light reflected off the buildings across the lake as we pulled into the poorly maintained parking lot. It was packed with cars, and I could feel the bass of the music pumping through the trees in the park to our right.

"What is this place, anyway?" I asked.

"Founder's Park. One of the most important places in the Indies."

I rolled up my window and stashed my bag under my seat. "Oh, yeah? Why's that?"

"There's a bonfire every Saturday at sundown. Best place to unwind." He winked and climbed out of the car. "And there'll be enough sorcerers here to nuke Kahanov to kingdom come if he shows up, so you'll be safe." He grabbed a bag of ice and a bottle of Jose Cuervo black from the backseat and handed me two insulated Yeti Ramblers. "Hold these."

"You know these people?"

"Some. There's always a good crowd, all ages—just not teenagers, thank fates," he added, grinning. "No one wants to deal with sloppy kids."

A black Beamer pulled into the lot, and a couple of girls who looked to be in their late twenties climbed out, holding a six pack of hard seltzer and a bottle of vodka. One of the girls shouted Casey's name and waved.

He glanced over his shoulder and gave her a thumbs-up but didn't stop. "But yeah, pretty much anyone is welcome. Just not the *wolves*."

"Right." A sinking pit of dread settled in my stomach.

Kahanov had that damn grimoire and was trying to hijack my dreams. He might still be after my blood. Shit was dire, and despite my anger at Jaxson, my feelings for him muddled everything. Could I trust him?

"You were with him today, weren't you?" Casey asked, as if reading my mind.

"I was." I narrowed my eyes at my cousin, trying to detect any hint of judgement. But there was none.

"A piece of advice, Cuz," he continued. "Stay away from Jaxson. I know you've heard it before, and I'm not one to lecture you, but you can't ever trust him or the pack. You're not one of them, and they'll never have your back."

"Believe me, I *don't* trust them. I just don't have many other options right now."

Casey veered off to the left. "Let me show you something."

We strolled down to a reed-lined pond and stopped by a cluster of large stones surrounded by little flowers. The central stone was longer than the rest and stood on end. Someone had carved hundreds of strange symbols and diagrams into its surface long ago. Casey ran his palm over the lines. "This is the founder's stone—the seed that created this part of Magic Side."

"What do you mean?"

"To make this part of the island, the LaSalles enchanted this stone with a powerful spell and floated it out into the lake on a raft. The magic spread through Lake Michigan and drew sediment and rubble up from the bottom to form an island. A small one, granted, but there weren't Magica living here at the time."

I ran my fingers over the weathered rock, tracing the symbols, which had grown shallow and worn from the rain.

"Those inscriptions on the stone were part of the spell. The ancient magic is spent, so technically, this is just an old rock. But our forebearers were sorcerers, and we work magic with our souls. That means the souls of our ancestors are in this rock.

Remember that fact if you ever question whether you really belong in Magic Side. I know this city must seem crazy, but it's part of you."

My heart ached at that thought. Of truly belonging somewhere.

Casey slung his arm around my shoulder and pulled me into his chest. "You have us, your family. We'll always have your back. Tomorrow, we'll sit down with Mom and bang our heads together until we figure out what to do about that prick, but now, it's time to forget all that shit and drink, got it?"

I nodded, pursing my lips to hold in the emotions that wanted to crawl out. I'd only known my cousin for a couple of weeks, and even though he was insane like the rest of the family, he seemed to genuinely care about me in his own twisted way.

Up ahead, the noise from the party filled the air. Dozens of people crowded around several cars that had driven into the park. A Jeep with lifted wheels sat beside a pair of coolers and lawn chairs, its speakers thrumming '90s R&B jams.

But it was the flames curling from the huge bonfire in the center of the gathering that drew my eyes. They weren't the normal orange, but instead cycled among a variety of colors— purple, blue, and green.

"A magic bonfire?" Just as I muttered the words, a woman across the way pitched a glowing blue orb into the fire like it was a baseball. The flames arced at least ten feet into the air, and shouts erupted from the crowd.

Casey shook his head as he put the ice in a cooler and pulled out a Coke. "Some of the sorcerers like to show off."

I raised a brow at him. "You don't say?"

Though I'd been suspicious that this gathering might be like the keggers I'd attended in high school, there were no keg stands, and the atmosphere was mellow. Most of the people here looked to be in their twenties or thirties.

Casey took the Ramblers and mixed us some tequila cokes. "I keep forgetting that this is all new to you. I'll introduce you to some friends."

An hour later, I'd met a handful of people whose names I couldn't recall. The bottle of Jose Cuervo was nearly empty, and the pop in my cup was flat. Casey was chatting up some woman with pointy ears who genuinely seemed interested in his humor. Shaking my head, I gulped down the last of my drink and set the Rambler beside one of the coolers. Two women exited a stone building that looked like a bathroom and stumbled toward the coolers, laughing.

"*Wolf bait.*" Behind me, a voice carried above the din of the music.

I spun, meeting the gazes of two guys. "Excuse me?"

Their eyes were glassy, and a cold darkness snaked around them. My skin crawled. *Run*, a voice deep in my mind said.

The tallest of them stepped forward, staring at me like a piece of candy free for the taking. He was built like Casey but stockier, and his blond crew cut and cocky expression dredged up memories of the bullies from my high school days. "My friend here was telling me that you're the alpha's little whore."

His words cut through the air and drew bile in my throat. My nails tingled, and I balled my fists to keep calm. It took everything I had to fight the urge to kick the guy in the balls, and if this hadn't been Casey's crowd, I would have.

The asshole stalked around me, poking and prodding with his eyes. "I told him *no*, that can't be right. She's a LaSalle." He stopped in front of me, and his eyes narrowed, revealing the hate simmering inside them. "And LaSalles don't *mingle* with wolves."

My heartbeat drummed against my ribs, and my senses heightened. The rustle of the leaves in the trees, the bead of sweat rolling down my spine, and the sour-rank stench of these bastards—a pungent mix of BO and cologne and whiskey that turned my stomach. My head spun. How much tequila had I drunk?

The other guy scoffed and waved his hand through the air, his movement unbalanced, his gaze distant. "She's no LaSalle, Jared. Let her chase Laurent's tail. Maybe she likes it doggie style." With a disgusting expression on his face, he pumped his hips in a thrusting motion.

I ground my teeth so hard that my jaw felt like it might crack, and my sweaty palms stung.

"What the hell is going on?" Casey shot forward and shoved the jerk in front of me. "Jared, get the fuck away from my cousin."

Jared stepped back and raised his arms in a non-combative gesture. "Easy, Case. Just getting to know the traitor in our midst."

Pure, unadulterated rage coursed through me, and my vision shifted. The sound of the music and the clamor of people talking were suddenly overwhelming, and my skin flushed. What was happening to me?

Chest heaving, I glanced down at my hands, which were burning. I blinked twice and jerked back. Blood dripped from punctures in my palms, and where my nails should have been, there were *claws*.

"*Fuck*," I squeaked as fear snaked into my heart.

Casey's gaze snapped to me and then to the other guy. My cousin had Jared's shirt in his fists, but he shoved him away. "What's wrong? Did that other fucker touch you?"

I hid my hands behind my back and shook my head, swallowing the panic in my throat. "Nope. I just need a minute. Alone."

Turning, I clutched my bloodied hands and jogged toward the bathroom, Casey's voice carrying behind me.

I slipped into the bathroom and locked the door. *Fuck, fuck, fuck.*

A beetle thwacked the lightbulb overhead, and I squinted, my eyes burning from the brightness. I took a breath and ambled toward the sink, bracing myself on the cool tile. My vision blurred before clearing. Trails of crimson blood streaked down the white porcelain sink, and my breath quickened as the pain in my jaw throbbed.

Stay calm, Savy. There's a perfectly reasonable explanation for this, I thought, though deep down, I knew better.

I inhaled and looked up, meeting the eyes of my reflection in the mirror.

A monster stared back at me.

11

"Oh, my God, no." My heart rate and breathing skyrocketed as I braced myself against the sink and studied my reflection in the mirror.

My eyes had gone amber. Auburn hair had sprouted along my forearms, and claws extended from my bloody fingertips, still aching from their release.

This wasn't PTSD or a trick of the mind. This was real.

My heart hammered against my ribs, but I couldn't move. The horror of the truth had rendered my body immobile.

There was no pretending anymore. I was turning into a werewolf.

I dug my clawed fingers into the side of the sink as I turned every scenario over in my head. How had this happened?

Jaxson had told me that it was practically impossible to catch lycanthropy from a bite, and while I'd been scratched and clawed and knocked around by werewolves, I hadn't ever been bitten.

I closed my eyes, recalling the events of the past two weeks. The rogue wolves had hauled me off to an old sanitorium and drained my blood. They'd also injected me with something. I'd thought it was designed to repress my magic, but what if it was something worse?

Had those bastards done this to me? Had they tried to turn a LaSalle into a werewolf?

Fuck.

Trembling, I leaned forward and bared my teeth in the mirror. They looked normal, despite the deep ache in my upper and lower jaw. I used my knuckle to push aside my lip so I could inspect my gums, and...fucking hell. They were swollen and red, and touching them made the pain worse.

This isn't happening, this isn't happen—

A jarring noise shook me from my thoughts, and I looked around wildly.

The door handle rattled again as someone tried to get in. I covered my ears as they started pounding on the door. The sound was almost deafening.

"This one's taken," I croaked, my throat suddenly drier than a bone. "Use the other!"

I had to find a way to fight this.

Agony exploded through my stomach, and I doubled forward, leaning my weight on the sink. Tears streamed from my eyes, mixing with the blood on the porcelain. I could *smell* the blood—just one of a hundred scents filtering through my mind, most of them revolting.

I gasped as a sharp pain erupted through my jaw, and I looked up in horror. Blood ran from my lips. I'd sprouted fangs. *Fuck!*

I had to get out of here, away from these people. If anyone at the party saw this, they'd crucify me. But where could I go? I had no one to turn to. Casey would never understand, and if Laurel found out, she'd kick me out or worse.

Run.

I could hide in the shadows. I just had to slip into the park without being noticed, then I could disappear into the woods and wait for this to pass. It *would* pass, right?

Of course it would. I'd seen my eyes turn this color before.

Having a plan gave me courage. Gut throbbing, I staggered over to the door and listened, but I could barely make sense of what I heard. My ears were drowning in noise. The light above buzzed incessantly, and the music sounded like someone had parked a loudspeaker right outside.

Even with all that, I could still hear the conversations of people by the bonfire.

The bathroom door beside mine opened and slammed with a reverberating thud as someone left. I could hear the soft padding of footsteps crossing the grass, though it was like the walker was stomping through hay right next to my head.

I shouldn't be able to hear that.

Gripping the handle, I unlocked the door and slipped outside and around the building. Casey was talking to some people, his back turned to me. Hopefully, he'd assume I'd left and wouldn't come looking.

I tried pulling the darkness around me, but my magic didn't flow. Too much noise. Too much pain. I gasped and shuddered as a piercing ache shot through my shoulder blades.

It was now or never. This wasn't going to stop.

I scrambled frantically for the deep shadows of the park, fear biting at my heels. My feet thundered over the ground, but when I looked back, no one had turned around.

Another bout of sickening pain hit me, and my vision skewed. When I looked up, the shapes of the trees and the leaves on the ground were brighter and clearer than they should have been. I could make out details of things that should have been impossible to see at night.

The scents of the forest were so overwhelming, I nearly

gagged. Hundreds of plants and animals that I could barely identify. Traces of creatures and people that had passed by hours or days ago. The aroma of ripe berries and dead animals and rotting vegetation.

Mind whirling, I pushed deeper into the woods with no idea of where I was headed, just that I had to get as far away from the bonfire and those people as possible.

The moon peeked through the leaves above. I ran and ran, stumbling every time the agony returned. My skin felt raw, and even the lightest breeze was too much.

This couldn't be how Sam and Jaxson experienced the world, could it? They'd go mad.

A wave of nausea hit me, and I doubled over and choked.

Deep breaths, Savy. You're a badass bitch, and you'll get through this.

Would I?

Gasping, I pushed forward into the trees, but the chafing of my clothes against my skin became unbearable. I yanked off my shirt and shimmied out of my jeans, cursing as they rubbed like sandpaper. My breathing came in huffs, and tears streamed down my face. I slowed, too exhausted to continue.

The buzzing of cicadas, the scurrying of an animal in the underbrush, and the creaking of branches—it was all deafening. I cupped my hands over my ears and craned my head upward, silently praying for this all to be a nightmare.

But it wasn't.

A gut-wrenching force exploded inside me, snapping my spine like a twig. I shrieked and dropped to the ground, my vision blurring from the pain.

When I opened my eyes, the moon was no longer visible through the trees. My body felt broken and wasted, like I'd been beaten to a pulp. I rolled onto my hands and knees, panting as sweat poured down my forehead, stinging my eyes.

Everything was wrong.

I'd seen werewolves transform. It happened in seconds, not minutes or hours. Had those bastards turned me into a freakish aberration? A half-human science experiment doomed to tear itself apart and die?

Agony struck again, and my back arched as my insides rearranged themselves, my ribs popping. A scream tore from my throat, stealing all the air from my lungs. Then the bones in my fingers cracked and shortened. My wrists couldn't bear my weight, so I rolled onto my side, wincing at the stabs in my chest.

Another snap, this time my thigh bone. And then the other one. I cried out, my voice sounding distant and feral. The pain was too much. My knees were next, and then my ankles. I didn't have the strength to scream, so I whimpered, my tears soaking the ground beneath me. Through my streaming eyes, I saw that my legs were twisted and covered in fur. My body quaked with fear and pain.

What had I become?

12

Jaxson

"What are you going to do about Savannah?" Sam asked as she crossed her arms and leaned back against the railing of Eclipse's rooftop terrace.

That was the question on all of our minds.

Savannah was confounding. Too independent to do as she was told, and too mistrustful to let us protect her.

When this had started, I'd thought that she was just an unlucky woman who'd gotten wrapped up in our business. Now it seemed the opposite had been true: the pack had gotten wrapped up in hers. She was a creeping vine that had entangled everything, dragging it down into a twisted mess.

But what could I do?

I swirled the whiskey in my glass and stared out at the moon, which was low over the horizon. "We hunt down Kahanov. It's the only way forward."

Regina was staring out at the same scene, leaning with her hands on the rail. "The reports of sleeping wolves keep coming in, Jax. We're at five now. If we hand her over, this could all end."

I turned and growled. "We're not bending to his demands, and we're not handing Savannah over. That's final."

She winced. "Just saying it's an option."

The deep ache in my chest that had started a few hours ago was growing, and my temper was shorter than it should have been.

"You okay, Jax?" Sam's brow furrowed as she watched me closely. Regina also had a concerned expression on her face.

"I'm fine." I checked my phone. Nothing more from Damian Malek, and I put it away. "Damian is still raking the Magic Side muck for the Viper, but last I heard, he thinks she's in the city. She may know what the sorcerer is after, or where he's headed."

"And if she doesn't?" Regina asked, her voice low enough to be a whisper.

"Then I seek a seer or summon the dead, or do whatever the hell it takes to find him."

Both women looked away, and I glared out at the moon.

I'd resort to that, but only if I had to. Dabbling in prophecy and fortunetelling was taboo in our pack. But was it any wonder? The fates were vile creatures, happy to give you just the right answers to lead you to your doom.

Two weeks ago, I'd sought a fortune teller to help me track down the person responsible for the abductions. She'd sent me to Savannah, and now here we were, in a bigger mess than ever.

Perhaps it had been a mistake to go to the seer.

To answer my questions, the fortune teller had drawn three cards. For my fate, she'd pulled the Hanged Man, and her reading of it still burned in my mind: *If you find the woman, you will find the answers you seek. But those answers will destroy you. You will lose that which you love and be parted from the thing you cannot live without.*

Well, I'd found the woman, and I'd gotten my answers. Now

my brother-in-law was dead, and my pack members were dropping like flies.

I could feel the noose tightening around my neck. Literally. I rubbed my throat.

Suddenly, a sharp pain exploded in my chest. The glass dropped from my hand and shattered on the ground as I doubled forward and clutched the rail.

Sam rushed to my side. "Jax!"

Confusion and agony clouded my mind.

A heart attack? Like the one that had forced my father to step down?

No. Something else.

The pain warped into a burning sensation, and then a tightness that felt like it was gnawing its way out. My vision darkened, and I heard Savannah's tortured cries in my head. What was this?

Savannah's fear and pain wrapped around my heart, tugging me toward her...and suddenly, like a cloak of darkness being pulled away from the sun, understanding dawned.

Oh, no. This couldn't fucking be happening.

I staggered back from the railing and went for the door.

"What's wrong, Jaxson?" Regina yelled.

Sam rushed after me, but I stopped her in her tracks. "Stay here. Don't follow me, that's an order."

I hurried downstairs, leaving the shocked and confused women in my wake.

I burst out of Eclipse and jumped into my truck. The engine roared to life, and I gunned it, heading west—the direction that the tether around my heart was pulling.

A deep dread filled me for what I would find.

My mate.

I'd heard stories about this from my sister, about what it felt like when a wolf's mate was close. Only it wasn't supposed to happen to me. Not like this. Not with *her*.

"Fuck!" I roared.

I could almost hear the cursed fates laughing. A LaSalle and a Laurent, entwined in a dance of self-destruction.

My heartbeat raced, and it was impossible to resist the pull. Savannah's pain was like an anchor dragging me toward the bottom of the sea.

I floored the accelerator and wove through traffic as confusion flooded my mind. Why had I only now realized this? Something had changed. *What?*

It didn't matter. I just needed to get to her, and then I'd deal with the rest.

I could feel her agony with every fiber of my being. Her mind was on the verge of shattering. Whatever was happening was fucking bad.

Hearing her screams in my mind had made me want to kill. But now there was only ominous silence. It was a mercy, but dread filled the quiet void. I gripped the steering wheel, my knuckles white, as I fought the urge to rage.

The burning tightness under my ribs intensified as I drew near West Shore Park, the largest wooded park in Magic Side.

Why had Savannah come here in the middle of the night?

Murderous thoughts flashed through my mind, and I cursed. Tires screeching, I pulled into the empty north lot. I parked and sprinted into the woods, letting the sensation in my chest guide me. I'd only made it a few yards before Savannah's shriek echoed through the forest.

My blood surged, and my senses sharpened to a razor. She was alive, but in pain and barely conscious. Perhaps a mile away. That would be near the border with the Indies.

She must have been attacked by the sorcerer. I *knew* that fucking cousin of hers couldn't keep her safe.

Sweat dampened my shirt as I leapt over rocks and wound through the trees. My wolf surged inside me, wanting loose, but if Savannah was inside the Indies, I didn't want any trouble with the LaSalles, and right now, my wolf would unleash a hell storm. I'd never felt him so agitated, and I struggled to keep him restrained.

I pressed on until Savannah's signature dulled all other senses. Her sobs wrapped around me, each whimper digging into my already aching soul. I slowed and stepped around a tree and froze.

It couldn't be.

Lying on the forest floor, crumpled and broken, was Savannah. Half woman. Half wolf.

My mate.

My fucking mate.

Her pulse was low, her breathing shallow. She was dying.

My wolf roared, demanding freedom, but I fought him down, though my bones cracked from the strain. He couldn't help her like I could.

I rushed forward and knelt beside Savannah's broken body. She was naked, her skin caked in blood, sweat, and dirt.

From our lore, I knew that the mate bond gave me the power to heal her. But I couldn't be certain I wouldn't kill her in this contorted half-human, half-wolf state. She was stuck in limbo and needed to shift all the way before she could heal.

When I touched her back, a tingling force shot up my arm, and her body jerked.

My mind burned with rage and denial and fear. It was impossible. This couldn't be happening. But it was.

I gently lifted her, cradling her in my arms. "Savannah, it's me. Open your eyes."

She needed to complete the shift soon, or she was going to die. Her skin already looked pale, and her pulse was erratic. I brushed a strand of her scarlet hair off her forehead. "Savannah, I need you to wake up."

She moaned, and her eyes fluttered open. "Jaxson?"

Her voice was hoarse, and her eyes were a rich amber gold. Beautiful. My wolf reared up again.

"Help me," she whispered weakly.

My chest calved in two, and I wanted to tear the world apart. But I had to focus. I cupped her cheek and rubbed away a tear. "You need to finish your shift, or you're going to die."

She pressed her eyes closed. "I can't. There's something wrong with me."

My heartbeat accelerated. What if that was true?

"There's nothing wrong with you. You're strong. Finish the shift."

She opened her eyes, and I saw the fear in them. I could sense she was resisting the change, rebelling against the transformation.

Of course she was. We were monsters, and she was a LaSalle. But resisting would kill her.

She shook her head. "I'm not a..."

"You are. And you're a fighter. The most stubborn woman I know—but the only way to win this fight is to give in. Let it happen. Or you'll die." I kept my voice calm and pushed my power into her.

She ground her teeth, fighting it again, but she finally whimpered. Too exhausted to fight any longer, she submitted to the change. Her body jerked, and she cried out.

My heart tore. "Easy, Savannah. Let the pain flow through you. It'll pass," I whispered, silently praying to the fates for one little mercy in the chaos they'd caused.

I felt her bones cracking and sinews lengthening and twisting beneath my hands. She screamed but let the transformation continue.

God, how long had she been fighting this?

I gently placed her on the ground and gave her some space. I could help guide her with my magic, but she needed to do the shift on her own. It was our way.

Her body jerked and arched, and I fought back the fear that had settled in my soul. For born werewolves, the first shift was painful, but according to our lore, the first shift was ten times worse for humans who caught lycanthropy. Not all made it through.

Would she survive this?

If she didn't, would my mind break? Or would I slowly descend into madness, like Billy had? That would destroy the pack.

Savannah cried out and clawed the ground, and I pushed all other fears and doubts out of my mind. Nothing but her mattered now. I just had to get her through this.

"Don't you dare give up," I ordered. "Let the shift take you."

Growling, she rolled onto her stomach and climbed to her knees. Her spine arched, and her legs and arms snapped and bent as her hands became paws and her face lengthened. Agony by agony, she completed the shift, until all that was left was a beautiful gray and auburn wolf.

She whimpered and shook her body, and my wolf rumbled in my chest, demanding to be set free. He wanted to meet his mate, but now was not the fucking time.

"Savannah." I slowly took a step forward, hands spread. "Savy." She snapped her head to me and growled, baring her teeth.

You did well, I said in my mind, testing our bond. She narrowed her amber eyes but didn't respond.

Perhaps that would take time.

"Easy." I took another step, sensing her pain. She was weak and favoring her left leg, and she snarled, limping backward.

She was afraid and confused, and she wouldn't be able to heal on her own yet.

I crouched low and spoke softly, letting my alpha presence wrap around her. "You're safe, Savy. Let me help you."

It felt wrong using this magic on her, especially during her first shift, but I couldn't risk her bolting off into the woods. Wolves normally shifted for the first time with their pack in a safe place where they could run freely and learn what it meant to let their other half take control. They also grew up with a community of support. Savannah hadn't, and the gods only knew what she was experiencing right now.

"Easy. I'm going to help you, okay?" I stepped forward with my hand outstretched. I paused, my fingertips a few inches from her nose.

Her bright eyes bored into me, reading my intentions. But then her shoulders relaxed, and she sniffed my hand. Her ears flicked up, and she brushed lightly against my fingers.

For a second, a smile tugged at my lips, but when she carefully lowered herself to the ground and began to whimper, that deep ache in my throat returned.

Her emotions overwhelmed my senses. Pain. Fear. Exhaustion.

I stepped forward and scooped her into my arms. "You can rest now. I'll take care of you."

She didn't fight me but nuzzled her face into my shoulder and closed her eyes. Her coat was soft and smelled like her— tangerines and sunshine. It was all I wanted to breathe in the world.

I carried her back to the truck, my mind churning. What the hell was I going to do?

My mate was Savannah Caine.

And she was a wolf.

13

I gently set Savannah down in the passenger seat and texted Sam as I slipped behind the wheel. *911. Meet me behind the apartment. Clear the guards up to my penthouse. Don't tell Regina.*

Sam was waiting for me fifteen minutes later when I pulled up out back.

"What's this about?" she asked as I got out of the truck.

What could I say? I just opened the passenger door and pulled out the exhausted auburn wolf.

"Who is..." Sam sniffed the air out of instinct, and her eyes went wide. "Oh. My. God...that's..."

"Yes, it is, and don't say a word. Get the door. I'm taking her up to the penthouse."

"*Your* penthouse?" she asked as she opened the door and called the freight elevator.

"It's warded with spells, I can put a dozen guards out front, and nobody will ask questions. You're going to stay with her tonight."

Sam lived in the building and served as my eyes and ears in

the pack. She was the only one I trusted to handle a sparking stick of dynamite like this.

The elevator binged, and the doors rolled opened. We got on for the long, awkward ride up. Sam's heartbeat was racing, and I could smell her distress.

I pushed my presence toward her. "This is going to be a shit-storm, but we'll ride it out, like always."

She swallowed and nodded. "How could this have happened?"

"I have no fucking idea. It has to be lycanthropy. But Savannah never told me she'd been bitten. Would she have covered that up? Did she say anything to you?"

Sam shook her head. "What about after the battle in the woods? Could Billy have been a carrier? Savannah was pretty beat up and left immediately after. I never checked her wounds...or what about when we were captured? Billy had access—"

"I don't know."

Could my brother-in-law have done such a thing? He was a bastard, but this...

Old memories tore at me, and silence lapsed between us.

When the doors opened at my penthouse, the normal guards were gone, waiting for Sam's word to return. I carried Savannah up to the magically warded door, which unlocked at my command and swung open. Hurrying through the house, I gently laid her on my bed—a beautiful red and grey wolf atop white sheets. She whimpered and set her head on her paws, then closed her eyes.

"She's still in shock, but I think she'll shift back sometime tonight. I need you to be here when that happens. If necessary, I'll help her through, but you'll need to clean her up. Calm her down. Get her clothes. And if you have to, explain what happened."

Sam frowned. "I don't think she'll be happy."

Savannah whined faintly.

A morose half laugh escaped my throat. "You think you've seen her angry before? She's going to be livid. Good luck."

"What are you going to do?"

"Dig into some of our old books of lore and see what I can learn about lycanthropy. And ways to reverse it."

My wolf strained inside of me, and I felt my claws extend, but I pulled them back.

A flicker of concern crossed Sam's face, but she gave me a small grin. "Okay. I'll hang out here and wait for her to go nuclear while you go read a book. Got it, boss."

I narrowed my eyes. "Sam, this is vital. No one can know about this."

"What about Regina?"

"Not now. I'll tell her and Savannah's guards as soon as possible, but we have to control the information here. That's your specialty."

"Okay."

"And Sam, no sleeping tonight. The sorcerer is hunting for wolves, and none of us can risk it. We'll take shifts tomorrow during the day if we have to."

She nodded. "We got the memo. What about Savannah, though?"

I frowned and growled low. It was a *fucked* situation, but we didn't have much choice. "She needs her rest. We'll have to gamble that the sorcerer is trying to capture her and not incapacitate her. If he tries that stunt again and she starts to sleepwalk, we'll be here to stop her."

"Got it." She didn't sound convinced.

I headed for the door. "Watch her."

"Of course. I know what she means to you."

I froze halfway out of the room, but my pulse started running.

There was no way Sam didn't catch my reaction, but I pitched my voice as calmly as possible. "Savannah is a liability. That's what she means to me. If we don't handle this right, everything could go up in flames."

"Jaxson," she said with deep incredulity, "I know she's your mate."

My gut wrenched with shock, and I spun around. "How? How do you know?"

Her gaze was steady. "I'm a master of information for a reason. Plus, I know the signs of bonded magic. I suspected it when you dashed out of Eclipse like that. But I'm sure this started long before tonight—I've seen the way you're pulled to her. You can't resist."

I braced myself against the door.

I'd been a fool to try to hide it from her. Sam's parents had been fated mates—she'd grown up with it. And she'd known my sister and Billy well. She intimately knew what to look for. And although she'd never spoken of it, I'd always assumed that she hoped to find her mate one day.

Why she would wish to tie herself to another's fate was beyond understanding, but it was none of my business.

I stepped very close, so my shadow fell across her. My voice was low and laden with warning. "You tell no one—not Regina, not Tony, not the guards. No one can know. We'll find a way to reverse this, to change her back."

My wolf tore at my chest, but I growled to rein him in.

Sam glanced over at Savannah and avoided my eyes. "Is that even possible? And if you *could* reverse the lycanthropy, do you think that would solve the mate problem?"

I scrubbed a hand through my hair. "I don't know, but I didn't feel the bond with her until she started shifting. From everything I know, the mated bond doesn't just develop. It's always there, and I would have sensed it the first time we met. This has to be lycanthropy. Or some kind of curse."

Could this have been a perverse trick by the sorcerer? The thought was too much to even contemplate.

Sam searched my eyes. "You've always been drawn to her, Jax. In the bar, in the woods..."

"No," I growled. "Not like this. Yes, she's gorgeous, but I don't want her. She is *not* my mate."

My wolf began to struggle, demanding to be let loose.

Sam rested her hand on my arm. "This could be a good thing for you."

I pulled away. "A *good* thing? This is a fucking disaster! The worst possible thing at the worst possible moment."

She crossed her arms and cocked her head. "Maybe, maybe not. This could be a bridge to the LaSalles."

I wrapped my hand around the doorframe and let my claws sink into the wall. It took all my restraint not to rip the molding off.

I tried to steady my breathing, but I was on the verge of shifting. "Are you insane? Do you have any idea what Laurel will do when she finds out that Savannah was infected with lycanthropy? On our watch? And potentially by my brother-in-law, who was also plotting to murder her entire family? It'll be a *war* like we haven't seen in generations."

Her eyes dilated as the gruesome reality sunk in.

"There's no option. We have to find an antidote. And until we do, we cover this—" My fangs erupted, and fur bristled along my skin as my wolf began to tear itself free. He was growing more desperate to get out every second that I was near Savannah. I staggered back.

"Fuck," I rasped. "He wants to meet her. Now. That can't happen."

Our mate! my wolf growled from deep inside of me.

Sam gripped my shoulder. "I'll take care of Savannah. Go. Run your wolf, clear your head."

Barely able to control my wolf any longer, I grabbed my keys and headed to the door. But I turned before I left as the chill of dread trickled through my veins. "Watch over her, Sam. And remember, do *not* fall asleep."

14

Savannah

I woke with a gasp. *Another fucking nightmare.*

At least the sorcerer hadn't invaded my dreams this time.

I turned over to go back to sleep, but I froze, eyes wide. These weren't my sheets.

Every sense in my body screamed at me. I sat up, and my heart clenched as I looked around. Holy shit. Where was I, and how did I get here?

Clutching the white bedsheet around me, I scanned the room.

Think, think, think.

Light streamed in from the floor-to-ceiling windows overlooking the lake, and I squinted. It was almost blinding. The décor was minimalist and sleek. Expensive. White floors, gray walls.

I racked my brain for any memory of how I had gotten here. Fragmentary images of last night filtered through my mind like rain. The sound of cicadas. Casey. The bonfire.

Panic flickered in my chest. Oh, shit, had I had a one-night stand with one of Casey's friends?

I squeezed my eyes shut. No. I'd been pissed, and I'd left.

After that, all I could remember was my nightmare of running through the woods. A shiver ran down my aching spine, and I shoved the dream out of my mind.

I slipped out of bed and wrapped the sheet around myself, sucking in a breath as pain trickled through my nerves. Not only did I have a massive hangover, but every bone in my body ached like I'd tumbled down a mountain a few times.

Whatever had happened, it wasn't cool.

A quick search of the room revealed neither my clothes nor my phone. *Shit.* I'd left the phone under the seat in Casey's car. Where my clothes were was anyone's guess.

I crossed the room and picked up the framed picture that sat alone on the dresser opposite the king-size bed that I'd just awoken in. A woman with dark, curly hair smiled at the camera. My blood froze. She was beautiful and had the same eyes as Jaxson.

The bedroom door creaked, and I spun, holding the framed picture out like it was a weapon.

"*Sam*?" I released my breath but didn't put down the picture. "Where am I, and why the *hell* am I buck-ass naked?"

"I think you should have some coffee." She stepped into the room and smiled, but I could read the concern on her face. She gave me a wide berth and set the mug on the bedside table. "Do you remember anything from last night?"

My mind still came up short. "I went to a bonfire with Casey, but the rest is missing. Tell me what the hell is going on."

My voice sounded distant and panicked. I realized that I'd set the picture down and was clutching my arms so hard that my nails were digging into my skin.

"You might want to take a seat," she said.

"Tell me!" I knew that whatever Sam was about to say would

be bad, and I didn't need her pussyfooting around it. Better to rip the band-aid off quickly.

Irritation flashed in her eyes, and her kind demeanor vanished. "You're a werewolf, Savannah. You shifted for the first time last night, and Jaxson found you in the woods broken and nearly dead."

Silence settled over the room, and then I broke it with a guttural laugh. I couldn't explain it—it was like the floodgates of a dam opening, and I just couldn't stop laughing. The absurdity of Sam's words was hilarious. Was she joking? Was I dreaming? I doubled forward, tears gushing down my cheeks as I cackled like a madwoman. It felt good, like a release of pent-up tension. The tears kept falling, though, and soon, my laughs turned into heart-wrenching sobs.

I dropped to my hands and knees, ignoring the pain because as the memories of my cracking bones and tearing muscles bombarded me at last, it was all I could focus on.

My vision blurred.

Sam dropped beside me. "Breathe, Savy!"

My lungs screamed, but I couldn't draw a breath.

I sat upright and pushed her away, gasping for air that never came. Now I remembered everything from the night before— the argument with those jerks, the bathroom where I'd begun to shift, my escape through the woods. And the pain. The excruci-ating, endless pain that had nearly split me in two.

Maybe it had.

I clutched my hair and screamed through my gritted teeth— at the circumstances that had landed me here, at my parents for leaving me in this shitty world, and at God for making this my cursed fate.

How was I ever going to face Laurel? And Casey?

I'd just met my estranged family, and I'd *actually* liked them.

Now? Now I had turned into one of the monsters they hated so much.

The room faded around me, and every sensation was drowned with gut-wrenching fury. My fingernails itched, and my skin burned, but my rage dwarfed it all. I was like a star imploding on itself. I was going to burn this fucking city to the ground.

But then, somewhere in the distance, I heard his voice. *Jaxson.* He was upset and yelling, but his signature enveloped me like a weighted blanket, pushing away my sinking despair. My panting breaths eased, and the pulsing in my temples slowed.

A tingling warmth spread through my cheeks, and my rage and pain slowly ebbed like a fading tide. I opened my eyes and met Jaxson's unyielding gaze. He was kneeling before me, clutching my face in his hands.

Mine.

"Savannah." He gently rubbed the dampness from my cheeks, and I realized that I was a sobbing, leaking mess.

I pulled away and rubbed the tears and snot from my puffy face. His jaw was set, and his brow furrowed as he watched me closely, either trying to read my thoughts or evaluate my sanity.

I climbed to my feet, brushing aside Jaxson's hand as he tried to steady me, and hurled myself into the bathroom. I slammed the door behind me and bent double with my arms across my aching chest.

Why was this happening to me? Of everything I had to face —abductors, demons, an insane sorcerer—why this as well?

"Savy? Are you okay? Can I come in?" Sam's voice came through the door.

"No. And no." I stumbled to the sink and stared at the reflection in the mirror.

I didn't even recognize myself, and it wasn't because of the swollen eyes and disheveled hair. My life had changed since that night at the Taphouse, and *I* had changed since coming to Magic Side.

What was I going to do?

I slumped down and put my head in my hands as I tried to grip the bull by the horns.

So, I was a werewolf now.

I tried the thought on for size, like a new pair of jeans. I didn't like it one bit, but I wasn't sure if this was something I could just *return*.

Inhaling deep breaths, I let my chest rise and fall. Okay. Where did being a werewolf leave me, other than screwed?

Worst-case scenario, this was now my life. Overwhelming sensory input, agonizing bone-snapping transformations, lots of hair everywhere. Potential for fleas. Benefits: none.

Best-case scenario, there was a way to fix this.

Either way, I still had a madman trying to abduct me, and being a werewolf didn't change that.

Impending death really had a way of putting things in perspective. I clambered to my feet with a low growl as my aches and pains reasserted themselves.

There was going to be a way to fix this. And after I found it, I was going to find whoever was responsible for this shit and make them pay.

I cleaned myself up as best I could and returned to the bedroom with the bedsheet wrapped around me like a toga. Sam was sitting at the foot of the bed while Jaxson stood by the window, arms crossed. He turned to me, worry and exhaustion clouding his face.

"Right, then, I'm a werewolf. How do we fix this?" I looked between Jaxson and Sam, feeling unexpectedly rational about the situation. Well, rational and pissed.

Jaxson took a step forward, but I shook my head as I stepped back. "I need answers. Is this lycanthropy? Is there a cure?"

He flexed his hands. "I'm not sure. Lycanthropy is extremely rare. There's a potion master who might know more."

"That's a start." A sliver of hope peeked out of the darkness in my soul. "Next question: how the *fuck* did this happen?"

Sam approached. "Did a werewolf ever bite you? The she-wolf whose mate you killed at the Taphouse? Billy? Someone you didn't tell us about?"

"No," I snapped.

Both of them were quiet, and Jaxson looked murderous. I suspected I knew why.

"Billy did it, didn't he? They injected me with some kind of lycanthropy serum while I was trapped in the sanitorium?"

"Possibly," Jaxson said, his voice gruff and strained. "We'll know for sure when we meet with Alia, the potion master. If we're lucky, she'll have an antidote."

I rubbed my face and took a deep breath. Somehow, I could face this. I'd faced blood demons and nightmares and murderous werewolves. I could face myself. Right? "Let's call her now, then. I need to know how screwed I am."

"Don't worry. We'll find a cure," Jaxson said. His words bit, and he wore a visibly pissed expression. Sam looked almost as upset.

And why wouldn't they be? They detested me to begin with, and now I was some sort of werewolf abomination. I was sure that the sooner they got rid of me, the happier they'd be.

But their feelings didn't matter right now. The sooner we got the cure, the better for *me*.

"How do you feel?" Sam inquired.

"Like I binge-watched horror movies all night, and then lost a boxing match." My stomach growled, and I shifted awkwardly. "That, and hungry."

Ten minutes later, Jaxson and I were sitting at the far ends of a black granite bar while Sam whipped up scrambled eggs and bacon in the most expensive-looking kitchen I'd ever seen.

She'd brought me a fresh set of clothes, thankfully, since the toga look didn't suit me. The jeans fit like a glove, but the sweater drooped over one of my shoulders. Fortunately, Sam lived on a lower floor, so the errand had been just a quick elevator ride for her.

"A lot of werewolves live here," she explained. "We like living together and near the alpha. Plus, there's a rooftop pool and bar and good amenities. Though my place is about the size of Jaxson's closets."

"I pay you better than that," he grumbled.

"Yes. But I like my view."

If it was anything like Jaxson's, I wouldn't blame her. His windows looked out over a vast green park and Lake Michigan.

I was doing my best to pay attention to anything but Jaxson. He looked good in the morning light. And as pissed as I was, my eyes couldn't seem to stop flicking his way. God, why was I so attracted to this man?

Maybe because he's hot and has a body I'd like to—

Fuck.

Cheeks blazing, I glanced around the apartment. White tiled floors, black cabinets, and chrome fixtures. The refrigerator was giant, and the glass lights that hung overhead were modern and simple. I knew Jaxson had money, but I hadn't expected his place to be so...chic.

I would have gladly murdered someone to have his bed and those *amazing* sheets. I could have nestled down in them forever.

Although I'd been too panicked to recognize or relish it, Jaxson's scent had been completely wrapped around me, and I regretted getting out of bed so quickly. It was easy to imagine the friction of my skin moving against those silken sheets. Heat pooled between my legs, and I crossed them.

Holy shit, Savy, now is not the time.

Jaxson tensed and cleared his throat, and I noticed that Sam was shaking her head as she piled the greasy bacon onto three plates.

Goddamned werewolves couldn't let a girl have a private thought.

You're one of them now.

My stomach twisted, and I buried my moment of desire with frustration.

"So," I said bitterly, "I'm a werewolf now. What do I need to know to get by until we find a cure? Like, how not to wolf out and eat people."

"We don't do that," Sam snapped.

"Well, as someone who's nearly been mauled by rampaging werewolves multiple times, it's a fair question."

"You know it's not."

"Your emotions and basal instincts will be heightened," Jaxson cut in, his gravelly voice instantly calming my fluctuating nerves and sending tingles up my spine. "You'll need to control them, or you'll risk shifting."

Just the sound of his voice heightened my basal instincts. I was so screwed.

"Anger is the worst of them." Sam shoveled a pile of eggs onto each of the plates and brusquely slid them across the counter with a lingering glare. "It's the primary trigger."

That checks out, I thought, recalling the events of last night. "If I trigger a shift, is there a way to stop it?"

"You'll have to calm your emotions enough to get control. If you don't, your wolf will take over, especially since you're new to shifting," Sam said.

If this morning was any indication, controlling my emotions was going to be difficult. "And if I can't control them?"

Sam arched her brows and fixed Jaxson with a discerning look. "Jaxson is the only one who'll be able to help you."

Of course. I was an out-of-control monster, and the only person who could help me tame my beast was Jaxson freaking Laurent. The same person who spiked my lust and anger with every move. The universe had a sick sense of humor.

I felt his burning gaze on me, and my pulse quickened. I didn't like the way things were between us. Something had changed, and I wasn't sure if it was a good or bad thing. I recalled hazy flashes of him finding me last night, and then I'd woken up in his bed *naked*. Shit, I hope we didn't—

"Sam put you into my bed last night," he said casually and took a sip of coffee.

Mother-fuc—

Choking, I dropped my fork and swiveled toward him. "Can you read my mind now, too?"

He paused, his eyes dropping to my legs, which were facing him and spread once more. "No, but you're like an open book when it comes to your emotions." Dismissively, he picked up his fork and began eating his eggs, his demeanor stony and distant. "Another reason to rein them in."

And just like that, Jaxson the alpha-hole was back.

I shoveled the rest of my breakfast into my mouth, silently cursing Jaxson.

His phone buzzed, and he answered, setting it on the counter between us. "Alia, thanks for returning my call. I have Savannah here with me."

"What can I do for you?" the woman said with a faint accent.

Before Jaxson could respond, I eyed him pointedly and said, "I have a wolf problem that I need fixing."

Alia was quiet for a beat, and then she said, "Surely she can't be referring to you, Jaxson?"

Sam laughed, and Jaxson's eyes blazed with impatience. "No.

The problem isn't with me, I can assure you. We think Savannah contracted lycanthropy. We need a cure."

She sucked in a sharp breath. "I'm sorry, Savannah. You... were bitten?"

"No," I said. "But I was recently injected with something against my will. We think that it may have given me lycanthropy. I've never been bitten, so it's the only possibility."

"Hmm...I've never heard of a serum that could do that. Have you, Jaxson?" Alia asked.

"No, but that doesn't mean it doesn't exist. We've been up against a pretty fucked-up blood sorcerer. The fates only know what he's capable of."

Though Jaxson's voice was assertive, I saw the doubt in his eyes. He didn't believe such a thing was possible.

Shit. Did he even think we could fix this?

My pulse started accelerating, and the bacon grease I'd just wolfed down curdled in my stomach. My palms began sweating, and Jaxson's apartment suddenly felt suffocating.

"Hmm...well, this might be tricky," Alia said. "There *is* a potion I can make that should cure you if you've contracted lycanthropy in the last few weeks. But first, I'll need to administer a test to confirm that you've actually got it. The problem is, I'll need concentrated wolfsbane to do that, and it might take a day or two to get that from my supplier."

Wolfsbane? *On it.*

"I can get that," I said quickly, leaping at the opportunity to take a little of my own fate into my hands, as well as a chance to get out of the increasingly claustrophobic apartment before I started hyperventilating again.

"Good. Bring it to my place. Oh, and Savannah..." Alia's voice faltered for a second, and I could sense her trepidation.

My breath stilled. "Lay it on me."

"The cure for your lycanthropy will be unimaginably

painful. Likely worse than what you experienced during your first shift, and it could take days to pass. You should prepare yourself."

Fear and dread clawed at my heart. I'd barely survived shifting into a wolf.

How was I supposed to survive the cure?

15

Savannah

The walls of Jaxson's massive penthouse were closing in. I could barely breathe.

I have to get out of here. Now.

A quick scan of the room revealed his truck keys lying on the counter. When Jaxson turned to Sam, I grabbed them and headed for the door. "I'm going to grab the wolfsbane and my phone from Casey. I'll call you when I've got it."

I slipped though quickly and shut the door. Then I scurried down the hall and hit the button on the elevator, hoping the car was there already.

It was not.

Jaxson was looming over me in a second. "What the hell do you think you're doing?"

"You heard the woman—we need wolfsbane. I'm going to get it." The elevator was taking way too long, so I hit the button again a couple times.

"*How?* You have no phone or wallet." Jaxson stopped me from hitting the button again. "I'll give you a ride."

The way he said it sent chills up my spine. He was so close.

His musky earth and pine scent addled my thoughts, and I couldn't keep my eyes from tracing the contours of his muscles beneath his taut button-down. The heat of my body was flowing.

Damn, I wanted him.

I tore my eyes away and prayed for the elevator to hurry the hell up. "I need to be alone."

Jaxson crossed his massive arms. "That's not a good idea."

Those arms.

I remembered him carrying me the night before. I'd never felt so safe. I wanted them around me again.

Shaking my head, I took a step back. "Alone is the antidote I need. Plus, Casey would be suspicious if you showed up with me asking for wolfsbane. I promise not to crash your ride."

The elevator doors opened.

Jaxson was quiet, his expression torn.

"I need this, Jax."

Sighing, he scrubbed a hand across his face and moved out of my way. "Fine, but I'm still sending a detail to follow you. My truck's in the garage. Call me as soon you get your phone. And *answer* if I call."

Clutching the keys in my sweaty palm, I darted into the elevator and pressed the button for the parking garage.

Jaxson's hulking form appeared in front of the closing doors, his expression dark and menacing. "I'm serious, Savannah. I'll hunt you down if I have to."

His voice was practically a growl, and it stoked a wild heat inside me. A part of me wanted the beast to hunt me down, but that was...crazy. As the doors closed, I realized I was practically panting.

"Shit!" I cursed into the empty elevator as it descended.

When it came to Jaxson, my body was unpredictable, and it was only getting worse. His power over me was like a drug, and when I was around him, I went out of my mind. Some twisted part of me had wanted him to ram his hands between the doors and shove them open. To take me back to his apartment. Hell, to take me in the elevator.

I'd wanted to feel his dominance. His power.

I slammed my palm against the wall. This wasn't me. I hadn't ever wanted that from him, and I never would. It was some twisted instinct, like my over-tuned senses, that was part of the monster I'd become.

Screw *that*. It wasn't going to be a part of me for long.

My chest strained, and I gritted my teeth, but I shoved the sensation down even as my fingernails began to itch. Now was not the time for a panic attack.

You're not panicking.

I ignored the thought and searched the garage. Jaxson's black truck was parked beside a Land Rover and a Lexus. Both probably his, I decided. He had nice wheels and gobs of cash, I had to give him that.

My fingers tingled with anticipation as I opened the door.

The bastard had taken my Gran Fury and stripped her to pieces less than two weeks ago. If I had any sense, I'd take his truck and get the hell of out Magic Side. Away from him, away from the sorcerer, away from all the bullshit. If I had to, I'd leave it in a ditch.

I sighed as I climbed into the cab.

If I lied to myself, I could almost believe that twenty-four hours ago, that plan would have worked. But not now.

Now I was being chased by a monster I couldn't outrun. It was part of me.

The truck rumbled to life, and the tires screeched as I beelined for the exit. The garage door opened, and I squinted as I careened onto the bright street.

I *hated* Jaxson Laurent. For what I'd become. For the mess I was trapped in. For the power he had over me. For the heat he made me feel.

The truck listed a little too much as I took the corner fast.

Easy, tiger.

My mind began to clear as I headed toward the Indies and *away* from Jaxson. All I had to do was act normal until I could get the cure from Alia. It might kill me, but I had to try. I couldn't live with a monster inside of me.

I let out a breath, feeling a modicum of relief as I passed the sign that marked the border of the Indies. *Welcome to Indiana*, it read, though someone had crossed out "Indiana" and replaced it with "Wild Side" in big yellow letters.

I pulled up in front of Aunt Laurel and Uncle Pete's house and got out. It was just after seven a.m., and I was certain Casey would be sleeping.

I was wrong.

The front door burst open, and my cousin stormed out. He was awake and looked like he was about to throw one down. Halfway through a string of curses, his gaze landed on Jaxson's truck, and his face contorted. "What. The. Hell?"

"Good morning to you, too," I said dryly as I strode up to his Rav4, which was parked in the driveway. It was locked. "Do you have the keys? I need my phone," I said, but as I turned toward him, I stopped short. His lips were pressed in a fine line, and his face was red.

"You fucked him, didn't you?"

I choked on my spit. "Excuse me?"

He pulled my phone out of his pocket and plodded down the front steps toward me. "I get it. Jaxson is a sexy beast. But next time"—he held my phone just out of my reach—"tell me when you're leaving. Don't just disappear."

I took my phone and noticed that it was fully charged, with ten missed calls from Casey. "Thanks. And I'm sorry, it wasn't—"

He held up a hand, motioning for me to shut up. "I don't want to know, and I'd rather not imagine you and Jaxson doing the nasty. Though I'm sure it was hot."

My cheeks blazed, which only seemed to confirm my cousin's suspicions. It was absolutely mortifying. I hadn't slept with the alpha-hole, but I assumed that the more I protested, the worse this situation would get. For the moment, he could believe what he wanted. The last thing I needed was him asking any questions I couldn't answer, so I'd have to go with it.

"Have you eaten?" he asked as we headed up the stairs.

"Uhm, yeah."

He smirked at me and chuckled as he ushered me inside. "Of course you have."

I wanted to kick him, though I couldn't help but smile because whatever he was thinking, I was sure—as he'd said earlier—it was hot.

We headed into the kitchen, and Casey poured himself a huge bowl of cereal. "Sorry about those jackasses last night. They aren't usually like that. Tensions have been high with the pack. Your boy toy is holding one of our containers hostage at the port, and a lot of the guys are pissed."

I crossed my arms and leaned against the kitchen counter. "Casey, let's be clear. Those friends of yours are *assholes*. I don't give a rat's ass what pissed them off. They never get to talk to me that way again."

He nodded. "Yeah, they know they did wrong. I was out of my mind with worry last night and took it out on them. They won't say anything ever again. Just don't, you know, add fuel to the fire."

"Trust me, I want as little to do with Jaxson as possible."

"Uh-huh," he said, as he scooped spoonfuls of Count Chocula into his mouth.

I rolled my eyes.

He smashed the cereal down into the milk. "Look, I'm not judging you for wanting a slab of hunk. As mom always says, never get involved in other people's business. I just want to be able to tell you *I told you so* when you come home complaining about fleas."

I put my face in my hands, wondering how long I was going to be able to stand this. But it did provide an opening. Plopping down in the chair in front of him, I leaned forward and whispered, "Actually, Casey, on that note, I need some wolfsbane."

He lifted a brow and stared at me while he chewed his kids' cereal, clearly in a sugar shock. "Sure...I've got a stack of cannisters in the closet. You didn't blast Jaxson again, did you?"

"No, I need wolfsbane extract."

He narrowed his eyes. "You know that's dangerous stuff in concentrate. What the hell do you need it for?"

I'd never been any good in drama class, and I silently prayed that Casey wouldn't be discerning enough to tell that I was full of shit. Mindlessly scratching at a dent in the table, I said, "Things with Jaxson have really heated up, and I don't like it. I found a potion-maker that can make me an anti–wolf attraction charm. But they need wolfsbane extract."

I stole a glance at my cousin, expecting him to call me out on the lie, but he was still spooning cereal into his mouth and nodding.

"Good idea," he mumbled. "If it works, can you get one made for me, too? That werewolf jammer keeps looking at me like she wants to eat me up. I don't need to go down that road right now."

Sam? *Really?*

I shook my head. "Great, I'll let you know if it works. Can we get the extract now? I found an apothecary who will make the... charm for me this afternoon."

"Give me five minutes. Then I'll take you over to the shop

and hook you up with some of our new batch." He slid his bowl into the sink and disappeared.

That had gone more smoothly than I'd expected. In the future, if I ever needed to have him do my bidding, I just had to load him up on sugar cereal.

Forty minutes later, I pulled up behind Casey's Rav4. He leaned out of his window and waved at the security guard, who laughed and pushed a button that opened a chain-link gate. The guard eyed me suspiciously as I passed through with Jaxson's truck. Whatever.

My phone rang on the seat beside me. Jaxson himself. I answered and turned on the speaker.

"You didn't call," Jaxson said, his voice rough.

"I was busy, but I'm picking up the wolfsbane now." I parked beside Casey in front of a three-story red brick factory. Plumes of smoke pumped out of the roof, and I frowned. Greenhouse gases much? This didn't look like a *shop*.

Casey climbed out of his car and headed over to my window.

Jaxson grunted and continued, "Where are—"

"Hold that thought. My cousin is here." I stashed the phone and unrolled the window as I smiled at Casey.

"Stay here. I'll be back in a few minutes, 'kay?" my cousin said.

I nodded. "Be sure to get the strong stuff, just in case I need to douse Jaxson...you know, if he gets freaky."

Casey laughed and disappeared through a door in the side of the building.

"You still there?" I asked the silent phone, wondering what the wolfsbane factory looked like inside.

"Yes." Jaxson's voice was even more strained than it was earlier, and I smiled, imagining the irritated look on his face.

"Where should I meet you?"

"My apartment."

I scanned the parking lot, making sure the coast was clear. "All right. I'll call when I'm headed your way."

"Wait, what? Where are—"

"Got to go. Talk soon." With that, I hung up and turned the phone on silent. Sliding out of the truck, I casually glanced around the building and slipped through the side door.

My feet stopped short as a mix of disbelief and shock snaked up my spine.

Before me, stretching the length of the building, were copper stills, steel vats, and tables manned by workers assembling parts. On either side of them stood floor-to-ceiling shelves with plastic shipping crates and an appalling array of arms—smoke bombs, grenades, cannisters, and boxes of what looked like ammunition.

It was an unholy cross between an industrial meth lab and a weapons manufacturing plant.

"Fuck," I gasped, my eyes watering and my skin puckering with blisters, no doubt from the wolfsbane in the air.

Casey was speaking to a woman who handed him a couple of glass vials. He looked over his shoulder, and his eyes bugged out when they landed on me.

"What is that?" I croaked to a man who was clicking several plastic pieces into an oblong object. My skin burned, and my throat was beginning to swell.

The worker looked up at me and frowned. "Uh, a pipe bomb. Who are you?"

"Heyyy!" Casey slipped his arm around me and pulled me close. "I thought I told you to stay in the car."

He glanced around wildly, looking totally suspicious.

I pushed him away and coughed. "What. The. *Fuck*. Casey?"

"Keep your voice down, and don't freak out." He ushered me to the door. "The last thing we need is for your magic to go haywire and blow us all up."

My jaw slackened, and I stared at him. "Are you serious?"

"Absolutely. This place would go up like a Roman candle if you detonated a burst of magic in here. *Hence* the reason I told you to *stay* in the car."

He shoved me out the door, smiling awkwardly at the workers who were now staring at us. Once we were outside, he slammed the door. "Don't say a word to Mom. She'll have a fit if she knew you were here."

My mind spun.

My family was involved in arms manufacturing. Jaxson had been right. And not just wolfsbane. Chemical weapons and shit.

"Casey, this place...it's wrong." I wheezed as I braced for a fit of coughing.

"Are you okay? What's the matter with you?" he asked, his face a mask of concern.

I strode toward the truck, tucking my sleeves over my hands and hoping he wouldn't notice the bright red blisters that covered them. It felt like someone was peeling my skin off with a red-hot knife.

"I'm fine. I'm just shocked," I said as I sucked in fresh air.

It was a lie. I was more than shocked. *Horrified.*

Casey appeared beside me and handed me two glass vials of a beige liquid. "Don't be. We produce this shit so people can protect themselves. This is no different than pepper spray or guns. You, of all people, should understand that."

I clutched the vials of wolfsbane, feeling sick to my stomach. This wasn't a mom-and-pop shop—this was a goddamned factory. My cousin was a nice guy, but how could I accept that he and his parents were involved in such evil?

"I don't understand. This is wrong, Casey, and *you* of all people should see that." I climbed into the truck and slammed the door.

As I drove past the guard's booth, I glanced in the rearview mirror. Casey was standing beside his car with a tortured expression on his face.

Was this what my parents had been wrapped up in, too? Had they blown themselves up while manufacturing chemical weapons that killed werewolves?

I brushed aside the tear that slid down my cheek as I drove toward the Midway Dens. Here I'd thought that Jaxson and the pack were the monsters, but the sad truth that was beginning to surface was far worse.

Maybe the real monsters had been my family all along.

16

Jaxson

I clenched my phone as I took the elevator down to the lobby. Savannah had called me ten minutes ago and ordered me to meet her outside. Ordered. *Me.*

I wasn't sure how much more I could take.

The doors opened, and I cursed the fates as I strode toward the glass door.

"Sir." The bellman nodded and opened the door for me, and I handed him a fifty.

My truck was idling in front of the building in the *No Parking* zone, Savannah Caine sitting in the driver's seat like she owned the godsdamned thing. The problem was, she looked fucking good driving my truck.

I reached for the door handle. It was locked. Savannah glanced at me and gestured with her thumb that I was going to be sitting in the passenger seat.

I would not have tolerated this shit from anyone else on the planet. Why her?

My patience dwindling, I crossed in front of the truck, not wholly trusting that she wouldn't run me down.

I climbed up and clicked on my seatbelt. Savannah tossed a vial into my lap. "Where to, grumpy?"

She gripped the steering wheel, and I noticed the pink welts on her hand. Anger and protectiveness flashed through me, catching me off guard. I slid the vial into my pocket, worried I might crush it.

"What the hell happened to you?" I growled, my jaw cracking.

Startled, Savannah tugged her sweater sleeve down to conceal her hand. "It's nothing. Don't worry about it."

She didn't understand, I couldn't simply *not worry about it*. That wasn't the way the mate bond worked. I could almost feel her pain and couldn't tear my eyes away.

But the last thing I was going to do right now was explain our mate bond. Hopefully, that would all go away with the cure. If it didn't, I wasn't sure what I would do. Maybe ship her off to Prague, or to another magical city.

The farther, the better.

I gripped the grab handle above the door, and something buckled in the roof of the cab. "I need to know."

My voice was low and charged with enough power to compel the answer.

Savannah's body tensed, and she stared at me. "Casey brought me to the family business. I went inside, and my skin blistered. It's fine and already better than it was."

Better? My head snapped to her, fury coursing through my veins. I'd torch that fucking place if I found out where it was.

Savannah glided her hand over the seat and placed it on my leg. "Are you okay?"

Her touch sent heat surging through my body, which only exacerbated my rage and added an unrelenting urge to claim my mate.

I glanced down at her hand, my chest rising and falling with each strained breath. I couldn't help but stiffen as indecent images filled my mind. "That's not helping matters."

Shock and then understanding crossed her face, and she removed her hand. "Sorry. What can I do to calm you down?"

"Drive." I punched Alia's address into my phone and clicked it into the holder on the dash.

She would be able to smell my rage and desire just as easily as I could sense hers, so I cranked up the AC and rolled down the window even though it was a blistering hot day. Sitting so close to her was abject torture, and it took twenty minutes in traffic before I managed to wrestle my murderous and lecherous urges into submission.

We didn't talk until Savannah pulled up beside Alia's building and turned off the car. "Feeling better?"

I narrowed my eyes at her, detecting the faintest trace of amusement in her concerned expression. She had no idea how attractive my wolf found her.

"Let's go," I said, climbing out of the truck. "And give me the keys."

After slamming her door shut, she stopped in front of the truck and dangled the keys out of reach. "Can't handle a woman in the driver's seat?"

I closed the distance and snatched them from her hands. There were only inches between us, and it was impossible to miss the swell of her breast as her pulse quickened. A bead of sweat rolled down her collarbone, and I leaned forward, wanting to taste it. I paused, breathing in her citrus scent like a fine perfume.

Instead, I dragged my nose up her neck, feeling the prickle of her skin as shivers worked their way through her. "You can drive my truck anytime, darling. All you have to do is ask."

One more hint of her fucking sweetness, and I was going to lose my damned mind. I stepped away abruptly, leaving her breathless and wanting. Her desire wrapped around me, taunting me like a siren's song.

Fuck, this was going to be harder than I'd expected.

Though instinct urged me to claim her and ravage her body like the queen my wolf wanted her to be, I couldn't let that happen. Sex would seal our fate, and that was a risk I wasn't willing to take, no matter how much I wanted to fuck Savannah Caine.

We needed to cure her today before both of us did something reckless.

Steeling my resolve, I opened the front door to Alia's building and waited for Savannah to enter.

She squared her shoulders and walked past me, feigning disinterest, though I could smell her heat, and it only aroused me further.

I dragged my hand through my hair and followed her to the elevator. The ride up was tortuously slow, and when the doors opened, Savannah bolted out.

The shifter standing guard in front of Alia's apartment tensed but recognized me and spoke into a small radio on his shirt. A recent break-in had changed the potion maker's perspective on the reliability of demons.

A few seconds later, the heavy wooden door swung open, and Alia appeared in a silky floral dress. "Jaxson." She eyed Savannah and smiled. "And Savannah, nice to meet you. Please come in."

She motioned for us to enter her loft.

"Thank you so much for helping us," Savannah said.

"Of course. I'm sorry you've been afflicted, and I hope I can help with an antidote. But I just want to make sure you understand that the cure may be worse than the affliction. Depending on when you were...infected, it might take several days to work through your system. Whatever you experienced before, this will be far, *far* harder on you."

Savannah's heartbeat raced, and I could smell the fear rising from her. It was one thing to hear this over the phone, another in person. She set her jaw. "Nothing could be worse than this. I need to be myself again."

My stomach twisted as my desire to protect her wrestled with deep resentment. Her blatant disgust and horror at being a wolf was infuriating.

The sooner we got rid of her wolf *problem*, the sooner I'd be rid of the bond.

Lies.

Alia nodded. "Okay, then. You have the wolfsbane?"

"Jaxson has it. I hope it's enough," Savannah said, taking in the huge space Alia had decorated with plants and books and faerie lights.

I gave the vial of the cloudy mixture to Alia, my claws aching at the thought of that poison. If Savannah knew how many people had been killed by that stuff, she might think differently of the LaSalles she called family.

Or maybe she wouldn't.

The apothecary shook the vial as she crossed to a table in the corner that was covered in bottles and bundles of dried herbs. "This will be more than enough. I just need one more ingredient—your blood."

Savannah spun around, her eyes dropping to the small gold knife and dish that Alia picked up from the table. She crossed her arms. "Absolutely not. If there is one thing I've learned, it's don't give your blood to anyone."

Alia shrugged. "Wise. I understand your mistrust. You don't know me, and blood is a very powerful magical component. Thankfully, we can make do with other things." She rummaged around on a shelf and held out a disposable plastic cup. "Fill this up a little. In the bathroom."

Savannah looked on for a second without comprehending, and then her eyes widened. "Seriously?"

"Your choice. We need to test how it reacts with an essence from your body."

Savannah turned red, and I could smell her embarrassment. I smiled and took a seat on the sofa, amusement replacing my earlier sour mood.

"Think of it like a pregnancy test." Alia handed Savannah the cup and motioned toward a room at the other end of the loft. "The bathroom's back there."

Savannah's jaw slackened, and then, glaring at me, she turned on her heel and stormed toward the bathroom.

After five minutes, she returned and awkwardly handed Alia the cup. "Wipe that grin off your face, Jaxson," she said.

I most certainly would not. Savannah took great pleasure in irritating me and was due for a taste of her own medicine.

"So how does this work?" Savannah watched as Alia plucked various herbs from the table and crushed them in a mortar.

"It's fairly simple." Alia grabbed a tincture from the shelf and poured it into a beaker, then sprinkled in a mixture of red and white powder and stirred it with a glass stick as it fizzed and turned pink. "I'll add the wolfsbane and urine, and the solution will turn red if you have lycanthropy."

Savannah put her hands over her face and sighed. "Can't you just give me the cure? I know it's lycanthropy."

Alia smiled. "I'm sure it is, but I need to be certain what you have before I administer you a potentially toxic antidote. Now, please step back as I pour in the wolfsbane. In concentrations like this, it'll burn your eyes."

Savannah didn't need much convincing. She crossed the room and stood beside me, arms wrapped around her. Alia put on a pair of safety glasses, then opened the vial of wolfsbane and poured two drops into the beaker. Even ten feet away, my throat tightened, and Savannah launched into a coughing fit.

"Sorry!" Alia vigorously mixed the potion, adding in several more ingredients. "As soon as I add the pee, the wolfsbane will be rendered inert and it shouldn't affect you."

Savannah's pulse was distractingly loud, and she nervously bit her lower lip. She wanted the cure to her lycanthropy, and though that's what I also wanted, something about it still stung.

A muscle in my jaw tensed as Alia dumped the cup of Savannah's urine into the beaker. I leaned forward, anxious for the solution to turn red. But it didn't.

Alia gasped and took several steps back as the contents of the beaker turned a blueish purple and began bubbling. "Oh, no!"

She dropped into a crouch as the beaker exploded, sending glass shards across the room.

I was up in a flash, drawing Savannah's body to my chest as the scalding projectiles embedded into my back. Growling at the pain, I looked down at Savannah, who was trembling.

"It didn't turn red," she whispered.

I said nothing because I'd seen it, too, and I had no fucking clue what that meant. The wounds on my back began to heal, and the glass shards dropped to ground as my body ejected them. Once I was certain Savannah was unharmed, I turned to Alia, who was inspecting the mess on her table.

"Damn. That's never happened before," she muttered.

"Yes, but what does it mean?" Savannah crossed toward Alia, wringing her hands in worry.

The potion maker inspected the base of the beaker with a frown. "Well, it means that it's not fucking lycanthropy, and now there's pee everywhere."

Savannah braced herself against the table. "So I can't be cured?"

My stomach knotted. *What the hell had they done to her?*

Alia sighed, traces of remorse in her beautiful features. "I'm sorry. I don't know what this is, and the only cure I have is for lycanthropy. If you were to take it, it would likely kill you. It's too risky."

Savannah strode to the window overlooking the balcony, hugging herself tightly. Her deep melancholy tore at me, and my wolf surged in my chest. I stepped close and gently touched my hand to her back, subtly pushing my alpha presence into her to calm the turmoil of emotion behind her sad eyes.

Perhaps there was no cure.

My wolf strained in my chest with excitement, but I shoved him down and bent my head close to her ear. "Let's go."

17

I let Jaxson drive. That was a clear indication of just how mentally messed up I was. To be fair, it was also his truck, and he'd taken the keys.

But I would have let him drive anyway. Probably.

I was a hollow shell of the woman I had once been. A husk. I leaned back in the passenger seat and put my face in my hands. "God, Jax, I'm so *screwed*. What am I going to do?"

"We'll figure this out," he said, pitching his voice low. It stroked the ends of my nerves, soothing me for a moment. But I knew it for what it was—an illusion. Just a product of his damned presence and power and the weird sway he had over me. A false calm.

"Figure this out?" I snapped, refusing to be mollified. "I have a sorcerer trying to kill me or abduct me or just mind-fuck me, and now I'm turning into a monster. How the hell am I supposed to deal with this?"

Jaxson's hands tightened on the wheel. "You're turning into a *werewolf*. Whether you act like a monster is up to you."

His bitterness was palpable, a caustic scent that burned my nostrils and made my stomach sink. "Sorry. I didn't mean it like that."

"You meant exactly what you said." His words were curt and resentful.

Man, he despised me.

I frowned, smelling my own embarrassment and shame. He was right—I'd meant what I'd said. He was a monster. A man that grew claws and fangs and turned into a ravening wolf. I was surrounded by monsters. Jaxson. The pack. The sorcerer. My family. And now me, too.

I leaned my head against the window. Trucks roared by us, the thunderous rumble of their engines straining my ears. People chatting on the street all sounded like they were shouting, and cars honking blocks away seemed like they were blaring their horns right behind me.

I gritted my teeth. "Everything is so loud all the time now. My ears are going to burst. How do you deal with this?"

"Don't worry, we're heading somewhere quieter. I expect it'll take time to get used to the sensitivity. Your hearing and sense of smell are probably ten times what they were before. You'll learn to filter. Hopefully, it'll be second nature before long."

"Hopefully not. We need to get this fixed, fast. I'm not supposed to be a werewolf."

You are, growled a voice in the back of my head.

"I'm not!" I snarled, then blushed as Jaxson raised his eyebrows.

Great. Now I was talking to myself.

"Sorry," I mumbled.

"Look, there are other people we can go to—seers, witches, maybe even the archmages. But for now, you're a werewolf, and you have a sorcerer coming after you. You have to learn to control your wolf, or it'll emerge at the wrong time and put you in danger."

I took a deep breath. He was right. If I lost control when a demon attacked, I'd be toast. Or what if Casey or Laurel or Uncle Pete found out? I'd lose the little family I'd gained.

My stomach churned. "How can I control it? I don't understand what's happening to me at all."

Jaxson turned down a side street and started driving east. "Practice. When your mood turns, when you get scared or angry, your claws will come out. We're going to start practicing so that you can pull them back and hide your nature."

I looked down at my hands and breathed slowly in and out, trying to calm my rising nerves. "Fine. Show me the ropes."

A deep rumble left his throat, and his lips curled up in a taunting smile. "If your wolf is anything like you, this could get interesting."

I glared. "What's that supposed to mean?"

The corners of his mouth twitched. "Well, it's just a guess, but your wolf might be a little unruly."

I bared my teeth at him, and when that did nothing to diminish his smile, I turned and looked out the window. "I don't understand werewolves *at all*. You talk about *your wolf* and *my wolf*. Do you just change into a different form? Or is your wolf...I don't know, a separate thing from you? You talk like it's a whole other entity sometimes."

Jaxson pulled into a desolate parking lot on the south side of the dockyards. Cranes were hoisting long containers from a cargo ship and stacking them on the shore with deafening thuds. It was sort of quieter, but at least there was nobody around.

He shut off the truck. "You and your wolf are the same. But just like your body changes when you turn into a wolf, your mind and personality change as well. They become more wolflike, and you might discover that your desires, instincts, and priorities change. That's why I generally find it easier to talk in terms of what I think versus what my wolf wants."

I opened my door and climbed out. The parking lot was little more than cracked and broken asphalt surrounded by an expanse of tall grass and native weeds.

I sighed. "So...what does a wolf think like? Will I just want to hunt rabbits?"

"No," he growled. "Could you be more insulting?"

"Sorry." To be fair, the scent of various unidentified animals lurking in the deep grass had definitely caught my attention. My stomach rumbled, and I blushed.

Jaxson made a path through the weeds, heading toward the lakeshore. "Wolves are cunning, proud, and loyal. Frankly, thoughts in wolf form generally make a lot more sense than those of most people."

That doesn't take much. People are nuts, said the little voice in the back of my mind. I shoved my rogue thoughts down and followed.

Jaxson continued speaking as we waded through the scrub. "When you're in human form, your wolf is repressed. But it doesn't go away entirely. And when its priorities are different than yours, it might speak up."

"Speak up?"

"Like a voice in your head. Your thoughts, but also not your thoughts."

I paused and gripped Jaxson's arm, pulling him up short. "Holy shit."

"What?" His eyes flicked to my outstretched hand on his arm. I could feel the energy flowing between us, but I was too lost in thought to care.

"I think it's been speaking to me. For a while," I whispered.

I've been doing this for a long time. I'm beginning to think that maybe you're not a great noticer of things.

"You didn't notice?" Jaxson asked, echoing the irritatingly snarky voice in my head.

"I thought...I thought it was just snappy inner dialog. I've always had that." My heartbeat accelerated. "Like...can I talk to it?"

Yes.

My jaw dropped, but Jaxson just watched.

"Um, hi?"

Hi. Let me out, already.

"It...wants out," I stammered.

And bacon or rabbits, the voice added.

"Not surprising," Jaxson said. "We'll get there soon. Claws first."

We stepped onto the three-tiered limestone seawall that lined the shore of Magic Side. Waves crashed below. Even though they were small, they were thunderous to my oversensitive ears.

My stomach twisted. This was a bit *too* much reality, but I stuck my hands out. "What do I do?"

"Concentrate on how they felt, what they looked like when they first emerged. Channel the experience," Jaxson suggested.

That was when Casey's friends had taunted me. I remembered the burning sensation in my fingertips. I pushed with my mind, trying to make them come out. When nothing happened, I tried flexing all the muscles in my fingers. Frustration began to choke me. "It doesn't work!"

Jaxson's eyes burned into me. "Often, we start to shift because of an emotion. Anger. Think about what happened that made them emerge the first time."

I groaned inwardly but closed my eyes and tried to recall the faces of the two pricks at the bonfire. I replayed their taunts and derision and inuendo. Rage crept across my neck and shoulders, and my muscles tensed, but no claws emerged.

That wasn't the first time, the voice in my head said.

It was.

But then I thought of the twisted horror that had called me from my house in the night—the noctith demon. Had I clawed it?

Not that. Look deeper.

No.

Deeper, the voice insisted.

I fought with all my will, but the thing inside of me forced an image of Billy into my mind. His face was frozen in horror and disbelief. Blood poured from his chest and across my clawed hands.

My eyes flew wide as pain erupted through my fingertips. My claws ripped free, and I stumbled back and cried out in surprise. Drops of blood trickled down my hands where my new talons had emerged, but the skin around them had already healed.

Blood-covered claws.

Stomach churning and near to vomiting, I bent over and tried to think of anything but Billy. I knew that somehow, he was responsible for all of this.

Jaxson steadied me, and warmth flowed from his hands. It mercifully drove the haunting images of Billy from my mind and the nausea from my gut.

"Good," Jaxson half-growled. His praise and lingering touch sent a shiver of delight along my spine. I hated that.

With a defiant snarl, I shook my hands out and wiped the tears from the corners of my eyes with the back of my wrist. "Fuck. Does it hurt less after a while?"

He shrugged. "Great transformations take pain. The first few times are always the hardest, when every sensation is new and raw."

I bit my lip and turned to gaze over the lake. I wasn't sure what I was searching for out there. A way out? Relief? Answers?

I watched the waves and cupped my throbbing hands.

Jaxson stepped up behind me, and his breath caressed my neck. Though our bodies didn't touch, his heat still warmed the skin beneath my clothes. My neck flushed, but I didn't move away.

He pressed his cheek against my hair and whispered, "Eventually, the line between pain and pleasure blurs. It becomes a symbol of your power to transform both your body and mind. To become something new."

His fingers slipped from my shoulders and ran down along my arms. His touch was so light, it felt electric, and I was certain that he sensed me shivering beneath his fingers. My control fading, I pressed my body back against the hard warmth of his.

His fingers continued drifting down my bare forearms until they came to rest on the back of my hands. Then, with an agonizingly gentle motion, he gently traced his fingertips backward from my claws, along my fingers, to the backs of my hands.

My claws slowly retracted, slipping inside my body, and I shuddered.

"Did that hurt?" he asked, low and gravelly.

I tensed and set my jaw. "Yes," I whispered. "But not like before."

He pushed his fingers along my hands. Pain tore through my fingertips as my claws extended once again. I winced and stifled a cry as I pushed my body against his.

Slowly, over and over, he slid my claws in and out, in and out, until the sensation was familiar, until I was drunk on his touch.

Jaxson's scent was all around me. Mossy earth and fresh forest, and the taste of melting snow. I could barely stand it with my improved senses. My legs quaked, but not from the ache in my hands.

"Now you try. Pull back your own claws, little wolf," he whispered into my hair in a voice that wasn't quite his. Something feral.

An hour ago, I would have stabbed him for calling me that. But now, I was intoxicated with his scent and his power. Something about the way his breath formed the words next to my ear made the heat rise between my thighs, and I wanted only to please him.

"How?" I asked, my question drifting out in a dreamlike state.

"Like before. Look down at your hands. Now they have claws. Think of how they look when you draw, when you paint. Focus your mind on your human form."

I did as I was told, bringing the image of my hands sketching into my mind. Nothing happened, and my body began to shake from frustration and the strain. I gritted my teeth and took a deep breath. How was I supposed to concentrate with his arms around me? With his powerful scent so close? I could feel every curve and dip of his muscled form pressed to my back, patiently waiting.

The idea of focus was preposterous.

But I didn't push him away. Instead, I gave up trying and savored his scent. I should have hated him. But in that moment, I was content to let my thoughts drift away, to imagine how it might feel to trace my own fingers across the contours of his chest.

With a spark of pain, my claws slipped back into my fingers. I choked in surprise. "I did it!"

Jaxson gave a low laugh, and I swelled with pride. I felt a force inside of me stir, desperate to be released. The wolf.

Let me out! the feminine voice demanded.

Be patient with me, I thought back, hoping that would work.

I concentrated on my hands and imagined my claws erupting from my fingers.

But with Jaxson so close, I couldn't focus on Billy or my rage or my fear. The sensations of his body drowned everything else out with my back and ass pressed up against him. He was rigid and powerful, and everywhere we touched, my skin burned with desire.

Stop thinking about boning Jaxson and let me free, damn it all!

The voice of the wolf brought me to attention like a slap in the face. My mind reeled, and I glared down at my fingertips, pushing with all my will as the color rose to my cheeks.

My arms jerked as my claws shot out, and I gasped in triumph. "I did—"

But before I could finish, my arms bent and began to twist. Hair burst from my skin, and I yelped as my shoulder popped out of place. My jaw and nose began to ache, and fangs erupted. My gut twisted in protest and rebellion.

I struggled in Jaxson's arms and tried to break free, even though I knew I couldn't outrun the monster tearing its way out of me.

"Too far," he growled, then grabbed my wrists. With a swift motion, he collapsed my arms against my chest and pinned me back against his body like a vise. But I didn't stop shifting. My legs trembled and my back arched as the transformation took hold. I was too scared to even scream or gasp for air.

Jaxson bound me tight and pushed his power into me. Wave after wave, it pulsed through my body, forcing the beast within into submission. Everywhere we touched burned with delight, and the monster finally calmed. Slowly, the hair on my arms withdrew, and my claws retracted. I collapsed in his grasp, horrified and spent.

"I like that you're ambitious, but you need to walk before you run," Jaxson said, his voice husky.

"She wanted out. I couldn't stop her," I whispered.

He relaxed his arms, and he stepped around to face me. "Of course she did," he said, and gently brushed the hair from my face. "Mastering a partial shift is hard. It requires control and dominance over your inner beast. The full shift takes less skill because you just let go. But I know you can do this. Out of all the women I know, your will is the most like iron."

"I can't. This is fucking insane!" I pushed away, but my legs were still unsure whether they belonged to a human or a wolf, and I stumbled to one knee.

Jaxson pulled me up. "You'll master this. That was good for a first attempt—though you haven't quite finished."

A subtle smile crept across his lips, and he placed his thumb gently against my upper lip and softly pressed on my canine. A dull ache spread through my jaw, and my eyes widened with shock as it withdrew.

"There. No more fangs. Now the shift is complete," Jaxson purred.

Rather than leaving my lips immediately, his thumb lingered. I closed my eyes, unable to think of anything but his finger softly pressing my mouth. My heartbeat quickened as the seconds passed, both of us frozen in place.

I parted my lips just to feel them drag against his skin.

The heat in my belly begged me to turn my head left and take his thumb into my mouth—to press my lips softly around it and trace my tongue along its length.

Instead, I turned my head right and stepped back.

He did the same and avoided my eyes. His voice turned hard. "You need to practice more. Now. We have time."

The stern tone was betrayed by the scent of his desire. It was overwhelming, a strong musk redolent with strength and power and possessiveness.

My heartbeat raced. If I could smell all that, what could he detect?

The scent of one-hundred-percent pure hussy, said the voice.

I gasped, and Jaxson raised an eyebrow.

My cheeks burned. How much of the feisty little voice was my own?

18

Jaxson

My phone dinged, and I glanced down. Damian.

Viper spotted heading into The Bookshelf. Still there.

Finally, some good news. "Okay, put your claws away. The Viper was spotted at an uptown bar. Time for happy hour."

Savannah retracted her claws. "Great, I could use a drink after today."

So could I.

Teaching her how to shift had taken every ounce of control I possessed. My mind had nearly broken when she pressed her ass up against me, and my wolf had howled with need. So now I had to ride beside her, smelling her body and desire, and hating her for it.

Savannah caught up as I headed to the truck. "Where are we headed?" The tension in her voice was palpable. This was what we'd been waiting for.

"A speakeasy called The Bookshelf over in the Circuit—downtown Magic Side. It's in the basement of a bookstore in one of the older buildings. Supposed to be hard to get into."

"But that shouldn't be a problem for you, right?"

"Of course not."

She looked down at her outfit. She was still wearing Sam's clothes. "Is it fancy? Am I dressed okay?"

Sam's jeans gripped her ass like a glove, and just watching the way her cheeks moved as she swayed through the weeds made me want to push her up against the side of my truck. Her sweater was too loose and kept slipping off her shoulder, revealing a smooth stretch of perfect skin.

I was losing my senses and my godsdamned mind, but it was hard to pull my eyes away. "You'll be fine."

When we reached the truck, she leaned against the door. "I can drive so you can navigate."

"Not a chance."

She twisted her hair alluringly. "Come on, I like your truck."

"Good." I unlocked the doors and swung into the driver's side. "Then load up."

A tortuous twenty minutes later, we parked along a side street and headed to the bookshop. It was on the bottom floor of an old, art-deco office building in an older part of the Circuit. On the window was an etched depiction of Death reading a book and drinking a cocktail. Underneath, old-fashioned letters spelled out *The Bookshelf*.

A bell on the door jingled as I pushed through. The place was a maze of overflowing bookshelves that smelled of musty paper.

A red demon with curling horns smiled at me from behind a counter and adjusted his spectacles at the two of us. "Can I help you? We have it all—everything your eyes and imagination could desire."

The only thing my eyes and imagination desired was my mate. I gritted my teeth. It was like lying down on the tracks and wishing for a train to arrive.

I scanned the place for the entrance. "We're looking to meet a friend for a drink. I think she's already here. Which way in?"

The demon folded his massive fingers together. "Do you have a membership or an invitation?"

"No," I growled.

"Well, then, we'll have to see if the bartender is interested."

We didn't have time for this sort of game. "Our friend is the Viper. She's waiting for us."

"In that case, the cover charge is a hundred. Pick a book off the shelf, and I'll send them down. If the bartender likes them, you can go in."

I put my hands on the counter and leaned into the face of the large demon. "Do you know who I am?"

He crossed his arms. "Do you know who *I* am? The guy who opens the door if I want to."

I growled low, but Savannah put her hand on my bicep. Her light touch cooled my temper even as heat crept along my spine.

"All we have to do is each pick a book?" she asked.

He nodded, arms still crossed and staring me down. "Any book. I'll send it down to the bartender, and if she likes your taste, she'll send you up a glass, and you can head down.

Savannah bit her lip, thinking. "What can you tell us about the bartender?"

"Nothing."

"This is ridiculous," I snarled. "We're supposed to be meeting someone there."

"Well, you can wait until that someone comes out. We have seats in our reading lounge."

My claws slowly began to extend, but Savannah tugged my arm. "Let's just do it."

I turned around, grabbed a book off the shelf, and dropped it on the counter. Savannah wandered to the back, taking her sweet-ass time browsing the titles.

"Just pick one," I grumbled.

"It needs to be the right one."

What was it about the woman that compelled her to be as frustrating as possible? After an interminably long time, she came back smiling.

"What did you choose?" Savannah asked me.

"No idea."

She held up her book proudly. It depicted a bare-chested man with a cropped beard sitting astride a motorcycle. The title was *Rumble Strip: Bayou Biker Bears, Book 1*.

My mouth dropped. "You've got to be kidding me."

"I like what I like." She shrugged and handed the book to the man. "Anyway, being in Magic Side has really broadened my horizons."

But biker werebears? *Disgusting*.

I crossed my arms. "Let's get this over with. Time is ticking."

The bookseller slid aside a panel in the wall and placed the books into a cubby. He closed it and pulled a cord. Soft squeaking sounded as the dumbwaiter descended, and the wheels of my impatience spun. After what seemed like an endless time, in which none of us spoke to each other, the dumbwaiter rumbled back up and dinged.

The bookseller opened the door, revealing two books but only one glass, which was filled with a finger of golden-brown liquid. He handed it to Savannah. "You're welcome to head downstairs, miss."

She took a sip. "Whoa. This is nice."

The demon grinned. "The bartender must have liked your taste."

"What about me?" I growled, warning resonating in my voice.

He handed me the book I'd selected. "You're welcome to sit

in our reading lounge and enjoy perusing *Enchanting Your Yacht.*"

I felt my wolf clawing at my chest with irritation.

Rip his face.

Teeth bared, I glanced at Savannah, whose smug expression did nothing to improve my mood.

I slammed my claws into the desk and leaned forward, letting my alpha presence wash over the demon. "You're going to let us both in."

The demonic bookseller backed up but didn't seem entirely cowed. Perhaps he had an innate resistance to being influenced.

Savannah pushed up beside me and wrapped her arm around mine in a way that immediately soothed my temper and aroused my body. "Please. My friend is a bit of a brute, and I don't think he was taking you seriously. How about I pick one for him?"

The demon, whose sudden nervous eye tic indicated he might be worried I would crush his skull, nodded. "Yes. Let's try again. Of course."

I waited while Savannah went to the shelves and quickly returned.

"That was mercifully fast," I grumbled.

"I saw it earlier and thought of you."

She handed it over, and the man lowered it in the dumbwaiter.

It came back moments later with a *very* full glass of whiskey.

He nodded and handed me the glass. I lifted it to my nose. The aromas were bold—honey, almond, and charred oak, with a soft hint of vanilla. I took a sip and let the warm liquid linger in my mouth. "This is excellent. What book did you offer?"

The bookseller held up a book with a couple of sweaty, steroid-pumped, bare-chested, and tattooed men on the cover.

Taming Bad Alphas. He leaned forward and whispered, "It's from our very spicy book section."

I clenched my fists tightly and glared at Savannah.

She smirked. "It got us in, right?"

The bookseller placed the books on the to-be-reshelved-rack, but she stopped him. "Actually, I think we want to buy those."

Then she looked at me expectantly.

The gall.

"Fine. Whatever gets us in." I slapped a fifty down. "Where's the bar?"

The demon bagged Savannah's books, then strode over to a shelf of historical fantasy novels and pressed an emblem carved in the side. The shelf slowly swung open, revealing a dark stairwell. A couple of red bulbs flickered to life, and the demon bowed. "Welcome to The Bookshelf. You have ten minutes of happy hour left."

I pushed past him and headed down the narrow stairs. We emerged into a long room with a bar on the left, booths on the right, and tables scattered around a stage at the back. The place was lit by deep yellow lights, and the walls were lined with dusty volumes. Most people were drinking, though there were a few enjoying a cocktail in the company of a good story.

The tattooed bartender smiled as we approached. "So, which one of you is into Biker Bears?" Savannah raised her hand, and the bartender winked at me. "Then *you* must be into those *baaaad* alphas. I flipped through it. That one gets hot fast."

My fists clenched. I would make Savannah pay for this. Her insufferable smirk was enough to make me want to rip the bar top off. Or her top off.

Trying to maintain some control over my emotions, I pulled out a wad of cash and placed a couple of fifties on the bar. "Two Manhattans."

"Sure thing." The bartender turned away and plucked a bottle of vermouth from a surprisingly wide selection on the wall. Manhattans must be their thing.

"Thanks for asking me what I wanted," Savannah hissed.

"We're not staying long."

She pouted. "You're more fun at your bar."

I turned and fixed her with a steady gaze. "Because it's my bar."

At my bar, everyone knew not to look too long at the woman I was with. Here, all the men kept glancing up at Savannah.

Our mate.

She was not. We hadn't sealed the bond, and we were going to reverse her condition. But it pissed me off, just the same.

I caught a vampire in the corner gazing straight at her with obvious intentions. He was looking right past the woman he was with and straight at Savannah's long, elegant neck and exposed shoulder. My claws slipped out, and it was all I could do not to flip his table over and ram a broken-off chair leg through his chest.

He looked away when he caught my gaze. I made sure the message was unmistakable. To my satisfaction, he whispered to the woman that it was time to leave.

While Savannah examined the selection of whiskey behind the bar, I looked around and made sure that every drooling male in the place got the same message: *Don't look. Don't touch. Or else.*

19

Savannah

I didn't recognize a single whiskey on the rack. That wasn't too surprising, considering I'd grown up in Belmont and learned to drink at a bar that had *well* and *Jack* as its only two options.

Everything about this place felt like it had been torn from another time.

The perky bartender returned with our Manhattans, served up in long-stemmed coupe glasses with a couple of black cherries.

I took a sip. The silky-smooth flavors melted in my mouth—herbal spice, with rich oak and a hint of underlying sweetness. "Oh, my God, this is good. Best I've had."

Jaxson gave me a grim expression. Apparently, he didn't appreciate competition for Eclipse. He turned back and leaned on the bar. "We're supposed to meet a *friend*. The Viper. Is she here yet?" When the bartender hesitated, Jaxson slowly put four more fifties down. "I'll probably keep an open tab."

She licked her lips, then took the money. "In the far back. Table by the early-twentieth-century horror section. Lovecraft and such."

I twisted so I could see. A single woman about my age sat way in the back. She had bobbed brown hair, black jeans, and a broad gold necklace. She was reading a book with an almost menacing intensity, and no one was sitting anywhere near her, despite the happy-hour crowd.

"Thanks." Jaxson took his drink and headed through the bar, and I followed behind.

There were probably twenty guys sitting in the bar, but not one looked at me as I walked past. Heat flushed my cheeks. Everyone was dressed in classy outfits, and I was wrapped up in someone else's jeans and an oversized sweater. Clearly, I wasn't even worth looking at.

Plenty of women looked at Jaxson, though, and I could practically read the thoughts of those who glanced my way.

You're not worthy.

It was true. I was just a LaSalle with dirty little mutant paws. I'd never be accepted by him or the pack or anyone in this city.

A vampire actually slipped out of his table and ran up the stairs after we passed. I hesitated.

Something didn't add up. I looked back. No one was looking at my ass, and I was certain it looked delectable in Sam's jeans. But the eyes of every man were stuck to a menu, to their girl-friend's smiles, or to the books on the wall. Everywhere but me. Not that I liked being ogled, but a little appreciation would have been nice.

Curious, I dropped my purse in front of a man at a round top and bent down slowly to pick it up. He practically crawled away from me and went so far as to pretend to be suddenly fascinated by the designs on the old tin ceiling tiles.

Jaxson.

Apparently, it wasn't just Eclipse for which he didn't like competition. What had he done?

"Why is every guy in here acting weird?" I snapped.

"You deserve respect," he grumbled as we made our way around an apprehensive cluster of drinkers.

"Do you mean *you* want respect? Maybe I like people looking at me."

He spun on me and stopped me in my tracks with his breathtaking golden eyes. "*I* don't like people looking at you."

Fire blazed through me, and heat flowed between my legs. He seemed like he was about to throw me over his shoulder or down on the ground. It was bullshit. But I liked it.

"I'm not your property."

He turned and kept walking.

I was about to let him have it when we reached the Viper. My pulse quickened.

In a way, the woman was responsible for all the shit that had befallen me since I left Belmont.

Pain ripped through my fingers as my claws slid out. I bit down on my lip and hid my hands behind my back as I fought to get control. Unfortunately, my limited technique for that amounted to thinking about how I would rub my fingers all over Jaxson's naked body.

Being a werewolf was really fucking with my emotions.

The Viper buried her face further in her book as we approached. It had a white cover with the tiny red face of a cat. I craned my neck to catch the title—*The Cats of Ulthar*. Never heard of it.

"May we sit?" Jaxson asked, his voice low.

The woman didn't bother looking up. "I don't know you."

He sat down across from her. "Then you've been lucky. But as it so happens, we know your friend the Ripper, and he had some interesting things to say."

She snapped the book shut and glared. "I don't know you, I don't know him, and whatever you've heard is total bullshit, so get lost."

"Funny. I've heard a lot of rumors about you in the Underground, and everything he said checks out. You were supposed to help him and another convict get out of town when Bentham was breached."

"Nope. I had nothing to do with that." She grabbed her pocketbook and rose to leave.

"Sit," Jaxson growled, naked menace in his tone. His power caught me by surprise, and I obeyed instantly, even though the order hadn't been for me.

The Viper resisted for a fraction of a second before following suit.

Jaxson jabbed a claw into the table. "You helped Ulan Kahanov escape. He's been fucking with my pack, and we need to ask you a few questions about him."

She sneered with obvious distaste. "Never heard of him."

I leaned forward and gave her my best *fellow girl in trouble* look. "Please. He's a sick freak, and he's turned my life into a living hell. Tell us what you know."

The Viper shot daggers at me with her stare. "No."

Jaxson's eyes flashed gold, and he loomed over the table. "I'll be frank. If you don't tell us, you'll have to slither out of here on your belly."

The scent of her rising fear filled the air. Good. She'd opened Pandora's box helping Kahanov escape. She could sweat.

She leaned forward and pitched her voice low. "Look, I can't talk here. I'd lose my reputation." She reached in her jacket and pulled out a business card, then placed it on the table and slid it across the table to Jaxson.

He picked it up.

The moment he touched it, a burst of static electricity made my hair stand on end, and then a shock blasted him backward. The tables and chairs behind us crashed to the floor, along with his body.

I leapt back and shouted in surprise as the Viper darted toward the rear. I dropped to Jaxson's side. "Holy shit, are you okay?"

His eyes were wide, and he wasn't moving. "Get her!" he slurred through clenched teeth.

Other patrons gathered around. I stood, but he didn't move a muscle to follow. "Go!" he hissed.

I scrambled after the Viper, who'd headed for the bathrooms at the back. The men's was empty, but the ladies' was locked. There wasn't anywhere else she could have gone.

I jiggled the knob. "Open up!"

No response.

I slammed my shoulder in the door, and pain leapt down my back and side.

Yeah, even with werewolf powers, breaking down doors wasn't going to be my strong suit.

The bartender grabbed my arm. "What the hell are you doing?"

"That Viper woman just hexed my friend and ran out on her tab. She's gotta be in there!"

The bartender took one look at Jaxson slowly beginning to move on the floor, then whipped out a key and unlocked the door.

It was empty. My eyes shot to the open half window high on the wall, which, by the look of it, led out of the basement and into the alley.

Oh, no. Not this again.

With no other options, I climbed up on the toilet and started squeezing myself through the window while the bartender shouted in protest.

I was halfway through when something hard slammed into the back of my head. My forehead rebounded against the rough asphalt, and I groaned in pain. Darkness crept into the corners of my vision, but I was just able to make out a dark shape standing within arm's reach.

I twisted, grabbed the shape with my claws, and yanked back as hard as I could.

It was a boot, and I cried out in triumph as the Viper toppled to the ground. I used her as an anchor to heave myself the rest of the way through the too-tight window.

She kicked me in the cheek, and I rolled away, releasing her leg. Then she was up and running. *Fast.*

I had boots of speed—at home—so I kicked off Sam's slightly-too-large shoes and raced after.

I could catch her, the voice inside me observed.

No way am I shifting, I thought back at it.

Fine. Suit yourself, slowpoke.

The gravel and asphalt tore into my bare feet, but the thrill of the hunt blotted any pain from my mind. The Viper was fast, but I was faster—way faster than I'd ever been before.

You're a werewolf now. It comes with perks, the beast inside me said.

The Viper darted around a corner. I released my claws and dug them into the brickwork to slingshot myself around after her.

Nice move.

It was a blind alley, and my prey was trapped. She backed up as I approached.

A week ago, I'd been a terrified girl running down an alley with a savage werewolf on my heels. The irony of the situation wasn't lost on me, but I didn't care.

I gave her *the look*. "You're going to answer my questions."

The Viper pulled a little flask from her pocket and a knife from her belt. "Don't come any closer. I mean it."

"What's that?" I asked, pointing to the blue vial.

She frowned, then gave an incredulous laugh. "A potion bomb. It'll stun the hell out you, and then I'll sink my knife into your throat."

Apparently, I should have known what a potion bomb was. I was way out of my depth. It was time for bravado and some desperate bullshit.

I began pulling the darkness around me and walked forward, drowning my fear. Her eyes widened as I made the shadows drip down the wall like ink, and I could smell her rising terror.

She brandished her blade. "Back off!"

I wrapped the shadows completely around myself like a black robe. "I'm a being of shadow. Your blade, your magic—it's meaningless to me."

I was lying through my teeth and was very much hoping that I wouldn't find out what a potion bomb was. Seeing as I couldn't throw fireballs like my cousin, bluffing was the best I could do.

"What are you?" she asked, pressing her back against the fence that cut across the alley. "Why are you after me?"

I hesitated. While I didn't know crap about Magica species or types of sorcerers, my life as of late had provided ample fucked-up inspiration.

I pulled a veil of darkness over my face—just like the sorcerer in my visions. "I'm one of the faceless ones. A stalker in shadow. And if you don't help me, you'll never walk in the light of day again."

I called more shadows from the walls and wrapped them around her legs.

She dropped her knife and raised her hands. "Please stop, I'll tell you what you want to know!"

Victory.

Was it? A pang of guilt tugged at me. She was practically cowering.

But then my guilt evaporated. She'd stunned Jaxson, threatened me, helped the Ripper—a serial killer—and also Kahanov, a kidnapper, murderer, and cult leader. She deserved worse than a simple haunting.

I drifted closer, an ominous, faceless specter of shadow. "You need to tell me exactly what you've done for Kahanov."

The Viper nodded. "I was supposed to transport him and the Ripper out of town, up to Wisconsin, where he had a contact who was going to hide him."

Billy. It had to be.

"The Ripper didn't show, and then Kahanov made me wait while he actually *sneaked into the Hall of Inquiry.* Can you imagine? You get out of jail, and the first thing you do is go by the police station. The Order Archives, technically, which is even harder to get into, although apparently, the place had just flooded. It was insane. He was a total lunatic."

"How so?" The first part we'd already pieced together. However, her assessment intrigued me.

"Traveling with him was really weird. He seldom responded to his own name. And he'd go on bloodthirsty rants."

"About what?"

She shrugged. "Some religious cult stuff. Also, getting revenge on the LaSalles."

My blood chilled. Once again, my family was at the heart of this.

"Who?" I asked, hoping for specifics.

"They're sorcerers. A shady family of arms dealers down in the Indies."

My mouth went dry as I thought of Casey's weapons manufacturing plant. It was wrong, but I knew they were good-hearted people. Weren't they?

The Viper looked like she might be getting ready to run, so I pivoted around her. "Do you know what Kahanov is after now?"

She shook her head. "No idea."

Lie.

I hissed. "You're not telling the truth, Viper. I can tell. I know when the truth is being hidden."

It was actually part of my wolf senses, but it sounded good. I made the shadows creep further up her body, and I felt my power sweep over her, pushing her into compliance.

She squeezed her eyes shut. "Okay, okay! Stop it. I'll tell you! But it's going to sound crazy. The freak came to me in a dream a week ago and demanded help. I know it doesn't make sense, but I swear it was real. He warned me if I ever told anyone, I'd never wake up again."

"I can make the same promise, right now. And you're not dreaming. So dish. What did he want?" I lengthened all the shadows of the alley until she was isolated on a shrinking island of light.

"He wanted information on a thing called the Soul Knife."

My heart leapt as the thrill of the chase rose again. *Now* we were getting somewhere. "What is it? What does it do?"

She shrugged as best she could with her arms up. "Some sort of ancient artifact. By the name, I guess you can use it to cut peoples' souls out? I don't know. I'm not paid for that."

I twisted my hand toward her, beginning to really enjoy the theatrics of the ruse. I even let a little madness slip into my voice. "And why did he want it?"

"No idea. He said something about needing to be complete. To be whole again. I didn't care. I just do the job and collect the money."

I pressed closer, and I could almost feel my power squeezing the truth out of her. "Did you discover where it was?"

She squirmed.

"What?" I growled.

The little snake glared at me. "You should really be paying me for this information. I'm a working girl."

I laughed. *The nerve.* "I'll be paying less attention to you. That seems a fair price."

"Okay, yes. I get it. You'll let me live." She still ground her teeth in protest. "The last known reference I could find was a bill of sale to a collector known as Alessandro il Mago. He lives in Italy, in a place called la città che muore—or something like that. That's all I know!"

My pounding heart was practically breaking through my chest. "And when did you tell him this?"

"Last night."

Fuck.

That night was ages ago. But we might still be able to stop him if we hurried.

I began to walk backward toward the walls, drawing the darkness in from all sides. "Get out of here. Don't tell him we spoke. And don't help him again."

I melted into the shadows along the wall, and she raced down the alley.

"Remember, the shadows are watching you!" I shouted in her wake, probably a little over-dramatically. Maybe I was drunk with power, but I didn't want her alerting the sorcerer.

Once she was gone, I dropped the shadows and strolled down the alley. I was confronted by the sudden reality that I didn't have my phone, and I had no idea how to get back.

A hulking shape thumped to the ground beside me, and I screamed and staggered back.

Jaxson.

I bared my teeth. "You asshole! You nearly gave me a heart attack!"

"Perhaps a little of your own medicine." His voice was low, but his eyes were full of amusement.

I narrowed my eyes at him. "You heard."

"Most of it. I was watching from the roof."

I wasn't sure if I was embarrassed or immensely proud. "Then you know I got the information."

"Remind me to ask for you when I need to scare the living piss out of someone."

I cocked my chin up. "At least my solution was more elegant than threatening to break her legs. I don't feel guilty in the slightest. She helped Kahanov get out of town and get the grimoire. She's at least partly responsible for the successive chain of shit that has happened to me. *And* your pack."

He was silent for a time as he studied my face. "You did well. Good work."

A shiver of delight ran down my spine, and my heart began to glow. His low, rich voice brushed against my nerve endings and made my skin pebble. By his scent, I could tell he meant it. That he was turned on by my confidence.

Suddenly, my heart was beating faster. I wanted him to step closer and press his body against mine and...

I slammed on the brakes. Why was I getting all hot and bothered for a scrap of praise from him?

I crossed my arms and tried to look pissed. "I'm glad you're not dead or permanently paralyzed. You wouldn't be very useful that way."

He shrugged, but something flashed through his eyes. "The Viper's business card was enchanted with a stunner spell. I should have felt it, and that mistake was on me. Thankfully, you chased her down."

"What next?"

"By the sounds of it, we're going to Italy to find this mage. He could be in danger. If he's still alive and has the artifact, we can negotiate. If Kahanov has beaten us to the punch, then maybe we can find some clues to what he's up to. I'll call Amal. She's been working there and knows the territory. She might even be able to find a way to call ahead and give the mage a warning and a heads-up that we're coming."

20

Everything began moving at high speed as Jaxson hounded his contacts for information and we grabbed supplies.

It turned out that Alessandro il Mago was a wealthy art collector and mage of middling skill. While he reputedly kept a large staff, no one answered the phone. An ominous sign that meant we were headed to la città che muore for a house call and going in blind.

Forty minutes later, I got the chance to travel by teleportation portal for the first time.

It was absolutely horrendous.

I clutched Jaxson tightly and screamed as the portal sucked us in and sent us spinning through a gray abyss.

My stomach lurched as I stumbled out of the portal and staggered halfway down a set of stone steps. Gasping for breath, I bent double and braced my hands on my knees as the world—and my stomach—continued to spin.

"That was horrible," I muttered. "Like riding the teacups at a carnival."

"Far better than a nine-hour flight to Rome," Jaxson said coolly.

I'd only been on a plane once, and an international flight with movies and cocktails seemed exciting and far less nauseating than being tumble-dried in some sort of magical netherworld.

When I was finally sure I wasn't going to puke, I righted myself.

Dark, bestial shapes loomed out of the moonlit forest around us. My pulse quickened, and I spun about. The screaming face of a hideous giant stared back at me.

I yelped and caught my foot on the stairs as I staggered away. Arms flailing, I landed on my ass on the stone steps. Pain shot through my tailbone, and I cursed as I slapped a hand to my butt.

Jaxson softly chuckled, and blood flushed my cheeks as I got a better view of the screaming stone face. It was a grotesque sculpture of an ogre's head. Stairs led up to its cavernous open mouth—apparently, the exit of the portal. It had two stubby teeth and hollow eyes, and its expression was contorted by rage.

He could have warned me. Prick.

I surveyed my surroundings.

A low mist covered the ground, and statues loomed up out from the trees around us—dragons, lions, elephants, and even gods. I recognized them and what they were now, and yet I still had to fight down my instinct to run. It was possibly the creepiest place I had ever been.

"What's all this?" I whispered.

The moon glinted in Jaxson's eyes. "Welcome to the sacred wood, garden of monsters. Don't worry, it's safe at the moment."

The "at the moment" clause rekindled my nerves, and I wrapped my arms around myself as a light mist chilled my exposed skin. At least I'd brought a jacket. "What are we doing here?"

"This is the closest portal to the mage's tower. Amal will meet us soon, but I wanted to get here early so you had a chance to shift and get accustomed to your wolf form."

My stomach dropped. Shifting hadn't been part of the plan. "I don't think I'm ready for that."

"I'm sure your wolf is."

Hell, yes, the wolf voice in my mind said.

I swallowed hard. "Is it necessary?"

"According to Amal, the mage's tower is in a tiny village without car access. We'll need to head overland through the woods, and we'll be faster and stealthier if we travel as wolves. You also need to know what it feels like to shift and how to change back. The transformation can be triggered by anger and fear, and the worst possible outcome would be for you to shift in the midst of danger."

I was definitely *not* ready for this.

I shook my head and lightly rested my fingertips on his muscled arm, pleading with my touch. "Jaxson, no. The first time I shifted, I passed out from the *pain*, and I've been exhausted all day. How can I face the sorcerer after going through that again?"

He leaned forward and whispered in my ear. "Because I'm here. I'll guide and help you through the pain. Most wolves wouldn't go through their first shift without their alpha near."

Jaxson was so close that the scent of his body overwhelmed my senses, and each breath I took sent liquid heat pooling in my core.

I licked my parched lips as a queasy sensation overtook my body. "So you're my alpha now?"

"Yes."

No, I didn't like that one bit.

Trust him, said the wolf voice in my mind.

That didn't help. I didn't trust it, whatever the monster inside of me was. My heartbeat kept accelerating.

"It'll be okay," Jaxson said as he placed his hands on my shoulders. "You can't be afraid of your wolf. You need to work together."

I shivered under his touch. "Work together? Aren't we the same?"

Well, I'm cuter, faster, and smarter.

My eyes went wide with surprise. It wasn't a part of me. It was like a completely different being. "I don't think I can deal with this right now."

"This is important. You need to be ready."

My palms felt as clammy as a dead fish, and my gut knotted even as I nodded consent. "All right, fine. What do I do?"

He unslung a small bag from his shoulder and laid it at my feet. "For your clothes."

My stomach plunged, and I gave him an apprehensive look.

"I'll turn away, but you'll need to take my hand when you're ready so that I can help guide you through the transition." He turned his back to me to give me privacy.

My mouth was as parched as the Arizona desert, and my heartbeat pounded in my chest. Unable to speak, I nodded, then tentatively began unbuttoning my shirt and listened for any sound of movement.

All was still.

Jacket, boots, jeans, bra, and panties—I dropped them one by one into a pile until I was clothed only in shadow and soft moonlight.

I crouched down and unzipped the bag. There was a pistol with a silencer packed in there, plus three clips of ammunition. Water. A few snacks. The oddity of the situation made me almost laugh. I was completely naked, crouching in a garden of stone monsters, prepping to turn into a wolf, and then, if I got lucky, find and murder a blood sorcerer. My life had gotten so strange, so quickly.

I stuffed the whole lot of clothes into the bag, and then, after a deep breath, I stood and wove a dress of shadows around me. "Okay. Let's do this."

"Take my hand," Jaxson said, his voice strained.

I turned around and stepped up behind him. My stomach spun. I was cloaked in shadow, but I was still naked and only inches away from Jaxson Laurent.

He held out his hand, and I clasped it. "Don't be afraid."

"I'm not," I snapped.

Liar.

"Is your wolf ready?" he asked.

Oh, my God, yes please, I'm dying in here.

"She says yes," I snarled.

"Good. Your wolf will know what to do. This time, let her come all the way forward and take over. I'll slow things down and push them along where I need to. It'll be easier every time."

"Oka—"

The monster inside slammed against my chest. The breath burst from my lungs as my ribs erupted in agony. Doubt strangled my thoughts. I couldn't do this. I wasn't a werewolf. I was just a girl from Wisconsin way out of her depth.

I fought back.

Release me! the wolf voice snarled.

I gritted my teeth. *I'm not ready! This is too much!*

Jaxson's voice brushed over my skin. "It's okay, Savy. Let her out. You'll still be you. It's time."

I screamed in protest and arched my back as the wolf inside took control. Hair ripped across my bare arms and legs, and I dropped to my knees. My skin stretched and my tendons strained as my muscles writhed. I cried out in agony as I dug one clawed hand into the earth and the other into Jaxson's palm.

The alpha turned and dropped to a knee beside me. He pressed his free hand into the small of my back, and his power sent wave after wave of relief through my body. His touch was warm and cold at the same time and felt like the ocean rolling across my skin.

I shivered in delight as much as I shook in pain.

The scent of the forest around us mingled with his signature, and in my daze, I couldn't tell one from the other. My skin was more sensitive than it had ever been, yet somehow, I couldn't feel where his hand stopped and my own skin began.

For a moment, we were one together beneath the stars—Jaxson, the wolf, and me.

His hands held me steady as I pitched and bucked, and his power drove through me, pushing me forward to the end. I gasped as my spine cracked and fur erupted around my back. And finally, sore and spent, I staggered forward on four clumsy paws and howled—a long, mournful cry that echoed with relief and release, agony and ecstasy.

I'm free.

The world was new.

My human senses paled in comparison to my out-of-this-world wolf perception. Hundreds of strange and exciting aromas hung in the air. Some I could pinpoint. Mushrooms. Moss. Different types of trees. Others I only had a vague idea of.

Suddenly, I had my nose against the ground and was sniffing. Shock rolled through me. I didn't have control.

I was supposed to think differently, but wasn't I supposed to be in control?

Apparently not. I was out of the driver's seat, and someone else was steering.

Fury and resentment boiled up inside of me, and I forced the head of my body up—but it went right back down as the wolf mind took over again.

It's my turn, the lupine voice snapped.

Jaxson crouched down beside me and held out his hand. "Hello, beautiful creature."

I sniffed it. Or more to the point, the wolf in control made me sniff it. A part of my soul withered with embarrassment, but the rest was filled with wonder as hundreds of aromas raced up my nose.

His scent had a clarity that I'd never imagined possible—the deep, earthy aromas of his skin and the salty and intoxicating depths of his sweat. His scent told me more than I'd imagined possible. His strength. Virility. Power. Status. I could barely interpret the information flooding into my mind.

Before I could gather my thoughts, I was trotting over the grass toward a sculpture of a stone elephant. With every part of my soul rebelling, I seized control and turned to the left—or at least I tried to. Instead, I stumbled and landed snout down in the grass.

I'm the expert here, the wolf voice growled. *You handed over the keys, so let me drive.*

Jaxson laughed. "Four legs takes a little getting used to."

It wasn't the four legs I was worried about. It was the *wolf* in control. *My wolf.*

I didn't think I'd get used to that thought. How was I even supposed to think of myself now? We were sharing a body—I saw what the wolf saw and felt what she felt. But was *I* walking or was *she* walking, or were *we* walking?

My mind spun in confusion, but the wolf's voice came through. *Relax, Savy. Just enjoy the ride.*

Fat chance. I was tired of others ruling my life.

Jaxson began unbuttoning his shirt, which immediately transfixed my—well, *our* collective attention. "I'm going shift now, too. Amal will be here soon, and we'll need to hurry as fast as possible. Normally, I would want you to have days running in the woods to get used to your new form, but we can't afford that luxury. Our clock is ticking."

Dread weighed down on me. What would we find at the tower? Alessandro il Mago or a corpse? The Soul Knife or the sorcerer?

Nothing good, my instincts told me.

Jaxson pulled the shirt free from his shoulders and dropped it onto the ground next to my satchel. Then he unlatched his belt and met my gaze. We averted our eyes, and he turned his back to us.

You were staring at him! That was so embarrassing! I thought, brimming with annoyance.

No. That was all you.

Was it?

Damn. This was going to take some getting used to.

Jaxson slipped out of his trousers in the corner of my vision, and the wolf's voice practically purred in my mind. *Look at those buns. He's going to be an amazing wolf.*

My heart froze as trepidation began to trickle through my veins. What would meeting Jaxson's wolf even be like? When I'd met it before at the fair, it had been a thing out of nightmares.

Jaxson met my eyes as his flashed gold. "Don't be afraid, pretty wolf. Just don't run."

Those were not the words I needed to hear.

With a low growl, he shifted.

His arms and legs bent and twisted, and silver-gray fur erupted across his moonlit back. His handsome face transformed into the muzzle of a beast, and sharp teeth sprang up, glinting white in the moonlight. He was enormous—two or three times my size, if not more, and rippling with muscle and power.

Then the beast that was Jaxson turned its glowing honey-gold eyes on me.

We cowered and began to back away over the grass as my wolf's fear entwined with my own.

This was not Jaxson. It was a monster out of legend.

We backpedaled, then darted left beneath the legs of the elephant statue with no destination in mind.

Jaxson snarled and chased. He was past us in a second, and with a few deft moves, he cornered us against a giant statue of a seated goddess with an urn on her head.

The silver wolf growled, and I understood the meaning, almost as if it was speaking in my mind: *Submit.*

Screw that! my wolf and I thought at the same time.

We jumped up onto the statue's lap, and when Jaxson stalked forward, we leapt into the air and landed on the grass behind him. We ran blindly, pushed by fear and the desire to run.

A strange, tilted shape loomed out of the darkness—a stone tower house that was listing to the side. Then Jaxson was on us, trapping us between the house and the terrace wall.

Submit, Jaxson commanded as he prowled forward, his unmistakable presence washing over us.

No! I said, but his power was a drug, compelling the wolf side of me to obey. Growling, she lowered her tail and sank down on all four paws. Then, with a noise somewhere between a snarl and whine, she bellied up.

You've got to be kidding me! I protested.

Jaxson lowered his massive head to sniff us, and then his bared teeth finally relaxed.

Resentment stewed in my chest.

I did *not* like wolf Jaxson. Not one bit.

21

Jaxson

My heart raced as my eyes drank in Savannah Caine. She was beyond beautiful, with a gray and auburn coat the likes of which I had never seen before.

I drank deeply of her scent, so different than when she was a woman. Richer, deeper, and utterly mesmerizing.

I wanted her to run, and to hunt her endlessly through the dense woods that surrounded the gardens. But there was no time.

She is ours. We should claim her.

Our mate connection was far stronger, but I knew it was a lie. She wasn't a wolf. She was a LaSalle.

Bitterness wound around my heart. The fates had ripped my sister from me and given me Savannah in return, making me relive the memory of what her family had done every time I looked at her.

Sorrow crushed in on my chest, and when I could bear it no longer, I tilted my head back and howled a long, mournful cry that tore its way out of my lungs.

Savannah sat up and tilted her head back, revealing the soft white fur of her neck. She howled, too. The thread between us pulled tighter, and my own howl caught in my throat.

She is one of us now. Part of the pack.

A voice echoed from the portal. "Jaxson!"

Amal was striding toward us.

Savannah's wolf went over and immediately sniffed her. I snarled, and Savannah looked at me, confused. We were definitely going to talk about manners.

Amal laughed it off. "Nice to meet you, too, Savannah, but we need to get going. Ready?"

She nodded.

Amal's eyes flashed gold, and a breeze of magic surrounded her, hot like the desert wind. Her signature flowed around us—a scent of fresh dates and apricots, and a taste like rich wildflower honey.

In a blur of radiance, she transformed into an Egyptian wolf, the dark fur along her back tinged with highlights of gold.

Unlike wolfborn, shifters like Amal transformed through magic, clothes and all. It meant she didn't have to lug equipment around, and she could shift almost instantly, without pain. Very useful for an assassin—though the senses, strength, and healing of wolfborn were far superior. We thought differently as well, so I kept advisers from both species in my inner circle and used teams of mixed operatives to exploit our different talents.

I was glad we had Amal with us tonight.

I lowered my head and snagged the strap of my gear pack. Savannah looked at Amal and then at her bag with a huff.

Yes. There were times where I was also a little jealous of magic shifters, too.

Heretic. You should be thrown from the pack, my wolf teased.

I laughed inwardly. *Bite me.*

With a burst of acceleration, Amal ran into the forest, and we raced after.

The thrill of the chase rose within me, and I glanced at Savannah. I could smell her elation.

This is what we're meant to do.

We dashed along faint game trails and wound our way through the hills, though I kept my eyes peeled. I could smell the traces of ancient things in these woods—ogres and goblins and worse. At least the soft light of the moon filtered down through the dark branches of the trees and lit our way.

After an hour, we crested a forested hill that overlooked a wide confluence of valleys. Our destination was an isolated plateau topped by a dense cluster of stone buildings. The mage's tower loomed above the edge of the town, a spire of golden-gray stone lit by the waning moon.

Our descent was heinous. It had rained recently, and cloying valley clay quickly caked around our paws. By the time we reached the base of the plateau, Savannah was wet and smeared with sticky gray muck from snout to tail.

She caught the laughter in my eyes and snarled. At least there had been a small drainage at the edge of town where we were able to wash off.

Amal paused as we neared the village and shifted into her human form again. The mud-coated Egyptian wolf disappeared, leaving a gorgeous dark-haired woman with bright yellow eyes in its place. Her clothes and boots were as clean as a whistle—another boon of her shifter magic.

Savannah looked down at her own feet and whined.

"We better proceed on two legs. They might shoot at wolves here," Amal whispered.

I dropped my filthy bag on the side of the road and shifted while Amal kept a lookout. I pulled on my boots and clothes and tucked my pistol in the back of my jeans.

Savannah was pacing back and forth, pretending not to watch me dress. I crossed my arms. "Time to shift back."

She planted her feet, arched her back, and growled. *No!*

Amal raised her eyebrows.

Apparently, Savannah in wolf form was just as obstinate as normal. I stepped up and released some of my alpha presence. "We need to get moving. Shift."

She sank to her paws and whined.

I gripped her by the scruff and used my alpha power to force the transformation.

She snarled, then began to thrash as her arms and legs lengthened, and the fur withdrew into her skin. I looked away, but I didn't let go.

Finally, the contortions stopped.

"Jaxson, if you don't take your hands off of me this second, I'll claw your damn eyes out."

Good ole Savannah, same as ever.

I released my grip and quickly moved to Amal's side. Just feeling Savannah's bare skin beneath my hands had made me stiff, and the scent of her sweat-soaked body was driving my mind wild with lust and desire.

"Don't look," she said. "I still need to change into my clothes."

"Wouldn't dream of it."

Lie.

I closed my eyes and tried to blot out the subtle sounds of lace sliding along her skin. My breath quickened.

What the fuck was wrong with me? She wasn't a wolf. Or at least she wouldn't be for long.

22

"Damn it all. I've still got mud on me," I spat. Though our surroundings were beautiful, I glared at the vile valley.

Jaxson grunted unsympathetically. "Kahanov had a head start. We need to catch up, so get moving."

"I know. Unfortunately, unlike some people—*Amal*—I actually have to slip into a bra and undies, and I've got clay in places I don't want to talk about."

The air stilled, and Jaxson's tension was palpable.

I yanked on my jeans and shirt, threw on my jacket, and grabbed the gun from my travel bag. I cocked my hip out and held the pistol casually in a *screw you* pose. "Okay. Let's rock it."

Jaxson crossed his arms and worked his jaw silently as he glared at me. "Next time, if I tell you to shift, do it. It might mean your life."

"It was the wolf! She's a tyrant. She wouldn't shift back."

You've spent your whole life on two legs. It was my turn, the beast muttered in my mind.

I felt a little bad. She'd been drunk with happiness...well, until the mud.

I tucked the gun in my belt and shoved the spare clips into my tight pockets, then followed Jaxson and Amal through the cobblestone streets of the tiny village. Ivy draped over the old stone buildings, and planters brimmed with flowers. It was like the village had been lost to time.

According to Amal, the town had originally been built by the Etruscans, who'd dug caves into the hard layer of volcanic tuff. Over the millennia, the underlying clay had eroded away, leaving the plateau isolated in the middle of the valley, and most of the population had moved away.

Only a few windows were lit, and we hugged the shadows. Jaxson was quiet, but Amal moved like a ghost.

Our plan was simple: knock on the door, and if no one answered, sneak in with the assumption that Kahanov was already inside.

The mage's tower was impossible to miss. It soared above the town. Built of ancient limestone blocks, it almost glowed in the moonlight. Problematically, however, there wasn't a door, just a brass knocker mounted on the wall above a set of stairs.

Amal kept a wary eye on the dark, crooked street while we climbed the steps. Jaxson casually slammed the knocker three times. No response.

After trying again, he ran his hand over the stone where a door should have been. "I have a bad feeling about this."

Amal nodded. "I think we need to assume the worst. Kahanov had a day's lead on us."

"Okay, so let's find an alternate entrance, seeing as there's no door to break down."

Amal slipped her phone out and pulled up an aerial map. "The mage has an isolated garden that protrudes over the cliff. We might be able to climb down into it from some of the houses at the edge of the butte."

Jaxson glanced up at the tiled roofs of the houses around us. "So, over the top?"

"My favorite way." Amal crouched and leapt. She soared into the air and landed lightly on the roof two stories above.

I glared at Jaxson. "How the hell am I supposed to do that?"

He turned, and his eyes glinted with yellow light. "Try parkour."

"Parkour?"

He ran three steps, leapt, and rebounded off the side of the adjacent building. He landed silently and gracefully on the roof, and made it all look impossibly easy. I'd seen him do similar moves when he'd hunted me down the alley.

Noticing my hesitation, Jaxson suggested, "I can probably jump back down and toss you up. You're light."

My blood boiled. I turned, ran three steps, and leapt with all my strength. I soared into the air—*waaay* higher than I thought possible.

Oh, shit.

The side of the building came up faster than I'd anticipated, and I ricocheted toward Jaxson with almost zero control. My chest slammed into the gutter, and I squeaked as I slipped and slid back, catching myself with my claws before I tumbled to the street below.

Jaxson was there in a second. He grabbed my jacket by the neck and heaved me halfway before hauling me up by the back of my jeans.

I scrambled up the roof on my hands and knees.

Lights went on in the house below, and we climbed over the top and ducked down. Someone started shouting in Italian.

"What are they saying?" I whispered.

Amal grinned. "That—and please excuse this, I'm only translating—that the fat cats are fucking on the neighbor's roof again."

I put my hands over my face and leaned back. I was so not awesome.

"Come on," Jaxson growled, and jumped up to the adjacent roof, a full story above us.

I sighed, got to my feet, and followed with more success this time.

The house was perched at the edge of the cliff, and as soon as I looked over the threshold of the roof, my stomach swam with vertigo.

The mage's garden was a narrow strip of green far below, protruding from the side of the plateau. Around the base of the tower, it expanded into well-kept grounds, but on every side, there was a steep drop-off into the deep valley.

A chilly breeze swept up from the mist-shrouded ground below, and my skin prickled. "I'm not jumping down there."

"Of course not. We'll climb," Jaxson said as Amal swung herself over the side of the roof and dropped to a narrow wall at the cliff's edge. Then she climbed down.

So this is how my crazy friends and I die in Italy, I thought.

Jaxson dropped down on the wall and looked back up. "I'll climb down beside you. Don't worry, the rock here is porous, and there are plenty of handholds."

My palms suddenly felt like seaweed, and my stomach tumbled. But I wasn't going to let him seem me squirm.

"I can't believe I'm going to do this."

I forced my claws out, sank them into some cracks in the top of the stone wall like Amal had done, and then levered myself over the edge.

It took ten heart-rending minutes to get down, and when my feet finally hit the ground, I uttered a quiet prayer of thanks and vowed to never climb anything ever again.

My fingers throbbed with pain, and I had to wrap my arms around myself to stop them from trembling. "What now?"

"We look for a way in," Amal whispered.

Tendrils of predawn mist wound around the garden. I could make out ornamental trees and flower beds, and a little gazebo in the distance. A series of busts were mounted on the low stone perimeter wall. I peeked over the edge, and my stomach dropped with a fresh twinge of vertigo. It was just darkness and mist below.

The garden was populated with statues of people in extravagant, lifelike poses. While the sculptures near the portal had been fanciful and grotesque monstrosities, these were absolute masterworks.

My eyes were drawn to a perfectly sculpted female warrior. She was thrusting her spear forward with a surge of force and momentum that I could almost feel. It was breathtaking.

Her target was a man mounted on another pedestal. He was naked and recoiling in fear, one arm raised. I wondered what message the mage was trying to convey.

We cautiously made our way through the misty garden toward the base of the tower. There wasn't a door there, either, but we found three caves in the cliff opposite the gazebo.

"Entrance might be in there," Jaxson whispered.

"Jax, I don't like this." Amal grabbed his arm, and a pang of entirely unreasonable jealously shot through me.

She pointed to another statue. This one depicted a man in a trench coat with arms thrusted forward as if casting a spell—I'd seen Casey strike a similar pose many times.

"Look at the way his coat is flying. These are *too* realistic, Jax. And modern."

"Shit." He spun, scanning the grounds.

I looked around. "What?"

He pulled me down behind the hedge, and Amal dropped beside us. "Basilisk. Or one of the children of the Medusae. Probably lives in those caves."

"What the hell are those?" I whispered, worry coursing through me.

"The first is a giant lizard. The second are serpents. Both can turn you to stone...like the statues around us," Amal answered.

Oh, goddamn it.

We waited. My heart was pounding so loudly that I was sure the mage could hear it all the way in his tower. But nothing stirred in the darkness.

Then a subtle scratching echoed from the cave. Jaxson tensed, and I held my breath.

From out of the shadows, a dark shape emerged. A massive reptilian head swung left and right. It flicked out its tongue, searching the garden for the source of the sounds.

Us.

23

Jaxson

Shit.

I yanked Savannah down behind the ornamental hedge. "Whatever you do, do *not* look at its eyes, or you'll end up like the statues in the garden."

Amal dropped beside us. "Stay quiet and crawl along the bushes."

I glanced through the gap beneath the hedge.

The six-legged basilisk moved cautiously, testing the air with its tongue. Every few seconds, it raised and lowered a frill along its back. It hadn't spotted us. That was something. I motioned for Savannah and Amal to start moving along the hedge.

Something rustled, and I checked beneath the bush again.

The thing had moved twenty feet, and I'd barely heard it. It was now only a few feet from where Amal and Savannah were still slowly crawling.

My mate. Protect her.

My pulse surged, and a wild madness consumed me. It was pure instinct, driven by the mate bond. Fuck.

I shot forward like lighting and slammed my claws into the

basilisk's back. It roared and thrashed as I tore away at its armored hide.

As long as I held on, it couldn't look at me.

The beast reached the same conclusion and dropped onto its side to roll. I thrust back before I was crushed and slammed into the side of the fountain.

Dirt and leaves exploded into the air as a massive reptilian claw swept the bushes aside, and a roar shook my bones.

I rolled onto my back and looked up to see—

Nothing.

Utter darkness in all directions.

I wasn't unconscious. My heart was pounding, and I could feel the damp, dew-covered grass beneath my body. Had its gaze blinded me?

Fuck.

The ground shook softly, and the creature's breath rasped a few feet from where I lay, drowning me in an unbearable carrion stench. The thing sniffed, and I felt a hot puff of air roll over my skin.

It was right there. How was I not dead? Was it blind as well?

The thing made a hissing noise, and I held my breath as I slowly and soundlessly readjusted my feet to leap away.

Gunshots rang out to my right. The basilisk unleashed a deafening roar, and my eardrum burned in pain. Then something swept within inches of my body as the beast charged away.

Suddenly, a hand grabbed my arm.

"Come on!" Savannah whispered.

"What the fuck's going on?" I couldn't see a thing.

She pulled me forward, and we started running. "This is my shadow magic. I can see. Follow me."

A blood-curdling roar sounded from twenty or thirty feet away.

"Hold on." Savannah skidded to a stop. "Amal, come to my voice."

"What's going on?" Amal whispered from the darkness.

"We're wrapped in shadows. It can't see us, and we can't see it. Nobody gets turned to stone."

"Brilliant, but—"

"Amal, take Jaxson's hand and follow me." Amal took one of my hands in the darkness, Savannah the other, and we moved through the garden.

Our feet crunched over a strip of gravel, and then we were pounding over grass again.

Suddenly a sea of stars and silhouettes of trees appeared. I stumbled out of the wall of darkness and to a halt just in time to avoid tumbling over the precipice and into the misty abyss.

Amal and Savannah were wide-eyed beside me. We needed a distraction to throw the monster off our scent.

I grabbed one of the stone busts along the wall and heaved. The marble head spun end over end into the darkness, and the sound of a heavy thud and rustling bushes echoed upward. The basilisk roared from behind us, and the deafening sounds of its footfalls rose as it scrambled over the edge of the cliff, scaling its way down.

Fuck, that was too close.

I nodded at Savannah and Amal and quietly moved forward along the wall toward the gazebo and the caves in the cliff.

A moment longer, I searched the entrances of the three caves for a clue. Pale light emanated from a pool in one, and steam rose off the water. Idyllic in any other circumstance.

Amal pointed to the middle cave. "A way in."

There was a thin seam of light. Before I could respond, an angry bellow erupted from the darkness behind us.

Savannah spun around. "The basilisk. Go, go, *go*."

We charged into the cave. The light was emanating from a

cracked door. I shoved both women through, then slammed the door behind me.

We found ourselves in a rough-hewn storage cave lit by dangling Edison bulbs. I pushed Savannah and Amal forward and around a corner just as the door exploded off its hinges, and shrapnel slammed me into the wall.

Savannah gripped my arm and hauled me out of danger as the darkness of her magic filled in behind me.

We scrambled up a narrow set of worn stairs cut from the rock. The walls shook, and the stench of carrion breath washed over us, trailed by the sound of claws scrabbling against the stone.

"It sounds stuck," Savannah said as we wound up the stairs and emerged in a long cave that served as a wine cellar. Relentless scratching and grunting echoed up the stairwell, but it didn't draw any closer. The basilisk was wedged. For now.

Savannah bent forward and braced her hands on her knees. "Thank God the stairs down there are narrow. I really hope there's a way out the front door."

To my surprise, her scent wasn't fear, but rather elation—the thrill of the chase. I inhaled deeply, delighting in her. "Nice move with the shadows. You saved my ass."

"It's a nice ass. Where the hell are we?" she asked, breast heaving. I had to tear my eyes away from the sheen of sweat that glistened hypnotically on her chest.

Amal traced the thousands of gouges that covered the stone wall. "In some old, hand-cut Etruscan caves. A lot of the buildings here use them for storage. Speaking of which..."

She pulled a silver case from her pack and clipped it on her belt, then passed one to Savannah. "This is a potion bomb cartridge. Just flip the lid to pull one out. They're labeled – firebomb, shockbomb, and stunner. I should have passed it out earlier."

"Yeesss," Savannah said. "I've heard of those."

Potion bombs were unstable, designed to break on impact, and they didn't play together nicely. I gritted my teeth. "Are you insane, running around with those?"

Amal shrugged. "The cases are pretty rugged."

I placed my hand on Savannah's arm. "Emergency use only."

However, I was pretty sure my warning completely missed the mark. Savannah had an eager gleam in her eyes that reminded me of her half-mad cousin.

I silently cursed as she clipped the bombs to her belt, then stepped around her before she started up the stairs. "I'll go first."

The door in the cave was already open, and I was betting that Kahanov had used the same entrance. By now, he probably knew we were here and had prepared an ambush.

Savannah sighed but let me pass. "Fine, you get blasted first and have all the fun."

We ascended the time-worn stairwell until we reached a narrow door, slightly ajar. I pushed it open slowly, revealing an expansive kitchen with white and black tile. A pot sat cooking on an old gas stove, and a body lay on the floor beside a knife. Blood was splattered everywhere.

"I don't think that happened chopping vegetables," Savannah whispered.

"Kahanov is here," I growled as a deep rage clouded my thoughts and a savage drive to hunt and kill filled my mind.

The bastard had attacked my pack and put five of my wolves to sleep. He'd also attacked Savannah, and with the mate bond, that didn't sit well.

My vision clouded as my body shook with fury. My claws ripped out, and my fangs erupted as hair bristled along my arms. I didn't push them back but remained in that liminal state between man and beast.

"We need to move fast," Amal said.

My senses blazing, I shot forward and out into a long, pearl-white gallery. The room's vaulted ceiling was covered with ornate gold decorations. Gold-framed paintings hung along the walls, and erotic marble sculptures stood in the corners.

It was absolutely garish.

"This place is gorgeous," Savannah murmured.

There was no door—the room simply ended and was followed by chamber after chamber, as far as I could see.

We moved on.

"I thought this was a tower," Savannah said, as she peeked out a window. Then she slapped her hand over her mouth. "Oh, God. I think I'm going to be sick."

I was by her side in a second. The skyline of the sleepy Italian town spread out before us.

Perpendicularly.

My head snapped around. The corridor was the tower. Somehow, the mage had turned gravity on its side, and we were walking upward.

"Man, that's freaky," Amal whispered.

"Then don't look out the window," I said. It didn't really make any difference, just as long as gravity didn't suddenly switch when we were partway up.

I moved silently from room to room, relying on my senses for warning. All we found were ravaged remains of golden automatons.

"Magic robots. Probably guards," Amal explained to Savannah.

Halfway through the interconnected galleries, we came to a room with a massive hearth ringed by red velvet chairs. I froze.

Someone was sitting in front of the embers. In an instant, I had my claws at the figure's throat—an old man, sleeping, and breathing slowly.

Not Kahanov.

I shoved my hand over his mouth and shook him awake, but he still didn't stir.

"He's like the sleepers," Amal whispered.

"What do you want to bet that Kahanov knocked out everybody here, the mage included?" Savannah asked.

I was too enraged to respond. He was close. I could feel it in my bones.

We passed through a library and halted in front of a dimly lit gallery.

The hair on my neck rose. The shadows were all wrong, and a scent of rotting fruit hung in the air. I tasted blood and copper, and my skin felt slick, like it was covered in oil.

Savannah met my eyes, pinched her nose, and mouthed *blood demon*.

Kahanov hadn't just been here—he *was* here.

My wolf surged in my chest with excitement. It was time for a reckoning.

I moved forward cautiously. Seven glowing glass cases occupied the center of the gallery. Each displayed a single object, most likely a magical artifact.

The furthest case was open. And empty.

Shit.

It had to have held the Soul Knife.

Suddenly, a voice called out from the shadows. "What a treat! You people are such a delight to work with. Here I sent you all sorts of invitations, and you turned them down. But now, when I'd lost all hope of you coming, you show up at the perfect time."

Kahanov.

24

My veins turned to ice. Kahanov's voice was just like it had been in my dreams.

Except now, the nightmare was real.

We were flanking the door to the gallery, our backs pressed up against the wall. My index finger burned on the trigger of my pistol, and my heartbeat was so loud, I was sure the entire town could hear it. I was going to finally be face to face with that asshole. He'd hunted, imprisoned, and haunted me, and if that wasn't enough, he'd turned me into a monster.

The writhing hatred that rose in my chest was so strong that I could barely see. Pain shot through my jaw as my canines erupted, and my fingertips itched.

Let me rip his throat out, the wolf growled in my mind.

I stood firm against her. *Not a chance. He's mine.*

Slowly, the itching subsided, but my canines didn't retract. I nodded to Jaxson. *Ready.*

On a three count, Jaxson and Amal swung into the room, claws out. I followed behind, pistol raised to cover them.

No one was there.

My heartbeat drowned out all sound as they rushed along the sides of cases. There wasn't enough cover to conceal a blood demon, but I could smell it.

Where is—

The breath exploded from my lungs, and my pistol flew from my grasp as a brutal force ripped me up into the air. Suddenly, I was face to face with a blood demon, suspended from the ceiling. My heart clenched with terror as the demon lurched along the roof of the gallery, holding me dangling from its claws.

In a blur of motion, Jaxson leapt to the wall and climbed. He was on us in seconds, and he sunk his claws into the thing's leg and pulled. The demon lost its grip on the ceiling, and we dropped.

Agony ripped through my shoulder as I slammed into the ground. I rolled over to get away from the sinuous monster, but the demon lashed out with its sickly green talons and dug them into my leg. Searing pain tore through me, and I screamed.

Jaxson jumped to my side and wrenched the demon's grasping hands away. It howled and roared, but the unearthly sound was cut short as Jaxson tore through its throat.

Blood sprayed over me as I scrambled forward on my knees, searching for my gun.

Wolf time?

No, I thought, my hands shaking from shock and pain.

Blasts of wicked green flames roared around us, and I scampered behind a display case just in time to see Kahanov *spider-climb* across the ceiling and drop down behind a case on the far side. What the fuck?

His voice echoed through the room. "Jaxson, let's be reasonable. Hand over the girl, and I'll wake your wolves. I'll even give her back when I'm done, to make things fair. On my own blood oath, I only need a part of her soul."

"She's mine. I'll never hand her over," Jaxson snarled, the sound verging on animalistic.

My wolf surged in my chest, but my stomach twisted. Two men arguing over who would have me?

Screw that.

"You want me, Kahanov? Here I am!" I stepped out and whipped a potion bomb at him, not even sure which type.

He peeked out, and his eyes went wide in horror. And then everything slowed down.

The momentary smug smile plastered across my face was torn away when Jaxson leapt forward and hauled me through the door.

The potion bomb plinked off the case where Kahanov was hiding and burst against the marble floor. A storm of lightning erupted through the room and threw Kahanov back toward the open exit of the gallery. Glass exploded through the air as all the cases shattered.

Then circles of once-invisible runes began glowing everywhere—around each case, on the walls, on the floor. The whole place buzzed with unstable magic.

Aw, shit.

Time sped up again as Jaxson yanked me around the corner and threw his body over mine beside a couch.

The tower shook with a series of ear-shattering blasts. I couldn't even hear them after the first—just bone-jarring thud after thud, followed by a long, constant ringing in my ears.

I buried my face in Jaxson's shoulder as the wall beside us lurched, and then the impossibly tall bookshelf listed and fell. It slammed into the back of the couch, just a couple feet above our heads. Books rained down on top of Jaxson's back, and one struck me in the corner of my eye.

Silence.

I struggled beneath the weight of Jaxson's muscled form and a hundred books. "Jax! Are you okay?"

I was shouting but could barely hear my own voice above the ringing.

He was breathing, though. I felt his chest rising and falling against mine, and the powerful scent of his body intoxicated my mind.

His deep growl reverberated through my body and down into my core. With a swift motion, he heaved himself up and hurled the shelf out of our way. Books poured off to either side of him as he climbed free. Then he held out a hand.

I grasped it, and he pulled me up and into his arms. His eyes burned with possessiveness and desire. It was too intense, and I looked away, my gaze landing on Amal's singed and crumpled form. "Amal!"

"Here," she said, picking herself off the floor with a groan.

Jaxson let me go, and I met his hard stare. I forced a smile. "Thanks for that. Who knew a little reading could be so hard on your body?"

Wordlessly, he extended his claws and moved toward the door.

I peeked around him. "Holy shit."

The room was blackened to its core. The paintings on the walls were gone, as were the cabinets and glass cases.

"Cases *like those* that hold dangerous and deadly magical objects are often protected with magical traps. You managed to detonate them all," Jaxson growled.

I nodded. "Okay. That's pretty obvious now, but it wasn't an entirely flawed plan. Maybe I got him?"

Jaxson shook his head and began making his way carefully through the smoldering wreckage. "Step lightly. If any of the traps survived the explosion, they'll be unstable."

Amal handed me her pistol. "I think you should maybe stick to this."

We moved gingerly through the gallery. I spotted a vase from one of the shattered cases, amazingly still intact. Apparently, magical objects were rather hard to destroy.

A ray of green light slammed into Jaxson's chest and sent him flying back into the smoldering debris. Then Kahanov skittered like a spider through the top of the doorway and leapt down toward me with a pale green blade in his hand.

The Soul Knife.

I dodged back as the metal swiped within an inch of my throat.

Before I could extend my claws, Amal flew into him and hurled him backward through the air. He slammed into the wall, and the knife clattered across the floor.

I froze, torn between going for Kahanov and for the knife.

He rose, hands burning with green light and blood dripping from his chest.

With no time to think, I called my magic and smothered the floor with shadows. Kahanov looked about wildly for the knife, and then, with a howl of rage, he released a wall of green fire that ripped through the room.

Searing pain blinded me for a second as the unnatural flames burned my exposed skin. It was all I could do to concentrate on the shadows hiding the blade. Agony took every lucid thought from me, save one—protect the knife.

I rolled over in time to see Amal whip a potion bomb through the air. There was a blinding flash of light, and when my vision returned, Jaxson was hauling me to my feet, and Kahanov was gone.

"Are you okay?"

"Get him!" I shouted. "I'll grab the knife!"

Jaxson and Amal raced into the next room as I staggered

over to where the Soul Knife still lay in the charred debris, cloaked by a veil of darkness that only I could see through. I scooped it up and slipped it into my belt.

That's one for our side.

I raced into the next room with Amal's pistol raised and skidded to halt in front of a massive bed, atop which lay two sleeping people, both buck naked. One of them had to be the mage, knocked out by Kahanov's dream magic.

But the feature that drew my attention was the open window.

"Fuck!" Jaxson snarled.

"Did he just jump out the window?" I shouted as I swept through the room.

In answer to my question, the floor and walls quaked as the window exploded inward and showered us with broken glass and shattered stone. A monstrous head rammed through the wreckage, and my heart seized with terror.

Noctith demon. *Fuck.*

Its head split open vertically, revealing rows and rows of savage teeth, and it sent a deafening screech pulsing through the room. Everything spun as vertigo overcame me, and I felt a trail of blood run from my ear down my neck.

The thing screeched again as it rammed its neck further through the opening. Stone and wood crumbled as the monster forced its way through, and I took cover behind a cabinet.

It was a living nightmare. Fear made manifest.

I froze as it swung its head toward Amal and spread its hideous jaws wide. A thick cloud of pink gas boiled from its mouth.

She staggered out of the way, but the gas surrounded her in seconds, and she fell to the floor. I recalled Neve's words and shuddered. These fuckers breathed clouds of sleeping gas, and we were trapped in a tiny room.

With a furious roar, Jaxson leapt forward and sank his claws into its neck. The thing shook, and Jaxson flew back against the wall. My heart stilled, and something in my chest pulled as the demon opened its mouth to breathe.

We can't lose him.

Without thinking, I burst out from the shelter of the dresser and hurled a potion bomb toward the demon's open maw. Unfortunately, the beast snapped its jaws shut, and the bomb ricocheted off its head and into the wall.

Oh, shit. Not ag—

I dove for cover behind the dresser as a fireball enveloped the room. The dresser lifted off its feet and flew over my head before smashing into the wall. Bits of stone debris rained down around me. Rolling over, I gasped and choked on the smoke.

Stars and town lights twinkled through a gaping hole where the window had been. The demon was gone.

"Jax!" I coughed.

He heaved part of the vanity off himself and stood. "Are you *insane*?"

"Yes." I scrambled across the debris to where Amal was lying beside the two sleepers, who had landed behind the overturned bed. She was still breathing. I shook her hard. "Amal!"

No response. She was out cold.

Jaxson was at my side in an instant. "Fuck. She's alive, at least." He pulled the rubble off her and lifted her sleeping form. "We need to get out of here. Did you get the knife?"

I stormed over to the hole in the tower. "Yes, but I can't believe that asshole got away."

"Doesn't matter. We got the Soul Knife. That's a win."

I touched the knife tucked in my belt as I looked out over the strange vertical horizon. The lights of the town twinkling on the left, and the starlit predawn sky on the right. I tilted my head to the right to correctly orient the view. The scene should have soothed me, but the circumstances only made my blood boil.

A set of black talons lashed through the open gap and tore into my jacket. I screamed in shock and dug my claws into the crumbling stone wall as the noctith demon yanked me toward the window.

My jacket ripped away, and Jaxson lunged for me.

Then my grip slipped.

25

I screamed in terror as I fell, the wind buffeting my clothes.

The night sky spun in circles around me as I tumbled downward. I caught flashes of stars. Of the misty valley. Of the garden far below.

I was going to die.

Not if I can help it, the wolf inside me snarled, and she seized control.

My body twisted, and my arms flailed out. The claws of my right hand ricocheted off the tower, then raked down along the stonework. Suddenly, they sank into the wooden lintel of a window. I gasped as my body jerked to a stop. My shoulder wrenched out of its socket, and an unbearable jolt of agony shot down my spine as my body slammed into the stone wall.

The Soul Knife slipped from my belt.

For a second, I watched it fall. Then the lintel split, my hand slipped, and gravity took hold once more.

I thrashed wildly. There was one brief moment of clarity when I saw the clouds and stars whirl by overhead, but then my body erupted with pain as I crashed into the bushes. Twigs ripped into my skin, and I howled as I rolled out onto the grass.

I groaned and wiggled my fingers. My shoulder was screaming, but at least my legs worked. I glanced up at the gaping hole in the tower high above. How was I even alive?

You're a werewolf now. We heal fast, and we're damned hard to kill.

It was a goddamned miracle.

A shadow drifted over me, and a new wave of adrenaline brought me to my senses. I rolled to my side and looked up. High above, a monstrous four-winged shape circled in the air, descending quickly.

The noctith demon.

It was coming for me. Could I find cover in the tower? I looked toward the caves, where light glinted from the shattered doorway, and my gut clenched. Was the basilisk still in there, lurking in the shadows? I was trapped between a demon that could put me to sleep and a monster that could turn me to stone.

Think.

Heart pounding, I looked around wildly. Where was the Soul Knife?

Something glinted in the middle of the garden.

Whimpering in pain, I pulled myself to my feet and staggered forward. I grasped the Soul Knife by the hilt and headed for one of the dark openings in the face of the cliff, praying the basilisk wasn't lying in wait. As I hobbled forward, I called the shadows around me. I just needed enough time to get inside.

The demon screeched above, and I could almost feel its wings vibrating the air around me. With as much speed as I could manage, I turned and ducked into the caves.

The earth shook behind me as the noctith demon landed at the edge of the garden. On its back sat Kahanov. That fucker.

Though I was certain he couldn't see me, he looked toward

the caves where I was hiding. "Savannah…you should be more careful. I need you alive. Let's not make this more painful than it needs to be."

The noctith demon shrieked and swung its strange head left and right, searching the garden with its hundreds of eerie, glowing eyes. I bit my lip until I tasted blood to keep from screaming, and pulled the shadows closer.

"Fine," the sorcerer called. "We can do this multiple ways. Nighty night."

The demon emitted another piercing cry and exhaled a plume of pinkish gas toward the caves. I looked around in desperation as the cloud billowed toward me. Did I have to inhale it, or would contact alone knock me out?

I searched the cave hopelessly. The only cover was the pool. I ran over, gulped in the biggest breath I could manage, and slipped beneath the water.

Closing my eyes, I began to count. Each second that passed was a prayer that the noxious gas would dissipate. I tried calming my mind, but every cut and gash in my body stung, and fear pressed in, heavier than the water around me.

My lungs began to burn, but I fought down my instincts. Every time a second passed, I vowed to stay one second more. Finally, when I could stand it no longer, I lifted my head slowly above the water.

The cloud of gas was gone.

While every nerve in my body wanted me to gasp in relief, I sucked a breath in through my teeth as slowly and quietly as I could.

The earth shook again as the noctith demon shifted position and released another plume of sleeping gas down the path outside.

A little relief trickled through me. They didn't know where I was. How could they not hear my heartbeat? It was practically ripping out of my chest.

Then my pulse skipped a beat as something scraped on the wall behind me—massive claws scrabbling on stone.

My stomach sank.

Death was coming.

26

Jaxson

Find her, my wolf howled in my chest. *She's in pain. Dying.*

I leapt from the hole in the wall where the window had been and hurtled down the face of the tower, using my claws as brakes to slow my fall.

The moment they found wood, I dug in and swung myself onto the windowsill. It was a fucking ridiculous way to get down, but speed was everything.

I heaved myself left to the next sill over.

The noctith demon shrieked and swung its head from side to side, searching for Savannah in the garden below.

Fucking Kahanov was on its back. I wanted to throw myself into the air and dive toward him, but it was too far to leap and have any chance of landing the attack. I had no idea what to do. Try to kill Kahanov? Take out the demon? Or simply find Savannah and get the fuck out?

I crouched and prepared to leap again, but I froze. Something was off. Then I saw it: the shadows below were moving. A dark velvet wall drifted closer to the demon.

Savannah's magic.

Damnit, what the hell was she doing?

I had to get to her. I leapt for the next window down. Stone rushed past me, and then I slammed my claws into another lintel and swung myself up onto the stone sill.

The noctith paused. Then both it and Kahanov looked up.

I'd been spotted.

The thing began beating its iridescent wings and started to rise. But suddenly, it spun to its right with unimaginable speed toward the caves and shrieked.

Savannah's cloud of shadows ripped away, revealing the hidden form of the basilisk. The noctith demon's mouth split wide, and it spewed a pink gas toward the monster.

But it was too late. The demon had looked the basilisk in the eyes.

The noctith reeled backward and gave a twisted, piercing wail as its head and legs turned into stone. It clawed the earth and tried to rise, but its dead and hardened foot caught on the low wall, and the demon feebly flailed its stone wings and limbs in the air.

It was already doomed. Half statue, half flesh and blood, the demon plunged over the edge of the garden, flinging Kahanov from its back. There was a flash of light, and he disappeared.

Transport charm.

Grinding my teeth, I leapt into the air and plummeted toward the garden below. I crumpled and rolled as I hit the ground, but my right shin shattered. Still, I roared and staggered to my feet, my bones already healing.

Find Savy.

I limped toward the caves, then slowed. The basilisk lay in the middle of the garden. I approached cautiously. Its chest rose and fell, but it made no movement in my direction. It was sleeping, a victim of the noctith's poisoned breath. But for how long?

I sprinted toward the caves. She had to be here. She'd been

controlling the shadows that had hidden and probably bewildered the basilisk. It had stumbled through the darkness, toward the loudest source of sound: the demon.

Gods, that woman was smart.

Her signature flooded my senses, and protectiveness coursed through my veins. "Savannah!"

"Here..." came a feeble response.

I ducked into the northern cave.

She was lying at the edge of the pool, soaking hair draped around her. Her skin had been shredded by hundreds of cuts, though they were already healing. I dropped to my knees and wrapped her in my arms. She was limp and cold. I pushed my magic into her, a torrent of healing fire.

She gasped and sat bolt upright in my arms. Her shoulder popped back into its socket, and the remaining cuts in her skin stitched closed, leaving white scars scattered like stars.

I gritted my teeth as I gave her everything I had, pouring my strength and life into her. She trembled in my embrace and arched her back as her mouth opened in a silent moan of delight.

I'd heard that the healing gift between mates was intimate, but I'd never seen it done. Not like this. It was the transfer of life. Of vitality.

Savannah's eyes flickered open. "My God, what did you just do?"

"I healed you."

"Remind me to fall out of buildings more often." She coughed, and as she turned to look around, a little bit of blood trickled down her lips. "Did I get Kahanov? With the basilisk?"

I could barely think. The drop of blood quivering at the edge of her ruby lips mesmerized my mind. I wanted to lick it from them. To press my lips against hers and kiss her with abandon.

My head began to bend forward as she turned her mouth toward mine.

Suddenly, she jerked out of my arms and scrambled down into the pool. "Holy shit, my clothes are shredded!"

She was looking at me like I was a filthy predator. And maybe I was. I scowled. "You're a werewolf now. Get used to it. Also, don't go adventuring in any outfits you're too attached to."

I looked away.

"Jax. Kahanov. Did we get him?"

I cleared my throat and sat back. "The basilisk got the noctith. And the noctith got the basilisk."

"But not *him*."

"No. He escaped."

"Fuck." Her head tilted back. "We were so damn close."

"It was a good plan."

She slammed her palm down on the edge of the pool. "I was so fucking close."

27

Savannah

Two hours later, I stepped up to the front door of Aunt Laurel's house, completely and utterly drained. I had the Soul Knife but couldn't shake the deep sense of failure. Kahanov had gotten away, and Amal was comatose, trapped in her dreams like the other sleepers.

Everywhere I went, I brought disaster.

Jaxson had called in the Order to secure the tower, and they'd transported the sleeping mage, his lover, and his staff back to Magic Side. Hopefully, the archmages could find a cure for the curse.

I couldn't bear much more guilt. Amal and the Italians had raised the number of sleepers to eleven. How many more would there be before this was over?

With a weary sigh, I shoved through the door.

"Savy? Is that you?" Aunt Laurel called from the kitchen.

While it was almost five in the morning in Italy, it was only ten p.m. in Chicago, and my family was apparently still kicking it.

I wandered into the kitchen like a zombie.

Laurel and Casey sat at their usual spots around the kitchen table, having dessert. She smiled and motioned to the freezer with her spoon. "You're just in time for ice cream."

It was like I'd strolled into a bizarre alternate reality, where everything was sane and homey.

Moving in a daze, I grabbed a bowl of country-style vanilla, topped it with a pile of Fruity Pebbles, and plopped down on a stool.

"You're so much like your father," Laurel said, eyeing my ice cream.

Casey stood up halfway, eyes wide. "Gods, Savy, what are you *wearing*?"

Oh, right. *That.*

"Uh." I looked down with no idea how to explain my current appearance. "An Italian man's clothes. I think they're really expensive."

My clothes had been incinerated by magic flames and shredded by a combination of demon claws, flying shrapnel, and plummeting into a bush. There hadn't been much left. And while the mage had a palatial closet, there'd been nothing for a woman. I'd grabbed a pair of slightly too-tight in-the-hips wool trousers and a not-busty-enough shirt that was currently ready to pop at the seams.

I was pretty sure Jaxson had appreciated that.

I'd also borrowed a scarf and a purse. Technically, a murse. It was real Italian leather, and no one would know the difference.

Casey leaned over to inspect the cuffs of my shirt. "Okay, I've *got* to hear this one."

Laurel raised her eyebrows. "Seems like you had an interesting night."

I leaned back. What should I even tell them? Nothing? Everything? I was too drained to care. "I went to Italy and sneaked into a mage's tower. I fought a basilisk, a blood demon, another one of those noctith demon things, and the blood sorcerer. I managed to live but didn't catch him."

My aunt dug into her bowl of ice cream. "My. That's a lot for one evening. No wonder you seem exhausted."

Casey waggled his spoon at me. "You haven't explained how you got the clothes, though."

I stared at them in disbelief. "Didn't you hear what I just said?"

My aunt leaned forward. "Well, give us some details. Sounds exciting. What were you after?"

"Whose clothes?" Casey added. "That's what I'm most curious about."

I pushed back from the table. "You two are mad."

My aunt was taken aback. "What?"

"What I just told you was literally insane. Like, out-of-this-world ridiculous. I don't know how many times I nearly died tonight. And you act like it was the most normal thing in the world! I know I'm in Magic Side, but this isn't normal, is it? Please tell me it's not normal."

My aunt gave me a knowing smile. "Normal? Of course not. But then again, you're not normal. You're a LaSalle. And clearly, you were up to the task, to your credit."

I ran my hand through my hair in disbelief. "How are you not yelling at me for running around and diving headfirst into dangers I know absolutely nothing about?"

My aunt narrowed her eyes and rested her elbows on the high table. "First, because it's not my place. I'm here to help, not run your life. Second, it's been clear from the start that the three ladies have their eye on you, and there's nothing anyone can do about that."

"Who?"

"The fates, of course. They have their favorites. From time to time, they pick a mortal and push as much on their plate as they can, just to see if they've got what it takes. Thankfully, I think you do."

My heartbeat rose as my temper twisted like a knife. "You mean this is all happening because some heartless cosmic entity is just fucking with me?"

"It's happening because you have the capacity to be great. To be special. And *that* draws danger like a light draws moths from the night. Trust me, my life at your age was an utter nightmare, too. But it made me like iron."

I gritted my teeth and glared at the table because I didn't want to glare at her. This was messed up. I despised the way Jaxson could compel me with his alpha presence. The way Kahanov had forced me to sleepwalk into the arms of a demon. The way the wolf inside me could take control of my body. I was tired of being pushed and pulled and thrown around. I wasn't going to give up control, even to the fates.

"I make my own destiny. I refuse to believe in fate," I hissed.

"Well, clearly, they believe in you," she said.

I shoved my bowl of ice cream back as frustration and resentment strangled me to choking. I did my best to broadcast *this is not acceptable* into the universe.

My aunt studied me silently for a while, then traced her spoon absently around her empty bowl. "What were you after in Italy, anyway?"

I didn't respond at first. Finally, with a sigh, I popped open my new, expensive-looking Italian leather handbag and pulled out the Soul Knife. Just touching the cool metal made my fingers sting. It felt evil.

I set it down carefully on the table. "This was what Kahanov was after, and we got it. Jaxson Laurent said that the Order should take it, but seeing as I don't know them from Adam, and since Kahanov is bent on using it to cut out my soul, I thought I would ask you where the safest place to keep it would be."

My family might be mild lunatics and weapons manufacturers, but they had been fiercely loyal to me. My aunt would know what to do.

She leaned forward and inspected the knife. "May I?"

I nodded in assent.

She picked up the blade and turned it over slowly in her hands. "Very interesting. And dangerous."

I bit my lip. "To be clear, I'm not asking you to hide it in the house. I'm certain Kahanov will come looking for it, and I don't want you two or Uncle Pete to be in danger. I'm just looking for advice."

She put the blade back on the table. "I have a place, but the Order's vault is more secure. Rumor has it that it's absolutely impregnable."

I stared down at the wicked blade. I could feel the wrongness of it with every nerve in my body. It wasn't just that Kahanov was probably going to use it to sever my soul—the blade itself was evil, I was certain of it.

I reached out but stopped my hand. "Actually, is there any way we could destroy it...maybe feed it to the Sphere of Devouring?"

My aunt smiled sadly. "That's a very good idea, but I'm afraid it's extremely hard to destroy an artifact like this. It's not ephemeral like a spell—it's magic made manifest. But I think I have a better idea of where to put it."

"Where?"

She picked up the knife by the blade and handed it hilt-first to me. "Right in your hands. I imagine, considering what you've accomplished already, that this is the safest place."

I kept my hands on the table and didn't move a muscle to take it. "No offense, Aunt Laurel, but that's a *terrible* plan. He'll just take it from me. It's like bringing your own carving knife to the Bates Motel."

"Nonsense. You won't carry it around in a belt sheath." She set down the knife and snapped her fingers. With a spark of magic and a twist of mist, an object appeared in her hand.

"Your car keys?" I asked.

"I store them in the ether. Along with my favorite wand, the *Demonic Tutelary Texts of Degobraxis the Infernal*, a purse, and a few other important or handy items."

My jaw dropped for a number of reasons.

Seeing as I didn't immediately protest, my aunt clapped her hands. "Casey, get my ethereal inscription kit."

"Uh...ethereal?" I stammered.

"The ether is a place between places. What's important is—" She snapped her fingers, and her keys disappeared. "It will be very hard for Kahanov to find the knife, and if, for some reason, he ever gets his hands on it, you'll be able to dismiss it at will. It's not foolproof, but I'm guessing he'll never suspect you have it."

Casey returned with a red leather satchel and handed it to Laurel. She opened it and pulled out a tiny vial of ink and a brush. "Give me your hand."

I did as she ordered, and she began painting little magical symbols on my palm. Her nutmeg signature rose into the air, and electricity flowed through my skin until my hand was vibrating with power.

I sat perfectly still, almost breathless, afraid that if I wiggled, she might mess up a symbol and blow off my fingers or something. Finally, she sat back. "Okay, the next step is to memorize the knife in every detail. You'll need those details to call it back to you. Tell me when you're certain you can imagine it exactly."

I traced my eyes over every inch of the Soul Knife. The bronze dagger was so patinaed that it was nearly pure green. The lancelet blade had a raised ridge down the center and was inscribed with fine runes, though none of the designs meant anything to me.

I turned my concentration to the signature of its magic, which tasted like wine and had the sound of ripe wheat blowing in the summer wind.

"Okay," I said at last.

My aunt placed her fingers on the back of my hand. "Now, imagine your hand completely empty. Unburdened."

I focused my mind on envisioning an empty palm, and my aunt began to chant. Her magic flowed along the symbols she had drawn and down into the knife. The scent of nutmeg and the sound of bees filled the air, and then the lines of black runes she had inscribed on my palm began to glow with purple light.

Suddenly, with a swirl of mist, the dagger and symbols disappeared.

I gasped. "It's gone!"

I turned my hand over, looking for any trace of her magical runes. Nothing.

"Now, the trick is to bring it back. Remember exactly how it was, how it felt in your grasp."

I closed my eyes and brought to mind the image of the knife. Every detail. Not just how it looked, but its weight and the way it fit in the palm of my hand. I imagined I could feel the signature of its magic, wine and rustling wheat.

With a puff, the knife appeared, and my hand sank with the weight. "Well, I'll be damned."

I looked from Casey to my aunt. "I mean, this is crazy powerful. I imagine airport security is impossible."

My aunt laughed. "Well, yes, but show me the terrorist who wants to pull a knife on a plane full of werewolves, vampires, and sorcerers."

Fair point.

She pushed away from the table. "And with that bit of hocus pocus, I'm headed to bed. I want to hear more, though, in the morning."

Casey crossed his arms and leaned back on his stool. "I'm not leaving until you explain why you're dressed like a man."

I turned my spoon on him. "Casey, I was considering spilling the beans, but you pestered me one too many times. I will never, ever tell you, and now you'll go to your grave haunted by the question."

I sure as hell wasn't going to tell either of them that I kept turning into a werewolf and was now at risk of ripping through every outfit I owned.

He glared at me with venom in his eyes. "I thought maybe you had a new Italian boyfriend. That's all."

"No."

"I hear you and Jaxson are a thing," my aunt said, far, far too casually at kitchen door.

The room spun, and the blood drained from my face. She knew. *Shit.* My eyes flicked to Casey, who looked away with suspicious speed.

I gave the side of his head a death stare. "Casey, you big-mouthed asshole. No, Aunt Laurel. We are *not* a thing."

She put her hands on the table and leaned forward. "Savannah, we all like the taste of forbidden fruit. I certainly did at your age."

"I don't want Jaxson's fruits," I blurted, sending the off-the-rails conversation over a bridge and into the chasm below.

She glanced at her son and frowned. "Keep in mind, I had to rear Casey through his teenage years. The women he brought into this house...there's a room I can never enter again."

"Too much. I don't want to know. Don't tell me."

"It's the room across from yours," Casey added.

I covered my face with my hands. This was too awkward.

"Do *not* trust Jaxson, Savannah," said Aunt Laurel. "The pack care only for their own. When you discover the truth of that, it'll break your heart."

My aunt left me sitting at the table in shock, with a half-eaten bowl of ice cream in front of me and an ancient, corroded blade in my hand. I pointed the blade at Casey and wordlessly let him wither beneath my glare.

He slowly got up and backed away. "Sorry?"

With that, he fled. I dismissed the knife and headed to bed, ready to sleep and hopefully wake without the persistent feeling that I was a fraud wearing someone else's clothes.

28

Savannah

My eyes fluttered open, and I gently closed them again as I did my best to hide from the day.

Ugh. No more murderous psychopaths, please.

At least my dreams had been free of demons and sorcerers and monsters. It had just been me and Jaxson, running free as wolves, with nothing to fear. Of course, that suggested a whole host of additional problems I didn't want to face this morning, either.

My jaw stretched wide in a yawn, and I forced my eyes open. Soft morning light filtered into the room, and dust motes softly danced in the rays. There was a peace in my soul that belied the danger that hung over all our heads. We'd disrupted the sorcerer's plans, but he was still out there, most likely scheming up a way to take revenge.

I stretched out my legs and froze.

Something was wrong.

I snapped my head down. Everything was fur and paws.

With a yelp, I leapt up, or tried to. My four legs tangled in the sheet, and I flipped over and out of bed with a thud.

I twisted and scrambled as I tried to disentangle myself from the sheets. Finally, I struggled free and paced back and forth.

Okay. I'm a wolf. I've done this before. All I have to do is shift back.

I focused my mind, straining with the human part of my being that was now trapped inside the wolf.

Nothing happened.

I felt the wolf's frustration as she took control and began to investigate the room. *No shifting. I need to run.*

I gritted my teeth and tried to shove her aside. *No. Not now. Please. We'll run later.*

My wolf didn't yield. Not even a hair on my body quivered. She was as stubborn as a—

Steps sounded on the stairs. God, no. Had someone heard my yelp and the following thump on the floor?

Shift now! Someone's coming, I said to my wolf.

No!

I let out a sigh of frustration, but it came out as a wolfy snarl.

Someone paused outside the door and my breath caught. "Savy? Everything ok?" Casey said. "I heard something fall."

Panic seized my mind. I couldn't speak as a wolf—just snarl, growl, and howl. A *mm-hmm* would probably come out as a whimper or sound like a wounded animal. That would have Casey breaking down the door in no time.

"Savy?"

Shit. He wasn't going to go away. My thoughts raced through my mind like Wile E. Coyote and landed on a single, desperate ruse.

I gave a snort, and then started snoring loudly. It sounded utterly ghastly, but it was as close to a human sound as I could make.

"Holy shit," Casey muttered to himself. The sound of his feet moved off into the hall. "That girl has one hell of a deviated septum."

If I'd been in two-legged form, I would have turned bright crimson.

My wolf paced back and forth. *I need out. This room is too small.*

Shift back, I pleaded. *Then I'll go to the park, and we can run there.*

No! I don't trust you. You walk beneath the sun every day. I've been trapped my whole life. I'm not shifting back.

Was this how it was for Jaxson and Sam? It couldn't be. Did they just have more control?

Do as I say, I commanded.

In response, the wolf shoved my soul completely out of the driver's seat and jumped up on the bed. She faced the mirror with teeth bared and fur bristling and growled. *Never.*

Too loud! I warned my wolf. Casey had to have heard her growl and would come to inspect. Sure enough, his footsteps sounded on the stairs again.

"Savy?"

Panic tore at me as my wolf looked around wildly. The window was cracked, and she darted over.

Oh, no.

I tried taking over, but my wolf pushed the window open and leapt out onto the eaves of the second-floor roof. Our feet stumbled and skittered across the shingles.

Fear tore through my mind as we slid toward the edge, but my wolf took control and planted our feet into the gutter just in time. She gave a low growl. *Don't try to take over! You'll get us killed. You drive on two legs, I get to drive on four.*

My mind spun. We were trapped on the roof. Casey had probably heard, and if anyone saw us, they'd shoot first and ask questions later.

Unable to control my rising fear, I submitted and withdrew into the shadows of my mind. *Okay, just get us out of here.*

My wolf padded quickly over the slanted shingles and landed gently on the porch roof like a wolf ninja. Then, with a burst of speed, she jumped off the roof.

My heart caught as we soared through the air and tumbled into the grass below. Paws digging into the turf, my wolf bolted across the lawn and scurried under the bushes on the far side of the yard as the front door burst open. I could smell the scent of my aunt. Breathing hard, my wolf pressed our belly down on the ground and waited, listening. I tried to call my magic to wrap shadows around us, but nothing came.

Apparently, I was completely powerless in this form, both in terms of control and of magic, and that scared me almost as much as Kahanov did.

Eventually, the footsteps receded, and the door slammed shut, though we waited silently to make sure my aunt was truly gone. Did the house have cameras? I hoped not.

What was I going to do?

We have to shift back. If anyone sees us here, they'll try to kill us. They hate werewolves in the Indies, I pleaded.

So I won't be seen, and we'll get out of the Indies, my wolf replied, scrabbling out from under the bushes and slinking down the street.

Please, I begged.

I need this. Don't you get that? You were chained to a bed and broke out. I helped you then. Help me now.

My mind swam. She helped me break out of the sanitorium?

I'd ripped through my bonds, though I couldn't remember how. *Of course* it had been her. I hadn't been that strong before. Kahanov and the freaks in white coats must have injected me with something.

They were the monsters I needed to stop. I could deal with the wolf later.

We should find Jaxson, I insisted, desperate for any kind of certainty or plan at this point. *You can drive.*

Okay. I like him. Both two legs and four.

It was a couple of miles to Jaxson's place. Maybe that would be enough...

A car door slammed up ahead, and a powerful engine roared to life.

Shit! We can't be seen!

Okay, I'll detour. My wolf looked both ways, then darted north across 74th Street. At that moment, a Mustang convertible swung out onto the road and squealed to an abrupt halt, pointed straight at us.

"Shit!" someone shouted. "Is that a fucking wolf?"

I recognized the voice. And the stench. One of the assholes from the park.

We ran.

Tires screamed on the pavement as the Mustang roared after us. All I could think of was that barren highway in Wisconsin where this had all started and how brutally that had ended.

If they ran me down, would I come back to life over and over again like the werewolf I'd hit?

My wolf swerved across the street and through the strip of tiny yards that fronted the rowhouses. She leapt and bounded, dodging around the bushes, flower beds, and little iron fences. A hedge of hydrangeas exploded into a shower of frozen petals behind us.

We juked and swerved as a ray of frost hit the ground beside us, sheathing each blade of grass with a thick coating of ice. *Those assholes are trying to kill us with ice magic!* I screamed at my wolf.

To my horror, she charged the Mustang. The surprised

driver slammed on the brakes, and the car twisted sideways. Its tires squealed and left stinking black streaks across the pavement.

We're going to die! I shouted in my head.

My wolf pounced on the hood, then launched over the guys' astonished faces, landed in the back seat, and spun, snarling and snapping.

The jerks screamed, flailed at the doors, and tumbled out of the still-skidding vehicle. My wolf bolted out of the car and raced across the street in the opposite direction. We ducked down an alley, jumped a fence, and hunkered down beneath someone's porch.

That was too close! I said.

But didn't you have fun? I should have ripped out their throats for the way they treated you the other night. I could feel my wolf's emotions, and it was hard to disentangle them from my own. Triumph. Rage. Protectiveness.

How was I supposed to relate to this new, very spirted, independent part of me?

We placed our head on our paws and waited until we heard the car drive off.

Some laundry fluttered on the clothesline in the adjacent yard.

Can you jump the fence? I asked. *We could shift, and I could put on those clothes and sneak back to the house.*

She readjusted her head on her paws. *No shifting. We're going to find Jaxson. My way.*

I tried to shove my wolf out of the driver's seat, but she wouldn't budge. Instead, she slipped out from under the porch and headed north.

I was a captive in my own body, forced to watch as my wolf darted across streets, dodged honking cars, and crept from alley to alley.

Our heart raced, and I could feel her terror as she pushed through the savage human world around us. But she kept going, refusing to let me or anything steer her from her course.

And then, amid my own fear and frustration and resentment, I felt the flicker of a new and strange emotion: kinship.

29

Jaxson

"What?" I growled into the intercom as shock whipped my thoughts into a frenzy.

The voice on the intercom echoed back. "There's an aggressive reddish wolf here who wants something, but we can't get close to her. I don't recognize her, but the scent's familiar. You'd better come down."

I ran my hand through my hair and cursed.

It had to be Savannah. At least that explained why the vixen wasn't answering her phone. I'd called a dozen times. I'd even considered calling that harebrained cousin of hers.

"Send her to me," I said, and hung up.

Of all the times to turn into a wolf and march across town.

I glanced at the images on my laptop. Nearly two dozen werewolves, none of whom had woken after last night. Things were fucked.

The elevator binged in the hallway, and moments later, claws scratched on my door.

I swung it open, revealing a beautiful wolf with silken fur

and pale blue eyes that sparkled with laughter like sun on a mountain lake.

My muscles stiffened as I caught the aroma of her body wafting through the air. I scented the subtle spark of lust that rose from her, hidden as it was beneath a storm of confusion, fear, and dread.

My own wolf surged in my chest, demanding to be free, to go to her, but I forced him down. I had to stay in control.

"Why the *hell* are you a wolf?" I snapped.

She raised her tail and trotted in, broadcasting, *Being a wolf is way more fun.*

"We need to talk. As humans. Did you bring...clothes?"

She shook her fur. *Don't need them.*

My skin itched as frustration took hold. As Savannah sniffed around my apartment, I texted Sam: *Savannah's here. Bring clothes. Urgent.*

I stalked into the bathroom and grabbed a towel.

If it had been any other wolfborn, I wouldn't have cared. We respected each other's natural form, which was part of who and what we were. But Savannah was still new to this, and I knew she wasn't comfortable in the same way.

Moreover, while I was used to seeing other wolves naked, I already knew there was no way I could see my mate standing nude before me and keep my thoughts straight. And with shit hitting the fan, I needed my mind sharp.

I thrust the towel forward and turned my head. "Shift. We have to talk."

She hopped up on the couch. Her lips pulled back to show her fangs, and the hair on her back bristled as she growled. *No. I am never shifting back. Ever.*

Had she lost her damn mind?

My patience ran out. With a snarl, I let my alpha presence wash over her, holding nothing back. "Shift!"

She staggered backward and whined in protest, but I pushed my power into her and forced the change.

Her body convulsed as her back arched and limbs extended with pops and cracks. She howled in protest as her fur retracted into her skin and bright red hair poured down from her scalp. Her lips curled in a snarl as her muzzle retracted, then relaxed into the familiar curves of Savannah's face.

Her expression of fury and betrayal faded into one of sheer relief. With a shudder and a cry of triumph, she dropped to her knees, naked on the stone floor—completely human once again.

I turned my head away and held out the towel.

Although my eyes were trained on the windows, the image of her body burned in my mind. The inviting dip of her back and smooth curves of her ass. The vibrant, bittersweet red hair draped across her skin. The way her chest and bare breasts rose and fell as she hung her head, and the exhausted smile of relief on her soft, full lips.

It was far more than I had meant to see but far less than I wanted.

I turned the rest of my body to give her privacy and to conceal my sudden stiffness, though she'd surely smell my arousal all the same. Even with years of practice, it was too much to hide.

I silently cursed.

What was happening? Women shifted around me all the time. It was who we were. Wolfborn. There was no shame in it, and we all understood when others in the pack felt glimmers of desire. It was instinct. Natural.

But I had never, *never* felt like this.

Heat flushed my neck as I imagined Savannah crawling to me across the tile, her pale eyes inviting me to join her on the floor. I was so aroused, it hurt. And worse, I could smell her readiness, a deeply repressed scent of desire that stirred beneath a storm of emotions.

She's our mate. It's right.

It was not.

The towel jerked out of my hand.

"Well, shit. That was a fucking nightmare," Savannah said.

"Are you okay? What the hell were you thinking, running across town on four legs?"

She snarled. "*Thinking*? I was thinking that my wolf is a treacherous bitch! She took control. Finding you was the only thing I could get her to do."

"You need to get control of yourself," I growled in return as I spun to face her.

She'd wrapped the towel tightly around her body and tucked it in the front. Savannah was tall, and the towel wasn't quite as large as it should have been. I followed her legs all the way up to the hem.

She tensed, and heat flooded my neck. A cool wave of her magic filled the room, and shadows swirled around her like a black evening gown.

I snapped my eyes up to hers. They were burning with hatred, which instantly killed my rising desire. But it wasn't my roving eyes she was angry at.

Her lips peeled back in a wolfish gesture "Damn it, Jax, I can't *get* control. It's like my wolf has a mind of her own. She locked me out!"

"You'll learn. I'll help."

"How is it that *you* can command my wolf when she won't even listen to me? I should have control over my own body. Not you. Not any man," she muttered.

"I do because I'm alpha."

"Well, I hate all your alpha bullshit," she snapped.

My muscles tightened as rage burned across my neck. I bared my teeth in warning. "It's who I am, so get used to it."

Her lip quivered, and she twisted away and stared out the window. "I hate that you have control and I don't. It's fucked up. She should obey me, not you."

I wanted to go to her, but my feet were frozen to the stone tiles. "You and your wolf are the same, Savannah. You need to stop treating her as something different or her feral instincts will have power over you. Accept that she's a part of you, and then you'll get control."

"She's *not* a part of me. This is something someone did to me." Savannah snapped her head around. "I fucking hate being a werewolf."

A knife twisted in my chest as bile tinged my mouth.

I let the silence hang in the air, softly inhaling the scent of her body and her emotions. Resentment. Bitterness. Loathing.

Savannah despised my power over her, despised being a werewolf, and despised everything I was and stood for. How much more would she hate me if she found out that we were fated mates? That she had no choice in the matter?

More than anything, Savannah Caine despised being told what to do. Her anger would be apocalyptic.

I gave a low, bitter growl. The fates rarely chose people who were good for each other. The three sisters generally made the cruelest pairings, then sat back to watch the world burn.

Billy and my sister had fed off each other. They'd fought and squabbled just as much as they'd fucked, and they'd pushed each other to drink and danger. But the thing that they'd bonded over more than anything else was their hatred of the LaSalles. Ultimately, that hatred had ended my sister, and then Billy.

I didn't want to be bound up in some twisted, ironic knot of fate with a woman turned werewolf who hated everything we were.

I had to fix this.

It's fate. You can't fix it.

"We'll fix it," I growled.

"What?" Savannah asked, suddenly shaken from her own silent stare.

I'd been talking to my wolf, but it could have just as well been her. "We'll fix your situation, Savannah. But first, we've got bigger problems."

"Fuck. What now?"

"Kahanov." I turned the laptop toward her. "He retaliated last night while we were sleeping. He has more power than any of us suspected. Twenty-one more members of my pack didn't wake up this morning."

Darkness settled over my soul. I wanted to hunt. To kill. To protect my pack.

Savannah's eyes widened, and she braced against the counter. "Twenty-one…"

"They're sleeping, not dead. We need to find a way to wake them and stop him."

Her voice broke with half a sob. "Oh, my God, this is all my fault. Why? Why do I bring an avalanche of shit down on everyone around me?"

Rage and protectiveness flared within me, and I steadied her as she swayed. "It's not your fault. He's a monster, and we're going to stop him."

She nodded, and I sucked in a deep breath. There was no good way to explain the next part. I let some of my alpha presence wash over her to calm and steady her before I spoke.

"There's something else you need to know. Kahanov sent dream messages to many, and rumors are flying. He wants you in exchange for the lives of the sleepers."

She clutched her towel, and her fear filled the room. "Your pack hates me. Someone will—"

"You're safe. My pack obeys me, and none of my men or women would ever do anything to harm you. Yes, they may resent you, but they'll protect you while we find a way to stop him."

Savannah shoved away from the counter and placed both hands against her temples. Despair tore into her breaking voice. "He's going to do this *every* night. It's not going to be twenty people, Jaxson. It's going to be forty. Sixty. A hundred. *Two* hundred. How many are in your pack? How many are you willing to lose for a LaSalle? You're going to *have* to hand me over sooner or later."

Her body quaked with tremors of anguish and betrayal, and my soul couldn't take it. My wolf howled in my mind and clawed at my heart.

With a lightning-fast motion, I seized Savannah's raised arms and pulled her to me. She gasped in horror and shock as she looked up into my eyes.

My fangs erupted, and I growled, "I am never going to hand you over to him. *Ever.*"

30

Jaxson's words hit my chest like a sledgehammer, driving the breath from my lungs. His hands dug into my forearms, but it was his voice that locked me in place. It had been feral—a primal growl just at the edge of being human.

I am never going to hand you over to him. Ever.

No one had ever spoken like that to me. Not with that kind of conviction. Or possessiveness.

It's the truth. I could smell it, clear as day.

He stared down at me with a golden fire burning in his eyes, flames of certainty and desire. His muscles rippled with a tension that vibrated down through my arms. I wanted to melt, to dissolve into him.

"Do you understand? I won't trade you. Won't hand you over," Jaxson growled in that unearthly voice.

I bit my lip and nodded. The fear and despair burned away inside me, leaving only embers of determination in their wake.

Emotions shuddered through my body as Jaxson's power pressed in around me like waters of the deep. His signature was out of control, wave after wave of forest scent rolling over me. It shook the air like an earthquake, and the sounds of icy streams cascading down a mountain slope filled my ears. I could taste the new snow on the air. It was so real, my tongue turned cold.

How I longed to warm it in his mouth.

My mind drained of its senses, and I pushed toward him, trying to reach his lips. But his hands, still clutching my raised arms, locked me rigidly in place.

I struggled and pulled back but couldn't move. A faint part of me screamed in rebellion against his control. But the rest of me reveled in his power, his mastery of the moment. So I let him hold me there, in silence and stillness.

My world was crumbling around me. A sorcerer was trying to cut out my soul. Dozens of werewolves couldn't wake because of me. And I didn't even have control over my own body or magic.

And amid the storm, for one moment, I'd found something steady. Immovable. A rock that I could hold on to. A promise that wouldn't be broken.

Our eyes didn't part as we stood in stillness. Finally, I let my arms relax—submitting, no longer pushing back or pulling, but content to just be in his steady grip.

The tension left his body, but he didn't let go. And then, slowly, his head began to drift downward toward mine.

I beckoned him with my lips, letting them part as I breathed him in. Did I really want this? The kiss of a man who hated my family and despised what I was? A man who had more control over my body than I did?

Yes.

Jaxson's hands released me, and he gently traced his fingertips down my forearms, around the bend of my arm, and softly up to my shoulders. My skin was flushed and sensitive, and almost burned at his light touch. He pulled me closer as he brought his mouth to mine. Our lips brushed across each other, quietly searching.

My own were soft and dry and desperate for his kiss. We'd done it before in the Michigan woods, in the heat of despair and chaos and barely surviving death. This was everything that hadn't been, yet the overwhelming sense of rightness was the same. My mouth didn't just want him—it *needed* him.

I pressed my lips against his.

He parted them, drawing in everything I had to give. My pulse raced as I kissed him back and let my tongue search for his, wanting nothing more than to taste him, to drink him in.

Heat rose within me as the waters of my body met, and my legs trembled. I needed more. His kiss was too hesitant. Too soft. I bit his lip and pulled him to me. He gave a low, possessive growl that sent shivers along my spine and raised the hair on my skin.

He dug his fingers into my shoulders, and I moaned with delight. He bit my lip in turn, but still, it wasn't enough. My flesh needed his. We were too far apart.

I shifted my arms and let the towel slip away, though the little dress of shadows I'd woven around myself stayed in place.

As the towel landed at our feet, Jaxson broke off our kiss and met my eyes. His pupils dilated, devouring me.

My arms were pinned between us. I pressed my palms to his chest. His steady heartbeat pounded against my fingertips as his hands began to drift slowly down my shoulders to my back and then down along my sides.

A shiver ran through me, and my skin prickled beneath his gentle touch.

At last, after an agonizingly slow descent, his fingers came to rest on my waist. I licked my lip, and he gently pulled my hips forward. He was hard and unyielding against me, and I wanted everything he could give.

I undid his shirt one button at a time, moving my hands deliberately beneath his steady gaze. Each button was a choice that I couldn't walk away from. It didn't matter.

After the last button, I slipped my hands beneath the cotton cloth, parting it so I could drag my fingers over the strong contours of his chest and around to his back. I pressed forward with my whole body, feeling his skin at last against my own in the space where his shirt was opened.

Warmth flowed between us like rays of the sun emerging from the clouds. My breath turned shallow, and I lifted my mouth to his.

A knock sounded from the door. My heart stopped, and suddenly, Jaxson and I were standing five feet apart. Had he pushed back from me, or had I pushed away from him?

It had better not have been him. Not again. Not like the last time. The shame. The embarrassment. The regret.

But this time, the only thing in his eyes was shock. Perhaps frustration. He glanced up and down at me and almost smiled.

The knock came again. "Jax?"

It was Sam.

My brain started working again, and I snatched my towel off the ground. The only thing I had under my makeshift robe of shadows was flesh, and it was suddenly very drafty in the penthouse.

There was no way around it. Sam was going to give us hell.

I pulled the towel tightly around me like a suit of armor. Jaxson paused at the door while he buttoned his shirt. He didn't meet my eyes.

What had I been thinking? Jaxson fucking Laurent? Attracted to a werewolf? It was madness.

This is your doing, you hussy, I thought furiously at my wolf.

Nope. That was all you, you horny harlot.

I gasped at the foul-mouthed and foul-minded wolf.

Jaxson raised an eyebrow at my outburst, and I shook my head.

Swallowing hard, I let a long litany of denials flood into my mind. I was not a werewolf. I didn't have to listen to the savage beast inside me. And I was *not* getting wrapped up with Jaxson Laurent. I plopped down on the couch, tightly crossed my legs, and let the towel and shadows settle around me.

With a click, Jaxson unlocked the door and swung it open.

Sam stepped in and cupped her hand to her mouth, covering a wide grin. "What did I interrupt? It smells like a Brazilian steakhouse in here, and you are a *very* rare steak, Savy!"

The scarlet drained from my hair and flooded across my face as my very soul withered.

Oh. God.

I should have let the sorcerer kill me.

Sam clapped her hands, laughing. "Oh, shit, I am so, *so* sorry, you two."

Jaxson closed the door behind her with a wry smile.

My neck burned with embarrassment and rage. Where had her enthusiasm been when we'd kissed the last time? She'd ripped me a new one.

But I hadn't been a werewolf then. Just a dirty, expendable LaSalle. Now I was some sort of half-breed. Did that really make things better?

Sam gave me a wicked grin and waved the spare clothes at me. "Are you sure you still need these? Should I come back later?"

"Cool it, Sam," Jaxson growled. "We're in fucking trouble, and we need a plan."

She nodded. "Yeah, I was just excited because you seem to be embracing the m—"

Jaxson gave Sam a look that practically made the walls of the penthouse shake. My skin chilled as his power washed over us both, and I was certain the temperature had dropped twenty degrees.

She shrank back. "Right. Sorry."

What the hell had *that* been about?

Clearly, I didn't understand a fucking thing about these wolves.

31

Savannah

I grabbed the clothes from Sam and rushed into Jaxson's bathroom while the two of them muttered about what to do next. It was hard not to eavesdrop with my keen hearing. Sam was distraught about the sleepers.

They were also talking around something else that they didn't want me to know about.

Ears burning, I tried to think of what to do as I slipped into Sam's clothes. Even though she was more toned, we were a decent enough size match. I zipped up and admired myself in the mirror. While Jaxson had seen my bare ass from plenty of angles now, I liked how taut it looked in Sam's skinny jeans.

I smiled when I unfolded the shirt. The front had an illustration of a derby skater beside big bold letters that said, *Warning: I Hit Like a Girl.* I flipped it over, and my smile melted. *Bitches With Bite. 2018 Derby Champions. You Can't Skate With Us.*

My canines started to inch down, but I held them back and pulled the shirt over my head. It was plenty tight, and as I didn't have a bra, Jaxson was going to see exactly how ready I was every time I got near him.

I sighed. He could smell it, anyway. I had to figure out how to mask it or get used to constantly being a horny beacon.

I returned to the kitchen and sat down on a stool at the high-top counter, trying not to look at the powerfully built man as he stepped up right beside me and poured me an espresso. "Have you eaten?"

I blushed. My wolf had stolen a snack of bacon strips off someone's plate at an outdoor café. Did that count?

"Sort of?" I breathed in the rich aroma that wafted up from the cup, though it couldn't mask his scent. "This is what I really needed. Thanks."

Sam put her palms on the counter. "Forget coffee. We're fucked and need a new plan. You got lucky when you caught up with Kahanov in Italy. And even if you find him again, he could slip away like last time. Meanwhile, each night, dozens more wolves will likely go to sleep and not wake up."

I cleared my throat. "It might not be wolves for long. If the pack doesn't hand me over, he might target someone more pliable. Vampires. Demons. Other...crime families. Anyone he could pressure to take me out. We need a way to break the spell."

Jaxson nodded. "I had a curse diviner look at the sleepers this morning, and I also called some folks in from the Order. They're still researching. Dream magic isn't well understood, and the best source of information was apparently that stolen grimoire."

"We've got to do something," Sam protested.

I chewed on my lip. "How old is the grimoire? Is the witch who wrote it still alive? Could we go directly to the source and ask her what to do?"

Jaxson and Sam both stiffened. He flexed his fist. "That would be...unwise. If the witch is still alive, she's probably not someone we want to risk dealing with. She could be worse than the sorcerer."

"Why? Because a powerful woman wrote a book?" I scoffed.

Sam leaned forward, eyes sparkling. "Grimoires aren't just books, Savy. They're tomes of dark, sinister magic that practically have a life of their own. Some are written in blood and wrapped with human flesh."

My skin prickled at the sudden chill that crept over me. I could smell the danger in her words, and I shivered.

Shadows crossed Jaxson's face. "Wolf legends say that witches and warlocks write grimoires to snare the souls of curious readers whose lust for power is greater than their common sense. Anyone who would create a thing like that wouldn't hesitate to trap us with their magic. It's too dangerous."

The two looked down at the table, and I swallowed hard. A long silence stretched between us.

I tightened my fists. "The clock is ticking, and we can't wait. If she can tell us how to undo the curse, it's worth the risk. Who knows? If this witch is really as bad as you assume and she's trying to snag powerful souls with that book, then maybe she'll help us just to get Kahanov's."

Jaxson frowned. "I don't think—"

"Anyway," I interjected, "you wolves have a pretty skewed sense of the dark arts—a label that seems to include a broad array of things like scrying and my own magic. So let's maybe ask someone less superstitious and see how crazy an idea this is."

"We don't even know if the witch is alive," he said, a knife edge of protest in his voice.

I raised my hands. "Who do we ask, then?"

Jaxson bared his teeth as he studied my face. Finally, he gave a reluctant grunt. "Fine. Sam, call Neve. She was the one looking into the book. See what she knows or can find out."

Sam pulled out her cell phone and stepped away as Jaxson drummed his fingers on the table in irritation.

I took a deep breath. "In the meantime, I have a stopgap plan."

"What is it? Make a deal with a devil? Summon the minions of hell to hunt him down?"

I froze. I hadn't thought of that. My aunt could summon demons, and I wondered...but no. I shook my head. "My aunt made a circle of protection around my bed to keep the sorcerer out of my dreams. Maybe we could make a big one where wolves could come sleep to protect them from Kahanov."

He shook his head. "I'm not sure wolves would be willing to sleep in the middle of a sorcerous enchantment, particularly one made by the LaSalles. They'd assume it was a trap."

"You're alpha. King Wolf. Can't you make them? By the second night, everyone would know it worked."

His eyes flashed gold, and I smelled his frustration and mistrust. His canines dropped and claws began to push from his fingertips. "Yes. The pack will do as I say, but I can't make Laurel do anything, and she won't help us. There's been too much bad blood over the years."

"Maybe not my aunt, but I might be able to twist my cousin's arm."

Jaxson gave a bitter laugh. "The lead distributor of wolfsbane in the world? I guarantee he's not going to help, *if* he even knows how to do anything else but blow things up."

Images of the weapons manufacturing operation flooded my mind, and my stomach twisted. But I knew deep down that my cousin was better than that. He had to be. I'd seen it.

I could make this happen.

"You don't know him," I growled defensively.

Sam, who was still on the phone—but apparently monitoring our conversation—just rolled her eyes.

Jaxson rose and stalked to the side of the room. "I know enough."

Pangs of protectiveness shot through me, and I snarled. "It *literally* can't hurt to ask. And if he doesn't know how to do it, maybe he knows someone who does."

I held my breath as Jaxson considered. His pack wasn't going to like this. They were in danger because of a LaSalle, and now the only way they were going to be able to sleep safely was in the middle of a LaSalle's hex.

Finally, Jaxson stirred. "Do it. Ask."

"Give me your phone." He handed it over, and I dialed Casey as I swiveled around on my stool.

Ragged breathing came across the line as he picked up. "Laurent, you motherfucker, is Savy with you?"

What was Casey doing? Running a marathon?

"Hey, Case, it's me. I'm borrowing Jaxson's phone."

"Where the hell are you?"

I put my finger in my ear to block the sounds of Sam on the other line, talking to Neve. "I'm in Dockside. And I need your help with some magic."

"Cool. Great. Let's play a different game. Do you know where the hell I am?" he wheezed.

I sighed and rubbed my temples. "In my room, rummaging through my shit like a drugged-out badger, by the sound of it."

"Close. I'm on a ladder trying to get to your open window to check if you're dead or not. Unfortunately, it's a little short and pretty unstable."

I leapt off my stool. "Are you nuts?"

"You weren't answering your phone, and your door is locked. When I saw the open window, I was worried you'd been abducted or something!"

"I'm fine!" I snapped. "I'm in Dockside with Jaxson and Sam, and we—"

Casey made a strangled sound. "Oh, my gods, Savannah, you didn't have him over last night, did you? I thought I heard a man snoring this morning. It was like a lumberjack choking to death on a muffin. Tell me you two weren't—"

"No! Seriously? I got up early and left. I locked my door without thinking and then couldn't get my cell." I thanked God that we were talking on the phone and that Casey never seemed able to pick up my lies.

"Okay. Good. Because Mom would kill you. What are you doing in Dockside, anyway?"

I ran my hand through my hair in exasperation. "Shit is going down up here, and we need your help. That circle of protection that Aunt Laurel made around my bed, do you know how to make one of those?"

"Yes. But I'm not making one for your wolfy love den, if that's what you're thinking."

"No! Damn it, get your head out of the gutter." My fingernails were beginning to itch. I tried to steady my voice. "Last night, the sorcerer put twenty-one wolves to sleep, and we don't know how to break the spell. He's going to keep doing it. We need a way to protect these people while we bring him down. Could you make a giant circle of protection in like, I don't know, a gymnasium? Somewhere a lot of people could gather."

Casey paused, and I could hear him gently sucking on his teeth. "Shit, Savannah. I don't know. I'm pretty sure they want to skin me alive up there."

"Tell the little punk he still owes us for the damage you two caused during your car chase," Jaxson snarled.

I bared my teeth at Jaxson and made a chopping motion in front of my neck to cut him off, but it was already too late.

"Was that Jaxson in the background? Tell that creep to shove a stick up his ass! He already stole our container to cover it! Screw this."

Casey hung up.

I growled and felt my fangs erupt. "Damn it! I'm handling this, Jax. Keep your mouth shut!"

Sam's eyes went wide, and Jaxson bristled at my command. "I told you he wouldn't help. He's a wolf-hating creep. He's probably laughing his ass off at the moment."

"Stay quiet this time!" I snapped. Sam cringed again at my blatant disrespect for her alpha, but I didn't care. I dialed Casey back.

He picked up. "No."

"Casey! Please."

He was breathing hard, and it sounded like he was climbing down the ladder. "No way, Jose! I'm not dealing with Jaxson and not coming to Dockside."

Jaxson looked ready to wolf out, so before he aggravated the situation further, I stormed into the bathroom and slammed the door. "Look, Case, I'm sorry about Jaxson. Please, do this for me, if not for the wolves. They're suffering because of me. Protecting them protects me."

Silence hung in the air, and then he sighed. "Fine. But I'm not going to Dockside."

I glanced at my reflection in the mirror, and the shirt sparked an idea. "What about the roller derby rink? It's big and has bathrooms. Could you make something there?"

"I guess? What are you thinking?"

"Like a FEMA shelter. Big circle of protection where werewolves can sleep safely."

He whistled low. "There's no way I can make one big enough to fit all the werewolves in Dockside. There are thousands of them."

"We've got to try something. There's a lot at stake."

Casey considered. "Okay. Fine. Tell *Hairy* that our debt is paid, and he's gotta release our stuff. He'll know what I'm talking about. I'm bringing backup to help make the circle, and if anyone looks like they're going to bite, we'll blast everyone."

"I'll tell him something like that, in a diplomatic and courteous way," I grumbled.

"Fine. I'll get my shit together and meet you all over there." He hung up.

I stalked out of the bathroom and gave Jaxson a glare. "He'll do it, no thanks to you. Also, give him his container of shit back." Before he could protest, I swung to Sam, who'd finished her call. "What did you learn?"

"Neve is hunting down the author and will give you a call when she knows more. She wanted me to remind you that the grimoire was committed to the Archive of Bound Tomes because it was dangerous. Anyone capable of committing that kind of knowledge to paper would be perilous, too."

"I don't see that we have any choice." My mouth went dry, and I met Jaxson's eyes. He was brooding in the shadows of the back corner, arms crossed. Waves of power poured out from him, and his scent gave off one clear signature: protectiveness. For his pack. For Sam.

He didn't like this plan. But I also sensed he would do anything to protect the pack.

Finally, he nodded.

I took a deep breath. "Okay. We have a plan. Make a circle of protection. Bargain with the witch. And stay alive long enough to hunt down Kahanov and kill him."

32

Jaxson

It took an hour to organize everyone and start setting up the shelter at the roller derby rink. The old warehouse bustled with activity as werewolves folded up bleachers and hauled in crates of water, food, and blankets. We'd bought out every box store in the area.

It was like prepping for a hurricane.

No one liked the idea of sleeping in a giant circle of magic created by the LaSalles, but as much as Savannah drove me to madness, I trusted her, and she trusted her cousin. That was something.

Stephanie would be rolling over in her grave.

I'd gotten pushback from every direction, but people complied. I was alpha. That was the way things worked.

Space was limited, so people would be sleeping here around the clock in shifts. Most of the signups were families afraid for their pups. I assumed many of the more conservative members of our pack would rather die in their sleep than accept help from the LaSalles.

I wouldn't make sleeping here mandatory, but I'd camp in the rink, and hopefully, the pack would follow my lead.

All the LaSalles have to do is not fuck this up.

The warehouse doors slammed open, and Casey LaSalle stepped through like a cowboy entering a saloon.

My eyes went wide. He had a bandolier of wolfsbane cannisters draped around his chest and a couple dangling from his side. Half a dozen werewolves spun around and extended their claws. Menacing snarls echoed throughout the vast room.

Casey thrust his hands out to the sides. "Nobody better fucking try to eat me! I'm here to help."

The fucking *lunatic.*

A tsunami of rage roared through me, and it took every ounce of strength not to shift. I wasn't the only one. Every wolf in the place was pissed.

"Everybody stand down!" I roared and pushed my alpha presence through the room, trying to maintain control over my pack as well as my own wolf.

I spun on Savannah. "Talk to your idiot cousin. *Now.*"

Her face was crimson, and the scents of shame and embarrassment poured off her. At least all the pack would smell it too and know how she felt.

Savannah rushed over and hissed at the moron. "Are you insane, Casey? You look like a terrorist!"

He slowly lowered his hands. "I'm just coming prepared."

"God. Please try not to start a fight. You're here to help. We're all on the same side, you idiot," she snapped, her voice cutting like a blade.

Casey huffed.

Seeing her upbraid him in public calmed my wolf, and half a smile twitched at the corner of my lips. I tamped it down and set my face with a stern, grim expression.

I strode over, trying to use my power to soothe and calm

the pack. There was no hiding the fury in my eyes. It took every ounce of strength I had to keep my voice steady, and I pushed my magic toward him to force him to calm the fuck down, too.

"Thank you for coming," I growled. "None of my people will do anything to hurt you or provoke you, I promise. Just don't do anything stupid. Like walking around here with a bandolier of *wolfsbane*."

Casey glared back at me. "Fine. But I know you're using that alpha voodoo on me to make my brain soft, so I'll be watching for any funny business."

"So will we."

Casey nodded and dialed his phone. "Okay, you guys can come in."

Two sorcerers Casey's age walked into the room, and Savannah tensed. The scent of her hatred boiled up, and she spun toward me, as her eyes had turned yellow and her fangs dropped. I could tell a full shift was coming, and her cousin was standing two feet behind her.

Help me, her golden eyes begged.

I touched her arm and pushed a wave of power into her to stop the shift dead in its tracks.

Her teeth retracted and eyes cleared, and I breathed a deep sigh of relief. She had a bit of blood on her lips. I pointed to my own, and she wiped her mouth with the back of her wrist.

Her anger wasn't gone, just repressed. Like mine.

"Who are those assholes?" I snarled as two pricks approached. If they'd done anything to Savannah, I'd break their backs over the bleachers.

"Two jerks I know from the Indies." She spun on her cousin. "What the hell are *they* doing here, Casey? I thought you weren't trying to start a fight."

He shrugged. "Penance. For insulting my cousin at the

bonfire. They'll behave. Anyway, I needed help, and I wasn't going to bring Mom."

Bonfire? Had they triggered Savannah's first shift? I'd hang their corpses from the dockside cranes.

Savannah turned on me, her eyes wide and pleading. "I think I've got this, Jaxson. Walk away."

She knew. The scents of hatred and murder coiled around me, plain for anyone to see. This was the curse of having a mate. I'd do anything to protect her, even murder two sorcerers who were offering to help our pack.

The pack had to come first. Savannah *couldn't* be my mate. We'd find a way to fix this.

I cursed, reined in my wolf and emotions, and buried them deep. But I did step up in Casey's face. "Wolfsbane stays outside, or you all stay outside. Not negotiable. You have my guarantee of protection."

He grimaced, then unslung the bandolier and handed it to one of his goons. "Put this in my ride."

"All of it."

He unclipped the canisters on his hips and passed them over. I could smell he still had some hidden somewhere, but I sensed this was as much of a concession as I was going to get.

"What do you have to do to make the circle?" Savannah asked him.

"Well, we've got to etch sigils around this whole warehouse. Even with three of us, it's going to take all day. We'll make it as big as we can, but it'll have to be really simple for us to get it done. It'll only protect against dream intrusion, but not demon attacks or spells. And I'm afraid it won't get rid of fleas or prevent rabies, either."

She reeled back and slapped him hard across the jaw. My wolf leapt in my chest. It was perhaps the sexiest thing I'd ever seen her do.

He staggered back and rubbed his chin. "Holy shit, Savy, I was joking. But dang, you pack a mean wallop. Are you on 'roids or something? Might explain the moods..."

"You are a complete asshole, Casey."

"Sorry." He pointed to her *I Hit Like A Girl* T-shirt. "Guess I was warned."

She stepped up, and a strange power emanated from her. She fixed him with a hard look. "You need to cut the funny business. Just look around. By tonight, this place is going to be crammed with werewolves. Mothers and fathers with frightened children. Families like yours. You're the only one who can make sure they sleep safely tonight and the only one who can prevent them from never waking up again."

Pride welled up in my chest. Everyone in the room was watching this showdown. They'd seen her take a stand and plead for their safety.

That was something. As much bad blood as there was in the room, everyone here knew we were depending on the little prick's spell tonight.

What stunned me was that amid all the scents of mistrust and resentment, there was a flicker of hope.

My people, getting hope from a LaSalle. Inconceivable.

Casey nodded, pondering Savannah's words. "Right...hero stuff. I can do that."

His gaze panned around the room, measuring the mistrust and expectation in the gathered faces. It paused on a she-wolf's backside as she bent over to pick up a large box of supplies and then heaved it effortlessly onto her shoulder.

His eyes dilated, and I could smell his sudden scent of...*gods, no.*

My claws slowly extended as Casey marched off to see if she needed help. "That lunatic is going to get the teeth knocked out of his face," I muttered.

Savannah crossed her arms. "Probably."

Revolting. A LaSalle.

But then again, one of them was currently my *fucking* mate. Not for long.

Savannah opened her mouth to speak, but my phone rang. Neve Cross. I picked up. "Tell me you've got a lead."

"I've tracked down the author of the book. A witch named S.L. Delamont. She lives on the outskirts of Magic's Bend," Neve said.

A witch. Better than a sorcerer or warlock. I worked with witches from time to time. They lived in covens, which were sort of like packs.

"What do we know about her?"

Neve sighed. "Not much, unfortunately, and I know quite a few folks out there. Apparently, she's a very private person and lives alone. She even has a girl named Molly do all her errands for her and never goes into town. I tried tracking down the girl, but I didn't have a last name."

My concern began to build. Witches that lived alone could be wildcards. Some were perfectly normal. Others weren't. They were like rogue wolves. Some were natural loners, seeking solitude in the wild. Others might be antisocial or rejected by their covens for participating in unsavory activities.

"That it?" I asked. There had to be more.

Neve hesitated. "Pretty much. She has some sort of side hustle, I don't know what it is, but I don't think it's legal because no one I talked to was sure. Pretty much everyone used the same words. Loner. Peculiar. Powerful."

I didn't like the way this was going.

"Okay. Do you have a phone number for her?"

"Nope. She doesn't use electronics," Neve noted.

I sighed. "Thanks for everything. We'll head out that way in a couple hours."

"Need backup?"

"Let's wait and see what we're facing. Maybe she'll be a sweet lady living in a gingerbread house."

Neve laughed. "If she tries to stuff you in her oven, I can get there fast."

"Thanks." I hung up.

Savannah, who had most certainly been listening in with her wolf hearing, narrowed her eyes. "You sound concerned."

"Maybe. The author is a witch living in isolation. Nobody knows much about her. It could be a bad situation."

She scowled. "Sounds to me like you have a preconceived social prejudice against powerful women who choose to live their lives alone."

I glared. "No, I don't. If she were a mage, it wouldn't be a red flag. But witches draw their power from their covens and tend to congregate with each other. Essentially, like wolves, they live in packs. And I trust that mindset."

Savannah scoffed. "So it's just a werewolf bias, then. That makes it all okay."

"Witches living in isolation don't have a coven to draw their magic from, so they often turn to outside sources for power. Demons. Devils. Dark beings. Piecing that bit of knowledge together with the fact that the woman doesn't like outsiders and wrote a little book called *The Grimoire of Nightmares*, which might very well be bound with human skin—*that* is what makes me concerned."

"Oh."

33

Dark images filled my mind. A lone hovel beneath the trees. An old woman with sharp fangs and long, cruel fingers, cackling softly to herself.

That couldn't be what we were dealing with, could it?

She wrote a grimoire. Possibly using human skin. How many humans would that take?

My stomach twisted a little. Perhaps looking up the author of a book used to summon nightmarish creatures and invade people's dreams was not, in fact, a good idea. Why couldn't things ever be easy?

"How do we get there?" I asked, dreading the answer.

"We'll take a portal to Magic's Bend. It's another magical city in Oregon."

Damn it.

"Or we could take a plane," I suggested, hoping against hope he'd bite at the suggestion.

Jaxson wasn't paying much attention. Instead, he was looking around the room and ignoring my input. "No time. We'll head out in half an hour. Hang tight until then—I need to make sure everything is running smoothly here."

With that, he stepped away to deal with logistics, leaving me to watch the bustle of activity. Casey and his team were busy inscribing runes in the floor of the warehouse. Every so often, they yelled at workers to back off and not step on their work. It was all posturing. The werewolves were obviously steering clear of both the magic ring and the sorcerers, and I could smell their mistrust and trepidation.

I glanced over at one of Jaxson's goons, who met my eyes.

"They're trying to help," I offered feebly.

He blinked. "Asking a LaSalle to cast a protection spell is like asking a serial killer to sharpen your knives while you take a shower."

The goon walked away to a part of the warehouse that was distinctly less filled with LaSalles.

And yet, they were letting Casey cast his spell. That spoke volumes. What Jaxson commanded, they did.

I had to shimmy closer to the bleachers to let a couple of burly wolves by, who were loaded down with water, food, and blankets. It was like preparation for a natural disaster. People had already started arriving, even though Casey's circle wouldn't be done for hours.

Sounds of children's laughter echoed through the warehouse. A mother slapped her hands together as she played games with her kids in the bleachers. It was only noon. Was she here in hopes of keeping them safe while they took a nap?

The enormous tragedy of the situation overwhelmed me. It was madness. We had to find a way to stop Kahanov.

Footsteps approached behind me, and a vitriolic scent filled the air. The hair on my neck stood on end, and my fingernails began to itch. I spun.

Regina, Jaxson's second.

"So, you're one of us now," she snarled, her voice brimming with disdain.

"I'm not," I snapped.

"Oh, yes, you are. You have claws, fangs, and turn into a wolf. More to the point, Jaxson has claimed you for the pack, so you're one of ours, no matter if you or I like it."

Jaxson had *claimed me* for the pack? Irritation simmered under my skin. That fucker.

Her eyes burned with barely controlled fury, and her voice quaked with rage and resentment. "You know this is all your fault, right?"

She tilted her chin toward a werewolf who was taping pictures of the sleepers on the wall underneath a string of cut-out words that read, *In our hearts and prayers.* "This mess is all because of you."

I swallowed hard as shame and guilt pressed in on all sides, and heat flushed my neck.

Did she think I didn't realize that? I was painfully aware of the situation. Jaxson, the pack, my family—everyone was at risk because for some reason, a half-mad sorcerer wanted to cut a part of my soul out.

Bile rose in my throat. I'd known about this world for two weeks. I'd turned into a wolf two days ago. I couldn't control my wolf or my magic and was desperate for answers, and yet, this bitch wouldn't give me a break.

My wolf strained at my chest, and my fangs shot out. *She needs a bite in the ass.*

I turned on Regina and bit off each word like the strike of a knife. "Yes. This is because of me. So why don't you just turn me over to the sorcerer? You'd solve the pack's problem and get rid of me all in one fell swoop. I'm sick of your reproach, so either try to take me or fuck off."

Regina snarled and shoved my shoulder firmly.

Pain erupted through my fingertips as my claws shot out. It took every ounce of control to rein my wolf in. I clenched my teeth and glared, ready for her to push things one step further.

"You don't get it, do you, Savannah?" Regina growled. "Clearly, neither you nor the sorcerer has any idea what it really means to be part of a pack. It's inconceivable that we'd turn over one of our own. Even someone we despise."

What was she saying?

I couldn't help my lips from pulling back in a snarl. "I have a hard time believing that you wouldn't dump me at the drop of a hat to get your pack members back. Do you really value a dirty LaSalle girl above them?"

Regina half-laughed. "You need to retrain your brain. You're a wolf and a pack member now. What you don't get is that we're wolves, not sheep. A pack, not a flock. We don't let outsiders prey on the weak and then stand idly by to watch. We fight to protect our own. I may not like you, but I'm not going to give you up to a terrorist."

I stepped up in her face. "If that's so, then why are you giving me shit? Just to make me feel guilty and more miserable than I already am?"

Regina's gaze didn't waver from mine, but she pointed to the pictures of the sleepers. "This is all your fault, and that makes it your job to fix it. Not Jaxson's. Not the pack's. You. Do what's right."

I couldn't help but look at the wall of pictures, and guilt dragged me down like a heavy iron chain. All those people.

Jaxson wouldn't give me up, nor would the pack—but there was an elegant solution.

My stomach tumbled as things added up, and I dug my claws into my palms. "So what, you want me to just give myself up? Because Jaxson won't hand me over?"

Her eyes were hard and unwavering. "I don't care what you

do—just end this without getting Jaxson or anyone else from the pack killed. This nightmare won't stop until the sorcerer's dead or you're in his hands. Do the math and figure it out."

My vision blurred as tears of rage filled my eyes. It was all too much. The pressure, the responsibility, the resentment.

In my chest, my wolf raged to be let free. But I just looked away and tried to stop from quaking. "Trade my life for a bunch of people I don't know, who've never shown me any compassion or kindness?"

Silence hung in the air.

Then she pushed her fingers to her temples and dropped down on one of the bleachers. "Fuck. I don't want you to give yourself up. If I were in your shoes, that option would be burning in the back of my mind, but I grew up with these people, and I love them more than my own life. I know you don't, and none of this is fair."

"It's not," I snarled. She didn't look up, and I could smell her shame and regret.

She pushed her hands through her hair. "Look, I'm sorry. I'm just afraid of how bad this could get. These are my people. But..." She paused and flexed her fists. "You're part of that group now. I'll fight with you and help you any way I can. But if the cost gets too high, if Kahanov starts killing—"

I put up my hand and walked back past the old bleachers and down the hall to the ladies' room, leaving Regina and her fear and resentment far behind me. I plopped down on a toilet, closed the door of the stall, and slid the latch shut. Then I wept.

It didn't last long. I'd used up most of my tears when my parents died and didn't have much in the way of reserves of self-pity. So after a few moments, I gingerly dabbed my face and eyes with some toilet paper.

Damn it, Savy, get a grip.

I took a deep breath, closed my eyes, and concentrated on

retracting my claws, just like Jaxson had taught me. Of course, they didn't budge.

Gritting my teeth, I thought of his voice. His scent. The feel of his presence, his command over me.

That did the trick.

Annoyance tugged at me. How was it that he still had control even when he wasn't there?

As my claws retracted, the turmoil of emotions churning in my chest slowly began to subside. The rage faded, my wolf let go, and clarity returned. I breathed a sigh of relief and opened my eyes.

It wasn't a nice toilet stall, and I instantly regretted my hiding spot.

Over the years, scores of girls, and probably quite a few guys, had carved hundreds of graffitied marks into the walls of the stall—phone numbers, dirty phrases, existential questions, and a few naughty stick figures on roller-skates.

One made me smile—a girl with large tits kicking a guy in the balls. The text beside it said, *Give your man what he deserves!*

"Kick 'em in the nuts" used to be my solution for most things. But then again, I was a lot more put together before I knew that sorcerers and werewolves existed. That had thrown old Savy for a bit of a loop. Where was that girl now?

Sitting on the crapper, hiding from a mean girl like she's back in high school, my wolf chided. *Let me go talk to her. I'll teach her a thing or two.*

"Regina's not my problem," I muttered. She was just a mirror of my own guilt. That was what I was hiding from in here. Guilt. Not her. Just the faces of the sleepers hanging on the wall.

I pushed my palms against my head. "What the hell am I going to do? Even if we can get the witch to help us stop the dream attack, how are we going to stop Kahanov?"

Kill him, duh, my wolf offered, somewhat unsympathetically.

"Easier said than done. He's crazy powerful with all sorts of demons and spells and God-knows-what. How am I supposed to stop him?"

Rip out his throat. Massive blood loss is an effective way to kill everybody. I'd be happy to do it for you, the monster inside of me eagerly chirped.

I knew where all of this was heading sooner or later: Kahanov and me, face to face. Him with all his magic and demons, me with my ignorance and lack of control. What edge could I possibly have?

Closing my eyes, I concentrated on the Soul Knife, trying to recall the way it felt in my hand and the sensation of its magic. After a while, electricity tingled in my arm, and the blade slowly took form.

I hefted it, measuring its weight. It was something, at least.

With a deliberate motion, I jabbed the tip of the knife into the door and started carving graffiti as I considered my options.

After few minutes, a series of light footsteps echoed outside, and the bathroom door swung open. Sam. I knew her instantly by her scent.

"Savy? Are you in here?"

"Yes." I started to gouge out another letter.

"You okay?" she asked.

"Yes."

"You coming out?"

"In a minute." I sighed.

I could see her leaning against a sink through the crack in the door. She crossed her arms. "Between us girls, if you're having trouble, I really recommend adding more fiber to your diet."

I stopped mid-scrape, and heat flushed my skin. "No! I'm not..."

"I know," she said, voice low and reassuring. "Regina told me she fucked things up. I'm here to sort it out."

I scratched out another letter. "She's a bitch, but that's not why I'm in here. I just needed some peace and quiet to think and to get my claws back in before my cousin and his idiot friends caught me. It's just all overwhelming. Having this wolf inside me. New magic. Being hunted for weeks on end."

She crossed over and leaned against the side of the stall. "I know, I'm sorry. I can't imagine."

I angled my blade to cross an A. "Thanks, but I'm not in here trying to host a pity party. I'm just trying to decide what to do. Regina's right. This is happening because of me."

"No. The bad shit is happening because of Kahanov. That circle out there is happening because of you. Our people have hope because of *you*," she said with conviction.

I almost believed her, but I shook my head. "The circle isn't enough. We don't know if the witch will help. And I need to solve this before things get out of control. Before we're talking about hundreds of wolves with sleeping loved ones. It's on me, and the truth is, I'm not up to it."

"That's where you're wrong. This isn't all on you to solve. You're part of this pack now, whether you like it or not. That means you don't have to face things alone. Not anymore. You have Jaxson and me, and when the chips are down, all the others will have your back. We look after our own."

"That's what people keep saying, but I don't believe it. I'm not pack. I'm not even really a wolf—just a LaSalle with a bad hair and nails problem. Maybe I look it, but I'm not part of this family. When the time comes, I'm going to be the first one voted off the island."

She hesitated a suspiciously long time. "You're more a part of this pack now than you can know. You have Jaxson's protection, and that means everything to us. Hell, I lent you my favorite shirt. I wouldn't do that if I thought there was the slightest chance someone would hand you over to the sorcerer."

I looked down at the faded purple *I Hit Like A Girl* shirt and blinked.

"This is your favorite shirt?" I said flatly. It was bottom of the hamper stuff.

I saw her flip her hair through the crack. "Absolutely. I like keeping trophies of all my conquests."

I laughed. "Oh, and what other trophies do you have?"

"That's a conversation for another time. After some *very* heavy drinking. But speaking of deviant behavior, what in the name of the gods are you doing to that door, anyway?"

I paused for a second, then started on the last letter. "Carving a sorcerous enchantment."

"Really?" Her voice hushed and had the slightest hint of trepidation. Wolves were so superstitious.

"No. I'm joking. I don't know how to do that yet. Bathroom graffiti is the best I've got." With a flick of the blade, I unlatched the door and swung it open to let Sam inspect my completed handywork.

I WILL KILL KAHANOV

She raised her eyebrows, and I shrugged as I dismissed the Soul Knife into the ether. "I figured that maybe if I wrote it down, that would make it true. Kind of like a spell. Of course, that's just wishful thinking."

She tightened her jaw and looked me in my eyes. "Savy...you understand how magic works better than you think you do."

I glanced back at the words. Silver sparks flickered to life in the etching, and soon, all the letters were shining with an ominous black light.

Oh, shit, what did I just do?

34

Savannah

Jaxson was waiting when I emerged from the bathroom.

"Ready?" he asked. Clearly, he'd been waiting for a while.

"Absolutely. Let's go on a witch hunt," I said, mustering as much confidence as I could.

I didn't tell him about the glowing black words. Sam had agreed to take care of the stall door, even if she had to take it off its hinges, as we didn't want any werewolves spooked away from the gym because of random glowing magical death threats in the women's bathroom.

But that was only one of my problems. Getting to Magic's Bend required another portal journey, and my stomach suggested returning to the bathroom and voiding its contents at the thought.

"You'll get used to it," Jaxson grumbled as I continued to complain.

It was, as I'd feared, horrendous—spinning and tumbling and a mass of gray, and then suddenly, we were standing in the middle of a museum. After a valiant show of restraint, and with only a slight sprint for the doors, I threw up in the bushes outside.

Thankfully, the rest of our journey was by taxi. Never had I so appreciated having four wheels beneath me.

We passed through a charming little town that made me long for home and my godmother, and then headed down a winding road through the forest. At last, our taxi pulled up opposite an isolated two-story cottage that looked like it had been pulled from another era. The blue paint was chipping, and several wooden shingles on the roof were missing.

"Are you sure this is the address?" I asked the driver.

He gestured to his phone on the dash, which had Wayz opened. "You tell me."

"Only one way to find out." Jaxson climbed out of the car, and I followed.

I had steeled myself for a twisted hovel in the midst of an ominous, rotting wood inhabited by a sinister crone who made books out of the flayed flesh of her victims. I had a very *real* image of it in my head.

"You know," I mused aloud, "somehow, this wasn't what I was expecting."

Jaxson opened the rickety gate in the white picket fence that surrounded the property. "Don't let the façade fool you. Keep your eyes open."

His body was tense and alert, like a predator stalking an enemy's territory. There was something utterly captivating about the way he moved. Power and grace. I'd never fully appreciated it before.

I tried to ignore my magnetic draw to him as we followed the concrete path that cut through the overgrown yard. The front steps creaked as I took them two at a time, glancing at the white rocking chair on the porch and the pots of herbs hanging from the railings.

My heartbeat accelerated.

The place was so unassuming that it was almost ominous. An incredibly powerful being lived here. She was capable of entering dreams and summoning nightmares, but there was no sign of her power. Something wasn't quite right.

A deep sense of unease rooted in my gut as I thought of Hansel and Gretel and the gingerbread house. Heart pounding, I picked up the brass knocker bolted to the door frame and rapped twice. "Here goes nothing."

The echoes died away. And then, just as I was about to knock again, my sharp ears detected the faint sound of footsteps gliding over the creaking floorboards. I sensed Jaxson tense, but before I could speak, the door flew open.

A middle-aged woman in a bathrobe stood in the frame. Her face was done up, but her wispy, red-dyed curls shot wildly around her head. "I told you, Molly, I'm not—*oh!*" she said in surprise as she locked eyes with me, then Jaxson. "You're not Molly." She narrowed her eyes suspiciously and slowly stepped behind the door. "If you're selling something, I'm not interested."

I'd conjured all sorts of terrifying images of S.L. Delamont, and the woman standing before me was *not* one of them. Perhaps we'd gotten the address wrong, or maybe the person we were looking for had moved.

I plastered on my best waitress's smile. "Hi, we're looking for S.L. Delamont. And we're not selling anything."

The woman peered at me curiously, then took in Jaxson's full form. "Well, that's me. Who are you, and what do you want?"

I opened my mouth, but Jaxson went straight to the point. "Jaxson Laurent, Dockside alpha, and this is Savannah Caine. We want to ask you a few questions about *The Grimoire of Nightmares*. We know you're the author."

She scrutinized us and pursed her lips. "The grimoire. How

odd. I haven't thought about that thing for years. Do you have it?"

"Unfortunately, no. That's why we're here. We're hoping you can help."

After a long pause, she gestured for us to enter. My skin prickled, but my instincts told me her intentions were sincere, so I stepped inside.

Flowery wallpaper covered the space, and the furniture was so quaint and homey, I nearly burst out laughing. This was *definitely* not what I'd imagined.

The woman crossed the living room and glanced over her shoulder. "Can I get you two some lemonade?"

Jaxson pressed his lips together, but I nodded and smiled. "Sure, that'd be great."

She disappeared into the other room, and I whispered to Jaxson, "Be nice."

He glared at me and continued scanning the space vigilantly, clearly not trusting the witch. That was fair. She didn't seem any more threatening than my aunt...who, in fairness, was an arms manufacturer, could summon demons, and kept the Sphere of Devouring in her closet.

The witch appeared a few minutes later carrying a tray and three glasses with painted lemons on them, and she set them on a coffee table in the living room. She took a glass and perched on the arm of a sofa, then eyed Jaxson curiously. "Tell me, what is it that you need, exactly?"

"Someone has stolen the grimoire from the Order's Archives and is using it to trap people in their dreams. We're hoping that since you're the author, you might know how we can help these people and put a stop to this." His voice was calm, but I could sense he was on edge.

I passed him a lemonade. He looked down and begrudgingly took it with a subtle shake of his head. The witch didn't seem to notice.

"Ah! So that's where the damn thing ended up. It always had a mind of its own." She frowned and took a sip of her lemonade, then drummed on her glass, seemingly lost in thought. "Yes, yes, your situation sounds unfortunate, but I'm afraid I haven't the faintest idea what to do. I'm not the author, you see."

"What?" My spine stiffened, and I slid my glass onto the table. "I thought you said you were S.L. Delamont."

"I am, and please call me Sorsha. I wrote the thing, but I'm not its *creator*."

I could sense Jaxson's irritation as he set his untasted glass of lemonade on the table beside mine. "Can you explain? We're short on time."

Sorsha raised her eyebrows. "It seems you're short on patience as well, but I'll bite." She stood and sauntered over to the bookshelf along the back wall, dragging her fingers over the spines. "The year was 1992. I was young and experimenting with all sorts of drugs. You know how that goes." She glanced over her shoulder at me and winked.

Um, no, lady, I don't. I smiled and nodded.

Her fingers stopped on a black leather tome, and she pulled it out. "Anyway, on one of my vision quests, I met an entity in a place of dreams. She was alluring and powerful, very persuasive, so I agreed to help her."

"What does this have to do with the grimoire?" Jaxson asked, his patience all but extinguished.

Keeping my eyes and smile locked on Sorsha, I slid my hand over the couch and squeezed his thigh to shut him up. Jaxson tensed, and I felt his gaze burning on my neck while I pondered how muscular his quad felt under my grip. *Shit.*

Luckily, Sorsha was lost in her story and didn't notice the exchange. "An entity named Cavra is the author of the grimoire. She said she had beautiful mysteries that she wanted to share with the world, but she needed a vessel. She dictated the work, and I transcribed it."

"And you just obliged?" Jaxson growled.

"I told you, she was persuasive, and I was young and enraptured with the magical world." She shrugged nonchalantly. "I might be able to help you for the right price."

She leaned forward and handed me the black book.

The rich leather was smooth and smelled of patchouli, and a silver bookmark peeked out from the middle. Instinctively, I opened it to the marked page, and shivers raised the hairs on my arms. A forested scene rose from the pages, veiled in shadows of blue and green and silver. It looked like a painting from a children's fantasy story.

"If you agree, I can get you to the Dreamlands, where you'll find Cavra. I can't promise that she'll agree to help, but you can try."

"Absolutely not," Jaxson said.

I jerked my gaze from the page and gave Jaxson *the look*, even though it generally didn't work on him. "Hold on a sec. If this is our one shot at stopping Kahanov from putting anyone else to sleep, we've got to take it."

He stood and gently gripped my elbow, towing me up. "We know nothing about the Dreamlands or this entity. It's too risky, and we're not going."

I yanked my arm free and turned to Sorsha. "Tell us about the Dreamlands."

Jaxson growled but stayed put.

Her eyes glistened and lost focus. "The Dreamlands is a magical realm, like the lands of the fey. It's where our dreams go once we've woven them—a strange mirror of earth, constantly changing and growing. It's unpredictable and deadly and wonderful."

Her words raised the tiny hairs on my neck, and I felt as if at some point, we'd already crossed a dangerous line. "How do we get there?"

She smiled and met my eyes. "Oh, I can guide you to Cavra. All you must do is dream."

35

Jaxson

Thirty minutes later, Savannah and I found ourselves sitting on thick rugs around a smoking brazier of fire-cracked stones and incense in Sorsha's sweat lodge. Well, she called it a lodge, but it was little more than a makeshift tent in her backyard.

I scrubbed a hand through my hair as a growing sense of unease settled in my bones.

Pack lore spoke little of the Dreamlands, mentioning it only in whispers at the dark edges of stories. It was a place of nightmares made manifest.

Trusting the witch to take us there was reckless as hell. Even if Sorsha didn't simply drug us and try to rob us blind, we'd have to find this entity, Cavra, and convince her to help us.

To be fair, I hadn't caught a scent of deceit or treachery from the witch. But while she seemed benign, the casual, practically offhanded way she talked about making a pact with a sinister being of unknown power and intent didn't bode well. But the clock was ticking, and we had to stop Kahanov before he put any more werewolves to sleep.

But I wasn't a fool. Rather than put our fate entirely in the witch's hands, I'd called Neve, who'd headed our way instantly and was standing watch outside the tent. In the event that Savannah and I didn't wake up, I trusted Neve to do what it took to extract an antidote from the witch.

Sorsha stepped into the sweat lodge carrying a brass tea kettle. She took a seat across from us and poured steaming brown liquid into a pair of terracotta cups. I watched her hands suspiciously as she pinched a variety of herb bundles that were strewn across the ground beside her and sprinkled them into the cups, swishing them carefully.

Finally, she reached over the baking stone pit and handed Savannah and me each a cup with a smile. "Drink this and relax. The brew will work quickly, so clear your mind and prepare yourself."

The brew smelled godawful and was likely laced with mushrooms or peyote or something worse.

Savannah sniffed her cup and wrinkled her nose. "Will we just wake up in the Dreamlands? How will we find Cavra?"

Sorsha smiled. "It's sort of like that. Your bodies will stay here while your souls travel there. I'll guide you through your dreams so that you'll arrive in the Vale. Once you're there, make your intentions clear, and Cavra will find you. Navigating the Dreamlands is more about your intent than geography."

Whatever that meant.

Savannah glanced at me. I could smell her trepidation, and I saw a momentary flicker of doubt in her eyes. But just when I thought she was going to back out, she downed the concoction in a single gulp.

"Ugh," she groaned, wincing. "This is worse than scrying potion."

"Fucking hell," I muttered, and shot back the cursed mixture in my cup. It was acerbic and bitter, and had a filthy, moldy taste.

Savannah had already gone pale, and sweat began beading on her face.

"Are you okay?" I slurred.

She forced out a faint laugh as her eyes began to cloud. "I regret everything. Mostly breakfast."

"When you wish to wake, envision me sitting as I am, in this tent," said Sorsha. "Call out my name and make it your intention to return to me. I'll pull you back."

I nodded even as my thoughts began to drift.

"And do *not* fall asleep in the Dreamlands. Where you'd go from there, I don't know."

"Okay," Savannah mumbled. Sorsha guided her down to the ground beside the fire and poured some of the liquid into the flames so that a fog filled the chamber. My vision blurred as my limbs grew heavy.

Savannah's eyes closed. My pulse raced, and I fought the drowsiness that snaked through my body.

"Stop fighting it, Jaxson," Sorsha whispered in the distance. "The Dreamlands has its sights on you, and there's no backing out now."

I cursed the woman and tried to crawl to Savannah, but instead, I found myself lying face down on the coarse rug beneath me. The world slanted, and darkness enveloped me, carrying me through a wormhole between dimensions.

A barrage of mutating images flashed through my mind— people and places I'd long forgotten or never met, shifting and falling into each other like a kaleidoscope. Possibilities grew from the ground like flowers and sunk into my thoughts like roots. The pressure in my skull increased, but when my head felt like it might explode, it stopped.

Sounds of the forest rose around me, and the scent of over- ripe fruit and anise burned my throat. I opened my eyes as sensations of wonder and astonishment blossomed in my heart.

Trees with twisted trunks towered overhead as the barest of light filtered in from the full canopy above.

I couldn't tell if the trees were real or a mirage.

I stepped forward, brushing a tendril of silver moss that hung from the branches. Tiny glowing lights drifted through the air like dandelions floating in the wind. I glanced down at my hands, unsure if I was dreaming or imagining this vision, but it was so real.

Savannah.

Dread focused my mind. I spun, but the forest around me was empty.

The thread that bound us pulled in my chest, and I shoved my way through the vines until I found her in a clearing beside a small pool that reflected a different sky than the one that hung over our heads.

"Jaxson! I thought I lost you," she said in a dreamlike voice as some of the strange motes of light settle on her skin. "This place…"

"Is perilous," I said gruffly as I took her hand and pulled her back from the edge of the strange pool. "As alluring as all this might be, don't let your eyes deceive you. In the few stories I know of this place, it's only ever mentioned as the source of nightmares. So stay close and don't touch anything. We need to find Cavra."

Before I could say a word, she raised her hands to her mouth and shouted, "Cavra! We need to speak with you!"

"What are you doing?" I snarled as her voice continued to echo unnaturally through the forest. "We shouldn't draw attention to ourselves."

"Sorsha said we only had to make our intentions known."

I didn't like this one bit. "Let's go find her. *Quietly.*"

We left the glistening pool behind us and pushed onward, gingerly stepping over the roots that snaked across the forest floor. The scampering and chittering of unseen animals preoccupied my senses.

Before long, a strange presence filled the air, and I suspected that we were being watched. I took Savannah's arm and raised a finger to my lips.

It wasn't a sound that caught my attention, but rather a feeling of power and silence. The noises of the forest died around us as a high-pitched humming reverberated through the trees. My claws slipped out, and my muscles tensed.

The smell of melon and sugar dulled my senses as a woman stepped through a curtain of moss dangling from the gnarled trees. Had it been there moments before? I couldn't remember.

"Blessed day, beauties," the woman drawled in a seductive voice, planting her hands on her full hips. She stood over six feet tall, and her wild, dark hair hung loosely around her, draped with vines and flowers. A crown of stag horns rose above her brow, and her nails were sharpened into points. "Now, which one of you summoned me?"

"I did," Savannah said, slipping around me.

"My, my, two wolf pups lost in my wood. What brings you here?" The woman's eyes darkened as she gaped at Savannah, taking a step forward.

"That's close enough," I growled. Cavra's head snapped to mine like an animal's, and her eyes brightened back to an emerald green. She smiled maliciously as she took my measure but quickly set her gaze back on Savannah.

I sensed Savannah's fear, but she stood tall, betraying nothing. "We understand that you dictated a book—*The Grimoire of Nightmares*—to a witch named Sorsha Delamont. That book was stolen by a blood sorcerer, and he's using it to trap people in their dreams. We came to seek your help in stopping him."

The woman tilted her head back and let out a hearty laugh,

the air around her vibrating with magic. Whatever she was, she was powerful, and I didn't like it one godsdamned bit.

After a moment, she clutched her chest and smiled broadly. "What a wonderful surprise. I haven't had visitors for so long, and to hear that my grimoire is actually being read is delightful."

"Will you help us?" I growled.

"So impatient, Jaxson. So keen for the hunt. You're asking a great favor."

Every muscle in my body warned me that this woman was perilous. A monster. I flexed my claws. "How do you know my name?"

"You knew *my* name, so it's only fair that I should know yours. Now, come with me and we'll discuss the favor you ask." Cavra shifted her body sideways and motioned with her clawed index finger—a talon unmistakably suited for ripping flesh.

We were stepping into the jaws of a dragon. But what choice did we have? We were committed to this path.

I stayed close to Savannah as we followed Cavra through the sinister forest. Birds with brightly colored plumage and curved beaks flitted through the branches overhead, feasting on the carcass of a small rodent. The stench of blood and raw flesh permeated the air, and Savannah gagged, covering her mouth.

Clearing her throat, Savannah asked, "Are you a sorcerer or a witch, Cavra?"

The woman chuckled heartily and glanced back at Savannah with an exaggerated sway of her hips. "Oh, gods, no, honey. I was a maenad once, though I outgrew it a long time ago."

This isn't good.

"What is a maenad?" Savannah asked.

Cavra lifted her arms above her head and twirled her fingers. Roots and vines uprooted from the dirt and twisted up her body like serpents. "Well, suffice it to say I was a celebrant of life in all its various forms."

Our lore spoke of the maenads as *the raving ones*. They were twisted beings of myth driven to frenzied rituals of excess and depravity. But that wasn't what worried me most.

"You said you *were* a maenad. What are you now?" I demanded, my voice low and tense. Cavra looked fucking maniacal, and if we didn't need her help, I might have tried to rip her throat out.

"The Dreamlands made me more." She turned and said, "I'm a lot like you, Savannah. I discovered myself in a new world, and it changed me. Perhaps it will change you, too."

"You're not native to the Dreamlands?" Savannah asked. She was much too calm and trusting of this monster.

"No. I moved to the Vale centuries ago, when my wicked sister ousted my mother from the throne and exiled me from the Summer Lands." The roots and vines that encaged Cavra withered and darkened, turning to ash.

I gently gripped Savannah's arm, pulling her to a stop. But she was unbothered, and her voice was tender and full of empathy. "I'm so sorry, that's terrible."

"No, terrible is what I will do to her when the time comes for revenge." Like a chameleon, Cavra's demeanor changed suddenly, and she smiled graciously at us. "But that's none of your concern. Tell me, what is it you want me to do about this sorcerer?"

Up ahead, the forest opened into a clearing that was illuminated by thousands of glowing lights strung through the trees.

"Can you stop him from entrapping more people? And set those he's captured free?"

"Yes," the maenad mused. "But whether I *will* remains to be seen."

No doubt, her price would be steep.

36

Cavra moved effortlessly through the dense forest into a brightly lit clearing. The folds of her long gown hugged her voluptuous curves, and her hips swayed gracefully. She was mesmerizing to watch, like her body was dancing even when she was standing still.

I could sense Jaxson's vitriol toward her, but for some reason, I felt a glimmer of kinship.

"You ask a favor. What can you offer me in payment?" she enquired, twirling a strand of hair between her delicate fingers.

"We can pay in coin, but I'm guessing that's not what you're looking for," Jaxson said roughly.

"Correct, wolf man. I live in a perfect dream. I have no need for currency."

What could a vastly powerful maenad possibly want or need? Unease settled over me. "There must be something we can do for you. A favor for a favor?"

Tilting her head, Cavra considered my words with a glint in her green eyes. "Now, *that* is a more interesting proposal."

Jaxson tensed, and I could sense his displeasure.

Cavra closed her eyes and stepped close to me, breathing in deeply and twisting her hand strangely in the air. My skin prickled as a cacophony of whispers filled the clearing, but I couldn't see where they were coming from—the space was empty.

Jaxson clearly heard, too. He scanned the area, his muscles twitching in anticipation of an attack.

Suddenly, the murmurs went quiet as Cavra opened her eyes, and a wide grin spread across her sharp features. "My. Apparently, you are far more than you seem, Savannah—so much strength lurking in the shadows of your soul. I do believe there *is* something that you could do for me. In return, I will cast a blocking spell on my grimoire, and your sorcerer will not be able to ensnare any further victims."

"And what about those who are already trapped? Will they wake up?" Jaxson all but growled.

"No, I'm afraid not. He has their minds sequestered in a place beyond my reach, and they will be trapped in their dreams until the sorcerer is killed or ends his spell. There's nothing I can do about that."

Disappointment tore at me, but at least we could prevent anyone else from getting hurt.

Then all we had to do was kill Kahanov.

I met Jaxson's steely gaze and knew he was thinking the same thing.

"What is it you want us to do?" I asked.

Cavra had an unabashedly predatory look on her face, and worry spread through me like a sickness. I had a sinking suspicion that whatever she was going to ask, we wouldn't escape unscarred.

"The payment I request is a bloodstone known as the *heart* of the forest. If you retrieve this for me, then I will cast the blocking spell."

"What is it?" I asked, warily. "And why do you need *us*?"

Cavra was a being of immeasurable power. It had to be a suicide mission.

She lifted my chin with a claw. "So suspicious."

Jaxson's eyes dilated, but I met her gaze without flinching.

Her eyes flickered with desire. "The heart is located on a basalt pillar in the center of the Glen of Shadows, not far from here. It is the one place in the Vale that my magic is useless, and as such, I've never been able to reach it. You, on the other hand share a certain kinship with the darkness, if I'm not mistaken."

I pulled the shadows around myself in answer, and she released my chin. "Good. It's almost like the fates sent you to me."

Even though I didn't trust the fates for a second, shadows were at least one thing I could control. Perhaps this wouldn't be *so* bad.

"A darkness inhabits the glen," Cavra continued, "and if the shadows catch you, they'll drag you down into the earth, where you will slowly be devoured."

I was wrong. We were screwed.

Maybe we didn't need to do this after all. Finding and killing Kahanov would solve all our problems. We could just skip Cavra and her forest of hungry shadows.

Jaxson was unusually quiet as he considered Cavra's words, and then he spoke. "What happens if the bloodstone is taken?"

"The shadows will be dispelled and no harm will befall you, if that's what you were wondering."

I studied her face and scent, but her emotions were a blank slate, and I couldn't tell if she was lying.

We shouldn't trust her, my wolf said.

"I'll go," Jaxson said, turning to me. "Stay here and keep your eyes open."

Irritation flashed through me at his protectiveness. "Like hell. I'm coming with."

"She must go with you, or you will fail," Cavra said quietly, though her words rang with stone-cold certainty.

For better or worse, this task fell to me.

Jaxson knotted his fists. "Together then."

I crouched and tightened the laces on my tennies, wishing I'd worn my magic boots today. "Any pointers you want to give us so we don't die?"

Cavra smiled down at me and raised her arm, pointing toward the forest to her right. A swarm of tiny lights shot from her palm and began winding their way through the dense trees. "Follow them. You'll know when you've arrived. Move quickly. Don't speak. And if the shadows envelop you, don't look at them directly."

How did you avoid looking at a shadow if it was surrounding you?

"Got it." Standing, I pulled my hair into a ponytail as I took a deep breath. "Okay, let's do this, Jaxson."

He glared at me, and I heard the rumble in his chest. "You lead. I don't trust this place, and I'm not taking my eyes off you."

Dread pooling in my belly, I took off after the lights as they disappeared into the trees. They reminded me of the lights in Alia's apartment, but they seemed to be sentient, or at least under Cavra's command.

Pretty little lights, leading us to our deaths.

We moved quickly, and my breathing became heavy. The forest was humid, and my shirt dampened with sweat. The whole place pulsed with a hypnotic drone that made me drowsy, despite the adrenaline pumping through me.

Every motion I made felt a little too slow. I ducked under a sheet of silvery moss that hung from a branch high above and tripped on a root. No—a rock.

Jaxson wrapped his arm around my waist, catching me before I faceplanted. "Keep your eyes on the ground."

His deep voice dragged over my damp skin, and I couldn't help the tingles that spread through me. Once I'd found my footing, he released his arm, though I could still feel the heat of his body behind me.

"Holy hell," I whispered, taking in the sights ahead. The dilapidated ruins of what looked like ancient stone buildings rose from the jungle, partially covered by the dense vegetation. "What *is* this place?"

"Legends say that the Dreamlands have been populated by different species of Magica for millennia. This must be the remnants of one the Great Cities," Jaxson said and softly pressed against my back. "Come on, let's keep moving. We don't want to be left behind."

I nodded and caught up with the lights, which had kept on winding their way deeper into the trees. God, I hoped we could find our way back.

We circled around a giant bust of a humanoid creature with almond eyes lying half buried on its side.

Taken by its unique features, I slowly stepped around it, but Jaxson grabbed my arm and stopped me short. His hand cupped over my mouth as he towed me down behind the stone bust, gesturing with his chin to the bushes on our right.

Heart pounding, I searched the trees for any sign of what Jaxson had seen, but all I saw were the same strange birds from earlier. I glanced around at Jaxson, whose hand was still covering my mouth, and gave him my best *what the fuck* look.

His body stiffened, and his gaze was locked on something behind me. Slowly, I turned my head, focusing on the trees. Still, I saw nothing, but then the slightest movement caught my eye.

At first, it was too subtle to make out its form, but when it moved again, my brain finally processed what I was seeing: a squat, hunched body, no more than five feet tall, with arms that hung to the ground. As it moved, its skin shifted and blended with the foliage, making it virtually impossible to see. Where there should have been hands, there were two hooked, obsidian talons.

I jerked backward into Jaxson, stifling the squeak that tried to rip from my throat. My claws and muscles ached as my wolf jumped in my chest, but Jaxson pressed his magic into my back, and I relaxed slightly.

Shit, Cavra hadn't said anything about these things. What else was lurking out here?

Movement to our left revealed a second creature rooting around under a rotten trunk. Something told me that that was what those hideous claws were for.

Jaxson slowly released his hand from my mouth and motioned for me to follow. We slipped back around the head of the ruined bust, keeping a wary eye on those things.

Apart from the shrill squawks of the birds and the skuttling of things in the underbrush, the jungle was quiet, which meant those creatures hadn't seen us. Probably.

The glowing lights that had been guiding us were long gone, and there was no telling in which direction the bloodstone lay. Still, Jaxson pushed forward, and I followed wordlessly.

We continued in silence searching for any sign of the lights, but they were gone, and everything looked the same.

Panic began to fester inside me, and my skin chilled. As if sensing something, Jaxson paused mid-step. He cocked his head to the right, scanning the trees, and then he whispered, "Run."

It took a second to register, but when he pushed me forward, I sprinted into the trees. Thunderous movement crashed behind me, and I stole a glance back, dread coiling in my stomach. Jaxson stood immobile, crouched with his claws out, ready. I spun behind a tree and peered around the side of the twisted trunk.

What was he doing? Why hadn't he come with me?

Suddenly, a giant *thing* launched out of the trees and soared through the air toward Jaxson. Its skin kept shifting colors, and its two hooked talons glinted in the light that permeated from the leaves overhead.

Jaxson shot forward and ducked beneath the monster's talons. In a flash, he'd grabbed the creature's arm and twisted. There was a snap, and then Jaxson hurled the monster backward.

The beast landed nimbly and paused. As if sensing my presence, it bent its reptilian head and looked right at me. It tilted its neck back and barked like a goddamned velociraptor. Seconds later, a similar bark echoed through the jungle, followed by another.

"Run, Savannah!" Jaxson roared as he leapt out of the monster's striking distance. "Get the damn stone. I'll find you!"

With my gaze locked on the monster, I took a step backward and spun. But my foot caught on a root, and I tripped, landing hard on my palms.

Fuck, fuck, fuck!

With my pulse pounding in my temples, I scrambled to my feet and sprinted away from Jaxson and that thing. More barking cut through the jungle, and the sound of something large moving through the trees toward me made my blood curdle. Was this a trap to lure us to our deaths?

No. I had the sense that if she had wanted to, Cavra could have killed us right there. I was certain she believed we had a chance.

But maybe just a slim one.

I skuttled behind a crumbled wall and listened. Apart from

the pulse of the Dreamlands and my pounding heart, there was nothing nearby.

I wished that Sorsha had prepared us a little more for this. All she'd told us was that *navigating the Dreamlands was more about your intent than geography.*

Maybe that was something. Hope dwindling like sand in an hourglass, I squeezed my eyes shut.

I need to find the heart of the woods.

Repeating the thought over and over like a mantra, I opened my eyes and began moving forward with a pool of dread in my chest. Ducking under branches and moss, I scanned my surroundings for any sign of that damn basalt pillar with the bloodstone.

Nothing.

I pushed onward, scrambling around and over the ancient ruins that the jungle had claimed. Finally, as my mind grew numb from repeating the mantra, the lights from earlier appeared ahead.

I brushed an oversized palm leaf aside. The lights had stopped and were clustered and hovering around a pitch-black void in the trees.

The Glen of Shadows. It had to be, judging by the way the darkness leaked out of it like tendrils of smoke. I glanced behind me, praying that I'd see Jaxson, but he was nowhere.

"Crap," I muttered, forcing my feet forward. I took several gasps, trying to get my breaths under control. I just had to go in, move quickly, and find the stone without looking at the shadows. Piece of cake.

I stopped just short of where the darkness started, and my skin tingled.

A chorus of faint whispers filtered out of the blackness: *Join us. In the darkness, you will find your answers. Take what you want. You belong here. You are one of us.*

Shit, I didn't want to do this.

I don't either, so now would be a great time to figure out how to get out of this, my wolf said.

I laughed. "I think we're out of options."

Well, glad you're driving this time.

Although that wasn't exactly a vote of confidence, warmth filled me. I wasn't alone.

I bit my lip. *I hope Jaxson is okay.*

He's fine. I'd know if he was hurt, my wolf said in my mind.

Would she? Why? There was so much I didn't understand about werewolves.

I pushed the nagging thoughts out of my mind and steeled my courage. Then I stepped into the glen.

37

Savannah

I blinked as my eyes adjusted to the dimmed light. Despite what it had looked like from the outside, it wasn't pitch black, but rather like the tail end of dusk.

Unfortunately, the shadows I'd seen snaking out were also inside, moving across the ground like liquid mercury. They must have sensed me because they began pooling and drifting in my direction.

Cavra's words rang in my mind. *If the shadows catch you, they'll drag you down into the earth, where you will slowly be devoured.*

I picked up a broken branch and tossed it into the shadows. It disappeared when they shifted away.

That was creepy.

A least I was good at seeing in the dark now—a byproduct of my own shadow magic. It was very easy to differentiate between shadows, and *the* shadows.

I moved as quickly as I could, while keeping my eyes peeled. The glen had the same flora as the outside but none of the animals, which hopefully meant there wouldn't be any of those monsters.

The shadows probably had eaten them all.

My sense of direction was shot, and the deeper I moved into the glen, the darker it got.

"Where the hell are you?" I hissed in frustration.

All around you, just take a look.

I jumped at the whispers. Was that the darkness answering?

"I'm looking for a bloodstone. Where is it?" It didn't hurt to ask.

The air cracked around me, and the whispers turned into growls. *You can't have it. It's ours. OURS... like you are ours, little sister.*

Oh, hell, no.

I kept moving, even though the fear that had taken root in my heart urged me to curl up in a ball. I kept my mouth shut and focused my intention on the heart of the woods.

Ahead, the crumbling wall of an ancient building blocked my path.

Want some claws? my wolf asked.

I've got this, I answered, feeling her challenge.

Grabbing hold of the vines snaking along its side, I hauled myself up, praying that I'd be able to see the pillar from the top.

Chest heaving, I finally reached the top of the wall, and my heart leapt. In a small clearing ahead was a black pillar of stone with a ruby-red gemstone sitting atop it.

I moved to climb down the other side when something beneath me shifted. Stones skidded, and then the face of the wall caved in beneath me. I landed hard as the limestone and rubble showered down around me.

I struggled to get up, but my body jerked. My foot was stuck.

Grunting, I shifted my weight backward and saw that my leg

was trapped beneath a huge limestone block that had tumbled over. *Fuck.*

Panic surged through me, and though I gripped the stone and pushed, it was too heavy and wouldn't budge. I twisted my foot and tried to angle it out of the hole between the blocks, but it wouldn't fit. Sighing, I took a breath and closed my eyes, attempting to calm my nerves. It would do me no good to panic, I needed to stay calm and figure out a solution.

When I opened my eyes, my heart froze. Shadows were snaking around me as dark tendrils moved down the ruined wall and across the jungle floor, shrouding everything they covered.

My chest ached, and my fingertips itched.

Let me take over! the wolf inside me shouted.

But I didn't trust her. What if she was still stuck after we shifted? And would she have enough sense to grab the bloodstone?

Shift, or we're dead, she urged.

No. I could handle this.

Magic coursed through me, and a wave of cool spread across my flushed skin. My darkness pulsed inside before pushing out and enveloping me in a shadow of my own creation. It strained against the darkness of the glen, pushing it back.

My teeth chattered as I fought to hold my focus. Every muscle in my body burned, and yet, I was barely holding back the shadows. I kept my gaze down, heeding Cavra's warning and avoiding any direct eye contact with the monsters.

My hands trembled with the strain, but slowly, with each agonizing second, the shadows inched backward.

I was stronger, but how long could I hold this?

I looked past my shaking arms at my trapped foot. "A little help, here?" I said to myself, hoping to God that the beast inside me was listening. She was stronger than me—physically, at least—and maybe she could give me a little of her strength.

Now you want my help? she answered.

"Can you help me move this block or not?"

Probably, but you'll owe me a bacon cheeseburger when we get home. And a run.

"Fine," I croaked, feeling my strength waning.

Okay, give it a shove.

I said a silent prayer and released my magic, dropping my hands to the stone at my foot. Taking a breath, I shoved it with everything I had. That *we* had.

My muscles strained with a power I had never felt before, and the block lifted and tumbled over to the side.

"Holy shit!" With my foot now free, I leapt up, shocked by my sudden strength.

My strength, my wolf chided.

"*Our* strength," I corrected, as I tested my ankle. It was scratched but fine.

The shadows of the glen crept toward me, and I choked on a laugh as I lunged toward the basalt pillar, which was just twenty feet ahead.

The whispers flooded my ears, taunting and warning me not to touch the stone: *You will die. Cursed for taking our heart. Ours, ours, OURS.*

But I was a bitch with one goal: get the bloodstone.

The shadows were on my heels, so I didn't slow when I reached the pillar, and my body all but collided into it.

"Now would be a good time for claws!" I shouted to my wolf.

My fingers erupted into talons. Ignoring the pain, I began clambering my way up. The stone was too hard to sink my claws into, but they were perfect for latching onto thin cracks. I heaved myself up, arm over arm, and finally drew a breath of relief when I saw the stone sitting unencumbered at the top.

Encased in a gold setting, it was the size of my fist and as red as blood. I reached forward and scooped it up. The instant my fingers touched the warm gemstone, a screeching hiss reverberated around me, and I moaned as my eardrums throbbed in pain.

Gritting my teeth and clinging to the pillar, I clutched the bloodstone to my body. Seconds that felt like minutes passed, and then the screeching stopped.

I steadied my heaving chest and looked around. The shadows and darkness of the glen had faded away, and though the place was still dim, it was a little less dark and creepy.

I leapt down from the pillar and landed hard on the jungle floor. "Okay, nice job. Let's find Jaxson."

You still owe me a bacon cheeseburger, remember, my wolf said.

I had full confidence in Jaxson's ability to take care of himself —I'd seen him fight many times. Still, I couldn't shake the worry and unease that had settled in my bones. Lately, the more time I spent away from Jaxson, the more I'd felt unsettled. It was strange and disturbing, and I didn't like it one bit.

I jammed the stone in my almost-too-small pocket, and hurried back in the direction I'd come, careful to watch my footfalls so that I didn't twist an ankle or get my foot stuck again.

When I finally stepped out of the glen, I recoiled as my senses were overwhelmed by the commotion ahead. Grunts and screeches cut through the jungle, and the iron tang of blood burned my nostrils.

Jaxson.

Fear wrapped around my heart, and I shot forward, following the sounds and smells. I broke through the trees but pulled myself back as Jaxson and one of those monsters nearly collided into me.

Jaxson's shirt was torn, and so was the flesh of his bicep, but he still managed to tackle the beast and pin it to the ground. It was missing an arm and looked worse for wear, and its shrieks cut out as Jaxson squeezed its throat. The thing struggled under his grip, trying to slice at Jaxson's back with its hooked claw.

Without thinking, I leapt forward and grabbed the claw. "I could use a little wolf power, now!"

My muscles surged, and I rammed the beast's arm into the dirt. It writhed as I pinned back the claw, while Jaxson kept squeezing. With each second that passed, its movements slowed, and then its body slumped, lifeless at last.

Jaxson released his grip and stood, turning to me with a deadly expression on his face. Blood caked his skin, and the wound on his arm began to slowly knit together. I dragged my eyes up his body, lingering on the patches of his sculpted chest visible beneath his torn shirt.

"Did you get it?" His voice was animalistic, and I had to fight off a wild urge to run to him and take him right here in the middle of this bloodbath.

What. The. Fuck?

My wolf was incorrigible.

All you, she quipped.

I squeezed my eyes shut, silently cursing as my cheeks blazed.

"What's wrong?" Jaxson stepped toward me, concern making his voice even more ragged.

"Nothing. I've got the bloodstone," I blurted, taking a step back because I didn't trust my traitorous body being so close to him.

He narrowed his eyes and watched me closely. *Too* closely.

"Are you...okay?" I asked, glancing down at the lifeless monster at his feet before meeting his eyes.

A slow, devilish smile spread across Jaxson's face. "Worried about me?"

"Of course. Those things were horrifying. Did you get them all?" I scanned the jungle and shivered.

"Yes, I got them all." Jaxson grunted and scooped up his phone from the ground. I couldn't help but admire how fine his ass looked in those jeans.

When he looked back at me, I knew from the glint in his eyes that he was reading my thoughts. "This way. We better get back to Cavra."

I nodded, and Jaxson led the way through the jungle. He seemed to know exactly where he was going, which was a mercy, as I had no freaking clue if we were heading in the right direction.

38

Jaxson

I sensed the maenad before she stepped out of the trees.

"You made it," Cavra whispered with a mixture of shock and disbelief, her gaze locked on the bloodstone. "What a delightful surprise."

She observed Savannah, and a dangerous light flickered in her eyes. The maenad couldn't be trusted. Her sweet voice hid a wicked cunning and lust for power, which made my skin itch.

I stepped between them, claws extended, blocking Cavra's view. "How does this play out now?"

It took every bit of strength to maintain my calm. My protective instincts were still in overdrive after what had unfolded in the jungle, and I was certain that Cavra was far more dangerous than anything we'd encountered there.

The maenad examined me with a deadpan expression, and then her lips twitched up in a faint smile. "Don't worry. I'm true to my word, wolf man. Give me the bloodstone, and I'll fulfill my end of the bargain...with your help, of course."

"What do you mean, with *our* help?" I growled.

"The spell you've asked of me is not a simple one. I'll need you to contribute a bit of your magic to bring it to fruition."

"What're you suggesting?" Savannah asked, suspicion ringing in her voice.

"I'm a maenad. I draw my power from passion and pleasure, so I'll need you two to join me and my family in our revel. Come." Cavra turned and motioned for us to follow with the flick of her wrist.

Savannah shrugged and stepped past me, but I caught her hand. She had no fucking clue how bad it was.

"No," I growled. "We will *not* be participating in your debauched rituals."

A maenad's revel involved wine, drugs, and sex. Cavra was dangerous, and I didn't want to risk losing focus. Moreover, I didn't want to risk losing control around Savannah—her scent alone, rich with sweat and desire, was enough to drive me wild with lust.

If passion took her, how would I hold myself back?

Cavra gave me a knowing smile that slowly took on a sinister twist. "Don't worry, Jaxson. All you two need to do is have a good time. I'll do all the rest. But don't delude yourself that your participation is negotiable. It's not."

Savannah pulled her arm from my grasp. "We've come this far. We're not backing out now."

She had no idea what she was dealing with.

"Delightful! I knew that you would see reason." Cavra held her hand out. "The bloodstone, please."

Before I could object, Savannah stepped forward and delivered it. My breath caught. The maenad cradled the stone like an egg, her gaze wild. After a few moments, she shifted her bright eyes up to us. "Thank you. Now, are you ready?"

"Let's get this show on the road," Savannah muttered as Cavra stepped up to the base of a massive, twisted banyan tree.

Cavra chuckled. "The show is just getting started, child. Watch out—you might even enjoy yourselves."

A wall of silvery moss hung from the lowest branch like a curtain, and with a wink, Cavra slowly parted it.

Closing my eyes, I begged the moon mother for strength. No matter what happened inside, Savannah and I could *not* fuck. If I could just hold that line...

Savannah stepped through, but I paused before the maenad. "If this turns out badly, I won't hesitate to rip your throat out."

"Oh, I *like* you. By all means, wolf man, go wild and don't hold back. After all, a revel wouldn't be complete without a little blood spilled. Desire is what makes us alive." She snickered and lowered her voice, her glance flicking toward Savannah. "Something tells me, though, that your desires have nothing to do with killing."

"Watch yourself, maenad," I growled, ducking under the curtain. But then I froze, my senses bombarded from an explosion of sounds, smells, and sights.

Scantily clad males and females danced and scampered through a garden wholly different than the jungle we'd just left. Faerie lights floated above a circular podium in the center that was ringed by white marble columns draped in vines and crimson flowers. Music drifted through the air, and the heady smell of jasmine and honey was intoxicating.

"What *is* this place?" Savannah asked, wonder glinting in her eyes.

"A trap," I muttered, and I fought against the haze creeping in around the corners of my mind.

"My home." Cavra motioned with outstretched arms. "You're safe here to explore your deepest desires. Drink and eat. Dance. Fight or fuck. As I was telling your mate, *just don't hold back.*"

I stiffened as Savannah laughed weakly. "My mate? Oh, no, we're not together."

"Hmm," the maenad mused, and gave me a wink. "What an interesting way to play it."

A male approached holding a tray of goblets. He had the legs and hooves of a goat but the upper body of a man with a bestial face. Savannah's jaw dropped as she took in his form, her gaze lingering on his upright ears and horns.

"What are you?" she blurted.

Cavra snorted as she scooped up two goblets from his tray and handed them to us. "This is Elias. He's a satyr and a great companion, but something tells me that you won't be requiring his services."

She eyed me playfully and took a sip from her cup. The silver goblet I was holding dented within my fist.

Mercifully, Savannah was taken by the satyr and missed the insinuation. She raised the goblet to her lips.

"Don't drink that." My arm shot out, and I gripped her wrist. As if waking from a spell, Savannah shook her head and frowned.

"Actually, you must drink that for this to work. Consider it part of your contribution," Cavra said. "I promise it's not poisoned, and no harm will befall you."

"Why do I doubt that promise?" I growled.

Cavra drummed her fingers on her goblet as her signature rose, vibrating the air around us and pressing in like the depths of the ocean. "Because I don't need to trick you or impair you to harm you. You are in *my* dream now."

The pressure released, and Savannah gasped.

"But you're my guests," Cavra said, in a cheerful voice. "So eat, drink, and be merry, and enjoy the safety of my protection."

Savannah narrowed her eyes at the maenad. "When will you cast the blocking spell on the grimoire?"

"I've already begun. I only need the power of the revel to

complete it, so drink up. Just one word of advice—don't fall asleep."

"I've heard that before, but why?" Savannah asked.

"There's no telling where you might wake up." Cavra turned and lifted her arms above her head, moving seductively toward the columned podium. The music amplified, and revelers flocked around her, drinking, dancing, and gyrating their bodies together.

"Fucking hell," I muttered.

Savannah turned to me, eyes wide. "Don't let me fall asleep, Jaxson."

"That's the *least* of our worries," I ground out, my voice rough. Heat coursed through me, and I knew full well that as soon as we drank that wine, we'd be doing everything *but* sleeping.

Worry wrapped around Savannah, and her lips pressed together. "We're not participating in an orgy, if *that's* what you were implying."

I raised the goblet to my lips and released my alpha presence, hoping it might help Savannah keep her head on straight. "Whatever happens, whatever you think you want, don't let me fuck you."

She swallowed hard and nodded.

39

The wine was fruity and tart and better than anything I'd ever had. Impossible flavors curled around my tongue—it tasted like tart cherries and the summer wind. It smelled of sunlight and filled me with a sensation like the world waking in spring.

Licking my lips, I moaned softly as the alcohol warmed my stomach. A man with a chiseled physique pirouetted across the grass, shaking an instrument with bells.

I laughed and took another sip of wine, then frowned when I noticed that my cup was empty. Looking up, I met Jaxson's intense gaze. He was watching me closely, and though his body was as stoic as a statue, his eyes were awash in emotions—desire, longing, and lust.

Warmth spread through me like the sun breaking through clouds, and it felt like my insides were alive with sparkling bubbles. An immense joy buffeted my spirits, and I raised my hands toward the sky and twirled. Somehow it was dark now, and thousands of stars twinkled from the heavens above like the lights hung around the garden, casting a warm glow over us.

"Let's dance, Jaxson!" I dropped my cup and took his hand,

trying to tow him into the crowd of revelers, but he was as immobile as a rock.

I frowned and was about to remark on his sour mood when a woman with flowers in her hair took my wrist, and suddenly, she and I were bounding into the frenzy of laughing people.

The thrum of the drums reverberated through my body, and I closed my eyes, letting my hips move with the tempo of the music. I felt free and alive, not a care in my mind.

Hours or seconds or minutes passed as I spun around the garden until an invisible force slowed me to a stumbling halt. I opened my eyes, and my gaze locked onto Jaxson's.

He stood at the edge of the crowd, his attention entirely focused on me, like a predator stalking its prey. His stare was so intense that I felt it vibrate the air between us.

Shivers inched down my spine, and a tightness spread through my chest, narrowing to a point above my heart. And then, like a thread wrapped around me, it tugged me toward the man with the honey-gold eyes. Jaxson Laurent. My alpha.

I moved nearer until our bodies were inches apart. Tilting my head, I looked up into his steely eyes. He wore a tortured expression, and now that I was close enough to touch him, I saw that every one of his muscles was tensed.

"Do you want to dance with me?" I asked.

"I don't dance." His voice was gruff and grouchy, and I couldn't help but laugh. I had a hard time imagining it, to be fair.

But we were in the most beautiful place. It was such a tragedy. How could this man be in such a foul mood?

How do I make a wolf come out of its den?

But I already knew.

I let the thread draw me to within an inch of him—so close I could almost feel his heartbeat. I gave him a demure look. "Chase me, Jaxson."

I took three steps back, not letting my eyes break from his. Then I turned and bolted across the garden, heading for the line of trees ahead that were completely different than the trees of the jungle outside. As I slipped into the forest, I glanced over my shoulder, catching the livid expression on Jaxson's face as he raced after me.

Though I wound deeper into the strange woods, those beautiful lights still floated in the branches, casting a warm glow over the space.

Movement behind me caught my attention, and stifling a giggle, I slipped behind a large tree, pressing my back to it. Jaxson was close. His woodsy pine signature permeated the area, and the pulse of his alpha magic pressed into me, *searching*.

Exhilaration coursing through me, I steadied my breath and carefully peered around the trunk. Where was he?

"Found you." His silvery voice skated over my spine, and I shrieked.

Clutching my heart, I spun and met his amused gaze. Thank goodness, his icy demeanor was finally thawing.

He took a step forward and planted his palms beside my temples, caging me against the tree. "You're terrible at hide and seek."

"Maybe I wanted to be found," I whispered, my chest rising and falling with each urgent breath.

Jaxson's eyes flicked down, deepening their honey tone as his desire flooded my senses. I studied his lips. I'd tasted them before, but damn, I wanted to run my tongue over them and taste them again.

He growled deep and low in my ear, and I shivered, feeling the rumble of his voice in every inch of my body. "Do you remember what I told you earlier?"

"No," I fibbed. I remembered everything he'd said to me before we drank the wine, but my body had other plans, and as far as I was concerned, nothing was going to stop me from getting what I wanted.

"Liar." His canines slipped free, and he lowered his face to my neck, lightly dragging his teeth over my skin. "Do you know what'll happen if you let me have my way with you?"

I swallowed and nodded, mindful of how close his incisors were to my throat. "You'll ruin me forever? No man will ever measure up?"

And though I knew it was the painful truth, I'd trade my future sex life for one night with Jaxson.

A throaty laugh rumbled from his throat, and he gazed down at me with a sinfully delicious look. "Oh, baby, you have *no* idea."

His whiskey voice lit up every nerve ending in my already sensitive body, but I was pinned to the tree, locked in place by his presence.

"And if another man were to touch you," he continued, lowering his head again and brushing his lips across mine, "I'd rip his heart out."

Old Savannah would have kicked Jaxson in the balls, but current Savannah was eating up his domineering possessiveness.

As I leaned forward and pressed my mouth to his, he released me and took a step back. "We should get back to the revel before things get out of hand."

His voice was strained, and his fists clenched, but I could sense his desire as strongly as my own. Why was he fighting this?

"Then go back. I'm going for a swim." I pushed off the tree and began marching toward the body of water that I could somehow smell. These wolf senses were more useful than I'd imagined.

"What are you talking about?" Jaxson demanded as he stalked through the dark woods behind me.

"My wolf wants to swim."

Liar, she said. *I hate swimming.*

I wound through the trees, following the crisp, fresh scent, until it grew so strong, I could almost taste it. I pushed through a bush and smiled. A large pool of water was set among the forest, surrounded by a neatly manicured lawn.

"Why must you always fight me?" Jaxson asked, his voice thick with pent-up irritation.

"I'm not fighting you. I told you, I want a swim." Kicking away my shoes, I peeled my shirt off and tossed it on the grass, catching the distressed expression that cut Jaxson's face. "You're free to go back to the revel, if that's what you want."

I slowly unbuttoned my shorts and slid them down my hips, bending a little further forward than I needed to slip my feet out of them. *You little hussy*, my wolf said.

"Fuck," Jaxson choked. "You're killing me, Savannah."

I turned to face him, wearing only my black lacy bra and panties. His body rippled with tension, and though he looked like he wanted to rage, his eyes drank in every inch of my body. I felt sexy and wanted.

Slowly, I moved toward him, locking him with my gaze so he knew my intentions.

"Stop before this goes too far," he growled.

I drew my hands up his chest, reveling in how hard and rigid it felt under my fingertips. "You want me, Jaxson, and I want you. We're both adults, so what's the problem?"

Gently, I began unbuttoning his torn shirt until his chest was fully exposed. I could practically taste the dried sweat and blood on his skin, and it sent a pulsing heat through me that settled low in my belly. This man was a god among mortals, and I wanted to claim him.

Mine.

I slipped his torn shirt over his shoulders and let it drop to the ground. He shivered as I traced my fingers down his chest, following the sexy trail of hair that continued from his navel downward, disappearing beneath his jeans.

A rumble escaped his throat, and his hands gripped my waist, locking me in place. "Once I start, there'll be no turning back. You'll be mine. Neither of us is ready for that."

His words only stoked the flames that were building inside me.

"You can have me tonight. No strings attached." I undid the button of his jeans with a wink, but his hands caught mine.

"You don't understand, Savy," he said gruffly. "My wolf is possessive. Once I bed you, there will be no escaping him."

Anger and hurt blossomed in my chest. Why was it that every time we got close, Jaxson pushed me back, making me feel like *I* was the one who'd led him to the edge?

Bastard. I pulled away from his grasp and turned, striding toward the pool.

Though the water was dark, I saw the glint of rocks ten feet below. I dove in, letting the cool water extinguish the rage that had risen in my heart from being rejected yet again. I swam until my lungs burned, and then I surfaced.

I turned to tell Jaxson what an asshole he was, but when I looked up, he was gone. Ripples lapped at my face as I treaded water, searching the area around the pool.

He left me here. The bastard actually—

I yelped in shock as a powerful force plunged me beneath the water. Then Jaxson's strong arms wrapped around me and lifted me back to the surface.

I kicked furiously to stay up. I wanted to punch him in the face, but I launched into a coughing fit.

His arm looped around my waist, and he swam toward the

shallows as I sucked in air. Once I'd recovered enough to say something, he swung me around and pressed his mouth to mine.

His tongue parted my lips forcefully, and I obliged, meeting his urgent kiss like this might be our one chance together. Our movements were frantic, driven by a need to close the distance between us. Heat pooled between my legs as I dug my fingers into his back and pulled myself as near to him as I could. Never had I been so turned on.

I moaned as his hand grasped my tangled locks, tilting my head at just the angle he needed to drink me in. My skin felt raw from the friction of his stubble, but I didn't care. I reached up and gripped his hair, holding him in place as I worked my mouth against his.

Everything about this felt right, like this was meant to happen. If Jaxson ruined all future sex for me, so be it. Right now, I needed him more than I needed breath itself.

But just as quickly as his lips had claimed mine, he pulled away, his hand still holding the back of my head. I drew in a ragged breath, thankful for the momentary reprieve but pissed that his mouth wasn't on mine.

"There's nothing I want more than to have you, Savannah. But trust me when I tell you that this can't happen tonight." He dragged his thumb over my lower lip, his honey eyes intense and full of lust. "And when I finally do claim you, it won't be when we're drunk on fairy wine."

Damn it all to hell.

40

Jaxson

Savannah's lips were plump from our kiss, her breathing heavy as she stared at me with disappointment. She was fucking gorgeous. "Then you better let me go, Jaxson, because I'm not in control of my body right now."

Her words were truer than she realized, I thought, biting back the curse that rose in my throat. I tried to push away, but my fingers sank into her skin, and my hold on her was stronger than before.

Fuck. The fates were in control now.

"I don't think I can do that," I said, my voice gravelly.

Savannah arched her brow, her pupils fully dilated and her skin flushed. "What are you suggesting?"

Her palms pressed against my chest, and though we were standing waist deep in the water, I could still smell and feel her damn heat. Like a drug, it was clouding my judgement.

I slipped my hand around her ass and lifted her to me. Just because I couldn't fuck her didn't mean we couldn't do other things.

Savannah wrapped her legs around me and moaned as she

pressed her heat into me. Thank fuck I'd left my jeans on, or all bets would have been off.

Cupping the back of her head with my free hand, I drew her mouth to mine, this time with less urgency. I brushed my lips against hers, inhaling and memorizing every note of her citrus sunshine scent. Her body fit so perfectly against mine, and though I knew it was only because of our bond, I couldn't deny how right she felt.

I nipped her lower lip, and then gently parted her lips with my tongue, tasting her desire.

"Jaxson, I want you," she whispered breathlessly into my mouth.

Releasing my fingers from her hair, I kissed her neck, dragging my tongue over her salty skin. She tasted so fucking good, I wanted to lick every inch of her.

"Tell me what you want, darling," I purred, delighting in the way her body quivered under my touch.

"You. Inside me. Now," she panted, arching her spine and exposing her neck to me.

My wolf surged against my chest at the sight, desperate to claim his mate. My intentions to move slowly were extinguished by the growing desire I felt building in both of us. With a quick movement, I positioned Savannah on my knee, supporting her back while I drew my other hand down between her breasts, following the curve of her body to the apex of her thighs. The sight of her hard nipples under the black lace threatened to send me over the edge, and a savage heat coiled inside of me.

She spread her legs, giving me access, and as my fingers slid under her panties and slipped inside of her, I felt just how ready she was.

"Fuck," I growled. My jeans were suddenly painfully restricting.

"Yes," Savannah groaned as I worked her heat, following

every whimper and shiver until she was on the edge. And so was I.

She slipped her arm between us and unfastened my jeans, then took my length in her hand. With a moan, she ground her hips against me, her body trembling as her fingers deftly stroked me. The forest around us faded away as my desire intensified to an agonizing height.

When she dropped her head back and screamed my name, my release hit me like an explosion tearing across every nerve ending in my body. Pure ecstasy like I'd never experienced before pulsed through me. I felt like a godsdamned teenager.

What the fuck?

My chest heaved as I cradled Savannah's spent body, our breaths mixing. She straightened her spine and looked up at me with a vixen smile. "That was amazing."

It was. Better than any sex I'd ever had. And that was alarming. Whatever connection I'd felt with Savannah had now grown tenfold, and I knew for certain that the image of me deep inside her would relentlessly haunt my thoughts until I gave in.

"*You* are amazing." I drew her close and kissed her gently, nipping her lower lip before releasing her and lifting her out of the water onto the grass. I kissed the pale skin of her inner thighs, feeling heat coil inside of me again. "Now *I* need a dip to cool off."

I pushed away from her, and she smirked at me. "You sure you don't want company?"

Hell, I could smell her own budding desire.

"You're torturing me," I grunted, not sure how strong my willpower was. Something had changed.

I turned and dove underwater, trying to focus on anything but the sweet taste of her mouth and the slick wetness I'd found between her legs.

I was a fucking goner.

When I surfaced, Savannah was lying on the grass, one knee raised as she gazed at the heavens. I finished cleaning up and climbed out.

Settling next to her, I scooped her up. She nestled her head on my shoulder and draped her leg over mine. Where there had been electricity before, there was now only the low thrum of a current passing between our skin.

"This was a good night." She sighed, resting her hand on my chest. I could smell her contentment, or maybe it was mine.

I traced her back, watching the stars above as my thoughts churned.

Savannah was everything my body desired. But she was like a bottle of fine wine. Every sip I took, the more I wanted, and the further from reality I slipped. From *responsibility*—my responsibility to my endangered pack. Theirs was the only future that mattered. While I might want Savannah, I had to think on behalf of thousands more.

I was bewitched and drunk. And I needed to sober up.

We had to find a cure for her condition. When she returned to being only a sorcerer, only a LaSalle, then maybe the bond would be severed, and I could resist her siren call.

But she's ours.

Savannah's soft snores filled the silence, and I smiled.

And froze.

"Savy, wake up!" I jerked upright, grabbing her shoulders, but her eyes were shut, her mind somewhere distant.

Then she began to fade away.

41

Savannah

I breathed in Jaxson's signature and sighed, letting my mind drift.

Everything felt right, for once.

Wake up!

My wolf's warning echoed through my mind, but I didn't want to. Jaxson and I were wrapped in a marvelous dream of dancing and swimming and kissing, and I never wanted to wake.

Suddenly, the firm warmth of his body was gone, replaced by rough ground and a seeping cold. I shivered as a chill brushed over my skin. Why was I so cold?

I opened my eyes and blinked, but there was only darkness. I reached out for Jaxson, but I was alone. Fear strangled my heart, and I bolted upright.

"Jaxson!" I searched the pitch-black void—a dark so deep that it made my skin tingle. The stars and moon and lights of the maenad's revel were gone, and the only sound was the faint echo of my voice.

Where the hell was I?

Calm down, Savy, and think.

The last thing I remembered was holding Jaxson, my cheek pressed to his warm chest. And then I'd closed my eyes...

Oh, no.

The maenad's warning echoed through my mind: *don't fall asleep.*

Fuck. I'd drifted off, and now I was God-knows-where.

My ass cheeks ached from the rocks that were jabbing into my backside, and the ground was damp and muddy. A faint but omnipresent sound of dripping water was maddening with my heightened hearing.

Don't panic.

I just needed to figure out where I was and then find a way out. That was possible, right?

I climbed to my feet, cursing when I realized that all I was wearing was my lacy underwear. Not good.

My eyes started to adjust to the darkness. A faint purple glow began to form shadows, and I could discern the muddy, root-ridden walls that rose around me.

I fought the fear that surged in my heart. I was entombed in the fucking earth, barefoot and practically naked.

Things could always be worse. Maybe.

My light source was traces of bioluminescent lichen that speckled the walls. At least it was something.

A steady current of fresh air blew through the passage, and a sliver of hope welled up in my chest. If there was air, then there'd be an opening, a way out.

I thanked the fates for my new wolf senses. One time only.

Gingerly shuffling forward, I began making my way toward the source of the air. It was slow going, but after a few minutes, my vision adjusted, and I'd blocked out the dull pain in my soles. I had to scramble over collapsed piles of stone and squeeze through a knifelike gap in the rocks, leaving scratches across my stomach and bruises on my knees.

Covered in scrapes and mud, I finally emerged into a forked passage. I paused. I'd seen this place before in a vision. When I'd last scried on the sorcerer right before we'd ambushed Billy's cabin. Fear crept under my skin. Both ways were constricted, but the current of air was blowing from the one on the left.

I started that way but froze as a faint murmur of whispers stilled my heart. What the hell was that? I craned my neck and listened. Words, but too subtle to make out.

I glanced at the passage to my left, the way out of this nightmare, and then at the passage to my right, the one with the voices, beckoning me to follow.

I had the uneasy feeling that I wasn't here by coincidence. I had no idea why, but something had pulled me here. My own intentions? Or perhaps another's?

While the way out was to the left, it wasn't the way that led to answers.

"Fuck," I murmured as I shook off my misgivings and went right, slowly making my way into the darkness with the voices.

This was how stupid people in horror flicks got themselves killed, I thought. But something inside of me, urged me to follow the whispers. A sixth sense.

Or a death wish.

The roots in the walls thickened as the voices grew louder, but still, I couldn't discern their words. As I pressed further into the underground hell, the smell of sweat and grime burned my throat. What was that?

My heart pounded against my ribs as I followed the musk, and then I froze.

Lining the walls of the cave, wrapped in roots, were bodies.

Horror coursed through me as I gazed up at the clusters of suspended people. Their skin was ashen and smudged with dirt, and apart from the barely perceptible rise and fall of their chests, they appeared dead.

I moved closer and sucked in a sharp breath when I recognized the face of a woman—one of the sleepers Jaxson had shown me on his laptop. These were the shifters who'd fallen under the sorcerer's curse.

I reached out to touch her, but a familiar voice stopped me: "Savannah, you know what they say. Let sleeping wolves lie."

My heart clenched.

Kahanov.

I slowly turned as his foul signature buffeted my senses.

"You bastard." My nailbeds itched, and my wolf stirred.

"I had a dream I would see you again," Kahanov said. "Funny how interesting dreams can get when they become real. What brings you here, anyway?"

I tensed to leap, but he whipped up a hand that erupted in green flame. "Ah, ah, ah. I could've already killed you where you stand, but I want you alive. We need to talk."

I froze. How fast could he move?

"Release the wolves," I snapped, trying to buy myself time to think.

"No. Not until you give me yours."

What the hell did he mean?

I'll rip his throat out! my wolf snarled in my mind.

My canines shot down, and hair erupted along my arms. I gasped as my shoulders started to stretch, but I shoved my wolf back and stopped the transformation.

"Wrestling with your better nature?" Kahanov laughed. "It's such a tragic thing."

I circled him cautiously, and he shifted, keeping himself out of reach. "I hate to see you burdened by your wolf, Savannah."

"You did this to me! You turned me into a fucking monster!" I snarled as bitterness flashed under my skin.

His lips pulled into a deranged smile. "Me? Not at all. You'll have to blame someone else for that. But I *can* help you get rid of your little wolf problem, if that's what you're aiming for."

My skin crawled under his gaze. "Fuck you. Stay the hell away from me."

He parted his hands, though the flames persisted. "Steady on. We can put our differences aside and help each other. You have something that you don't want—a wolf—which just so happens to be what I need. Give me the Soul Knife, and I can free you from your beastly burden, once and for all. Everything will go back to the way it was."

The way it was. What a foreign thought. I wanted that so desperately—to not be ruled by another spirit, to not have to worry about hiding the monster that I'd become. She wasn't supposed to be inside me. We were complete opposites, and she fought me at every turn. I was broken, and maybe this was a chance to fix that.

Don't you dare, my wolf growled.

But I couldn't, could I? She wasn't a part of me—yet she *was* part of me, bonded in some twisted way.

Doubts whirled through my mind, and I desperately needed to keep Kahanov talking until I could figure out a way out of this mess. "Why my wolf? You're surrounded by werewolves. Why me?"

"Because you're different, and your wolf is different." The flames surrounding his hands flickered in his eyes, and the air hung with rage. "Because your family took mine and left me incomplete, forced me to inhabit this pathetic shell of a body. This is their fault, but you can fix it. Just tell me where the *fucking* knife is."

"No," my wolf and I growled together.

"Okay, Savannah, how about I sweeten the pot?" He strode toward the sleeping shifters and drew his fingers through the hair of a man in his twenties. "You give me your wolf, and I'll let you and all these people go. I'll swear a blood oath on it. If you don't—well, I can't ensure their safety."

My stomach dropped.

I had to do something.

My wolf reared up in my chest, and I stumbled backward. *I'll fucking tear your throat out if you hand him that knife*, she said.

"I'm not giving up the knife!" I shouted, both to him and to my wolf, as I wrestled for control.

"Fine. I guess we'll have to do this the hard way." He dismissed the flame from his hand, drew a vial of red liquid from his pocket, and took a sip. Magic swirled around him, and he raised a hand. "Stop."

To my horror, I froze in place. I could feel his magic inside me. In my blood. My eyes darted to the vial.

He grinned as a trickle of red slipped from his lip. "You forget—I'm a blood sorcerer, and I have your blood. Now, let's start with something simple. What are you doing in the Dreamlands?"

"Visiting Cavra," I said before I could even attempt to resist. I clapped my hands over my mouth.

His eyes widened. "*Cavra*? You little minx..." Suddenly, he stiffened as a realization struck him. "What did she ask of you?"

"The bloodstone," I replied through clenched teeth, willing my voice to be silent.

Kahanov swore and spat, then stepped closer to me and lowered his voice. "Tell me where the Soul Knife is."

"It's here," I heard myself say.

He laughed. "Really? Clever girl. Show it to me."

I fought his control, but my blood began to boil.

Help me, I begged my wolf.

I felt her strength rise within, a snarled torrent of rage. *Tell that bastard to—*

"Fuck off!" we roared together as my body shook with her fury.

"So much stronger now!" Kahanov hissed. Then he gritted his teeth and pointed his finger at me. I felt his signature surge, a vile, dominating presence pushing down on me from every direction.

I let out a single sob of frustration as my resistance broke, and I summoned the Soul Knife. The cursed thing materialized in my hand in a swirl of purple smoke.

My heartbeat raced. It was happening all over again, just as he had dominated me in my room. Every muscle strained in protest.

He opened his palm. "Give it to me. Put it in my hand."

He was so powerful, I knew that even with the strength of my wolf, I couldn't resist.

But his words gave me a slender opening.

"Here, asshole!" I lunged and put the blade in his hand—point first. The vial shattered in a burst of glass and blood, and he screamed in rage.

A green wall of fire erupted from his hands. The shockwave seared my skin and threw me backward. I crashed into the wall and gasped as roots dug into my spine.

"Give me the damn knife!" Kahanov sprang forward and grabbed my wrist, but I kneed him in the groin.

He roared and, seizing me by my waist, threw me to the ground.

I screamed as the rocks jabbed into my side, but I kept my hold on the Soul Knife.

A crazed grin cut his face, and he lifted his arm and pointed at me.

Run, Savy. Get out of here, my wolf shouted in my mind.

The panic in her voice sent a fresh wave of alarm through me. I rolled onto my knees, but as I was climbing to my feet, his magic slammed me back against the wall. Piercing pain shot through my wrist, and the Soul Knife flew from my grasp. It clattered against the ground, and Kahanov laughed, delight clear in his voice, as he raced toward it.

Get out of here. NOW! My wolf pressed against my ribs.

No. This had to end.

As Kahanov bent down to scoop up the knife, I launched forward, crashing into his back. The force knocked him off balance, and together, we hurtled to the ground.

He grunted and cursed, then swung his elbow back, catching me square in the cheekbone. My adrenaline and fear dulled the pain, though, and I grabbed a fistful of his hair and slammed his face into the dirt. "Die, you psycho prick!"

He roared and swung his arm around. I didn't see the blade until it sank into my thigh. Searing pain shot through my leg, and my vision doubled.

As Kahanov pulled the knife free, I slammed my hand into him and released an uncontrolled burst of magic. He flew back as I scrambled backward across the floor of the cave. My chest heaved, and I shook my head, trying to quiet the tortuous noises in my mind.

I can still summon—

Before I had time to act, pain shot through me as the bones in my body began snapping. A scream tore from my throat, and I couldn't be sure who it belonged to, me or my wolf.

When the agony subsided, I looked up at Kahanov through wolf's eyes.

He was laughing like a goddamned maniac.

We're injured, and he's too strong, I said to my wolf. *We need to get out of this cave.*

But she didn't respond. Not to me, at least. She bared her teeth and snarled, then attacked. The metallic taste of blood filled our mouth as she sank her teeth into his skin.

Her elation mixed with my panic. Kahanov still had the Soul Knife.

Get us out of here! I screamed to my wolf.

But it was too late. The blade sank deep, and we howled in agony. Then a wave of magic burst into us, and we were hurled backward through the air. The wall of the cave broke our flight, and the impact sent a wave of pain through our ribs.

Yet my wolf climbed to her feet and met Kahanov's murderous gaze.

"Come here, little wolf. You belong with me," he growled. "Savannah doesn't respect you, but I will. You can be free, just come to me."

For a second, terror seized me, drowning out the pain. I was helpless and out of control.

But then my wolf turned and bolted down the cave.

Green flames licked at our heels, but we were faster than him, even cut and bleeding.

We didn't slow. The fork in the passage appeared ahead, and the scent of briny sea air pulled us forward.

She darted down the passage that I should have taken from the start, and after a few minutes, light appeared, then the azure blue of water.

Thank God.

42

The sun was high in the sky, and the brightness in contrast to the darkness of the cave was painfully blinding. Fresh air had never tasted so good. Relief flooded me at being out of that cave, but where the hell were we?

My wolf sniffed the air, then took off down the pebble beach. She was remarkably quiet, which was unusual.

Are you okay? I asked. *Where are we going?*

Now you're concerned about me? she responded. *You were ready to hand me over to that asshole.*

I would never! I insisted, but I sensed she didn't believe me, and maybe she was right not to. She stumbled slightly but pushed on, despite the pain of our open wounds.

Where are we going? I asked.

Getting help. Be quiet. I need to focus. She sniffed the air, then hurried onward.

I guessed she was giving me a taste of my own medicine. I shut up and let her guide us down the beach. We were tired, and the wounds on our thigh and shoulder throbbed.

Fear tore at me. *Kahanov will be hunting us.*

Silence.

Finally, a few cabins appeared among the pines along the shore. She limped into the trees and sneaked through the shadows toward the closest cabin.

What are we doing? I asked.

Get clothes. Become human. Find Jaxson. Her thoughts were tired and broken.

At least she was willing to hand over control.

Guilt tugged at me.

She slinked behind a bush, and then I saw where we were headed. A clothesline was strung between two trees, loaded with at least ten sets of clothes. Mercifully, there was a pair of leggings and a sweater that looked vaguely close to my size. My wolf leapt up and grabbed them with her teeth, and then slunk back into the bushes.

Once she'd put some distance between us and the cabin, she stopped and dropped the clothes. *Your turn*, she said, utterly exhausted.

Never had she been so willing to shift back to human form. I was both shocked and saddened. That fight had taken a little of the fire out of her.

Let's do this. Quickly, this time, I told her, worried that it might not work without Jaxson here. But what choice did we have?

My wolf lowered herself to the ground, and then our body strained as the shift took hold. I gritted my teeth as I jerked and bent, and the horrors of the shift began. I had to stifle a scream as I felt the ligaments and muscles in my legs and arms tearing, and the wounds in my skin reopened.

Pain blotted out my thoughts. Why wasn't it over? The shift to wolf form had been fast.

But the agony only increased. We were stuck between forms. Dread coiled in my chest.

We need Jaxson, my wolf snarled in pain.

Like hell we do! Jaxson wasn't in control of our body.

I tried to calm my mind so I could let the shift take me. My wolf seemed to sense my cue and settled, and we both embraced the pain that worked through our body.

This time, when our joints popped and sinews stretched, the agony eased until it was gone.

Panting, I finally opened my eyes and stared up at the trees. The pine branches swayed in the ocean wind.

"We did it," I whispered and rolled onto my hands and knees.

I was exhausted and achy, and pangs of hunger knotted my stomach. I glanced down at the wound on my bare thigh where Kahanov had sliced me with the Soul Knife. The skin was red and inflamed, but the bleeding had stopped. Maybe my wolf's healing power was kicking in.

"Well, we could have gotten off worse," I muttered as I inspected my naked body.

Speak for yourself, my wolf piped up. *I need food and rest.*

I smiled. "You and me both, sister."

My shoulder was swollen, my ribs bruised. There were cuts all over my body, but the only ones that weren't healing quickly were those made by the Soul Knife...which Kahanov now had. I tried to summon it, but nothing happened. I could still feel my bond with the blade, but I was too far away.

Shit!

I'd failed to kill him, and now I'd lost the knife. My stomach clenched as the weight of failure pressed upon my heart. I wiped the tears from the corners of my eyes.

Hey, we lived. We broke that vial of blood. And we can get the knife back. Focus on the task at hand. Find Jaxson, my wolf said calmly.

My heart warmed. If she could think clearly, then so could I.

I staggered to my feet. I needed to call Jaxson to tell him

where I was—so where the hell was I? My ears picked up the sound of cars on a road, so I headed that way.

When I finally reached the highway, I stuck out my thumb. I was barefoot, scraped up, wearing twigs in my hair and clothes that clearly didn't match. I looked like a survivor of a plane crash.

Hey, at least you're cute enough to make it work, my wolf chirped.

Where was this positive attitude before? I asked, annoyed.

You didn't need it then.

I wasn't sure how to interpret that.

Thirty minutes later, I caught a ride with an older man in a Crown Victoria. Old Savannah would have never hitchhiked, but the man seemed harmless, and if he'd turned out to be a serial killer, I would have just clawed him to pieces.

Luckily, he was genuinely nice and helpful, and I learned that I was in Washington. I'd never been to the Pacific Northwest, but I decided I liked it, and so did my wolf.

Lots of good smells in the woods here. Let's not go back to Chicago.

It was tempting to hide out here so I'd never have to face my werewolf-hating family or the psychopath sorcerer or my condition. If only I could just forget it all and start a new life.

Or we'll be a wolf all the time, and you can be a human when the moon is full.

Deep down, we both knew there was no escaping things.

The chatty old guy dropped me off at a strip mall in a small town called Forks. He even gave me twenty bucks to grab a bite to eat.

I ordered a large turkey club from Subway and put on my best smile when I asked the cashier to borrow his phone. Thankfully, he was a teenage boy, and I could tell he had the hots for me. He unlocked the phone, and I slid into a booth and pulled up Google. I hadn't memorized Jaxson's or Casey's numbers, so I looked up the number for Eclipse.

As the phone rang, I prayed to God that Jaxson was there and not still stuck in the Dreamlands. Just the thought of that place had my mind wandering, and I couldn't shake the image of Jaxson's lips pressed against mine as his fingers worked me in all the right places. Had that really happened, or was it all just a dream?

My cheeks blazed when I realized that my skin was flushed and there was a mounting tightness in my center.

Jaxson's rough voice answered, and tingles worked their way up my thighs.

"Jaxson, thank fuck," I blurted, clenching my legs together.

"Savannah! Where are you?" His words vibrated with agitation and exhaustion.

"I'm in Forks, Washington," I answered. "And I found the bastard."

43

Jaxson

I pulled into the crowded parking lot of the strip mall, my frustration mounting. Why was this small town so packed? Who'd ever heard of Forks?

I ground my teeth.

Savannah was close. The bond between us was taut and pulling uncomfortably in my chest.

I had to get to her. She was hurt and alone, and it was all my fault. I'd let my guard down. I'd lost my focus while drunk on wine and lust, and I'd let her fall asleep. After she'd disappeared, I'd nearly turned Cavra's revel into a bloodbath before getting a hold of Sorsha and exiting the Dreamlands. I'd woken in the tent, but Savannah was gone.

I'd been almost overcome with relief when I'd heard her voice on the phone. She'd survived, but that didn't absolve me of anything.

"Do you think she's still here?" Neve asked. As soon as I'd gotten off the phone with Savannah, I'd grabbed Sam and headed to Neve. She'd used her planes-walking powers to teleport us to SeaTec airport, the closest location she was familiar with.

"Yes, she's here," I growled as I wedged the rental SUV into a handicap spot.

Sam raised her eyebrows and glanced at Neve. "Somebody's in a rush. I think we'll give you two a mo—"

I was out of the SUV and striding across the lot before she finished.

The bell of the door rang as Savannah stepped out of the Subway. She was barefoot and dressed in black leggings and a poorly fitting sweater. Her gaze instantly locked on me, and my heart missed a beat.

She'd known I was here. Was she also feeling the pull of our bond?

I wove through the parking lot. A car slammed on its brakes and squealed to a halt in front of me as I crossed the street. The driver blared the horn, but I paid him no attention.

Savannah leapt into my arms as the driver gave one last defiant honk. I shot him a look that stilled his heart and had him throwing his car into reverse. I pulled Savannah close, burying my face in her hair. Her familiar scent wound around me, and my wolf stirred, excitement filling us both.

"Glad you're here," she whispered.

I set her down, and anger surged through me when I noticed the swollen red welt on her cheekbone and the scrapes on her skin.

"Are you hurt?" I gently cupped her cheek. My voice was ragged, strained by the emotions flooding through me—relief, contentment, desire, anger. And most of all, guilt.

Fuck, it was too much.

"Just a little bruised and tired."

Exhaustion pulled her shoulders down, and I could tell she was lying about the severity of her wounds.

My chest churned with guilt and shame. I should have been more careful, should have protected her.

I shook my head. "I'm sorry—sorry you had to face Kahanov alone, sorry I let my guard down, sorry for what happened in the fore—"

Her cheeks flushed and she lowered her eyes, cutting my words short. "So that *did* happen."

My pulse raced.

Gods, the woman was getting under my skin. What had happened between us couldn't happen again. I knew I was playing with fire, and I needed to shut this down before it got any more complicated.

We'd deal with Kahanov, then we'd cure Savannah. Once she was no longer a wolf and the mate bond was broken, we'd be free of these irrational emotions.

Lies.

"The Dreamlands is just that—a dream that's best forgotten. Kahanov almost got you, and every second we linger, he might slip away. Come on." I nodded toward the SUV and walked away. She trailed behind, and I could smell her offense and anger.

Good. It was better if she hated me. It'd be easier for both of us.

The SUV's taillights went on as we approached, which meant Sam had slipped into the driver's seat, forcing me to share the back with Savannah.

Shit. It wasn't the time for her to play matchmaker. The emotions flooding me were too intense, and I needed space. That, and I needed to heal Savannah, and sitting side by side wasn't going to make that any easier to deal with.

"Wait." I turned and stopped Savannah as she approached the SUV. I placed my hand on the small of her back, and she gasped as I poured a short burst of healing magic into her.

Though it weakened me each time I used it, it would cure a few of her cuts, and hopefully, her exhaustion.

Her eyes dilated with surprise, and I could smell her undeniable arousal. "Did you just...heal me?"

"You need to be on your A-game for what's coming. I could tell you weren't."

Savannah's eyes turned cold, and the scent of her desire waned. Good. It was going to be hard enough to think just sitting in the same car as her.

I opened the door for her, and she slipped into the back seat without sparing me a glance. I kicked Sam out of the front, loaded up, and gunned it out of the parking lot.

We headed out of town, looking for the place where Savannah had been picked up. My fists tightened on the wheel at the thought of her hitchhiking alone, but I pushed it from my mind.

Sam hefted a cheap gym bag onto Savannah's lap. "I brought you some spare clothes."

"Thanks," she said as she met my eyes in the rearview mirror. "I don't think I'll change right now, but I'd kill for some shoes."

"There's a pair of old sneakers."

I heard a zip as Savannah opened the bag. "Thank God, my feet are killing me and super gross. You're a saint, Sam. I owe you...like, a new wardrobe."

"Deal. We kill the sorcerer, and then you take me shopping. But for now, tell me how you lost your clothes in the first place."

As Savannah yanked on Sam's old sneakers, she gave us the details of everything she'd seen and what Kahanov had said.

"Apart from Kahanov and the sleeping shifters, did you see anything or anyone else in the cave?" I asked.

Savannah shook her head. "No, but I wasn't in there long. It looked like the place might go quite a ways back, though."

"If he's expecting us, I'm betting he's summoned some back-up," Neve said.

I tightened my grip on the wheel. "He's expecting us."

The bastard had been one step ahead of us the whole time. I hated going into his fucking lair, but I had to find my pack members before he learned the extent of what Cavra had done.

About thirty minutes down the road, Savannah leaned forward. "This looks familiar. I think I saw it on my way into town." She'd unclicked her seatbelt before I even finished pulling over. "Once we get to the beach, I should be able to find the cave again. It was crazy looking."

We climbed out, and I reined everyone in. "Okay. Backup is on its way, but for the moment, it's just us. We need to go in quietly and take him out as quickly as possible, or drive him back further into the caves, away from the sleeping wolves. Savannah, can you cloak us in shadows once we're inside?"

She nodded and led us past a few cabins along the forested slope toward the ocean. I could have followed the path just as easily myself. Her wolf had come this way, and the scent drove my own wolf to the edge of madness.

Savannah slid down a sandy rise onto a deserted beach. Stacks of sun-bleached driftwood scattered the waterline. After we'd walked at least a quarter mile down the rocky, empty stretch, she whispered, "There it is."

A chill ran up my spine.

A twisted, storm-hardened tree clung to the eroding coastal bluff, its roots framing a dark cave that looked like a hole leading to the heart of the earth. A steady breeze blew onshore, smelling of kelp and fish, and Savannah shivered as she stared at the entrance.

"I hate caves," she said.

Sam snorted. "You and me both."

But this place wasn't just a cave. It was an entrance into

something far worse. I could feel the magic radiating from the opening—a low, hypnotic pulse. I'd felt a similar pulse in the Dreamlands.

It was some kind of portal or rift between that strange realm and our own. It had to be, and that must have been how Savannah was able to physically exit the Dreamlands.

We began to move toward the cave, but I held up my hand and froze. A sickly-sweet scent of rotting fruit burned my nostrils, and my adrenaline surged.

I knew that smell all too well. A noctith demon.

In the darkness of the cave entrance, a shadow twisted and unfolded.

"Watch out!" I grabbed Savannah's waist and yanked her aside as the dark shape burst out of the cave.

Sam cursed and dove out of the way, while Neve launched skyward.

The monstrosity reared up on its six legs, and its head split open, revealing rows of pointed teeth. A pink gas billowed from its throat and spread across the ground.

I pulled Savannah along. "Sleeping gas! Run!"

Sam scrambled to her feet, but just as the gas was about to consume her, a wind tore across the muddy beach.

Neve. She floated in the air, hands outstretched, and called a gale.

Flying sand and grit cut into my skin, and I had to brace myself to hold us upright, but the gas dissipated instantly.

The noctith demon staggered back and dug its clawed feet into the earth. Then it shrieked into the howling wind.

Savannah clutched her ears and doubled over in agony, and as my eardrums burst, I felt a warm trickle of blood seeping down the side of my neck.

Gritting my teeth against the pain, I ran and leapt into Neve's torrent of wind and sailed through the air. The second I landed on the demon's back, I sank my claws into its segmented carapace. The thing was momentarily shocked by the impact, but then it let out another shriek, and its body thrashed.

I dug my claws deeper and began tearing off pieces of its hard exoskeleton. It screeched louder and bucked, and one of its hairy legs reached up and gripped my calf. I snarled as its claws tore into my muscles. My grip loosened, and I was thrown sideways. I slashed one of the beast's wings before I hit the ground hard, my shoulder screaming.

The demon tilted its head back and opened its razor-lined mouth, but its shriek was cut short.

"You guys go! I'll take care of this thing!" Neve roared. Her voice shook the air like a thunderclap, and her eyes burned with fury. Her hand stretched toward the demon, whose neck was throbbing and spasming. She slammed the beast down onto the ground, and it clawed at the sand and rocks with its legs and tail.

She was suffocating the thing with her magic.

Savannah gaped in horror. I grabbed her hand and towed her into the cave after Sam.

Darkness enveloped us.

44

My ears rang, and I shook with fright at what I'd just witnessed.

Between Neve and the demon, I didn't know which terrified me more.

Kahanov.

I sucked in a slow breath to steady my nerves as we moved deeper into the cave. What the hell was I doing? I'd just escaped from this nightmarish place, and now I was headed back in.

I rubbed my ears, but nothing would get rid of the pain. Suddenly, I felt the light touch of Jaxson's hand on the base of my back. I took a sharp breath and closed my eyes as his magic pulsed through me. The pain in my ears subsided, but my heartbeat still pounded.

"Stay close," he said gruffly as he flicked on a flashlight and stepped in front of me. His woodsy pine scent wrapped around me, and a deep ache settled in my chest at the memories that rose in my mind.

Sam pulled out two flashlights and gave me one as we followed behind him.

Jaxson's power to heal me drove me to the edge of fury. I hated the way it aroused me, the way I suddenly found myself warm and wet and breathless. Fuck.

I bared my teeth at his back. He'd made his position clear: what had happened in the Dreamlands stayed in the Dreamlands. Wasn't that what I wanted, too?

What an idiot, I thought. I should have known better than to have opened myself up to him like that.

Do you ever stop thinking about him? my overly snarky wolf asked.

She was right. I needed to get my head in the game, but that was the last place it wanted to be. As long as I distracted myself with Jaxson, I wouldn't have to think about walking into doom.

I could smell it on the air. The cruel death the fates had planned for me. I didn't care anymore. Just as long as I got to take Kahanov down.

The dripping of water grew louder as we pushed deeper into the cave.

I glanced back toward the entrance, fear fluttering in my stomach. We'd left Neve to deal with the noctith demon, but after seeing what she could do, something told me she could take care of herself even if its friends showed up.

Jaxson stopped abruptly.

"What's that?" Sam whispered behind me.

I inclined my head and listened. A low, faint scraping noise came from the passage ahead.

"It sounds like something scratching or digging," Jaxson said.

Hope and dread flared in my chest, and I cautiously stepped around Jaxson. "Maybe Cavra's spell woke the shifters. They might be trying to get free."

It was a long shot, but if there was any chance, we had to get them out of there before Kahanov noticed. I drew the shadows around me and sneaked ahead down the hallway.

"Savannah, wait," Jaxson hissed as he grabbed for my arm.

I slipped out of his grasp and pushed forward, moving toward the fork in the cave that I knew was ahead. I flicked off my flashlight. "I've got this. I'm practically invisible."

"Damn it," he growled behind me, and I could smell his frustration. But he wasn't my alpha—or at least he wouldn't be for long—and he held no power over me.

I ignored my wolf's snicker and paused where the tunnel split to let my werewolf vision adjust to the darkness. The stink of sweat and bodies was so strong, I almost gagged.

I peeked into the cavern, and my heart dropped. The sleepers still hung from the walls, roots snaking around their bodies. They hadn't awakened. Their chests still rose and fell softly like they were deep in a dreamless sleep. The strange scratching sound wasn't coming them, but from the roots digging into dirt.

I covered the end of my flashlight with my hand, flicked it on, and let a thin ray slide over the cave walls.

The sorcerer wasn't here, just slumbering wolves.

I breathed a long sigh of relief, and waved Sam and Jaxson into the room. "The coast is clear."

Sam froze as the beam of her flashlight illuminated the suspended bodies, "My gods..."

A dark rage spread across Jaxson's face as he shone his light from one body to the next. The muscles in his arms twitched as his signature boomed around us. My body trembled even as heat pooled in my center.

Shit, my wires were seriously crossed.

"We need to get them out of here," Jaxson growled.

Sam shot forward and began pulling the roots away from the closest shifter. "How are they here and in Magic Side as well?"

I could hear her heartbeat and practically taste her panic.

"I think we're in the Dreamlands," Jaxson whispered as he counted the figures. "Shit. It's not everyone."

The Dreamlands? Fuck. I helped Sam rip the roots from around the sleeping body as a shudder worked its way up my spine. The moment I pulled the last root free, the woman's eyes shot open, and I gasped.

She turned her head as if looking at someone behind my shoulder. "Mary? Where am I? I was having a nightmare..."

Then the sound of her voice and her form faded away into nothing.

"What just happened?" Sam asked, stunned.

"I think she woke up," I whispered as I looked from Sam to Jaxson. Suddenly, I was certain of what was going on. "Jaxson's right. This isn't just a cave in Forks. It's a portal to the Dreamlands. If we free the people here, they'll wake in the real world."

Jaxson spun his light around the room. "We need to cut these people down before Kahanov returns."

A familiar chuckle sounded from the passage ahead, and a sickening dread crawled down my spine.

"But that wasn't our deal, Jaxson."

I spun. Kahanov stood at the far end of the chamber with a shit-eating grin on his face.

Jaxson's claws extended. "This ends now, Kahanov. Release my pack."

"The deal was your shifters for the girl. Why would I release them when you haven't met my demand?" The sorcerer paused, and his eyes flicked to me. "Unless, of course, you've reconsidered."

Irrational dread flooded my veins. I knew Jaxson said he would never hand me over, but if it came down to several dozen members of his pack or me, would he really keep his word?

"Wrong answer." Jaxson dropped his light and bounded

forward in a blur of violence. The sickening sound of claws connecting with flesh was masked by Kahanov's scream.

Before I could react, a flash of green flame hurled Jaxson into a wall.

Sam rushed toward Kahanov, but he scrambled up the wall like a spider and out of her reach, then drew forth the Soul Knife. "Fine. That's the way you want to do it? Then I'll take what's mine. Savannah's soul."

He lunged for me, and I scrambled back. In my terror, I focused on one thing: summoning the knife to my hand.

With a puff of purple smoke, it vanished from his fist and appeared in mine.

Kahanov grinned as he leapt back to the wall. "What a clever trick, Savannah. I wish I'd thought to do that, too. Oh, wait. I did."

He snapped the blade back to his hand.

My jaw dropped as I looked down at my empty palm.

Shit. This is going to be a problem.

"Die, asshole!" Sam shouted as she pulled out her pistol. She braced it on her hand with the light and unloaded three rounds at him as he scrambled along the ceiling of the cavern. I flinched as the deafening gunshots rang through the cave, making my already damaged ears throb with pain.

I searched wildly for Kahanov, but he was gone.

"Fuck!" Jaxson shouted. "He ran."

He shone his light over the sleepers dangling from the wall. "Sam, get these people free. Savannah, you're with me. There aren't enough bodies. We need to find the rest of the pack and take Kahanov down. Time for stealth mode."

As Sam turned to the root-bound shifters, I drew the shadows around us, and we headed into the dark passage.

45

Jaxson

We wound our way through the jagged, twisting cave. A strange blue glow glazed the wall ahead with color. We moved cautiously until the narrow, rocky corridor bent and opened into a vast subterranean landscape that bathed us in eerie light.

Bioluminescent moss covered the walls and ceiling of the massive cavern, and its unearthly glow reflected off a shimmering pool that filled the center of the chamber. Gnarled trees with silver, tendril-like leaves grew around the edges of the water, and their roots snaked across the walls.

At any other time, it would have been breathtaking.

Savannah pointed. There, in the middle of the room, was the grimoire, floating in the air above the pond.

Still wrapped in Savannah's shadows, we stepped cautiously through the entrance, and guilt settled in my heart. I could already see that the roots of the trees around the pond entombed more sleepers. Many faces that I knew and loved, others less familiar.

All of them were my responsibility.

I looked behind us. A massive tree rose over the entrance, much like the one on the shore. It was the only exit.

Savannah's whisper echoed through the chamber. "Where is he?"

"I don't—"

Her scream cut me off, and I spun.

Hundreds of roots sprang out from the walls and started wrapping around her like the tentacles of some alien beast.

Dread and rage filled my chest, and I leapt forward with a growl. I released my claws and began ripping at the roots—but as soon as I did, new ones snaked around my own ankles.

Savannah had her claws out and was tearing through the roots as they grasped at her, but she couldn't keep up. My heart lurched as a tendril whipped around her neck and she gasped, "Jaxson!"

Fighting my way to her, I tore the root away from her throat and tried to pull her free, but two of the tendrils snaked around my arms and started dragging us apart.

"No!" I growled, my muscles straining.

Savannah summoned the Soul Knife to her hand and sliced through the roots binding her leg. They withered and died, and I heard the trees wail silently in my mind.

Suddenly, the knife vanished from her hand, and she gasped. The voice of the sorcerer echoed over the pond: "I'll be taking that."

I turned to see Kahanov standing by the edge of the water, next to a cluster of trees. He waved the knife.

"Screw you!" Savannah shouted from the knot of roots. The blade vanished and reappeared in her palm, and she began desperately cutting again as I fought my own restraints.

She would be a sitting duck if Kahanov attacked, but as long as I held my ground beside her and gave her time to cut herself free, he wouldn't be able to get close.

As if reading my mind, the sorcerer laughed. "Let's play a game. It's called 'Jaxson Makes a Choice.'"

He positioned his empty hand in front of the chest of a woman entwined in the roots of one of the silver trees. She wasn't any older than Savannah—maybe a year or two younger. Cara? I couldn't be sure.

"Touch her, and you're a dead man!" I bellowed.

Kahanov smiled. "The moment I summon the Soul Knife, I'll sever her spirit. So you get to choose: Savannah or her."

"Save her, Jaxson," Savannah said. "Save them all. *Please.*"

Her voice cracked with sadness, and the anguish and fear in her eyes was like a dagger to my heart.

The world spun. I was alpha, and my duty to the pack came above all else—but Savannah was my mate, and there was nothing I could do but protect her.

My wolf thundered inside me. *Kill him.*

Mindless rage churned in my body, and I unleashed a primal roar as I wrenched the roots from around my legs.

"Time's up!" The Soul Knife disappeared from Savannah's hand and appeared in Kahanov's. He rammed it through the woman's chest, and a trail of smoke rose from the dagger as he yanked it back. The woman's sleeping eyes shot wide, and her mouth opened in a silent scream.

Savannah's cry of despair echoed through the chamber as she summoned the blade back from Kahanov's hand and began cutting frantically at the roots.

The woman faded away, her body vanishing.

"No!" I roared as the roots snaked around my body and began squeezing like a vise, slowly dragging me toward the wall. They cut into my skin, but I couldn't feel the pain through my shock and rage.

Kahanov began to warily approach. "Once, I thought that if I could teach you to submit, you might be useful. But what kind of pathetic alpha are you? One who'd put a single foolish girl above your whole..."

The sorcerer paused mid-step, and then started to laugh. "*Oh*, this is too good. How did I not see it before? You two are fated! No wonder you're willing to let them all die. You don't have a choice."

"Fuck you!" I roared.

"What does he mean?" Savannah shouted as she ripped her claws into a root.

"It means he's about to watch all these poor souls die while futilely trying to save you," said Kahanov.

Planting my feet, I seized the biggest root I could find and began to pull. My body strained, but the walls of the cave shook, and dozens of rootlets ripped away as rocks tumbled to the ground.

I would rip this cavern down to protect her, if I had to.

The sorcerer laughed as he leapt to another rootbound wolf. "Who's next?"

Tears filled Savannah's eyes, and she stopped struggling. My stomach clenched as roots wound around her instantly and started pulling her in.

I strained to get to her. "Don't you dare stop fighting!"

"Trust me, I'm not," she rasped. "He needs me alive. I'm buying you time to save your pack. I'll save myself."

With that, she let the roots flow over her, and panic seized me. I released the massive root and grabbed her hand. She screamed as the tendrils pulled her in.

Agony and guilt tore through my body as her hand slipped from mine. In the split second before it vanished, the Soul Knife appeared in her grasp.

Then she was gone.

Rage like I'd never known surged up from my soul. I ripped

away the roots around me and fought my way forward. "I'll fucking kill you, Kahanov!"

"Not quite, Jaxson. I don't need you or these people anymore." Laughing, the sorcerer leapt to the walls and unleashed a searing blast of flame, setting my clothes alight. I growled with pain and tore free of the roots around me even as my skin burned away.

Almost blind with pain, I grabbed a torn root in my hand and whipped it at him. Kahanov's laugh was cut short as the whip wrapped around his leg. I pulled, and his body flew from the wall, crashing to the jagged stone of the cavern floor beside me.

I was on him in a second, ramming my claws into his body.

Warm blood splattered across my face.

He screamed, and a billowing cloud of fire burst around me. The blast sent me flying back, and I tumbled across the jagged floor of the cavern. Growling, I rose in time to see the sorcerer stagger to the base of a tree. I lunged, but the roots swallowed him whole.

Suddenly, I was alone. Savannah was gone. And Kahanov was gone.

The shock of it drove the breath from my lungs.

Panicking, I tried to find a way through the cluster where he'd disappeared, but there was only dirt behind the immobile wall of roots.

I tilted my head back and howled with rage.

As the reverberations died through the chamber, Savannah's words echoed in my mind: *I'm buying you time to save your pack.*

I looked to the faces of those I'd failed.

My heart clenched. The roots were moving and winding around their necks. Horror filled me, and the weight of what the sorcerer had said sank in: *I don't need you or these people anymore.*

I leapt for the nearest body and tore the roots from the man's throat as I shouted for Neve and Sam.

Savannah had bought my pack time. But time was running out.

46

Savannah

The writhing roots dragged my body downward through a long, snaking tunnel. I screamed as rocks ripped into my skin and tore my clothes. Suddenly, I was falling, and then agony shot up my spine as my body slammed into the ground.

Groaning, I rolled to my side. I was in a large, dark cavern. Small patches of bioluminescent moss cast a dim light, enough that my shadow magic let me see clearly in the dark.

Clutching my aching arm, I got to my feet and looked up. Far above, the hole I had fallen from was closing as roots filled the tunnel and knit together.

Panic fluttered in my chest, and I quickly searched the chamber for hidden exits but found none.

I was trapped.

At the far end of the cavern, another cluster of roots on the ceiling began to move. They slowly descended from the ceiling with Kahanov in their grasp.

He raised his hands, and three giant balls of light formed in the air, illuminating the dank interior cavern. "Ah, Savannah. Alone once again. This time, there's nowhere to run."

"Let me go, Kahanov, or I'll fucking kill you."

"Kahanov? Dear, no. You all keep calling me that, but Ulan hasn't been here for a long, *long* time. His body has been very useful, though."

I backed away and extended my claws. "What the fuck are you talking about, and why are you after me, you asshole?"

He summoned the knife as the roots set him down, and menace and foul magic vibrated the air. "Your family killed my wolf, and so I'm going to take yours in return. I'll be whole again, and then I'll bring your family and the Order and the pack to their knees. They'll beg the dark god for his mercy, but the only mercy we will offer is death."

The dark god? An image of the black wolf in the sky outside of my aunt and uncle's house filled my mind. But before I could process it, he lunged.

I spun away from the blade and suddenly extinguished the magic lights high overhead with my shadow magic.

Kahanov lurched forward, blinded for just a second.

I summoned the blade and struck.

Some sixth sense made him turn, and the tip only grazed his skin. He bellowed with anger and released a blast of green fire where I'd been—but I'd already moved away.

The blade vanished from my hands and reappeared in his.

He laughed. "You think you can hide in the dark, Savannah? You think that will save you?"

A stream of emerald fire poured from Kahanov's hands like the jet of a flame thrower. He spun, sweeping it through the room. I dove out of the way, but the flickering light betrayed my location.

I rolled to the side and tried to scramble out of his reach, but the knife found my shoulder in the fading light of the flames. White-hot searing pain shot through my body, but it was the agony in my soul that sent terror through my veins.

My wolf howled, and a deep sense of wrongness flowed through me as the knife caught on something that wasn't flesh— my soul.

Before he could strike again, I screamed as I rammed my claws into the bastard and sent him flying back across the room.

With my heart thundering in my ears, I crawled to my feet and stumbled deeper into the cave.

Kahanov looked down at the blood-covered knife in his hand and laughed maniacally.

"Come, now, Savannah, stop cowering in the shadows. I don't need to see you to hurt you. I'm a blood sorcerer, and as long as I have your blood, I can torture you all I want." Before I could react, he licked the blade, and the blood trickling down his fingers suddenly began to smoke.

Then it burst into flame.

I screamed in agony as the blood in my veins turned to fire. I staggered to my knees, gasping with pain.

Help me, I begged my wolf.

She growled in my mind. *We are wolfborn. Pain is part of who we are. It's nothing to us. Channel it, master it, like when we shift.*

I tried to master it, but I couldn't. It hurt too damned much.

Kahanov laughed again. "I've tasted your blood, and now I can sense where you are. Your shadows won't hide you anymore, little wolf."

The fire surrounding his hand went out, but the fire in my veins only worsened.

I lay gasping and choking as his magic incinerated me from the inside out. I had no idea how to fight this. His magic was living flames in my veins...

My breath caught. My aunt had taught me how to deal with fire. Could it work?

I steeled my mind and summoned my magic. The darkness trickled through me like ice water, slowly extinguishing the blaze within, just as I'd extinguished candles a thousand times before. Though the pain wasn't all gone, my mind flickered with a momentary sliver of clarity, and my vision cleared.

Fuck.

Kahanov was almost on top of me—creeping silently forward with the knife out, guided by my moans and by the pull of my blood. But why sneak?

It hit me like a flash.

He doesn't know I can see in the dark. He thought I was just hiding with my magic.

That was an opening. Hope pounding in my chest, I let my cries of pain lure him in like a siren's song.

Looming over my whimpering body, he raised his hand and rammed the Soul Knife down. His fist slammed into my chest...but it was empty because I'd summoned the blade to mine.

With a swift stroke, I drove the Soul Knife home, and Kahanov let out a blood-curdling shriek. I jerked it back to strike again, but the blade caught—not on flesh or bone, but on something deeper. Something primal.

Kahanov's soul.

I twisted the blade and pulled with all my strength. His flesh cut easily, but his soul didn't.

As he screamed, I instinctively poured my magic into the knife. The shadows drained from the room and flowed as billowing tendrils of black smoke poured into the blade itself. My arm went deathly cold, and the sorcerer howled.

And then his cry was cut short as his soul was severed, and the knife swung free.

I rolled away and tried to stand, but before I found my footing, a spectral shockwave rammed me back against the wall. My vision blurred, and the vibrations shook my head. Then an unearthly wail ripped through my mind.

The twisted form of a screaming face rushed toward me and dissipated into mist.

I'd seen that face before, but where?

The specter's wail lingered in my mind like an echo in a canyon, repeating five words over and over: *I will have my vengeance!*

My skin crawled with dread. What the hell was that? And what did it mean?

Nothing good, my wolf said. *Also, I don't think we're done here.*

Kahanov rolled over and gasped. "You bitch!"

His voice was somehow different with traces of an accent that hadn't been there before. Blood covered his chest and trickled from his mouth, and he began to crawl toward me like a deranged animal.

I backpedaled and leveled the knife at the creep. "You should be dead. I cut out your soul!"

"Not mine. Dragan's. And now, thanks to you, I'm free of him and bleeding to death."

Dragan? *Dragan.* The twisted, screaming face. I *had* seen it before...in my aunt's old clippings.

But Dragan was dead.

My mind reeled. I pulled my knife back, preparing to strike the moment he came near. "What the hell are you talking about?"

"The bastard's ghost possessed me. Ironically, he was the one who needed you alive. I don't."

None of this made any goddammed sense. "But...I just freed you!"

"What would you have me do, then? Let you drag me back to Bentham?" He chuckled in the darkness. "Thank you, Savannah. You've been useful. And now, the only thing I need you to do is die."

With a freakish burst of speed, Kahanov—the *real* Kahanov

—summoned the blade and charged toward the sound of my voice, lashing out recklessly like a rabid animal. Before I could call it back, the Soul Knife sank deep into my leg, and I gasped with pain. But at least it wasn't the soul-wrenching agony from earlier.

With a snarl, I twisted away, wrenching the hilt from his hand. Then I spun and rammed my elbow into his face and sent him flying back.

Blood gushed from the wound in my thigh. *Oh, shit.*

Kahanov staggered unsteadily on his feet and grinned with maniacal glee. He raised his hand. "Now this ends."

The blood still pouring from the knife wounds in my back and leg began to burn my skin. I looked down, and to my horror, the flowing rivulets began to writhe and take shape, bubbling and expanding until they had shifted from trickles of blood into a pair of crimson serpents.

I yelped and staggered back as the two blood snakes wrapped around me.

Panic clouding my thoughts, I tried to tear them away, but the serpents reared back and lashed out. One sank its fangs into my breast and the other into my back. Agony racked my body, and I stumbled into the wall.

I seized the one on my chest. It wrapped around my hand, and then it struck my face with unbelievable speed. Pain shot through my right eye, and half my vision turned red.

I stumbled to the ground in agony. My mind swam, and I couldn't think.

Embrace the pain, my wolf said as she suddenly seized control.

She didn't ease the transition but rather shifted in a single fell swoop.

Fur sprang from my skin, and my back twisted. My jeans and sweater tore, and my face lengthened into a muzzle as my fangs erupted. Unimaginable anguish ripped through my body, and in the span of two breaths, I'd transformed from girl to monster.

The snakes had lost their hold during the transformation. With lighting reflexes, my wolf clamped the larger serpent in our jaws and bit down. The snake's head was severed, and its body exploded in a spray of red.

Before the other snake could bite, my wolf dashed through the darkness. Even limping, she moved with utter silence.

Kahanov spun around slowly, listening and searching the darkness of the cavern.

As we crouched down, a pebble scrapped beneath our foot.

The sorcerer's head whipped toward us, and he unleashed a torrent of flame.

But my wolf didn't dodge it. With a howl of pain, we leapt through the inferno. Fur burning, we hurtled through the air and rammed our paws into Kahanov's chest, slamming him down onto his back.

He sank the Soul Knife into our belly, but my wolf ignored the pain. With a savage movement, she bit down on his throat.

And tore.

The metallic tang of blood coated our mouth, and I gagged as Kahanov's body twitched and then went deathly still.

My wolf rose, and we leaned against the wall, panting. *It's done. I can't climb. Can't take the knife. We need to shift.*

The horror of the moment was replaced by a new fear. *Shifting will kill us! We're bleeding out. We need to wait to heal*, I said.

My wolf weakly shook our head. *We're too hurt to heal. Have to risk it. Must find Jaxson, our mate. He can heal us.*

Our *what?*

She didn't wait to argue with me.

Agony tore through me as the shift began. My back arched and popped, and I howled as every wound we had taken cried out in agony. My forelegs lengthened into arms and hands, and my bloodstained fur withdrew into my skin.

Soon, I was human again, trembling and naked on my hands and knees. I had deep knife wounds in my gut and thigh and shoulder, but I still had my soul.

The world spun, and I hauled myself to my feet with a root and looked at the body of the sorcerer. Kahanov...or Dragan. Both. They had died as they had lived—stained with blood.

"Thank you," I whispered to my wolf as hope and sorrow overwhelmed me.

She whimpered. *Find Jaxson. Nothing else matters.*

For a second, doubt chilled my skin, but I shoved it away. Jaxson was still alive. He had to be. I knew it somehow in my soul.

The room rumbled, and dirt trickled from the ceiling. The place looked like it was going to cave in.

I looked up at the dense cluster of roots at the top of the chamber—the way I'd fallen in. "How the hell do I get out of here?"

You're the monkey—climb, my wolf said weakly. Joy raced through my heart. She still had a little strength for snark.

"Here goes nothing." I grabbed hold of the roots, then began to haul myself up.

I would never have been able to make the ascent without my claws and new werewolf strength. Even so, I was gravely wounded, and it took the last reserves of my strength to reach the top.

Hundreds of thick roots blocked the way, so I summoned the knife and began to hack.

Silent, unearthly screams echoed through my mind. The roots recoiled and slowly began to wither as I sliced through their flesh and souls.

I buried my sudden guilt for the screaming roots and envisioned each as a blood-red snake. Teeth gritted against the pain and exhaustion, I hacked my way through with abandon, even as I felt the roots wrapping around my feet.

We have to get to Jax.

He was pulling me to him somehow, like I was tethered to him by an invisible thread wrapped around my chest.

It was just the delirium of exhaustion, of course, but it gave me strength and dragged me onward all the same.

47

Jaxson

"GIVE HER TO ME!" I roared as I ripped through root and stem.

My battered, blood-slick hands could no longer grip, so I wrapped a long root around my forearm and pulled. My muscles strained as I braced against the rock wall, and then the thick root tore free as tendril after tendril ripped.

I'd broken a passage through the roots where Savannah had disappeared, but the barricade of living roots kept shifting and growing back. We battled for every inch, each of us trying to tear the other apart—but I would be victorious.

The mate bond pulled me downward like an anchor falling toward the ocean floor. She was so close. Weak, but alive. And she needed my help. I could feel it with every bone in my body.

A tremor shook the cavern. It wasn't the first, and I silently prayed to the gods that it wasn't the last. The tremors were growing closer together, and the weak rock was unstable. I didn't care. I had to reach her. Not because she was my mate, but because she was my responsibility—she'd trusted me, and I'd failed her.

Lies.

Desperation drove me forward with relentless fury, and I ripped and raged and tore until a patch of pale skin appeared between the roots.

Savannah.

She was bound and wrapped in roots, fully restrained and covered with blood with the Soul Knife clutched limply in her hand.

The sight of her sent me into a frenzy. I seized the knife and began chopping away, but as soon as I severed some of the roots, they shifted, and she started to sink again.

I grabbed her arm before she slipped out of sight, and her eyes shot open. "Jaxson...they're pulling me back!" Her voice was weak and strained with pain.

My chest rumbled, and I slashed through the great root that had wound itself around her waist. The tension on her body eased, and another tremor shook the cave. With one hand around her, I carefully sliced the remaining roots that had entangled her body and pulled her, cold and naked, from the knot.

"You have the knife," she murmured. Then she waved her hand, and it vanished from my grip. "No one should have that knife." She wrapped her arms around my neck. "I almost made it to you."

"You did," I growled as I lifted her up.

The root-infested tunnel shook, and more rocks clattered down around us.

Time to go.

I turned and climbed up the tunnel with Savannah in my arms. My legs were exhausted, but the faint beat of her heart against my chest drove me forward, giving me strength.

"I killed him," she whispered, her words fading into almost nothing. "Your pack is safe..."

"You did well," I said softly as I pushed my way back up the tunnel. Tendrils and roots snaked around my arms and ankles as I lumbered up the slanted shaft, but I tore through. She was in my arms, and no force could stop me.

At last, I burst forth into the dim cavern with the pond. "Jaxson!" Sam shouted from below a tree. "Time to go!"

"Have you finished? Are they all free?" I braced myself as another earthquake shuddered the cave.

"Yes!" Sam yelled. "Let's get the fuck out of here!"

With Savannah unconscious, I charged toward the exit as the chamber quaked and roots began to writhe along the walls.

Sam pointed to the grimoire floating above the pond. "The book!"

"No time, leave it!" I shouted over my shoulder. The only thing that mattered was getting Savannah and Sam out of there.

We ran through the trembling tunnels as the roar of falling rubble echoed up the passageway from behind.

I ran with all the strength I had.

Neve found us in the first chamber of sleepers. "This cave won't last long. I'll planes-walk us out of here!"

"No! The shift will kill Savannah. She's too wounded. I need to heal her. Get Sam out!"

"We're not leaving you!" Sam shouted. "The entrance isn't far!"

We ran together through the crumbling paths as stone and sand rained down around us. Neve summoned a whirlwind ahead, keeping the debris off our heads and out of our way.

At last, I saw the glimmer of daylight. I charged headlong out of the quaking tunnel and down the pebble-covered beach.

The tunnel roared as the sound of collapsing earth followed me out.

I dropped to my knees in the ocean and laid Savannah's body in the shallows. Plumes of red clouded the water. She had so many wounds—cuts, lacerations, fang marks. She was a new wolf, and her healing powers weren't yet as they needed to be. But *she* was as strong as she needed to be, and still hanging on by a thread.

My stomach quaked and my arms trembled as I summoned the power of our mate bond. I was drained, but the touch of her skin gave me strength.

I poured all I had left into her.

48

Ecstasy coursed through my body like a wave breaking against the shore. It was fire in my veins and ice burning my skin. It was pain and pleasure and absolutely unrelenting.

I gasped and arched my back as Jaxson's magic surged along my spine, and my eyes sprang wide.

The world was radiant.

Every color was new and more than my eyes could handle. I could feel the infinite blue of the sky and taste the golden sunlight beating down on my bare skin.

I was in *his* arms.

Where his flesh began and mine ended, I didn't know. But I felt every one of his heartbeats thundering through the world around me.

"You're alive," Jaxson's voice rumbled, and my blood surged.

I reached up and brought my fingers along the edge of his jaw, his beard prickling my fingertips. "More than ever."

I slid my arms around his shoulders and pulled myself to his lips. We flowed together like the rolling waves, and when his fingers caressed my bare skin, it felt like a rising dawn. His taste, his kiss, and his passion were everything, and my body was blind to any sensation that wasn't him.

I'd never been more alive.

But amid the bliss, a moment of clarity cut through my mind, followed by a flood of memories and fear. I sat up straight. "Where am I?"

"Safe. On the beach."

The ocean stretched infinitely into the distance and rolled softly along the shallow shore. Clouds raced through the sky high above, though the wind along the coast was nearly still.

I was naked in Jaxson's arms, but I didn't care. We'd just shared something that went beyond bodies. Something deeper, something magical.

I pulled myself closer and kissed him again, then twisted so that I could see behind us.

The entrance to the Dreamlands beneath the strange tree was gone, replaced by only a collapsed, dead-end cave.

I bit my lips. "The sorcerer..."

"You killed him."

Had I? It was hard to believe, and doubt gnawed at me. What about Dragan? The image of his ghostly face haunted me. I'd have to tell Jaxson what had happened, but exhaustion weighed me down. I turned my eyes to Jaxson's. "And the sleepers?"

He brushed my hair. "We freed them. They're all safe, thanks to you."

My heartbeat slowly began to accelerate. Memories surfaced, and my breath caught. "But you weren't going to save them—you were going to save me. Kahanov...he said you didn't have a choice. That you'd let them die to protect me. *Had to.* What did he mean?"

Jaxson looked out over the ocean, and I felt his trepidation.

I grabbed a handful of his tattered shirt. "What did he mean, Jaxson? There's something you're not telling me."

Anger burned in his eyes, and worry wrapped around my heart.

He tensed his jaw, but at last, he spoke. "We're bonded. Mates. It's...impossible for me to allow harm to come to you."

I pushed away from him. "What the hell are you talking about? *Mates*?"

My wolf had used that word, right before she shifted back. I didn't like the sound of it one bit.

Jaxson's gaze was hard, his voice cold. "We're fated to be together. Bonded. True mates."

I scoffed. "That's ridiculous. I don't believe in that kind of thing."

He gritted his teeth and spoke with a bitter tone. "It doesn't matter whether you believe it or not, or whether either of us wants it. The fates have woven our lifelines together. We have no choice."

We're mates, my wolf said, but I shoved her aside as shock and resentment boiled up inside of me. I was *not* going to be told who to be with, not by Jaxson or my wolf or the fates or anyone.

I disentangled myself from Jaxson and stood, pulling what shadows I could find around me to cover my nakedness. "You realize how fucked up all this sounds, right? This can't be real."

He climbed to his feet and glared back at me. "Fated mates are as real as magic or werewolves or prophesies. The mate bond is part of our world. I didn't know we were bonded until you shifted the first time. Suddenly, I felt your pain from miles away, and I knew exactly where you were. That's how I found you in the woods."

He came to us when we were dying, caught between forms, my wolf said.

Panic seeped in through the corners of my mind.

Jaxson touched his chest. "Our bond—it's like a string stretched between our souls, always pulling us back together."

I sucked in a sharp breath. This was hitting too close to home.

I'd felt that sensation, a tug on my chest pulling me out of the cavern and to Jaxson even when I was almost too weak to hold the knife.

He placed his hand lightly on my shoulder and released a burst of magic that sent a shiver along my spine. "Our bond is how I can heal you. Only true mates can do that. I can't do it for anyone else in my pack."

My heartbeat accelerated, and I fought for air as my lungs tightened. Jaxson was cornering me just like he'd done in the alley behind his autobody shop, like he'd done in the garden of monsters in Italy.

"Please. You can't do this to me," I whispered, pleading for him to declare it was all a lie.

His eyes flashed with anger. "Do this to you? Do you think I'm any happier about this than you are? Do you think I want this? Because I don't."

His words were a slap in the face, and resentment welled up in my heart.

So *that* was how he truly felt. I should've known.

I knotted my fists and vowed to find a way out of this fucked-up mess. "So this is like some sort of curse? There must be a way to break the bond."

His jaw tensed, and his eyes flashed a honey-gold. "I don't know. Maybe if we find a way to cure your lycanthropy..."

"Fuck! You can't be serious!" I clenched my fists, and the bitter truth dawned on me. "Is that why you were so eager to see Alia? To find a cure? Because of *this*?"

His silence was an answer in itself.

Of course he would be desperate to get rid of me. I was a dirty LaSalle.

Jaxson raised his hand, but I started backing away. "No. This is too much. No one has the right to control my body or my heart. Not the sorcerer, not you, not my wolf, and *not* the fucking fates."

"Savannah, I know this is a lot. Calm down. We can talk this through."

Talk me through losing my right to choose my own partner? Talk me through being fated to someone who despises me and my family?

Anger burned in my chest, and I wanted to scream—at Jaxson, at the fates, at everything.

"No. I will *not* calm down." I rubbed my throbbing temples. "*I* control my own fate. Nobody else. I'll decide if I'm your mate or not, and *I'm not*. No fates or magical bond can make me. I reject this."

His eyes blazed with resentment and rage, like my words had been a blade rammed into his chest, cutting out his soul.

It made my heart ache—but was that really my heart feeling for him, or was it a product of our so-called bond? Were any of my feelings for him real?

I didn't know any more. It was too much to process.

"Savannah." He stepped forward, but I stepped back, keeping my distance.

"Sorry, Jaxson, but I can't do this."

Then I turned and left, pulling a dark cloak of shadow around me.

My thoughts pounded in my mind as I strode down the beach. Were we really fated mates? Did I really have no choice?

The implications were staggering. If it was true, then everything between us was fake. A *lie*. A byproduct of our mate bond.

My heart felt like it was cracking, and a lump of sorrow and embarrassment rose in my throat.

Jaxson hadn't tried to save me because he cared. He hadn't healed me because he cared. He was compelled to. Forced to by the bond.

The sorcerer had said almost as much. Jaxson would have watched everyone die before he let me go. Because he *had* to. Not because he chose to or wanted to.

And everything he felt, it was because of our mate bond. Not because of his heart.

Hell, I'd smelled his bitterness and resentment when he'd told me we were fated. He said he hadn't wanted it—because of course, how could he have truly cared for me? I'd killed his brother-in-law, and my monstrous family had killed his sister.

He'd had to watch Kahanov start to cut the souls from his pack, helpless to choose them over me. Helpless to save his wolves and to do his duty as alpha. It was horrific.

My skin suddenly felt overheated, and my breaths were coming too quickly. I couldn't breathe, I needed to get out of there.

I began to run.

Sam's voice erupted from behind me. "Savy! Where are you going?"

She was running after me, but instead of slowing, I quickened my pace.

"I don't fucking know!" I shouted over my shoulder. "Away from here. Away from Jaxson and Magic Side and the pack."

"Come on, Savy. Stop this. I know it's a shock. You just need time to get used to the mate bond."

I skidded to a halt and spun in horror. "Wait a minute, did you already know about this?"

She nodded. "I've known about you two since you first shifted. It's impossible to miss. Your bond is so strong th—"

"You both knew, and you kept this from me all this time?" I clenched my fists to keep my thoughts and hands under control as waves of betrayal and anger burned through my veins.

She reached out, but I pulled away. I didn't need her pity or comfort. It was too late.

Sam let her hand drop. "You'd just been turned into a wolf. You had a sorcerer trying to kill you. We knew it would be overwhelming. Too much was at stake."

"So you just left me out of the loop, like always." My voice cracked, and I fought back the tears that were pooling in the corners of my eyes. "I'm done with all of this. You, Jaxson, the pack. I can't trust anyone."

I turned to head back toward the collapsed cave to find Neve —who was mercifully something other than a werewolf—but Sam caught my arm. "He cares about you, Savannah. And I know you care about him, too."

"You know nothing about how either of us feels. Now let me go!"

I tried to jerk my arm free, but she held on. "*I* care about you. And that's not because of some bond."

Her words made my throat catch, but I pulled away and started walking. I couldn't handle this rollercoaster ride of emotions, and I didn't know what to believe anymore. There were too many unspoken words, too many hidden truths.

"Please don't shut me out. You're a werewolf now. You need someone to help you through this."

"I'll find my own way." Until I found the cure.

"That's not how being in a pack works," said Sam. "I'll help get you through this transition, and I'll tell you everything I know. About shifting. About moon cycles and pack etiquette. About the heat."

I stopped short in my tracks. "The heat?"

She gritted her teeth and made an apologetic shrug.

God help me.

We're gonna need her, my wolf said.

I closed my eyes and begged for strength. "I'm going to find Neve and return to Magic Side. And when I get back, I'm leaving. I don't want to see you or Jaxson again. I want you to leave me the fuck alone."

49

We arrived in Magic Side in a whirl of wind and magic. I staggered over to the wall and braced myself until the warehouse stopped spinning.

Teleporting with Neve was like skydiving into a hurricane.

Sam placed her hand on my shoulder. "Are you okay?"

"Fine," I lied, and shrugged her off.

Jaxson took a step toward me, but I flashed him a vengeful look that told him to stay the fuck back. I couldn't be near him, and I couldn't trust my mind or body around him.

I glared at the floor as it kept spinning around. I was still mad at Sam, but I was also wearing *another* set of her clothes, a track suit that she'd brought in the gym bag.

And she hadn't even mentioned the fact that I'd lost her favorite shirt in the Dreamlands. That said quite a lot...though potentially, she hadn't figured that one out yet.

I stood and looked around.

The warehouse was packed with werewolves, and a cheering throng had formed around Neve and Jaxson. Heroes. Word had traveled fast. We'd woken the sleepers. We'd defeated Kahanov.

The pack was safe.

Time to get the hell out of here.

I started to slink toward the shadows, but Sam caught my arm. "Nuh-uh. You just saved the lives of dozens of wolves. The pack is going to want to see you."

"I don't wan—"

She shoved me forward, and then, to my shock, she howled.

Howls erupted around me, and my wolf surged in my chest, understanding some unspoken message that I couldn't. Suddenly, I was surrounded by werewolves, laughing and embracing me and patting me on the back.

What the hell was happening? These people...they *hated* me.

Sam gave me a shove. "Welcome to the pack. We get rowdy."

But I *wasn't* part of the pack.

My surprise mixed with unease as voices rose around me and people cheered. Not long ago, these people had wanted to string me up. And now, they were treating me like a hero. One of their own.

But I'm not.

Still, something stirred deep inside of me. The same strange feeling I'd felt when I'd met Casey, Aunt Laurel, and Uncle Pete.

We belong, my wolf said.

I shook my head. *No.*

They were drunk in the moment. None of it was real—a delusion, just like my feelings for Jaxson, and his for me.

Amid the fray, a woman caught my arm and pulled me to her. Did I recognize her face? She took my hands. "I saw you in my dream."

My cheeks burned under the attention and the avalanche of emotions washing over me. "What?" I croaked.

"That *man* trapped me in a nightmare. It wouldn't stop, and I couldn't escape. But then I saw you in my dream, moving in the shadows. I didn't know who you were, but in that instant, *I knew* someone was coming for me, that someone was fighting for me, and that even in the darkness, I wasn't alone."

She wiped her eyes and wrapped her arms around me before I could escape. My thoughts drifted from the rejoicing werewolves around us to my own dark dreams and the face of the fortune teller, whispering from the shadows.

Deep down, I knew my nightmare wasn't over.

I will have my vengeance! The voice of Dragan, the deranged lunatic my aunt had killed, echoed through my mind. I'd cut his soul out, but was he really gone?

Not a chance. But maybe, just maybe, I wasn't fighting alone.

My gaze drifted through the crowd and landed on Jaxson. He stood apart from them like a lighthouse over the sea. Despite the commotion that surrounded us, his piercing honey-gold eyes didn't waver from me. Shivers raked over my skin, and my wolf surged toward him.

I felt his irresistible magnetic pull drawing me into his orbit, summoning me to him with every breath I took.

Jaxson Laurent, my fated mate.

I turned and walked away from it all.

I'd find a way to fight this. A way to break the bond and make my fate my own.

Thanks for joining us on this wild adventure!

Ready for Dark Lies, book 3? Read it now: mybook.to/Dark-Lies

And if you'd like to keep up to date with our writing progress and get access to exclusive, insider-only content like deleted scenes and short stories, sign up for our newsletter: https://www.veronicadouglas.com/newsletter

Finally, if you've got an extra minute, please leave us a review on Amazon (mybook.to/Untamed-Fate) and Goodreads or Bookbub. Reviews make a *huge* impact. They help us become better writers and keep us motivated through the difficult pages!

Up next: keep reading for an author's note on the archaeology, history, and adventures that inspired this book!

AUTHOR'S NOTE

Thank you so much for reading *Untamed Fate*!

As archaeologists, we love to include historical tidbits and exotic locations in our stories. Savannah and Jaxson's Italian adventure was inspired by a trip we took with Linsey Hall, long before we began to think about writing. One of the places we stayed was Civita di Bagnoregio—a tiny village perched on a plateau in the middle of a heavily eroded valley. It served as the basis for la Città Che Muore, the town where the mage lived. The only way to reach Civita di Bagnoregio is to either ascend the donkey path up from the valley floor or cross a long narrow bridge that stretches out from the rim of the valley (we removed the bridge for our version of the town).

Civita di Bagnoregio was founded two-and-a-half millennia ago by the Etruscans, who excavated caves in the hard volcanic tuff. The local geology has put the town in a precarious position. While the city was constructed atop the hard layer of tuff, the underlying layer is clay, and it is continuously eroding (we actually saw several landslides while we were there). The plateau continues to shrink, undermining the picturesque city, which is on verge of collapsing into the valley—giving it the nickname 'the dying city.' We spent time hiking in the region, and got just as mud-covered as Savannah did!

Savannah and Jaxson arrived in Italy through a portal in a garden of stone monsters. This location is based on the *Sacro Bosco* (Sacred Grove) in Bomarzo, also known as the *Parco dei Mostri* (Park of the Monsters). The wooded garden is filled with towering grotesque sculptures, some of which were sculpted directly into the bedrock. They include a giant ripping a man in half, a war elephant with a Roman legionnaire wrapped in its trunk, and a massive turtle, among many others.

The garden was commissioned in 1552 by Prince Pier Francesco Orsini as an expression of grief. The prince returned from a brutal war in which he'd been held for ransom and lost his best friend, only to have his beloved wife die soon after. The garden defies all conventions of a well-manicured and orderly Italian renaissance garden. It is an expression of chaos, with grotesque sculptures, an asymmetric layout, wildly growing trees and shrubs, and even a tilting tower house.

Perhaps the most striking sculpture in the garden is the massive head of Orcus, whose screaming mouth opens into a cave, and which directly inspired the portal Jax and Savy traveled through. Orcus was an Etruscan/Roman god of the underworld and known as a punisher of broken oaths. In many ways, his open mouth is like a gateway to hell. Over the entrance, the words *ogni pensiero vola* are inscribed on his lip, which translates as "all thoughts fly" or "all reason departs." If you are brave enough to enter the screaming mouth, you find a little table where you can have lunch, and thus take part in eating while appearing to be eaten.

Speaking of portals, you might be wondering why, of all places, did we put a portal to the Dreamlands in Forks, Washington—the town of Twilight fame? While on a writing retreat in the upper Olympic Peninsula, we were inspired by the Tree Root Cave in Olympic National Park. The cave is in the side of a cliff along the coast. The top is formed by a massive spruce which appears to be floating in midair. The dirt has eroded from around its roots, leaving them to dangle down freely. The tree clings to the cliff above the cave like a gangly spider or octopus. While the tree looks like it should topple over, it continues to thrive, which has earned it the nickname, the Tree of Life. Once we saw it, we knew that *this* had to be a way into the Dreamlands. We used the imagery of the twisted roots throughout the book, a metaphor for the strange connections between the waking world and that of dreams, as well as the interwoven fate of Savannah, Jaxson, and her wolf.

Untamed Fate is set in the wider Dragon's Gift universe created by Linsey Hall. Magic's Bend is the setting for many of her early stories, and you might recognize Alia from her *Wolf Queen Book 1, Darkest Moon*. She actually makes her first appearance in *Infernal*, book 1 of Linsey's *Hades & Persephone* series. Definitely check them out! You can expect a lot of crossovers between the folks from Guild City, Magic's Bend, and Magic Side in the future.

That's all that we have space for in this book, but we'll be posting more detailed notes about the archaeology and history that inspired this book in our newsletter. You can sign up at: https://www.veronicadouglas.com/newsletter

Dark Lies, the sequel to *Untamed Fate*, is available now. You can read it on Amazon here: https://mybook.to/Dark-Lies

And if you'd like to chat more about the books, interact with fellow readers, and get the scoop on what's up next, you join the Veronica Douglas Facebook reader group (Veronica Douglas' Magic Side Insiders) here:

https://www.facebook.com/groups/veronicadouglas

That's all for now! Sweet dreams and thanks again for reading!

-Veronica Douglas

DARK LIES
MAGIC SIDE: WOLF BOUND, BOOK 3 OF 4
PREVIEW

My nightmare's not over. It's just beginning.

I killed the sorcerer that turned my life into a living hell, but instead of getting better, my world is falling apart. New threats lurk in every shadow, and I still don't have the answers I need.

The cops want me to betray the pack, the pack wants me to betray my family, and servants of a dark god are hunting me for my blood. I've turned into one of the monsters I feared most, and I have no idea why. Worse, I can't control the beast inside me.

I need to find a way to break this curse before my family discovers my secret—before my fated mate, Jaxson Laurent, claims me as his own. He's as hot as sin, and I can barely restrain myself when he's near, but I won't let him rule me and I won't let the fates determine my path.

When I finally unmask the dark lies that have haunted my life, will I be strong enough to face the truth?

You can read Dark Lies now on Amazon here: mybook.to/Dark-Lies

WICKED WISH
DRAGON'S GIFT: THE STORM BOOK 1
VERONICA DOUGLAS
LINSEY HALL

WICKED WISH

DRAGON'S GIFT: THE STORM, BOOK 1 PREVIEW

If you're ready for more Magic Side adventures and want to read a complete series right now, try: Wicked Wish (co-authored with Linsey Hall).

I'm at the mercy of a fallen angel.

I work for the Order of Magica, the supernatural version of the FBI. Sounds fun, right? Except I spend my days chained to my desk, writing reports, and wishing that I was out solving crimes. *Well, be careful what you wish for.*

When my best friend is abducted, my life in Chicago turns upside down.

I'll do anything to get her back—even work with Damian Malek, a wanted criminal, notorious crime lord, and dangerous fallen angel. He's hot, lethal, and he's the only one who can help me master my dangerous powers. I don't want anyone to know about my magic, but I have no choice if I want to save my friend.

Here's the catch: if the Order finds out that I'm working with Damian, I'll get canned. Maybe even be hunted for what I am. But if I don't give him what he wants, he'll reveal my secret to the world.

Wicked Wish features a rebel heroine, a dark angel hero, and slow burn romance. Prepare yourself for edge-of-your-seat adventure amongst ancient ruins and fantastical worlds.

If you enjoyed the archaeology, history, and daring in Linsey Hall's original Dragon's Gift books, this adventure is for you!

Begin the adventure now: mybook.to/Wicked-Wish

ACKNOWLEDGMENTS
VERONICA DOUGLAS

Thank you to everyone who has been so supportive, especially Linsey and Ben—we could never have done this without you guys! Our adventures together inspired this book.

Thank you to Jena O'Connor and Ash Fitzsimmons for your patience and amazing editing skills!

Thank you to the amazing readers on our advanced review team! Extra special thanks to our beta readers Penny, Susie, Aisha, and Amanda—your eyes are so sharp!

Many thanks to Lauren Gardner for all of your hard work. You are absolutely a lifesaver! And thanks to Caethes, for all your efforts to get us rolling. You both made the launch of Wolf Marked an amazing success.

And finally, a huge shoutout to Orina Kafe for designing another mind-blowing cover! You are truly the best!

ABOUT VERONICA DOUGLAS

Veronica Douglas is a duo of professional archaeologists that love writing and digging together. After spending an inordinate amount of time doing painstaking research for academia, they suddenly discovered a passion for letting their imaginations go wild! A cocktail of magic, romance, and ancient mystery (shaken, not stirred), their books are inspired, in part, by their life in Chicago and their archaeological adventures from around the globe.